THE COCOA GIRLS

ANNIE DOYLE

To,

Auntie Ann

Best Wishes,

From,

Barbara

x

For my mam, with love and admiration.

ACKNOWLEDGEMENTS

This story would never have been created without certain people. My nana's life and that of her grandmother, mother and aunt gave me the inspiration for The Cocoa Girls. They were remarkable women who achieved extraordinary things when opportunities for women were extremely limited. Ena, Theodosia, Mona and Ivy; I hope my story does credit to your incredible legacy. Add to the list of remarkable women my mam, Pat. She asked me to research her female ancestors' histories, and the facts I uncovered inspired me to put pen to paper.

I must pay particular tribute to Susan Gallacher for her interest and support and getting me started with genealogy. Tragically, Sue was taken from us much too soon and she didn't see *The Cocoa Girls* in print. Tremendous support at home allowed me to work without distractions; to him indoors and the crazy hound, thank you. So many others contributed to enable me to do this. My family and friends; thank you for your support and never squashing my dreams. In particular, thanks from the bottom of my heart go to: the incredible Jacky Collins, aka Dr. Noir, dear friend, powerhouse of all things fiction and the provider of wise words whenever I need them; Fiona Veitch Smith, wonderful creative writing tutor, editor, friend and author of the '*flapulous*' Poppy Denby Investigates series; everyone who attended Fiona's creative writing classes with me; Glenda Young, friend, constant supporter of my writing journey and author of powerful historical sagas and cosy crime stories; Shelley Day, friend, supporter, insightful critic and author of *The Confession of Stella Moon* and *What Are You Like*; my lovely, constructively critical beta readers Debbie, Jo and Tracy; Sue, Jill, Steph, Eleanor, Noosh, Margaret and all the other Saturday morning writing women; Jo Eaglesham for the inspiration behind my eccentric dancers Jim Colvill and Annie Tate, based on her paternal great grandparents; Rob Barnes for typesetting, a terrific cover design and fabulous chapter illustrations; Valerie Speed for my wonderful author photographs. Many more people helped me along the way. To each and every one of you, thank you.

FICTIONAL CHARACTERS
GATESHEAD

Eveline Dinah Annie Brown (Evie)/Ena Leighton –
abandoned four-year-old child. Our central character.

Dinah Jane Brown/Ivy Dinah Jane Leighton – Evie's aunt.

Margaret Patricia Brown/Mona Leighton – Evie's mother.

Louis Levy/Lewis Leighton – Evie's father.

Elizabeth Ann Brown/Lizzie – Evie's nemesis. Dinah and Margaret's
cousin.

Mary Glass – Lizzie's elder sister.

Andrew Glass – Mary's husband.

John Todd – postman.

Jack Todd – Evie's friend. John Todd's nephew.

Nancy Glover – Evie's friend.

Miss Kinghorn – Evie's teacher at South Street Infants School.

The Registrar/Arthur Armstrong – official at Gateshead Registry Office.

Matron – matron at Gateshead's Union Workhouse.

George Green/Geordie – rough Pipewellgate resident.

The Crone – homeless woman and skilled eavesdropper.

Miss Trudy – Dinah and Margaret's dance teacher.

Harry Campbell – local criminal and wheeler-dealer.

Harriet Armstrong – Arthur's sister.

PARIS

Theodosia Labouriming/Tee/Frannie le Fleur/Theodosia Brown –
Evie's grandmother.

Jacques Labouriming – Theodosia's younger brother (deceased).

Solomon Zettler – director of the Zettler Girls dance troupe.

Jeannie – dancer with the Zettler Girls. Theodosia's friend.

NEWCASTLE-UPON-TYNE

Henry Brown - railway fettler. Theodosia's husband.

William Brown – Henry's brother.

Agatha Brown – William's wife.

Ernie Redford - railway fettler. Jeannie's husband.

Jacques Redford – Jeannie and Ernie's son (deceased).

Mrs Swann/Madame Desperéaux – guest house owner at Springbank Lane.

The Captain – Mrs Swann's parrot.

Corky – clown. Springbank Lane resident.

Jim Colvill and Annie Tate – husband and wife. Eccentric dancers. Springbank Lane residents.

Fatima Ferrari – belly-dancer. Springbank Lane resident.

Sully Sullivan – juggler. Springbank Lane resident.

Ora, Petra and Kora – tightrope walkers. Springbank Lane residents.

Monsieur Olivier Desperéaux – French singer. Springbank Lane resident.

LONDON

Kitty – dancer who befriended Jeannie as a girl.

Fred – stage-hand at the Metropolitan Music Hall. Jeannie's beau (deceased).

Samuel Levy – Louis's uncle.

Violet, Nellie and May – dancers at the Diamond Music Hall. Mona's friends.

Billy Shaw – manager at the club.

Esther and Jacob Levy – Louis's wife and son.

Mrs Newbold – guest house owner at Parkview.

Mr Newbold – Mrs Newbold's husband (deceased).

Clara – Mrs Newbold's house maid. Suffrage supporter.

Harold Barnes – music hall performer. Parkview resident.

Celia and Lawrence Stratton – husband and wife. Trick cyclists. Parkview residents.

Monsieur le Grand – director at the West London Theatre.

Bessie Bentley – actress. Parkview resident.

Wilhelmina Ponsonby-Smythe – Bessie's character in '*Olympic Contests.*'

Rémy Sand – French actor.

Herbert Joseph Primavesi/Bertie – Ivy's beau.

The Waitress – waitress at the Lyons Cafe on Shaftesbury Avenue.

HAMPSON HALL - NORTHUMBERLAND

Mrs Foley/Cook – cook.

Mrs Jackson – housekeeper.

Mr Foley – head gardener.

Mr Jackson – butler.

Ruby Rogers – scullery maid. Dinah's friend.

Winnie Smith – scullery maid. Dinah's friend.

Edward/ *'the lad'* – Mr Foley's assistant. Lord Hampson's unacknowledged son.

Rose - Winnie and Edward's baby.

Lord and Lady Hampson – owners of Hampson Hall.

Master Walter Hampson – Lord Hampson's elder son.

Master James Hampson – Lord Hampson's younger son.

Reverend Ash – local vicar.

Grace Opal – opera singer and actress. Master Walter's fiancée.

VOYAGES / NEW YORK CITY

Peggy Willow – English dancer and actress. Mona's friend.

Alberto – doorman at Peggy's apartment building.

Marvin Marvel/Marv – American director at the Paradise Theatre.

Lottie Linton – Peggy's character in *'The Night Of The Season.'*

Chuck Chancer - character in *'The Night Of The Season.'*

Frankie – dancer in *'Marv's Fabulous Femme Fatales.'*

Isabella Holliday – wealthy American. Mona's companion on her voyage to England.

HISTORICAL CHARACTERS
(NOTABLE REFERENCES AND CAMEO APPEARANCES)

Céline Celéste – French dancer and actress (1815 – 1882).

Emma Livry – French ballerina (1842 – 1863).

La Goulue – stage name of Louise Weber. French cancan dancer and star of the Moulin Rouge (1866 – 1929).

Francesca Caccini - Italian composer, singer, lutenist, poet and music teacher of the early Baroque era (1587 – after 1641).

Emma, Lady Hamilton - English maid, model, dancer, actress. Mistress of Lord Horatio Nelson (1765 – 1815).

Horatio Nelson – Vice-Admiral and English flag officer in the Royal Navy (1758 – 1805).

Camille Pissarro - Danish-French Impressionist and Neo-Impressionist painter (1830 - 1903).

Jules Verne - French novelist, poet, and playwright (1828 – 1905).

Maximilien Robespierre - French lawyer and statesman (1758 - 1794).

Robert Louis Stevenson - Scottish novelist, essayist, poet and travel writer (1850 – 1894).

Enrico Caruso - Italian opera singer (1873 - 1921).

Millicent Fawcett - English politician, writer, feminist and women's suffrage campaigner. (1847 – 1929).

Ralph Lynn - English actor, best remembered for playing comedy parts (1882 – 1962).

Harry Gordon Selfridge - American retail magnate and founder of the London-based department store Selfridges (1858 – 1947).

Margaret Getchell - American businesswoman, manager of Macy's during the department store's early years (1841 – 1880).

Emily Wilding Davidson – English suffragette and member of the Women's Social and Political Union (1872 – 1913).

Percy Bysshe Shelley – major English Romantic poet (1792 – 1822).

Harriet Westbrook – first wife of Percy Bysshe Shelley (1795 – 1816).

Mary Wollstonecraft Godwin - English novelist and second wife of Percy Bysshe Shelley (1797 – 1851).

Charles Dickens - English writer and social critic (1812 – 1870).

Arthur Conan Doyle - British writer and physician (1859 – 1930).

PRIMARY LOCATIONS
GATESHEAD

The Union Workhouse – where Evie's story begins.
Pipewellgate – Lizzie's room in a rundown tenement building where Evie stays.
South Street Infants School – Evie's school.
The Globe Hotel – Lizzie's second home.

PARIS

The Folies Bergère – where Theodosia meets Solomon Zettler and Jeannie.

NEWCASTLE-UPON-TYNE

Central Street Music Hall – where Theodosia and Jeannie work.
Springbank Lane - Mrs Swann's Guest House, where Theodosia and Jeannie stay.

LONDON

The Metropolitan Music Hall, Shaftesbury Avenue – where Theodosia and Jeannie work.
Leighton Mansions, Maida Vale – where Louis's uncle, Samuel Levy lives.
The Diamond Music Hall, Warwick Street – rundown music hall where Mona works.
Parkview, Chestnut Tree Avenue – Mrs Newbold's Guest House, where Ivy stays.
The West London Theatre, Shaftesbury Avenue - where Ivy works.

NEW YORK CITY

The Casino Theatre, Off-Broadway – where Mona intends to seek work.
The Paradise Theatre, Broadway – where Mona and Peggy work.

THEATRICAL PRODUCTIONS

At the West London Theatre, Shaftesbury Avenue - *'Olympic Contests'* and *'Toujours Belle.'*

At the Paradise Theatre, Broadway – *'The Night Of The Season'* and *'Marv's Fabulous Femme Fatales.'*

MUSIC

'Frère Jacques' - earliest printed version on a French manuscript (circa 1780). Some evidence that composer Jean-Philippe Rameau wrote the music.

'I dream of Jeannie with the Light Brown Hair' - written by Stephen C. Foster (1854).

'Annie My Own Love' - music composed by Stephen C. Foster, poetry by Charles P. Shiras (1853).

'A Bird in a Gilded Cage' - composed by Arthur J. Lamb and Harry von Tilzer, sung by Hamilton Hill (1900).

'Sur le Pont d'Avignon' - dates back to the 15th century.

'I love You Truly' - words and music by Carrie Jacobs-Bond (1901).

'O sole mio' - music composed by Eduardo di Capua, lyrics written by Giovanni Capurro (1898).

'The boy I Love is Up in the Gallery' - written by George Ware (1885), performed by Marie Lloyd (1886).

'Petite fille Evie' – words taken from *'Frère Jacques'*. Earliest printed version on a French manuscript circa 1780. Some evidence that composer Jean-Philippe Rameau wrote the music.

Bonny Mary of Argyle (I Have Heard The Mavis Singing)' - written by Robert Burns (circa 1850).

'Oranges and Lemons' - first published in Tommy Thumb's Pretty Song Book (1744).

'The Entertainer' - written and performed by Scott Joplin (1902).

'Let Me Call You Sweetheart' - music by Leo Friedman and lyrics by Beth Slater Whitson, published (1910).

'Three Little Maids from School Are We' - written by Gilbert and Sullivan (1885), part of the comic opera *'The Mikado.'*

'Beautiful Dreamer' - written by Stephen Foster (circa 1862).

'Tell Me Pretty Maiden' - written by Leslie Stuart (1899), part of the Edwardian musical comedy *'Florodora.'*

'Alexander's Ragtime Band' - written by Irving Berlin, sung by Collins and Harlan (1911).

'Le Temps des Cerises' - music by Antoine Renard, lyrics by Jean-Baptiste Clément (1866).

'Plaisir d'amour' - music by Jean-Paul-Égide Martini (1741-1816), lyrics by Jean-Pierre Claris de Florian (1755-1794).

Prologue

Gateshead, England – August 1903

Four-year-old Evie Brown clutched her aunt's hand. Her long auburn curls escaped from her white cotton bonnet and bounced against the back of her blue dress. Aunt Dinah did a funny half-walk, half-run to try and keep up with the tall, thin man striding ahead of them. His long black tailcoat flapped behind him as he marched. Evie didn't know who he was or where he was taking them or why they had to walk so quickly. Her little boots clicked on the cobbles as she hurried to keep up.

A sudden movement to her left made Evie turn. She screwed her eyes up but could only make out a dark figure. Was it her grandmother? Had her grama, with her warm cuddles and sweet voice, come to take her home? Home, where they would have Grama's warm, sweet drink. Where Grama told stories about a place called Paris. Despite the warm day, an icy chill crept up Evie's spine. Her bottom lip quivered as she remembered Aunt Dinah saying her grama had gone to be with the angels. Evie didn't understand why her grama had done that when she could have stayed with her, but Aunt Dinah's eyes filled with tears when she said Grama wasn't coming back, so Evie didn't ask her anything else. The figure moved again, and Evie saw it was a man. He stepped out from the dark shadow of the building and Evie shook. Who was he? What did he want?

The workhouse, vast and forbidding, loomed into view. Aunt Dinah stopped and Evie, small for her age, hid behind her aunt's dark linen skirt. She peeked out, her eyes following her aunt's as she stared at the high, black walls. The iron gates creaked open, and Evie jumped as a rat shot out. A sturdy woman in a long black dress followed, brandishing a rusty poker. The rat darted past; its sharp teeth embedded in the soft body of a small brown mouse. Evie watched it turn and run back, its long slimy tail disappearing through the workhouse gates. She stayed hidden as the woman marched towards them. Almost as wide as she was tall, her ruddy cheeks shone as her beady eyes sought the rat. She shoved the poker into a large pocket in her voluminous dress and faced them.

'Mr Glass?'

The man who had led Evie and her aunt to this terrifying place removed his high black hat.

'Yes. Good day to you, Miss...?'

'The child will address me as Matron. Well, where is she?'

Evie flinched and her aunt's skirt twitched. She cried out as Matron reached around Aunt Dinah and grabbed her hand. Evie's other hand shot back to her aunt as Matron pulled her away. Aunt Dinah reached out, but Matron crossed her fleshy arms in front of Evie and held her fast.

'No! Let me go!'

At Evie's shrill cry a swarm of crows lifted from the festering sewage pools outside the workhouse. The huge birds hovered, vulture-like, black eyes fixed on the filth below.

'Stop that nonsense!' Matron continued to hold Evie.

Evie's large, dark-brown eyes darted around. Aunt Dinah studied the ground, and her shoulders shook. The man's spectacles slipped as he looked down his long nose at his pocket watch and tutted. Evie's eyes searched for the man in the shadows, but he had gone. Aunt Dinah raised her head. Her piercing blue eyes met Evie's and she mouthed, *'no crying, remember?'* Evie sniffed and nodded as her tears fell. Aunt Dinah held out Evie's bag, but Matron let it fall into the mud. Aunt Dinah retrieved the bag and clutched it to her chest. Evie screamed as Mr Glass turned away and gestured for her aunt to follow.

She wanted Aunt Dinah to refuse, to pull her back into her arms and for them to run away from these horrible people and this scary place. Evie sobbed louder as her aunt lowered her head and stumbled away. The last image Evie had was her aunt putting her hands over her ears. Evie's desolate wails bounced off the walls of the workhouse and a deafening clang echoed around her as the huge gates slammed shut, claiming her in their menacing embrace.

Chapter 1

21 years earlier
The Folies Bergère, Paris – 1882

Theodosia smiled into the darkness of the music hall, her piercing blue eyes bright. The Zettler Girls took their final bow and the curtain stayed down. Every sinew in Theodosia's body tingled with excitement; music and dancing brought her to life. When the odd little man had introduced himself and the English-speaking stage manager explained his question, Theodosia hadn't hesitated. Solomon Zettler's star dancer had been taken ill. Medium height and of slender build, Theodosia was the perfect replacement to join his dance troupe for one matinée performance. She revelled in the precise nature of their disciplined routines. The straight lines and geometric figures, an exhilarating display of perfect high-kicks and taps, had left the crowd clamouring for more. As the Zettler Girls broke their line and hurried to their dressing room, a gentle hand stopped her.

'You were excellent, considering you only joined us at the last minute! So graceful!'

Theodosia understood 'excellent' and blushed at the young woman's compliment.

'Merci beaucoup, er...'

'Jeannie, my name is Jeannie.'

Theodosia pointed at her chest. 'Bonjour, Jeannie. Je m'appelle Theodosia.'

'What a beautiful name! Tee-o-do-seea?'

'Oui.'

As the women removed their make-up in front of the grainy mirror, the door banged open. Theodosia turned as Mr Zettler's eyes settled on her. She watched him push through the throng.

'Mademoiselle? Would you consider joining my dance troupe when we return to England?'

Theodosia raised her eyebrows; she had only understood *'dance troupe'* and '*England.*' She looked at Jeannie who pointed at Theodosia, then at herself and the other dancers. Theodosia shrugged and shook her head. Mr Zettler tutted and left the room. When the door opened again, the stage manager stood beside Mr Zettler. Theodosia stared open-mouthed as the stage manager explained. How could she accept? Through the stage manager she expressed her gratitude, saying Mr Zettler's offer flattered her. She said it needed careful consideration and she didn't know if she could be released from her current contract. Could she leave the Folies Bergère? The grandeur and extravagance of the music hall, with its comic opera, ballet, acrobatics, popular song and circus-style acts, had been her home since her parents died. The elegant exterior of the music hall belied the internal environment, where people from different levels of society met without the traditional restrictions of class morality. Visitors sat in the lavish auditorium or strolled in the galleries as performances unfolded. Theodosia had never set foot outside Paris. She wasn't sure if the prospect of leaving France terrified or excited her. Outside the music hall, the dancers gathered around her. The women twittered as they shared their views of Mr Zettler's surprising question. Standing in the middle of the noisy group, Theodosia raised her hands. The women fell silent.

'Y a-t-il quelqu'un qui parle français?'

Theodosia's question elicited blank stares, none of them spoke French. She tapped a well-manicured finger against her lips and tried again.

'Chocolat?'

The word, similar enough in both languages, produced nods and smiles.

'Et, 'ot chocolat?'

As the women dissolved into laughter Theodosia took Jeannie's arm. She led them to Café de Flore in the 6th arrondissement, close to her own small, rented apartment. She had lived alone since her parents died and had no other relatives or close friends. Dancing and music were her escape from loneliness. Her parents' deaths had left a gap in her life which only family could fill. She dreamed of having a husband and children of her own. She motioned to the women to sit outside the pretty café, pointing out the flowers and foliage blooming from the terrace. She ordered hot chocolate (or cocoa in England, according to Jeannie's faltering explanation). Theodosia closed her eyes, recalling her first taste of hot chocolate. Her mother calling for her *'petite fille au chocolat,'* her *'little chocolate girl'* as she prepared the delicious drink, and the sweet, comforting aroma filling her nostrils as she held the warm cup. The perfect remedy in so many situations, according to her mother. To herself, Theodosia promised to carry on this tradition with her own children. She appraised the women and smiled as Jeannie attempted to speak French. As twilight fell the women stood and made their apologies. Some performed a dance move, others pointed in the direction of the music hall. Theodosia knew they had at least one more performance that evening. Her dark curls bounced as she shook her head at Jeannie.

'Non ma chérie, pas ce soir.'

To make it clear she wasn't going back to the music hall, Theodosia called the waiter and ordered another drink then stood to embrace her new acquaintance. Jeannie's eyes glistened and Theodosia reached for her handkerchief. Jeannie studied the pretty lace edging and the small blue flowers embroidered in one corner, surrounding a blue letter *'T.'* Theodosia kissed Jeannie, to the side of one cheek then to the side of the other. The light kisses caressed the air to the sides of Jeannie's cheeks. Jeannie flushed and returned Theodosia's handkerchief before running to join the others. As she reached them, she turned and waved. Theodosia raised her hand and smiled. As the *'allumeurs'* started lighting the gas lamps at the corner of Boulevard Saint-Germain and Rue Saint-Benoît, Theodosia left Café de Flore. She turned; the waiter was busy with evening clientele, but he stopped. He nodded and she smiled before walking away.

Chapter 2

Theodosia touched her face. What had made her cry in her sleep? She sat on the edge of the bed and recalled the image of her mother, sitting in the same place. She shivered and reached for her robe. She stroked the delicate silk bedspread as she replayed the vivid dream, her mother here, asking if she still used the trapdoor trick. She smiled as she remembered her mother explaining about the magic of daydreams, a trick to escape in difficult times. She could open a trapdoor in her mind and go anywhere. Her mother called it 'le truc de la trappe,' the trapdoor trick. In her dream Theodosia had touched her mother's face, closing her eyes at the familiar softness.

She walked to the window. On the street below people went about their business. She frowned, she had been flattered by Mr Zettler's offer the previous day, in the company of Jeannie and the others. Now, in the cold light of day, she hesitated. She rested her forehead against the window and closed her eyes. The trapdoor trick returned her to life before everything changed. Her parents were poor, but she had never wanted for anything. They worked hard to give their only child a warm home, decent clothes and good food. Before becoming pregnant her mother had danced in the Paris music halls. Her father, a labourer on some of Paris's ambitious building projects, helped to bring fresh water and light to the city and to improve sanitation, railways and roads. He worked long hours and had few days off, but when he came home, she ran into his arms. He lifted her high, twirling her around until she saw stars. Her mother scolded him, *'fais attention avec elle, mon chéri!'* He *was* always careful, her strong, handsome father who lifted and twirled her and told stories of places beyond Paris. They drank hot chocolate and sang songs from the music hall, including Theodosia's favourite, '*Frère Jacques,*' Brother Jack. She didn't have a brother, but as a girl she decided his name would be Jacques, when he arrived. He never did arrive and when her mother sang, the longing and heartbreak in her voice had captivated the young Theodosia.

'*Frère Jacques, Frère Jacques,*
Dormez-vous? dormez-vous?
Sonnez les matines, sonnez les matines,
Ding dong, ding dong.'

Theodosia was 16 when her mother died. Her parents explained they were expecting the long-awaited Jacques (it had to be a boy) and she shared their joy. Jacques's much-anticipated arrival was short-lived when Theodosia's mother went into premature labour. Her piercing cries, '*Non! C'est beaucoup trop tôt!*' were seared into Theodosia's memory. Her mother's terror was justified, it *was* too early for Jacques to enter the world. Despite everyone's best efforts, Theodosia's mother and the baby boy died. Her father fell into a deep depression and began drinking, not coming home until the early hours of the morning. The days of being lifted high and twirled around were over. Her father died exactly one year after her mother, his liver ravaged and his heart broken. Alone in their once joyful apartment, Theodosia grieved, but not for long. She had to pay her rent or face eviction. She hid her sorrow and went in search of a job. As she entered the music hall on the Boulevard de la Madeleine she straightened her shoulders, determined to leave as part of the chorus line. Her hopes were soon dashed, she had no experience and no letters of recommendation. Her discomfort grew as the director looked her up and down and motioned for her to turn around.

'C'est ça! L'assistant du magicien!'

Theodosia raised her eyebrows. The director hushed stifled giggles from the chorus line as the dancers waited for her reaction to becoming the new magician's assistant. She heard their whispers; the previous incumbent hadn't lasted long. A combination of being folded into tight spaces and the magician's shaking hands as he wielded his swords, had proved too much. If she hadn't needed to pay her rent, she would have turned her back on the director. Instead, she lifted her chin and accepted his offer. She watched the dancers leaving the stage, determined to join them before long.

Theodosia shivered and moved away from the window. She tightened her robe around her slender frame and sat where her mother had been in her dream. She longed for her advice, what would she have said about her daughter going to England? Her mother had insisted women should fight for their rights and refuse to allow society to overlook them. She encouraged Theodosia to be ambitious, to strive for a better life and recognise her value. Theodosia adored the beauty and fashionable sophistication of Paris, walks beside the Seine and to the majestic Notre-Dame Cathedral, the mouth-watering food and good wine, but she had never been anywhere else. Most people of their social class lived and died within a few miles of their birthplace. Her mother had made her promise to marry for love, to wait for *l'étincelle,'* the spark. The tongue-tied stage manager at The Folies Bergère often waited for Theodosia at the stage door. At Café de Flore the handsome waiter's eyes followed her every move. She hadn't experienced the spark with either of them. Perhaps in England she would find her man with the spark. Once she found him, they would have their own family. Her mother had always posed a question when any of them faced a decision. '*Ça te fait sourire?'* She hoped her mother would be proud of her now and in answer to her question, yes, travelling to England and dancing with the Zettler Girls did make her smile.

The French director accepted her decision to leave when he discovered Solomon Zettler's star dancer wasn't returning to England. Theodosia gave notice on her apartment, sold her belongings and bought a new hat and coat for the journey to England. The long duster coat would protect her jacket and skirt from the inevitable dirt, rain and soot. The lightweight, loose-fitting, blue linen coat had a long slit at the back. Alone in her apartment, she practised sitting, flipping the

sides of the coat up as she lowered herself onto a chair. She also practised her introduction.

'Good day, 'ow do you do? My name? My name is Theodosia
Labouriming.'

She frowned; she was proud of the name her parents had given her,
but she knew it wouldn't be easily understood. Friends called her Tee,
but she needed a name for the stage in England. Something short and
easy to remember that would make people smile. She closed her eyes,
recalling her mother's stories. Her mother had delighted in telling her
about remarkable women, insisting Theodosia could also create a life
for herself. Could she use one of their names? There was Céline Celéste,
the ballerina who enjoyed great success in New York City. Tee wondered what America was like and whether she would ever go there.
Now she was leaving Paris, she allowed herself to dream of a happy
future, full of dancing and glamour. To believe she would find her man
with the spark. That they would have a family. Perhaps she would have
daughters who would visit New York City. Daughters who would make
their own choices and lead happy, independent lives. She recalled
Emma Livry, a ballerina with the Paris Opera. She shuddered; if she
used Emma's name she would always be reminded of her tragic accident. Poor Emma died after her clothes caught fire on stage. An image
of 'La Goulue' flashed through her mind and she cringed. She was a
Moulin Rouge can-can dancer with a shocking reputation for risqué
dances and worse. No, her name was no good. Tee remembered her
mother's story about Francesca Caccini, the first woman to compose
an opera. She played five instruments and worked at the court of the
Medici family in Italy. Tee smiled; her mother would be proud she
remembered her stories. She decided to use Francesca's name but
shorten it. Her new surname was easy, 'La Fleur' for her mother's love
of flowers. Frannie La Fleur (Tee to her friends) smiled as she prepared
to leave her Paris apartment for the final time.

With a satisfying clunk, Tee clicked the solid brass buckles adorning
the top of her mother's carpet bag shut. The stylish dark-gold tapestry

fabric had faded and the leather handles were frayed, but the buckles had stood the test of time. She pictured her mother. Most of their belongings were second-hand but everything was polished until it shone. Her mother believed in dressing in the best clothes she could afford and approaching every new day as if it held promise. Tee had little of value apart from her mother's silver necklace, set with small sparkling stones. Her mother had worn it the day she announced she was expecting Tee's long-awaited brother. They dressed up and went to Café de Flore for hot chocolate. Tee smiled; her mother had sparkled that day. She wrapped the necklace in her handkerchief, promising her mother she would keep it safe and wear it often. Reassured her belongings were secure, she fastened the ribbons of her soft velvet bonnet under her chin. Her dark curls were pulled back at the sides and fastened in a low knot at the nape of her neck. Contrasting blue tones transformed the simple bonnet into something luxurious, its elegance belying its price. She caught her reflection in a window as she walked, a Parisienne lady travelling to England. She smiled; she had much that was precious. The handkerchief from her mother with the blue 'T' embroidered in the corner, feet that could dance and songs in her heart. Her parents had given her strength and determination to take with her wherever she went.

Tee's heart soared as the women gathered at the Gare du Nord. Her eyes sought Jeannie among the throng. Despite their communication difficulties friendship had blossomed, and Tee hoped to learn more about Jeannie on the journey. It involved two trains in France, a ferry from Calais to Dover and a train in England, to Charing Cross, London. It would take two days, if they weren't delayed by bad weather. She expected Mr Zettler would be taking them by the cheapest, most uncomfortable route. She spotted Jeannie and stepped forward, her embroidered suede boots peeping out from under her long skirt. She saw Mr Zettler clap his hands and gesture towards a large black shape approaching the station. As the train drew closer clouds of thick, dusty smoke filled the station and she lost sight of Jeannie. She coughed and her eyes ran as the dirty, sooty smoke surrounded her. She covered her ears as a deafening squeal from the huge locomotive engines brought the black monster to a halt. As the smoke cleared Mr Zettler shouted at them to board. She hurried towards the open door where Jeannie held out her hand.

Chapter 3

The chatter started the moment they took their seats. Before stowing her bag, Tee had removed her diary, intending to record as much of the journey as possible. She opened the small black leather-bound volume and checked her travelling documents were tucked inside. The whistle shrieked and the iron beast lurched from the station. Her parents' descriptions matched the reality of the lush green landscape the train chugged through. The fields rose then dipped then rose again and the train's engines beat a steady, rhythmic tone. She added words to the tone in her head.

'Je pars pour l'Angleterre. I'm going to England.'

In the early evening they reached Lille, where Mr Zettler instructed them to change onto another train. Tee's diary remained almost blank; her good intentions hampered by the womens' chatter. As they hurried to the next train, she repeated place names in her head, resolving to record the details later. She saw even less of the journey from Lille to Calais because Jeannie wanted them to learn more of each other's language. After a while Jeannie fell asleep. Tee moved her friend into a more comfortable position and settled into the train's rocking motion. As her eyelids grew heavy, she sensed someone watching her. Mr Zettler nodded before wrapping himself in a blanket and placing a pair of small black spectacles on his nose. If he was typical of Englishmen, she feared the man with the spark would continue to elude her. The sun dipped into a darkening sky as the train pulled into Calais. The engines wheezed as if they too, needed to sleep. Steam and smoke concealed Tee's view of the station as gritty dust and dirt swept through the coach. The women coughed as noxious air caught their throats. Mr Zettler motioned for them to collect their bags. Tee and Jeannie stepped onto the platform, stamping their numb feet to return them to life. Tee savoured the fresh air as they left the station, a warm breeze caressed her back as they walked. Mr Zettler strode at the front of the weary group, his umbrella raised as if in salute.

'Allez, Calais!'

He laughed, his eyes seeking Tee's. She tried asking Jeannie how far it was to the quay, praying *a short walk* meant not far. Her toes pinched against the tight fabric of her boots and the soles of her feet ached. Her stomach growled and she hoped there would be time to eat before the next stage of their journey. She looked around, smiling. For the first time she heard as many people speaking English as French. When they reached the quay, she looked towards the town. She could just see the tip of the *Tour du Guet,* the Watch Tower. Her father had said the tower's telegraph office was used to announce the death of Napoleon I in 1821. She gazed towards the Calais lighthouse, distinguishable from other coastal lighthouses by its white colour and black lantern. Her mother had told her another story of Calais, about Emma, Lady Hamilton and Horatio Nelson.

'Here was real romance but hidden behind a gentleman's arrogance and social standing!'

Despite their deep love and Nelson's honour, Emma's was an unhappy story. Tears welled in Tee's mother's eyes when she said Emma was destined by her low birth and gender to die in poverty. After Nelson died Emma fell into debt and spent time in a virtual debtor's prison. Tee's mother explained genteel prisoners could pay to live within three-square-miles of the prison. Tee questioned how Emma could pay and her mother just raised her eyebrows. In July 1814 Emma and her daughter escaped from their creditors and fled to Calais, where Emma died and was buried the following year. The sadness of Emma's story had never left Tee. Recalling it now strengthened her determination to build a prosperous life in England and marry for love or not at all.

They were due to catch the ferry to Dover at ten o'clock that evening, giving them time to eat in the refreshment room at the quay. Tee removed her gloves and inspected her hands. Her skin itched and the journey's dirt was thick under her long fingernails. She pointed to the *'Toilettes'* sign.

Jeannie replied in her limited French. *'Oui, je dois me repoudrer les yeux.'*

Tee didn't have the heart to explain Jeannie intended to powder her eyes, not her nose. Inside the powder room, the fragrance of her mother's soap escaped when the carpet bag's buckles clicked open. She had understood little of Mr Zettler's instructions about what to pack but, along with her mother's necklace, had brought the soap. As she unwrapped it, the clean, fresh scent of roses filled her nostrils, transporting her to Le Jardin des Tuileries in the 1st arrondissement. She had visited the elegant gardens separating the Louvre from the Place de la Concorde with her mother. It was the perfect landscape for walking and appreciating Parisian culture. Tee's parents didn't have a garden, but everyone benefited from the aromatic roses in Paris's beautiful public garden. As she lathered the delicate soap under the water, she pictured her mother breathing in the perfumed blooms. The soap washed away the dirt and soot of their journey. She smiled and passed the soap to Jeannie.

As they prepared to board the steam-powered passenger ferry to England, Tee looked for Mr Zettler. His short, wheezy cough and the tap tap of his silver walking cane alerted her to his presence. At the bottom of the gangplank a uniformed man stopped each passenger, checked their documents and inspected their baggage before allowing them to embark. As Mr Zettler reached him, his behaviour changed. His eyes darted around as Mr Zettler slipped a brown envelope into his gloved hand. The uniformed man tipped his cap and allowed Mr Zettler and the women to embark. Clutching her redundant travelling documents, she watched Mr Zettler take small, quick steps up the wooden gangplank. He paused and tied a bright red scarf over his hat.

Some of the women giggled at his outré attempt to triumph over the gusty wind. He turned and they were silenced. When the stage manager at the Folies Bergère had hinted at Mr Zettler's unusual behaviour and warned her not to trust him, Tee had brushed off his suspicions, thinking him resentful of her decision to leave. Now she wondered whether her new employer had something to hide. She continued to watch Mr Zettler as the women gathered on the wooden deck. He carried a large leather medical bag. He had placed it on the seat beside him on their train journeys, always keeping one hand on it. When he slept, he put it under his blanket and in the refreshment room he had placed it on a chair beside him. Why did the director of a dance troupe carry a medical bag? What did it contain to make him so determined to never lose sight of it? He spoke and she blushed, she had been staring.

'Avez-vous le mal de mer, Mademoiselle Labouriming?'

She had never travelled on water before and didn't know if she suffered from seasickness. She took a chance. 'Non, Monsieur Zettler.'

Another of the women approached him, her face ashen. She stumbled as if drunk and pointed at his bag. She attempted a pleading smile before vomiting. Mr Zettler led the woman away. Tee longed to ask Jeannie what was happening. She raised her eyebrows and tilted her head towards Mr Zettler. Jeannie shook her head. Tee walked to the rail; the leaden water churned beneath the ferry. She hoped Mr Zettler was tending to the woman with a seasickness remedy from his mysterious bag. She looked around. Some passengers stood at the rail or sat in one of a small number of chairs. Jeannie motioned for Tee to follow her towards a door in the middle of the deck. Tee pointed to the chairs, but Jeannie shook her head and gestured towards the ship's funnels, where a thin trickle of steam and smoke curled. Tee nodded, understanding Jeannie's concern. Once the ferry got underway thick steam and smoke would overpower anyone on deck. The door led them down some steps into a seated area. The hard seats provided little comfort and Jeannie removed her coat and placed it over her knees. Tee copied her friend, making herself as comfortable as possible. Some of their group sat nearby. Mr Zettler and the woman with seasickness had disappeared. Tee tried asking Jeannie about Mr Zettler's bag.

'Monsieur Zettler, son sac?'

Jeannie's brow furrowed.

Tee tried again. 'Le mal de mer?' She stuck her tongue out and used her hands to outline the shape of a bag. Jeannie nodded. The ferry's deafening whistle signalled their departure. Above the blaring whistle Tee caught one word of Jeannie's reply. It was the same in French, poison.

Tee didn't know how long the journey would take, only that they should arrive in England the following morning. Once the whistle stopped, she tried again to ask Jeannie about Mr Zettler. Her friend's eyes darted around the small seating area and she shook her head. Jeannie soon fell asleep, and Tee took out her diary. As they travelled to Calais the places they passed through had evoked wonderful memories of her parents' stories. Tee knew little of her parents' lives before she arrived, other than her mother dancing in the Paris music halls and her father working as a labourer. What she had were their stories, told on cold winter evenings as they drank hot chocolate, and on warm summer days as they walked by the Seine, the cool blue water sparkling in the sun's rays. The truth of the stories had never mattered. She longed to tell her mother her own stories in person. Instead, she decided to write reflections of her new, independent life as letters to her mother. Her mother would never read them, but the action brought her closer, in Tee's mind and in her heart.

'Dearest Maman,

Your little chocolate girl has left Paris! While dancing at your beloved Folies Bergère I was invited to travel to England with a dance troupe. I think you would be pleased, you always insisted I should strive for a better life. I remember your stories, full of romance, colour and music. Papa often strayed into tales of fighting for the glorious revolution, and you guided him to subjects more suitable for a young, impressionable girl. Maman, I delighted in Papa's stories!

What of my journey? We travelled north-west of Paris, passing the little town of Pontoise. I recalled the artist Camille Pissarro, who lived there and in London. Soon I shall be Theodosia Labouriming, the dancer who lived in Paris and London! The fields were as you described, so many shades of green. I longed to find the places you talked of, Jalais Hill and The Hermitage, but the locomotive chugged on, across the River Oise. Looking into the water I remembered our walks by the Seine, and I prayed for a river to equal it in England.'

The ferry lurched and Tee stopped writing. Screams rose as the vessel ploughed through the heavy swell of the cold waters. Jeannie stirred but didn't wake.

'Maman, what a beautiful little station is Gare de Beauvais! Papa bought your smart carpet bag there when he worked on the railway. When he returned, he told us about the magnificent tapestries he watched being made. He teased he had brought no presents. Then he produced a delightful pencil set for me and the elegant bag for you. I have it with me and will keep it always. My heart's desire is to buy you a new one, if only I could give it to you.'

The ferry hit rougher waters and her pencil scrawled a violent black line across the page. Jeannie woke as the vessel rocked, shaking them like dice in a cup. A woman was thrown to the floor. Mr Zettler's limited French stretched to blasphemous exclamations.

'Sacré bleu! Mon Dieu!'

Tee shared his dismay at the woman's injury, the deep cut bled heavily. Mr Zettler muttered and searched through his bag. Tee could see a vast array of drugs; she also saw the glint of a large, sharp knife. Her suspicions grew. She backed away as Mr Zettler tended to the woman. The cut bandaged; Mr Zettler led the woman away. Tee turned to Jeannie and raised her eyebrows. Her friend shook her head. The weather worsened. Some women vomited, others lay on the floor and tried to move with the vessel. Tee and Jeannie leant into one another and closed their eyes as wind and rain tossed the ferry around. After a while Jeannie's breathing changed but sleep eluded Tee. She prepared to continue writing but sensed someone watching her. As she turned, Mr Zettler inclined his head and smiled. She shuddered. There were men who recruited women as dancers then demanded they carry out less respectable work, like the women in the Folies Bergère's *'promenoir.'* At the back of the music hall, prostitutes walked freely during performances. Their behaviour gave a different meaning to the act of promenading, despite them being required to conduct their business with discretion. She shook her head. Mr Zettler had brought her to England because she was a good dancer, nothing more, nothing less. She returned to her writing.

'Dearest Maman,

I am sailing to England! I had not imagined such a bumpy passage; I am lucky not to have fallen victim to seasickness. Back to my journey. Further north from Gare de Beauvais, we passed Amiens. I remember Papa's story about the author Jules Verne and his surprise that Monsieur Verne left such a handsome city. How he could have left the canals, delightful promenades and the magnificent cathedral with its nave, such a masterpiece of architecture. Papa said Amiens was famous for the conclusion of the treaty of peace between France and England in 1802. Perhaps I shall remind my new English friends of that!

Maman, in the powder room at the Calais quay, I used your favourite soap, "Savon à la rose." It reminded me of our happy walks in Le Jardin des Tuileries. When I find my man with the spark, I shall insist on having a rose garden outside our house. I will love and protect my children as you and Papa loved and protected me. I have such dreams, Maman!'

Tee squinted; it was too dark to continue. She closed her eyes and slept until the whistle signalled their arrival. Dover's overcast early morning greeted them. Thoughts of seeing the famous white cliffs or the sun's rays casting a golden glow on the ancient castle were gone.

The exhausted women wanted to get to the train station and complete their journey. Mr Zettler corralled them and moved towards the exit. The woman with seasickness and the woman with the bandaged forehead reappeared. Once again Tee clutched her documents. She showed them to Jeannie and raised her eyebrows. Jeannie pointed towards Mr Zettler. Tee frowned as they disembarked in the same manner, following another mysterious exchange between Mr Zettler and a uniformed man at the bottom of the gangplank. She suspected Mr Zettler had paid to conceal the contents of his bag. On the train from Dover to Charing Cross she blinked to keep her eyes open, excited for her first view of London. She pushed her suspicions about Mr Zettler away and carried on writing.

'Maman, I am in England! This train will take me to London! Did you ever imagine your daughter travelling so far? Back to France. After Amiens, we arrived at Arras. This was one of Papa's favourite stories! His hero, Maximilien Robespierre, was born in Arras in 1758. Papa hailed him as the best and most influential figure of the French Revolution. I remember you stopping Papa when his eyes grew wide, and he threw his arms around as the story ventured into a tale of bloody murder and atrocity. I thought it a fantastic story, I loved Papa's excitement! We took another train at Lille, near France's border with Belgium. We went straight from one station to another and I learnt nothing of Lille or Belgium. Maman, I must tell you about my new friend Jeannie and our employer, Mr Solomon Zettler.'

Tee stopped writing as Jeannie stirred, stretching and yawning herself awake. The sun rose into a pale blue sky and dirty grey clouds scudded past as the train chugged into London. Tee's first impression of London was its greyness. Dusty clouds, stone-dark smoke enveloping the train and, as they approached their destination and crossed a river, dreary, muddy water. Even with the sun rising above it, the Thames could never rival the Seine. Tee shivered as she stepped from the train, pulling her thin coat around her. Mr Zettler narrowed his eyes and called the women towards him. He bent low, forcing them to move closer. Some of them gasped and drew together as he spoke, whatever could he be saying? The words Tee recognised because they were similar in French had no place in her new, exciting life in London. Why was Mr Zettler talking about *'meurtres brutaux,'* brutal murders, *'la criminalité,'* criminality and *'les prostituées,'* prostitutes?

Tee linked her arm through Jeannie's as they walked. Derelict warehouses and high tenement buildings blackened by smoke made her question her decision to leave Paris. She held her breath as they passed narrow, shabby alleyways. She covered her nose with a gloved hand as the stench from gutters overflowing with sewage crept over their weary group. London's poor were packed together in sordid sinks of poverty. There was nothing appealing in the overcrowded area of warehouses, abattoirs, pubs, cheap music halls and lodging houses. She pictured Paris and the Seine and shook her head. What had possessed her to leave that behind for this cold, stinking place?

When Mr Zettler stopped, he tilted his head towards the door of yet another grey building. Tee raised her eyebrows. Jeannie pointed at the building and Tee's bag. Mr Zettler crossed the road and entered the Metropolitan Music Hall. Tee followed Jeannie and the other women into their lodging house. They dumped their bags then trudged across the road. Their first show was the next day and Mr Zettler had instructed them to meet him on stage in five minutes, ready for rehearsals.

Chapter 4

The Metropolitan Music Hall, London

The Metropolitan Music Hall's terracotta granite facade made it the most imposing building on Shaftesbury Avenue. Tee took in the elaborate, artistic carvings adorning the grand, modern entrance. The women walked to the side of the building and entered by the stage door. Mr Zettler tapped his cane as he ushered them into the dressing room, packed with performers in varying states of undress. The Zettler Girls were one of several variety acts scheduled to perform the next day. As the women squeezed past tightrope walkers and clowns, Mr Zettler twitched and shouted.

Any doubts Tee had about coming to England vanished the moment she stepped on stage. She took comfort from the familiar; the sweet, waxy smell of the greasepaint, the cacophony of noise as the musicians tuned their instruments, the thrill of anticipation as the dancers lined up in the wings. The Zettler Girls' twittering stopped when they linked arms and prepared to dance, like a nest of baby birds about to fledge, they readied themselves. They shimmied and swished, using every ounce of energy in their bone-weary bodies. They were determined to give the performance of a lifetime the next day. The loyal London audience had missed their favourite dance troupe while the Zettler Girls were in Paris, the women wanted to reward their followers with a spectacular show.

They waited two weeks for a day off. Once she had accepted London would never be Paris, Tee settled into her new life. Their lodgings were clean and they had enough to eat. She and Jeannie became inseparable, and their knowledge of each other's language grew each day. As they left Shaftesbury Avenue on their day off, Jeannie said she had a surprise for Tee. As they approached their destination, Jeannie told Tee to close her eyes. Tee didn't need sight. A wonderful, sweet smell filled her nostrils and she could taste it, chocolate.

'Open your eyes, we're here!'

Tee opened her eyes slowly, wanting to savour Jeannie's surprise. They were outside The Paris Chocolate Company on Regent Street. Tee caught her breath as the smell transported her to Café de Flore, drinking hot chocolate with her parents. She swallowed to dislodge the lump in her throat and turned to embrace her friend. Jeannie's eyes were bright as Tee thanked her. They giggled as they pushed the heavy, ornate door. A bell tinkled and a uniformed waitress appeared and led them to a small table. As they waited for their cocoa, Tee's eyes were drawn to the large glass counter and its vast display of chocolate in all its forms, tablets, powder, bonbons and medallions. Behind the counter, the pièce de resistance of the display, the French syrups. Bottles full to the brim with the choicest condensed fruits, each one a different colour, bursting with flavour and sweetness, waiting to be brought to life with cold water. After two cups of cocoa Tee and Jeannie left the delightful smell of chocolate behind. As they crossed the road towards Hyde Park, Tee spotted Mr Zettler. His jaunty walk and short, wheezy cough were unmistakable. She pulled Jeannie into a doorway and they held their breath as Mr Zettler's cane tapped closer. When it stopped Tee heard a whispered greeting. She peeked out. Mr Zettler's hand rested on his silver cane as he spoke to a man in the next doorway. The men were reflected in the window, heads close together. They exchanged something, a small package to Mr Zettler and a brown envelope to the stranger. She ducked back into their hiding place as Mr Zettler cleared his throat and bid the stranger farewell.

The women hurried towards the park, keen to avoid their mysterious employer. Tee listened as Jeannie told her what she knew about the park. Henry VIII had created it for hunting deer in 1536. Opened to the public in 1637, in addition to being the venue for the Great Exhibition of 1851 in the famous Crystal Palace, the park's exciting history included duels, demonstrations and summer parades. Speakers' Corner was a focal point for free speech and debate. Tee slowed her pace, taking in the beauty of the popular destination. They joined the throng of walkers and horse-riders on one of the tidy paths, bordered by avenues of trees. Tee smiled, appreciating the tall oaks and elegant silver birch. They followed a footpath running alongside the bank of a lake. At the first bend of the Serpentine, they sat on a bench. Tee turned to Jeannie, determined to learn more about Mr Zettler.

'What does he keep in his medical bag, Jeannie?'

Jeannie leant in and lowered her voice. She looked around before answering. 'Medicines.'

'Why? He's not a doctor. Is he ill?'

Tee considered Mr Zettler's constant cough and the wheezing. Had their employer fallen victim to the deadly effects of the London air? When they had arrived at Charing Cross a thick, choking smog hung over the city. The yellow fog was a constant, unwelcome companion and Jeannie urged Tee to cover her mouth and not inhale the noxious pollutants. Once enough of the irritant-carrying fog settled in your lungs, a slow and painful death would follow. The sulphurous fog swirled around the shadowed streets, offering a protective cloak to criminals and predators.

'Does the fog make him cough and wheeze, Jeannie?'

'No, he has asthma.'

'What else?'

Jeannie's words were quick. 'Poison. He takes poisons.'

Mr Zettler had asked Tee if she suffered from sea sickness. Icy fingers crept up her spine. If she had accepted his remedy, what would he have produced from his sinister bag?

'Did he give one of the dancers poison on the ferry, Jeannie? The poor woman looked worse by the time we reached Dover.'

'The so-called remedy is something called creosote. He gives the foul-tasting liquid to anyone who's desperate enough to take it.'

'What do you suppose was in the package he took from the man in the doorway?'

'I don't know. You wouldn't think it from his coughing and wheezing but he takes something for his asthma. Have you noticed those little cigarettes he smokes?'

Tee nodded.

'They contain something called stramonium. It brings on hallucinations and delirium. I saw an advertisement for them, they're called *"Cigares de Joy"* and they tell you to hold the smoke in as long as possible.' Jeannie shuddered and twisted her lips before continuing. 'Can you imagine? It would be like breathing in the foul London fog. The tobacco brings on vertigo, nausea and vomiting, you get cold sweats and can't speak or think properly.'

'Why would anyone choose to smoke them? And why does he risk carrying everything around in his strange bag?'

Jeannie shook her head. 'Perhaps he thinks he can pass as a doctor so no one will ask awkward questions. Or perhaps he's terrified of losing any of his precious drugs.'

'What else does he take?'

'I don't know, but don't ever accept anything he offers you. Promise?'

Tee nodded, unnerved by the exchange. Something else troubled her about Jeannie's hushed indictment of their employer. 'How do you know all this, Jeannie?'

Jeannie's body stiffened and she turned away. Her shoulders shook as she sobbed. Jeannie, the woman with a ready smile who now wept, grief-stricken. As Jeannie's sobs slowed Tee stroked her back and repeated the question. Jeannie sniffed and took a deep breath. When she had finished speaking Tee embraced her. 'Come on, we need to get warm.'

Back at their lodgings, Jeannie slept. Tee's heart ached as she opened her diary.

'Dearest Maman,

I promised to tell you about my friend Jeannie and our employer, Mr Solomon Zettler. You always said looks are unimportant, a person's value is in their behaviour towards others. Mr Zettler's appearance can be forgiven, but his habits leave much to be desired. His craving for the "Cigares de Joy" is not the worst thing, but he is dependent on drugs and poisons. He carries a large medical bag and I have seen some of its contents, laudanum, morphine, and arsenic. It is no surprise he keeps such vigilance over the bag. Jeannie is everything I could wish for in a friend. She is kind and cheerful, although I have learnt that cheer is applied anew each day, masking a deep, dark sorrow. A sorrow caused by Mr Zettler.'

Jeannie stirred but didn't wake. Tee continued writing.

'This is Jeannie's story Maman, as she told it to me. Jeannie lived a happy life with her parents until she was 12. That year the ever-present London fog was unusually thick and persistent and carried within it an invisible killer. Tragically, Jeannie's parents were among the hundreds who contracted fatal bronchitis. Jeannie escaped the deadly infection but with no other family, was taken in by a charity. Her expectation of being safe and cared for did not last. With little to eat and beatings from those meant to protect her, she had to escape. She left and no one looked for her. Her swift descent took her to the workhouse and then onto the streets, where Mr Zettler found her, begging to survive. He offered her work at his music hall, in exchange for food and a bed. She accepted this upturn in her fortunes, only to find herself trapped in Mr Zettler's sinister world. A dancer called Kitty took Jeannie under her wing, without her protection Jeannie's story would have been very different. Kitty kept Jeannie safe. Jeannie only learnt of the agreement later; Kitty sold her soul in exchange for Jeannie's safety. One day Kitty missed rehearsals and Jeannie listened in horror as the rumour spread around the dance troupe. Kitty had been taken to one of Mr Zettler's seedy brothels. He owned several of the feared establishments, situated well-away from the respectable Jewish community in London.

Jeannie never saw Kitty again. She became a dancer and grew up learning how to look after herself, but she never forgave Mr Zettler.

A few years passed but history repeated itself when Jeannie met Fred, a stagehand at the music hall. Remember you told me to wait for the spark? Well, Jeannie and Fred found it! Fred came to London from the north of England, seeking his fortune. He worked for Mr Zettler and as soon as Jeannie saw Fred, she knew they would fall in love. She said how happy they were and how they talked of their plan to flee the music hall and Mr Zettler. Before they could save enough, Fred had an accident and everything changed. The stagehands had to move props and equipment around quickly, in-between acts. One day Mr Zettler bellowed at Fred and Jeannie's beau, fearful of their employer, attempted to lift a heavy piece of scenery on his own. He fell and injured his back. Mr Zettler appeared with his bag and Fred made a good recovery. Then Fred's behaviour changed. He became sullen and withdrawn and Jeannie feared he had fallen out of love with her. One day she saw him whispering in a dark corner with Mr Zettler. The director poked his cane in Fred's face, demanding money. When Jeannie confronted Fred, he snarled it was none of her business.

"This monster wasn't my Fred, Tee."

As Mr Zettler's grip tightened, Jeannie was powerless to halt the change in Fred. His back injury left him with a permanent stoop and Mr Zettler's drugs made him moody and unpredictable. Jeannie tried talking to him but the Fred she had fallen in love with was gone. This Fred no longer kissed her gently or shared secret plans of their escape. This Fred snarled and stole from her to satisfy his cravings. This Fred, either deeply depressed or euphoric, constantly sought the oblivion Mr Zettler's drugs provided. Like many addicts he chose a life without the person who loved him, rather than a life without the substances he craved. At the end of a gruelling performance a hunched Fred, slurring and racked with pain, searched for Mr Zettler. Jeannie seized her opportunity and said their employer was waiting for Fred in the lodging house. Once there, she locked Fred in.

"It was the longest, darkest night of my life, Tee."

When Mr Zettler failed to arrive, Fred turned on Jeannie. He shouted and pummelled the door with his fists, demanding to be let out. He threw

Jeannie onto the bed and spittle flew into her face as he growled. His sweat dripped into her eyes, mingling with her tears. As she wept, he paced the room like a caged animal, hands clenched and fists ready. He continued to pound on the locked door. Eventually he passed out and Jeannie covered him with a blanket. The body she had once embraced and delighted in, now drug-ravaged and convulsing. By turns Fred sweated and shivered. All night long he moaned, his arms and legs cramping and twitching as his body tried to rid itself of Mr Zettler's poison. He vomited on the bed, the floor and on his beloved Jeannie as she mopped his brow. Fred, who had never raised his voice or his hand to her, ranted and raved as if the devil had claimed his soul. Eventually, exhaustion took over and he slept. Jeannie's eyes grew heavy as she too succumbed to the horrors of their evening.

Jeannie woke to an empty room, the key hanging in the lock. She heard a commotion outside and saw a dancer running towards the lodging house. She froze. Fred had gone straight back to the danger she had tried to save him from. She found a shell of a man. His ruined body lay slumped against a wall behind the music hall, rain plastered his hair to his head and soaked his clothes. She knelt beside him and gently removed the dirty needle from his arm. She stroked his grey face and kissed his blue lips. The gentle man from the north of England who came to the capital to seek his fortune, had lost his life to the dark side of London that lurked in the shadows. The depraved underbelly of the city had claimed an innocent man. Kneeling by Fred's body Jeannie made a vow, she knew not how or when, but she would ensure Mr Zettler paid for his brutal treatment of Fred.

After Fred died Jeannie tried to find a job elsewhere. Dancers never left Mr Zettler's employ of their own accord. They were sent to one of his brothels or submitted to life on the streets. When the opportunity arose to perform at the Folies Bergère, Jeannie decided to slip away and stay in Paris. Meeting me and learning I intended to return to London with them changed her mind. With me by her side, Jeannie's spirits rose, and she resolved to put her grief behind her. Jeannie is like family to me, Maman. I will try to protect her as I would a sister or a daughter. I know she will do the same for me.'

Tee avoided Mr Zettler, but his ominous shadow was ever-present. She listened for his wheezy cough and the tap tap of his cane, making herself scarce when he came near. She and Jeannie stuck together. They got changed and removed their make-up together and they linked arms when they left the music hall.

Tee had been in London for a few months when Mr Zettler joined them on stage as they took their bows at the end of an evening performance. She saw the women stiffen at his presence. Once the music hall was empty, he raised his hands. Increasingly dependent on the vile *'Cigares de Joy,'* he was overcome by violent coughing. No one helped as he bent double to control his breathing. As he recovered his stance, he met Tee's eyes, an angry red vein pulsating in his neck. His eyes were hooded and bloodshot, and his smile belied an ominous threat. The women were silent as he delivered his menacing monologue. As he spoke, toes tapped and arms twitched as the womens' anxiety grew. Tee understood enough, he smirked as he told them about brutal attacks and murders. Pointing at them, his hissed whispers declared the victims were dancers and prostitutes. While these attacks were less common in the more respectable west end of London, he warned of depravity spreading from the east. A few miles away, he cautioned, were women so reduced in circumstance as to be forced to sin or starve to death. He grinned, saying he told them this not to scare, but to protect them. He ended with a sibilant assurance; they were safe working for him. As the dancers left the stage, he reached out a dirty, wizened hand. The dancers scattered like autumn leaves in the wind as he approached. Tee recoiled as his long, dirty fingernail traced a line down her arm.

'Worry not, my French beauty. I will keep you safe. You can work in my house.'

Jeannie pulled Tee away and they ran. They knew what working in his house meant and Tee had no intention of being trapped in one of his seedy brothels. She stared at Jeannie; her friend's eyes were steely.

'He took Kitty from me, then he took my beloved Fred. He will not take you!'

'But where can we go?'

Jeannie smiled. 'Newcastle-upon Tyne!'

Tee had never heard of Newcastle-upon-Tyne. She listened as Jeannie explained Newcastle was Fred's hometown. She said she knew nothing of any family Fred had left behind, but it was somewhere she could feel close to him again. A few days later, their plans were in place and they fled. Between them they had enough money to pay for the train journey and their surreptitious exit from the lodging house. A friend of Fred's arranged for them to be hidden inside a wagon delivering supplies to the Capitol cafeteria and restaurant, next door to the music hall. They slipped silently from the lodging house as the sun rose. The wagon took them to Kings Cross station where they caught the first of two trains. They were heading towards an uncertain future in a place where they knew no one. It was preferable to living with the threat of Solomon Zettler's next sinister move.

Chapter 5

Newcastle-upon-Tyne

Tee smiled as they passed through lush countryside and pretty villages. They took two trains, one from London to somewhere called York and another from York to Newcastle-upon-Tyne. As the train gathered pace and moved further from the capital's outskirts, Tee frowned at the changing landscape. Verdant fields and quaint villages were replaced by dark industrial buildings and rundown cottages. She narrowed her eyes to make out a mysterious structure with huge chimneys, positioned on top of a small hill a little way from the railway. Intricate systems of ropes, pulleys and wheels supported the monoliths. Huge black seams cut through the hills, like rough, jagged scars. Tee knew about mining but had never witnessed the harsh reality of the conditions in which men and boys risked their lives, to bring the precious black gold to the surface.

Jeannie spoke sadly. 'That was one of the reasons Fred left the North-East, Tee. His father took him to the pit head and said unless Fred wanted to go into the hot depths of hell every day, unless he wanted a life in the dark and possibly a death there too, he had to get away.'

'Do you know any more about Fred's family, Jeannie?'

'No, his father died in a pit collapse not long after that conversation. His mother was already dead and he had no brothers or sisters. The only person I know of in Newcastle is Mrs Swann.'

Tee smiled; she had understood enough of the story to want to hear it again. She asked Jeannie to regale Fred's tale of the spirited woman he met before he left Newcastle. He had saved enough money to get to London and pay for a few nights' lodgings. He arrived at the station early, worried if he waited at home, he would change his mind. He found a spot on the platform and watched the comings and goings. As he waited a strange scene unfolded, involving a stout woman and a bird in a cage. The woman's bright clothes and hat festooned with colourful feathers and ribbons marked her out on the otherwise drab platform. Fred had never seen such a hat. The women in his village only wore hats on Sundays, for church. Instead, they wore white cloths, tied at the nape. The functional coverings were designed to protect them from dust and dirt as they cooked, cleaned and scrubbed. This woman's hat was something else. Her large bosom quivered as she argued with the station porter. She called for the stationmaster and a second uniformed man appeared. Fred moved closer. The stationmaster's imperious tone left no room for doubt.

'No Madam, I am sorry, it is impossible.'

'My man, as I have already told you, the Captain has accompanied me on the train ever since my dear husband passed away.'

'That is as may be, Madam. Today the answer is no. The Captain cannot travel with you.'

The woman was alone, Fred couldn't see the mysterious Captain. A high-pitched squawk made Fred jump. 'Man bad!' The woman hid a smile and her eyes held the stationmaster's glare.

'What am I expected to do? My train is due. There is insufficient time for me to return the Captain to Springbank Lane.'

'I am afraid I cannot help you, Madam. Perhaps someone could take it home for you?'

'It? The Captain is a most handsome he, and I thank you to remember it, sir!'

Tee giggled, knowing what was next in Jeannie's story.

A blanket draped over a cage at the woman's feet jutted out repeatedly as the Captain pecked at the article of his captivity. 'Train! Train!'

Fred laughed and the woman turned her heavily powdered face towards him. Kind, mischievous eyes sparkled beneath sweeping dark lashes.

'And you are?'

Fred shook the woman's gloved hand and soon found himself heading to Springbank Lane. People turned to look at the handsome young man with the parrot in a cage. 'Man good!'

Tee smiled. 'Fred was kind to her, Jeannie.'

'He *was* kind, Tee. Before Mr Zettler's filthy drugs controlled his every waking moment.'

Fred could take the precious Captain home and still catch his train. Mrs Swann offered to pay him, but he refused to take her money. Instead, fascinated by the sound of her guest house, he accepted the invitation to join her for tea when he returned from London. Mrs Swann offered accommodation to music hall performers. She loved the gaiety and entertainment her guests brought into her home. Friends with more conservative boarding establishments balked at the idea of serving evening meals at midnight and breakfasts at lunchtime. Mrs Swann was the perfect hostess for artistes and performers. A voice greeted Fred outside Mrs Swann's guest house.

'Oh, you got the job of bringing the Captain home this time, did you?'

Fred laughed, realising this was a regular occurrence. He was one in a long line of people to have the pleasure of meeting Mrs Swann and the Captain. He nodded. If the remnants of make-up on the man's face hadn't given away his occupation, the Captain did.

'Clown! Clown!'

Faded black marks on the man's cheeks, forehead, chin and the tip of his nose confirmed the Captain's identification skills. The man wobbled towards Fred, twisting his hat in his hands.

'Late night, see.' The man blushed.

'I was waiting for my train, and...' Fred gestured towards the Captain.

The man guffawed. 'She does it all the time! I'm Corky. Are you coming in?'

Fred wanted nothing more than to see the inside of Mrs Swann's guest house. 'No, thank you. I have to catch my train. I'll visit when I return from London.'

Corky took the Captain. The high-pitched squawk reached Fred as he walked away. 'Ta-ta!'

Jeannie's eyes filled with tears as she finished her story. Fred had never made it back to Springbank Lane. Tee touched her friend's arm.

'We will visit her, Jeannie, and tell her how special Fred was.'

Jeannie sniffed and her shoulders shook as she nodded. Tee forced her weary eyes open as the train slowed to a halt. Jeannie stood and stretched then gathered her belongings together.

'This is York, Tee. We need to change trains here.'

Tee yawned as she collected her carpet bag. As she stepped from the train, her eyes were drawn to the huge roof arches and elegant iron lamp posts situated at intervals along the platform. York was the most beautiful of the stations she had seen since leaving France. Splendid, polished copper lanterns at the top of each lamp post illuminated the charming station. She smiled at the orange light, reflecting downwards and casting colourful muted shadows over the platform. York could never rival the chic Gare de Beauvais, but it came close. As she boarded the train to Newcastle, Tee hoped their destination would be as delightful as York.

Once they were settled Jeannie turned and patted Tee's hand. 'Thank you, Tee.'

Tee raised her eyebrows.

'When I told you what happened to Fred, you didn't judge him. You are a true friend.'

Tee smiled. 'Ma chérie Jeannie, you are the best friend I have ever had. My parents brought me up to treat others as I hope to be treated.'

'Have you ever been in love, Tee?'

The question took Tee by surprise, she shook her head as she answered. 'No, Jeannie. I loved my parents, but I have never found a man with the spark.'

Jeannie smiled. 'Well, you might find him in Newcastle!'

Tee's eyes grew heavy as the engines chugged onwards and she moved to position her head on Jeannie's shoulder. She felt a tug at the sleeve of her coat as Jeannie shook her awake.

'Look Tee! The bridge to Newcastle!'

Tee blinked as the dark structure loomed into view. A man's voice boomed around the carriage, regaling a tale of Queen Victoria opening the bridge in 1849. The redoubtable monarch described it as *'a handsome stone bridge built across the river, 132 feet above low water, the river being full of shipping.'* On the other side of the bridge lay Newcastle-upon-Tyne. Two tall church spires bore down on the hillside above the inky river, dominating the industrial landscape.

'Remind me, Jeannie. What is the name of the river?'

'The Tyne, Tee. As in Newcastle-upon-Tyne.'

Tee peered into the oily waters. Queen Victoria had provided an accurate description. The river was a hive of activity, plumes of dirty smoke from the factories and workshops curled along the length of the riverbank. Foul smoke from the iron foundry and the engine works belched into the air. This river, like the Thames, bore no resemblance to her beloved Seine. Below them a young couple held hands as they ran across another, smaller bridge. Tee understood the couples' carefree escape, anyone would flee from a life in the dilapidated tenement buildings dominating the other side of the Tyne. She dragged her eyes away from the couple as the train crossed into Newcastle. A porter directed them towards a decent, reasonably priced guest house. As they left the station through the *'grand porte cochère,'* Tee relaxed into her new surroundings. They started walking in the direction of the recommended guest house, then Jeannie stopped.

'Tee, you said we could visit Mrs Swann and tell her about Fred.'

'Yes.'

'Why not now? Fred said she kept late hours. I think Springbank Lane is quite close.'

Tee studied Jeannie, she understood her need to pursue the link to her lost love. Although Tee's mother would never read anything she wrote, keeping a diary helped her feel she was close. Tee agreed and they hurried back into the station to seek directions to Springbank Lane. In their excitement, the women were oblivious to two railway workers watching their every move from further along the platform. Henry Brown and Ernie Redford had spotted the women the moment their elegant toes stepped from the train.

Chapter 6

Mrs Swann set her glass down and bustled to the front door. Her residents were all at work and she wasn't expecting anyone. New guests were always welcome at Springbank Lane and she smiled as she opened the door with a theatrical flourish. Her usual effusive greeting stuck in her throat, which lucky wind had blown these two beauties onto her front step?

'Mrs Swann?' The brown-haired woman's eyes filled with tears.

'Oh, my dear, whatever is it? Quick, come in. Gins all round, I think!'

Sometime later, after the exchange of tears, gin and life-stories, Tee and Jeannie found themselves unpacking in Mrs Swann's pretty attic bedroom. She had insisted they stay, and suggested they seek work at a nearby music hall. Jeannie kept the full details of Fred's harrowing death from Mrs Swann. She said nothing about drugs, only that he was involved in a fatal accident in London. Mrs Swann put her hands over her mouth at the news of Fred's demise.

'He was so young. And so kind to help me with the Captain, I had hoped to meet him again.' Mrs Swann nodded her head towards the covered cage in the corner of the room where an oblivious Captain snored gently. 'He will be so upset when I tell him.'

Over breakfast the following morning Mrs Swann provided directions to Central Street Music Hall and told them to mention they were her guests. 'A number of my residents are engaged there; I am confident they will find places in their chorus line for two talented dancers!'

Tee and Jeannie performed a few routines by way of an audition and were quickly accepted into Central Street's theatrical family. The previous evening Mrs Swann had explained they wouldn't meet her other residents until the following night, because they didn't appear for breakfast until late morning. Now the friends were dressing for dinner, excited by the prospect of an entertaining evening. Mrs Swann smiled as Tee and Jeannie stepped into her decorative parlour. She jumped at a loud clatter of cymbals from the hallway. The proffered drinks wobbled precariously.

'It sounds as though our resident clown is home!'

Mrs Swann moved closer to Jeannie and whispered. 'I have already told him the sad news about Fred.'

The rotund man filled the doorway, his laugh as large as his girth. He dropped his cymbals and tipped his hat towards them. 'Ladies, how delightful! Corky the clumsy clown at your service!'

Corky's stomach prevented him from completing his bow. He shrugged and barrelled towards them; arms outstretched. His large chubby arms enveloped them in a warm, sweaty hug. When he released them, he looked from one to the other, his kind eyes settling on Jeannie.

'I only met him one time when he brought the Captain home. Nice man, Captain said so.'

'I am Jeannie. Thank you, Corky.'

'And I am Theodosia. I am pleased to meet you, Corky.'

'See-o-doo? Sorry, Miss. What?'

Tee and Jeannie laughed. 'Call me Tee, Corky.'

Corky twisted his hat in his hands, blushing as Mrs Swann handed him a drink. The gentle giant cradled the delicate glass in his large hands. Tears pricked Jeannie's eyes. She swallowed and turned away, waiting for the emptiness of Fred's absence to pass. As her tears started, a welcome distraction arrived. Jeannie wiped her eyes and turned back.

A young couple fell into the parlour, laughing and shouting.

'I tell you it was!'

'And I tell you it wasn't! How could you have seen a giraffe in Newcastle?'

'Then it must have been a very tall horse with a very long neck!'

The couple's infectious laughter spread around the parlour and Jeannie's sadness went unnoticed as she slipped it back inside her heart.

'Ladies, let me introduce you to our very own eccentric dancers, Jim Colvill and Annie Tate!'

Tee and Jeannie had known comedy entertainers in London and Jim and Annie's high spirits were welcome. The well-dressed, handsome young couple kept them entertained with an endless stream of jokes and funny stories. Next to arrive was a beautiful young woman whom Mrs Swann introduced as Fatima Ferrari. Corky wasted no time in sidling up to Fatima and revealing her occupation. He placed a chubby finger on his lips then made his pronouncement.

'Miss Fatima, she's a belly-dancer! She's very flexible, very good if you drop something under the table!'

Everyone laughed. Corky beamed as Mrs Swann topped up their drinks. As Tee and Jeannie introduced themselves to Fatima, a booming voice interrupted their conversation.

'Sully's home!'

The room erupted with cheers as a tall, handsome man made a dramatic entrance. He flung the parlour door open and juggled his way into the room, continuously throwing coloured balls into the air and never failing to catch them. Tee marvelled at his balletic action, he kept at least one ball in the air while handling the others. She watched as he expertly juggled towards the drinks cabinet.

'Sully Sullivan! Not the lemons! They're for the gin!' Mrs Swann's generous bosom quivered as she blushed, she was sweet on the athletic juggler. Sully turned away from the lemons.

'Who do we have here?'

His unusual accent puzzled Tee. Corky solved the mystery. 'Sully pretends he's from a big place called Australia but he's from London, a Cock-a-knee.'

Sully approached Tee and introduced himself, without the fake accent. 'Guilty as charged. Ladies, Sully Sullivan at your service!'

Sully bowed low in front of them. As he rose his eyes fixed on Jeannie. The friends exchanged a glance as they sipped their drinks. How fortunate that Fred had met Mrs Swann and this happy assortment of friendly, entertaining characters had welcomed them. Sully returned to the hallway and packed the juggling balls into a suitcase along with hammers and knives, ready for his next performance. The last of Mrs Swann's residents floated into the room as if on air. Corky delighted in making the introductions, blushing in front of the petite, beautiful young women.

'This is Ora, Petra and Kora, they walk the tight high-rope!'

'No Corky, the high tightrope!' Mrs Swann corrected the bashful clown as the women each stretched out a graceful hand to first Tee then Jeannie. They moved in unison as if they were one, not three separate individuals.

'Very well, I think we are all present and correct. Let's eat, drink and be very merry!'

After eating her fill, Tee looked around. Her maman would have revelled in the company of these kind people. As she enjoyed her new surroundings, someone started singing. The dulcet tones belonged to Corky. The bumbling clown who struggled to utter simple words had no trouble when he sang. His bashful expression and hat-twisting gone, he held his head high and his arms outstretched as his pitch perfect tenor filled the parlour.

'I dream of Jeannie with the light brown hair,
Borne, like a vapour, in the summer air.
I see her tripping where the bright streams play,
Happy as the daisies that dance on her way.'

As Corky sang, compassionate eyes turned towards Jeannie. Her grief revealed itself and she lowered her head. Tee reached for Jeannie's hand under the table. Fred should be here. She knew Jeannie would never forgive Solomon Zettler for stealing her true love away in such cruel fashion. Jeannie squeezed Tee's hand back. Tee knew that here, Jeannie would try to make a new life, to find happiness again. The table erupted as Corky bowed. As Mrs Swann replenished their glasses another singer took to the floor. Jim Colvill turned to face his wife as his deep, mellifluous tones filled the room.

'There'a wound in my spirit,
No balm can e'er heal:
In my soul is a sorrow,
No voice can reveal.
And deeper the furrows,
Will sink on my brow,
For Annie, my own love,
Is gone from me now.'

As Annie Tate embraced her husband, everyone sang the chorus. Tee smiled at their well-practised perfect pitch and timing. She and Jeannie joined in as the merry group raised their voices in joyful song. Sometime later Tee and Jeannie made their weary way to bed, their stomachs full of good food and wine and their hearts full of gratitude. Springbank Lane's cast of colourful characters had accepted them as family and enveloped them in their warmth. They belonged.

Chapter 7

Tee and Jeannie's lives settled into a happy rhythm. After their final performance each evening, the entertainment continued at Springbank Lane. They usually returned to Mrs Swann's in between matinee and evening shows, but as they left Central Street one Saturday afternoon, Jeannie led Tee in the other direction. As they strolled along the grey cobbles, they were dwarfed by the shadows of magnificent buildings. When they reached the impressive Grey Street, Tee turned to Jeannie.

'Where are we going?'

'We don't have long before we have to be back so I thought we would have a treat.'

'What treat, where?'

'It's a surprise.'

Tee followed her friend along the street of smart buildings. As they rounded a corner she clapped her hands, Jeannie had found a Paris Chocolate Company in Newcastle! It was smaller than the London one, but as Jeannie pushed the heavy door Tee smiled at the bell's familiar tinkle. In a small area with high stools at the back of the shop, they relaxed and enjoyed their cocoa. It became their regular haunt in between matinee and evening shows. During one visit Tee asked Jeannie about Sully Sullivan. Jeannie blushed.

'I don't know what you mean.'

'Come on Jeannie, everyone knows he's sweet on you!'

'What about you? The men who wait at the stage door always ask for you.'

'Don't change the subject! Don't you like him?'

'Who?'

Tee shook her head; she wouldn't pursue it. Sully followed Jeannie's every move and Tee had hoped her friend might give him a chance.

'It's...' Jeannie hesitated.

'What?' Tee raised her eyebrows.

'I loved Fred so much. What if I fall in love and the same thing happens? My heart wouldn't recover a second time, I'm not sure it will ever fully recover from losing Fred.'

'I know. But what if you try again and find true love with Sully?'

Jeannie's bleak, empty eyes tore at Tee's heart. 'I found it, Tee. I found the spark with Fred. I can't imagine finding it twice, can you?'

Tee looked away. Her maman had told her to wait for the spark but it was nowhere to be seen. Jeannie was right, how could anyone expect to find true love more than once in a lifetime?

'I'm sorry, Jeannie. Let's agree not to think about Sully Sullivan or any other man. We can be happy, independent women who work hard and enjoy their leisure time.'

Tee linked her arm through Jeannie's as they left the Paris Chocolate Company. As they made their way back to Central Street two men stood unnoticed on the opposite side of the street.

*

Henry studied his dusty shoes as Ernie pulled at his sleeve.

'Henry, it's them!'

Ernie had been determined to discover where the beautiful women went after they left the train station, and it hadn't proved difficult. The women left then returned to speak to the station porter. The porter's discretion vanished when Ernie promised to buy him a drink. The women had asked for directions to Mrs Swann's guest house. Ernie had delivered a triumphant punch to Henry's shoulder.

'They must be dancers or actresses! Mrs Swann only takes in people from the music halls.'

'Alright Ernie, calm down.'

'They were the jammiest bits of jam I ever saw! Didn't you notice?'

'Yes, of course.'

'Well then.'

'What?'

'We need to find out where they're performing and get ourselves along! Don't you think?'

'I suppose so.'

'Well, you might sound more enthusiastic, man.'

In truth, Henry Brown was terrified. Everything about the women terrified him. Their appearance, their smart, fashionable London clothes, even how they walked. But what terrified him the most was what had happened as the dark-haired one stepped from the train. She had turned in his direction, it was a split second, a moment in time, before her friend demanded her attention and she turned away again. It had surged through his body. The electricity. Ernie hadn't stopped talking about them, determined to involve Henry in his plans. Henry tried to tell Ernie the women were out of their league, but Ernie wasn't having it. Once he knew where they were staying, he asked around and learnt they were dancers at Central Street Music Hall.

The men's days as fettlers on the railway were long, heavy ones. Vital maintenance of the lines ensured the safety of travellers, and Henry and Ernie worked hard at their important jobs. Days off were rare, and Henry watched Ernie's excitement grow as the next one approached. He insisted they should wait for the women outside the music hall that afternoon. Henry shifted his position and tried to stand behind Ernie. He moved away when the stage door opened.

'There they are! Quick, let's see where they go!' Ernie hurried after the women.

Henry knew it was pointless trying to stop his friend's determined pursuit. He was relieved Ernie hadn't approached the women the moment they appeared; he would happily postpone that for as long as possible. They walked behind, at a distance Henry found uncomfortable. The women didn't turn around. Further evidence in Henry's mind that they weren't interested. Ernie wouldn't be swayed. As the women left the Paris Chocolate Company, Henry picked fluff from his jacket. He worked hard, but his wages would never stretch to smart suits or shoes, the clothes he wore for best were anything but. A woman like her wouldn't give a man like him a second glance.

'We'll go and watch them tonight then?'

Henry nodded, knowing nothing good would come of it. The beautiful dancer wouldn't even notice him, but perhaps Ernie would be lucky with the brown-haired woman.

Ernie clasped his friend on the back. 'That's the ticket, man! We'll have a great time!'

Henry sighed. Years of living with his late father's put-downs had taken their toll and turned him into a pessimist. He had never understood why his father treated him and his elder brother so differently. Perhaps it was simple, his father liked William and disliked his younger son. If so, Henry didn't understand why. Perhaps it was because Henry's mother favoured him, her younger son. William sailed through life unaware of feelings one way or the other, and always landed upright in any given situation. He had married well; his wife Agatha, a woman of independent means, had inherited her father's fortune along with several properties. For all her money Agatha had a heart of stone. Why had William fallen for her? His brother wasn't so shallow as to marry for money, but Henry lost respect for William as he saw his brother cowed by his cutting wife. Henry discovered his mother in tears on William and Agatha's wedding day, her despair revealed a deep sorrow for her elder son, and she made Henry promise to marry for love.

'Kind, handsome boy. Promise you will wait for the woman who stops you in your tracks.'

Henry had promised, and his mother died not long after William and Agatha were married. Now the woman who had stopped him in his tracks was here, in Newcastle, he feared he wouldn't be able to keep his promise. He took his reservations with him to the music hall that evening, as Ernie insisted they arrive early for a space at one of the tables closest to the stage. Four other men, already in their cups, joined their beer-soaked table. As the master of ceremonies introduced the acts for the night's show, he whipped the men into a frenzy and Henry found himself caught up in the thrill. His heart thumped as the rowdy crowd stood on tables and jostled for position closer to the stage. The crowd roared as the music rose to a deafening crescendo, the curtain flew open and there they were. The air left Henry's lungs as if he'd been punched. He hadn't imagined her. His first sight of her in the station hadn't been an illusion. He was propelled forward as a throng from tables further back surged into him, their excitement fuelled by alcohol and lust. Beside him, Ernie joined the raucous shouts. He grabbed Henry's arm and pointed towards one of the dancers.

'Look! Isn't she a bobby-dazzler?'

Henry's eyes were elsewhere. The dancers were all a similar height and size but the dark-haired one from the station stood out. He sensed movement and noise around him, but he was alone, trapped in a slow-moving space in time. A space in which only the two of them existed. She performed the same high-kicks and taps as the others but held her head differently, majestic and proud. She smiled and his heart stopped. He dragged his eyes away as something tugged at his sleeve. Ernie's lips were moving. Henry turned back to the stage, mesmerised by the woman's flowing, sinuous movements. Hours or seconds could have passed, he was oblivious to the passage of time. He was cheering and applauding when Ernie pulled him away.

'Quick! We need to get to the stage door before everyone else!'

Henry's fervour carried him out of the music hall and round the corner. He floated to the stage door. He mopped his brow with his handkerchief and brushed imaginary fluff from his jacket. He licked his index finger and tried to tame a stray hair.

'You look great, man! She'll love you!'

Henry froze, what was he thinking? He turned, conscious of the reality of his situation. Crowds of men had gathered behind him. As he struggled to breathe, Ernie shouted.

'There they are!'

The crowd surged forward and Henry tried to hold his position. He found himself propelled towards the women. He stumbled as a large man barged past him. As he righted himself, he found a space near the wall and stood, breathing deeply. He closed his eyes and covered his ears to drown out the noise as Ernie disappeared into the crowd.

'Are you all right?'

Henry's eyes flew open, he didn't know how long he had been there. The voice matched the woman, the gentle lilt of her accent told him she wasn't English. What was the word his mother would have used? Exotic. Her striking blue eyes locked onto his.

'Are you unwell?'

Henry shook his head and she smiled.

'The show was not so bad?' Her gentle laugh floated into the space between them, that and her kind eyes acted like a magic potion and his fears evaporated. They stood, surrounded by crowds, but saw no one else.

'This is Jeannie, we're going for cocoa, are you coming?' Ernie's question went unanswered.

'Tee?' Jeannie touched her friend's arm. 'Are you coming?'

'Oh. Sorry, I do not know...' Tee's eyes were fixed on Henry's.

Henry held her gaze. 'Yes, if you want to.'

A sky full of extravagant stars followed them to the Paris Chocolate Company. Tee never tired of telling Henry she fell in love with him that night. She admired his difference; he hadn't pushed himself forward with the other men. She wanted to learn more about the handsome man who left the crowd to stand by the wall. She didn't mention his dusty shoes or second-hand suit. When he opened his dark-brown eyes it had surged through her body. The spark. The foursome fell into a companionable routine. Jeannie insisted it wasn't serious between her and Ernie, until she admitted it was. The men were welcomed by the women's friends at Central Street and Springbank Lane. Tee longed to tell her mother about Henry Brown, the man with the spark.

'Dearest Maman,

Your little chocolate girl has fallen in love! I have found him, the man with the spark. 'Enri works on the railway, he does heavy, honest work like dear Papa. Oh Maman, I know you would love him. He is kind and thoughtful and so handsome. The best thing about 'Enri, is he does not know how special he is. He has no airs and graces, going about as if he is the most ordinary man. I will have my happy family with 'Enri, Maman. Jeannie has found love again, with 'Enri's good friend Ernie. He is a good man who will treat Jeannie very well. Jeannie and I stay in Newcastle-upon Tyne, at Mrs Swann's guest house for theatrical types. How delighted you would be to meet the kind, entertaining people who stay here. We are happy as we go about Newcastle, we have such fun and are made welcome wherever we go.'

Life had dealt Tee and Jeannie a good hand, they had escaped from Solomon Zettler's sinister shadow, found good jobs and a safe place to stay. Now they had both fallen in love and their lives were light, no clouds darkened their horizons.

Chapter 8

11 years later
Gateshead – 1893

Theodosia Brown's daughters played happily in the summer sun. Tee closed her eyes and basked in the heat of the day. The People's Park provided some consolation for the lack of green space anywhere else in Gateshead. When Henry had first brought Tee to the other side of the Tyne years before, she had turned as they neared the end of the Swing Bridge.

'How can two places on opposite sides of a stretch of dirty water be so different?'

Henry shrugged, used to the comparison. Newcastle and Gateshead were both areas of heavy industry, but Tee was unprepared for the poverty on the other side of the water. She remembered the young couple running over the bridge when she arrived on the train from York. In her imagination they were fleeing from a pitiful existence in the run-down tenement buildings dominating the Gateshead side of the Tyne. Now she considered them fortunate to have escaped.

'Come, mes filles au chocolat, Papa will be home soon.'

Dinah and Margaret ran to their mother, taking a hand each. They made their way back to Dorney Street. Tee swung her daughters into the air, one at a time. Their innocent laughter warmed her heart. Despite the depravation of Gateshead, she had never been happier.

As autumn had turned to winter in 1882, she told Henry she was pregnant. Henry dropped to one knee and proposed. Not to be left out, Ernie proposed to Jeannie. Jeannie, having allowed herself to fall for Ernie, accepted. Mrs Swann asked Tee and Jeannie about accommodation for their wedding guests, saying she could ask other local landladies. The women shook their heads, Mrs Swann and her residents were the closest thing to family they had, apart from Henry and Ernie.

In 1853, two catastrophic events changed the course of Ernie's life. As a railway engineer, Ernie's father was promised a railway cottage. Before they could move to their more salubrious surroundings, cholera claimed his wife's life. The disease was rife in the areas of Gateshead with no sanitation or fresh water; Pipewellgate's position on the banks of the Tyne made it one of the worst. At the back of the tenement building Ernie's parents shared with five other families, a dirty trench served as a toilet. The mess was cleared out, stacked against a wall and removed every six months. Pipewellgate swarmed with infection and Ernie's mother succumbed to cholera, dying swiftly and in terrible pain. Not long after his mother's death Ernie's father died in an accident at work and the Railway Orphanage took Ernie in. At the age of 13 and it being the only occupation he knew, Ernie followed in his father's footsteps and sought work on the railway.

Henry also had no guests attending their wedding. He explained his only close family, his brother and sister-in-law, were unable to attend. He hesitated when Tee asked why. She pretended not to notice his discomfort and made a joke by pointing at her stomach.

'This is an embarrassment for some people, non?'

'No. Agatha is busy with her charity work, that's all.'

Tee was disappointed for Henry; his brother had been bullied into missing their wedding by his domineering wife. Henry turned away, embarrassed to be caught out in a lie.

The couples were married at Gateshead Registry Office on the 1st of January 1883. The following day Dinah Jane Brown entered the world. Fifteen months later, on the 10th of April 1884, Margaret Patricia joined her elder sister. Henry and Ernie's jobs didn't place them in a category where they would be offered railway cottages, instead they rented rooms on Dorney Street in Gateshead. Tee was delighted to have her dearest friend as a neighbour. Their houses, along with others in the street, were owned by Henry's sister-in-law, Agatha. Henry presented the arrangement as an act of generosity on Agatha's part. Tee suspected there were no generous bones in Agatha's body, there must be some benefit in the arrangement for her.

'How much rent does Agatha charge us, 'Enri?'

'You don't need to concern yourself with the rent, Tee.'

She flinched at her husband's stern response, anger from Henry was rare.

'I think I do, 'Enri. I suspect she charges us too much.'

Henry clenched his hands and turned away. He spoke, his voice calm. 'There are things I can't tell you because I don't know. But believe me, Agatha Brown is not a woman we want as an enemy. Mention her name and watch how people react.'

Tee didn't pursue the matter but resolved to discover why Agatha Brown provoked anger in her normally equitable husband. She was the only cause of tension between them. Tee didn't trust Agatha, but Henry changed the subject when she asked about his sister-in-law. What was the English expression? Tee frowned, something to do with smoke and fire. While Henry and Ernie worked hard on the railway, Tee and Jeannie were busy at home, Tee as a mother to first one daughter then another. With two babies born in fifteen months, she didn't know how she would have managed without Jeannie. Jeannie was a natural with Dinah and Margaret and for years Tee's heart broke for her friend, she and Ernie hadn't been blessed with children. Not long after Dinah's tenth birthday, a tearful Jeannie arrived at Tee's door.

'What is it?'

Jeannie fell into Tee's arms and revealed her news, she was pregnant.

The rooms they rented from Agatha were small and functional, but Tee insisted on one having a particular purpose. In Paris her mother had created a magical world in the room she called her *parloir,* her parlour. In this joyful room Tee's parents sang and danced and told stories.

Tee didn't waver in her determination to replicate her mother's parlour, to create the same sense of joy for her own daughters. She and Henry were far from rich, yet despite the poverty and despair outside, once they closed the parlour door, they were in an oasis of beauty a world away from Gateshead. Nothing was new, she repaired and restored each piece of old, discarded furniture with painstaking care. She discovered a talent for turning unwanted things into precious items to be cherished and enjoyed, for breathing life into things long-since abandoned and left to rot. As she and Henry toasted Jeannie and Ernie in her beautiful parlour, hidden away from grim Gateshead, Tee beamed.

Jeannie's pregnancy started badly with terrible morning-sickness, and the warm summer had turned her into a bloated, grumpy friend. As Tee rounded the corner into Dorney Street she called out to Jeannie. Her friend sat on her front step, fanning herself with a newspaper.

'You should be inside, it is too 'ot out 'ere!'

Jeannie folded the newspaper, 'it's too 'ot indoors as well!'

Tee laughed and promised to bring her some cool lemonade.

'Thanks, Tee. I don't think I can get up!'

Tee was delighted for Jeannie and Ernie, despite the difficult pregnancy and the heat, their long-awaited child was on his or her way. She poured the lemonade, watched Dinah and Margaret polish theirs off then the three of them went back outside. Dinah and Margaret played happily in the street as Tee sat next to her friend. Jeannie smiled as she took the welcome drink, nodding at her swollen stomach. 'He's grateful too, thank you, Tee.'

Tee laughed. 'Oh, you have decided it is a boy?'

Jeannie nodded. 'Yes, a little boy for your girls to mother. His name will be Jacques.'

Tee's eyes filled with tears as she embraced her friend. Jeannie had remembered the story of Tee's much-wanted brother. She and Ernie had taken his name, Jacques. Tee left Dinah and Margaret playing and went inside. As she waited for Henry, she wrote to her mother. Her diary entries had been very rare since Dinah and Margaret were born.

Once, Henry had asked why she wrote to her dead mother. She took his hand and looked into his dark brown eyes.

'Oh, mon chéri, 'Enri. Of course, I know my dear maman will never read my words, but this helps me feel closer to her. Also, I write for our daughters, one day they will want to know something of where they came from.'

Henry frowned, 'but you can tell them everything they want to know.'

Tee's striking blue eyes filled with tears. 'I thought my maman would always be with me but one day she wasn't. Then my papa was gone and with them their histories. All I have are memories. I want our daughters to have more.'

Henry embraced her. 'I'm sorry, Tee. Of course, I understand.'

The heat of the day continued as she started to write.

'Dearest Maman,

Your cocoa girl could not be happier. 'Enri and I have a good marriage and rent some pleasant rooms from 'Enri's sister-in-law, Agatha. Our beautiful little daughters are now nine and ten years old, how I wish you and Papa had met them. Dinah is kind and sensible, Margaret is a wilful dreamer. I knew their natures the moment they entered the world. Margaret slept soundly from the day she was born. Dinah was still only 15 months old and happy to share her toys. She put her small woollen dolly into Margaret's chubby hand, the baby clutched it and wouldn't let go. Their personalities were clear even then, Maman.

'Enri works hard on the railway, he is a good man, like Papa. He takes good care of us and tells stories to the girls; their eyes sparkle as he speaks. They run to him the way I ran to Papa. You now have trois filles de chocolat, Maman, or three cocoa girls as they say here in England. Jeannie and Ernie live beside us, and Jeannie is pregnant with their first child. I must tell you about Mrs Swann from the guest house in Newcastle. She now lives in Paris! A handsome French singer called Monsieur Olivier Desperéaux came to stay at Springbank Lane. When he returned to Paris, he took his luggage and Mrs Swann with him! Her other guests are scattered to the four

winds, being entertaining elsewhere. I am so glad 'Enri and I have Jeannie and Ernie living nearby, we are each other's family, Maman.'

A noise outside made Tee look up. Henry and Ernie were home. She moved to the door, ready to call for Dinah and Margaret to come and greet their papa. The words stuck in her throat. A scream. Jeannie. The baby. She ushered Dinah and Margaret indoors then hurried outside. She found chaos; Dorney Street's residents were shouting and screaming and running towards the river. Jeannie clutched her stomach, doubled over outside her house.

'Jeannie, what's happening?'

Jeannie pointed at the crowds. A neighbour clutched Tee's arm as she hurried past.

'It's the men, an accident on the railway!'

Tee's hand flew to her mouth and her heart skipped a beat. She instructed Jeannie to breathe. As Tee joined the hysterical crowds, she prayed to every god she knew.

'Not my beloved 'Enri, please not him.'

A different group returned to Dorney Street sometime later. Those who had lost fathers, husbands, brothers and sons trudged back from the railway, desolate. Those who returned with their men and boys were desperate to get them indoors to rejoice in private. Tee returned alone.

Jeannie was where Tee had left her, sitting outside the house she shared with Ernie. The house she *used* to share with him. How would she tell her best friend that her husband and the father of her unborn child wasn't coming home? She didn't need to. Jeannie met her eyes and started to scream. She dropped to her knees. As Tee went to her, the screams became a guttural wailing, Jeannie howled like a wounded animal. Arms embraced Tee and she turned to see two of her neighbours. One took Tee's arms and shook her head. The woman turned Tee to face her house. In the doorway, Dinah clutched Margaret's hand; their faces streaked with tears. The woman pushed her gently towards them and a bereft Tee took her daughters in her arms.

How much time had passed since she left the house? She was aware of each minute. The minute she took her daughters inside, when their empty eyes broke her heart all over again. The minute after she told them about their papa when they cried like never before. The minute she cuddled them and said she would never leave them. Now she had managed to settle them, and in this minute, she needed to breathe. She also needed to check on Jeannie. As she closed her eyes and tried to take slow, deep breaths, unwelcome images from the accident returned. That afternoon, a train of carriages with passengers coming to Newcastle from York had an addition, a truck loaded with a casting and other ironwork. The large casting, part of a weighing-machine to be installed at Newcastle station, weighed around 2½ tons and overhung both ends of the truck. As the train approached Newcastle, the large casting fell from the truck onto the lines. Henry and Ernie, along with other railwaymen, rushed to right the truck. As the men pushed at the heavy bulk the weight shifted and the casting fell towards them. Nine men died instantly, including Henry and Ernie, and others were injured as the ironwork did its brutal damage. Tee blinked the images away, she had to see Jeannie. As she turned the door handle, Henry's best cap fell from a hook on the back of the door. Sobs racked her slender frame as she bent to retrieve the cap Henry would never wear again. She opened Jeannie's door and called out. She held her breath against the hot, heavy air. Inside was silent and dark. She called again and her words dripped into the empty room. She turned towards footsteps on the stairs. A neighbour. The woman shook her head.

'I'm so sorry pet, there was nothing anyone could do.'

Tee frowned. 'Where is Jeannie?'

The woman looked upstairs and started to speak. Tee put her hands over her ears. It wouldn't be true until she heard the words. The woman gently removed her hands.

'She's gone, pet. And the baby. The poor little mite never stood a chance, it was much too early. The shock, you see. Brought him too soon.'

Tee gulped for air, first Henry and Ernie and now dear Jeannie and her baby.

'Him? Did you say him?'

'Aye, pet. A little boy.'

Tee's legs gave way and she thumped onto the stairs. She was 16, hearing her mother's screams as her long-awaited and much wanted brother Jacques tried to enter the world. History had repeated itself. Night crept into Dorney Street as she kissed Jeannie and Jacques good-bye. Jeannie, her dearest friend and Jacques, who would never be. The neighbour arranged for the doctor to have the bodies taken away and Tee closed the door on the silent, empty house. As she stepped into her own house, Henry's best cap fell from the back of the door. She left it on the floor. She walked to the parlour and closed the door behind her. The unfinished letter to her maman lay on the table, the words blurred as her tears soaked the paper. If she wrote the letter now, many of the people she had told her mother about would be missing. She had no one to turn to, Henry's ineffectual brother William offered nothing, he asked his wife's permission to speak. She had no family in Paris, she and her daughters were alone. What would become of them? In a bed-room above her bowed head one of her young daughters slept soundly. The other lay curled at the top of the stairs, eyes wide open as she listened. Her body shook as the sound of her mother's desperate sobs reached her.

Chapter 9

Ten years later
Gateshead – June 1903

Dinah

Dinah waited in the dismal corridor at the Union Workhouse Hospital. She pushed her unruly auburn curls back under her black bonnet and tugged at her tight, restrictive collar. She wished she could be anywhere else.

'Miss Dinah Jane Brown? Daughter of Theodosia Brown?'

She followed the tall man into a small, stuffy room. Without looking at her he gestured towards a wooden chair and pointed at a piece of paper on the desk.

'Are you able to read this and confirm the information is correct?'

She ignored the insult and read the document. She stared, he expected her to sign this? She clenched her hands and met his steady gaze. She shook her head. How dare they? What gave them the right to insult her mother? Would this one cruel line of information be recorded as the sum of her mother's achievements?

'This says nothing about my mother or her life!' Her voice trembled as she tried in vain to defend her dead mother.

'It is a legal document, Miss Brown. It is required to state when, where and how the individual met their end.'

The Registrar stated the facts as he appraised Dinah from his seat behind the large desk. Dinah pictured her mother; Theodosia Brown, Tee to her friends, Frannie La Fleur on stage. A Frenchwoman living in Gateshead. Dinah was proud of her mother's allure, her difference. She met the Registrar's eyes with quiet confidence.

'It is incomplete, my mother was born in Paris. She was a dancer there and in London before she married my father. She lived her own life; she was much more than someone's wife!'

Dinah stopped. Her mother would receive no credit here for her independence and determination to create a life for herself. She hid her frustration and signed her name where instructed. Through unshed tears she studied the concise information set out on the death certificate:

'The 16th of June 1903, at the Union Workhouse Hospital, Theodosia Brown, female, age 41, the widow of Henry Brown, a railway fettler of Gateshead, cancer of the uterus.'

Dinah swallowed her frustration at the lack of information about her mother's achievements. Her descendants would learn she was a widow who died from cancer of the uterus. Dinah wanted those who followed to know of her mother's intelligence, beauty, kind nature and style, not her cancerous uterus. She wanted them to know her life had meant something, Theodosia had followed her own path, insisting women could achieve anything, if they set their minds to it. Dinah looked up from the scornful document and caught the Registrar staring.

'Is there something else?'

'No, I...' he stumbled over his words.

Dinah's piercing blue eyes held his gaze. She waited for him to criticise their unconventional family, but he was silent. Everyone knew Theodosia had kept them together after their father died, even when Dinah's younger sister Margaret discovered she was pregnant. Theodosia had spent her final days in the bleak Union Workhouse hospital. Dinah wanted better for her family.

Lizzie

'Quick! Run! It's the stinking witch!'

'Go to the devil!'

The filthy urchins fled as Elizabeth Ann Brown shoved at the rotten door of the house on Pipewellgate. Lizzie exhaled, thankful to have her room in the rundown tenement to herself. The building's other inhabitants were packed in like rats in a festering sewer. She sometimes had money for wood, so despite the squalor outside, there was warmth near the small fire. The room was thick with silence and she muttered to herself, overwhelmed by the need for another human voice. She poured sherry into a stained, chipped cup. She had first tasted it at her sister Mary's wedding. At 15 the bitter taste had made her gag. Now it took the edge off her misery. How could she have known she had a predisposition for alcoholism? Her mother used whatever spirit came to hand to pacify Lizzie when she was teething and later when she had any form of malaise. Agatha Brown had two daughters; Mary was the apple of her mother's eye. Lizzie was one daughter too many. Agatha did anything she could to silence her younger daughter and make her sleep, including using spirit laced with laudanum as a sedative. Lizzie put her hands over her ears to drown out her mother's words.

'I have told you before, you will take the abstinence pledge, or you will leave my house!'

How ironic the mother who used alcohol to silence her younger daughter now refused to have the substance under her roof. And now Lizzie needed it to get through the day. She had chosen to leave her family home, the draw of the bottle outweighing any sense of commitment to her mother. This room was a good price because Pipewellgate's position parallel to the Tyne made it one of the worst areas in Gateshead. The rotten stench from the dirty, muddy river clogged the air and filthy sewage water gushed down the narrow, cobbled streets. Rats outnumbered people and rough, desperate prostitutes waited for business on every corner. Lizzie knew what the locals called her; *the ugly spinster seamstress*' or *'the stinking witch.'* At 35 she had been written off; she would never get married. She never went anywhere to meet anyone suitable. She didn't bother styling her hair or wear fancy dresses like her stuck-up cousins Dinah and Margaret, but she worked hard. Years ago, she had hoped to find a man like her, plain and direct, someone to take walks with and go dancing with. She had longed to be a good wife. As the years passed and no invitations came, she lost hope.

Lizzie stitched a hem on a pair of men's dress trousers. She had started working as a seamstress's assistant at the age of 14. It didn't pay well, but her attention to detail meant her customers were usually satisfied. She took another mouthful of sherry. She had something to smile about. One of her customers, a widower, had recently started paying her attention. The stitching blurred before her eyes as she poured more sherry. She had no experience of men, other than the rough, vulgar types who frequented the Globe Hotel. When the widower had arrived with his alterations, he looked her up and down. A new, unfamiliar sensation gripped her and she imagined a faint glimmer of hope. Was he interested in more than her sewing skills? She had never paid him much attention. He was smaller than her, of tidy appearance and acceptable enough. She wasn't in a position to be particular, unlike her cousins, who were convinced they would marry rich, handsome men. This plain, ordinary man would suit Lizzie very well.

'They will be ready on Wednesday week?'

'They will.' She tried to hide her Geordie accent and sound more like her cousins.

'Alright, Miss Brown. Good day.'

'Miss Brown!' She could count on one hand the number of times she had been addressed so formally. She imagined how it might be, to like someone and for them to like her. She had never been close to anyone; she didn't like herself much and disliked most of the people she met. She was so used to being lonely, she couldn't imagine happiness. She had expected to end her days alone, as a universally pitied spinster. She deserved to celebrate, she had convinced herself the man was about to propose and remove her from a pointless existence. She smiled and reached for the jug.

Margaret

Margaret Patricia Brown fidgeted as she waited for her sister. Her little girl played on the floor, unaware the woman she had spent so much of her young life with was dead. Theodosia had adored her granddaughter and without her, Margaret didn't know what would become of them.

They had lived without a male head of household since Dinah and Margaret's father died. Theodosia, determined to give them a secure home, ignored local disapproval. The sisters admired their mother's independent nature, but Margaret didn't know how Theodosia had managed after their father died. They always had enough food, were warm and well-dressed. Mysterious packages arrived every so often, Theodosia called them *'petites surprises.'* Colours of every hue exploded from the delicate paper; silks, satins, ribbons and feathers for the beautiful dresses their mother made. Margaret could still smell the French cologne that wafted from the paper as her mother unwrapped the wonderful gifts. Theodosia said they came from their French family. Margaret prayed the surprise parcels would continue to arrive.

She stood at the window. The dirty grey of the cobbles merged into the crumbling dark stone of the rundown houses. She sighed. Theodosia had told her daughters they could do anything and go anywhere, if they were determined enough. She told them stories of the Seine, the magical river running through the heart of Paris, explaining how it changed with the seasons. In the spring and summer, you could sit under the beautiful willow trees and watch the boats on the twinkling water. In the cooler autumn months, the dramatic browns and golds of the trees warmed your skin. In the winter, people flocked to the atmospheric city to marvel over the ice-skaters venturing onto the frozen river. Theodosia said her French relatives had written to her about the Summer Olympics in 1900, describing in glorious detail the events hosted on her favourite river, the rowing, swimming and water polo. Margaret could have owned a painting of it, so vivid were her mother's descriptions. She smiled as she remembered Theodosia teaching her and Dinah about the magic of daydreams, giving them a trick to escape from dreary Gateshead. They could open a trapdoor in their minds and be anywhere. She called it *'le truc de la trappe,'* the trapdoor trick.

'Close your eyes, mes belles filles. Now, imagine the most wonderful place you can and put yourself there. Have you done it?' The sisters had nodded.

'Now, Dinah, where are you?'

Dinah described a meadow full of beautiful summer flowers and a lake, the water cool and refreshing in the sun's heat.

'Tres bon, ma chérie. Now, Margaret?'

Her dream-place was a glittering ballroom full of people in beautiful dresses, dancing to the latest music, laughing and having fun.

'Tres bon aussi, ma chérie. Now, if you feel afraid or sad, use the trick to escape to those wonderful places in your mind. Trust me, it works.'

Margaret never missed an opportunity to open the trapdoor and escape from the stinking Tyne, which could never rival the elegant Seine. She knew her irresponsible actions had put them all at risk. She had approached her mother with dread when she discovered she was pregnant.

'Will I have to leave home?'

'No, you can stay here with me and your sister.'

'Will my baby be adopted?'

'No.'

'Will my baby be brought up as my younger brother or sister?' She viewed this as the best of a set of dreadful options.

'No. This is your child and my grandchild. I will keep us together, no one will separate us.'

She had embraced her mother. She knew what could happen to women in her situation. Unmarried pregnant women disowned by their families ended up in the Union Workhouse. Once there they were left to fend for themselves. Many died giving birth or soon after. The babies were tainted when they entered the world, and many endured painful deaths as poverty and illness pervaded their short-lived, miserable existences. In the workhouse, rife with disease, many babies only lived for hours or days, dying of malnutrition or diarrhoea. Those who lived might receive some schooling but were also expected to work. There were horrific stories of beatings and heart-breaking tales of children who had never seen the light of day or breathed fresh air.

Theodosia kept Margaret calm during her labour, telling her how to breathe and soothing her through the pain. When Margaret visited the Registrar's office after Evie arrived, she conducted her business quickly then rushed out, clutching her daughter's birth certificate to her chest. She grew hot, feeling the Registrar's serious eyes following her every step, and sensing his unspoken judgement hanging in the air. She hurried home and handed Evie's birth certificate to her mother.

'22ⁿᵈ of May 1899, at Seymour Terrace, Gateshead, Eveline Dinah Annie, a girl, born to Margaret Patricia Brown, a Factory Hand.'

Margaret longed to protect her daughter from the inevitable name-calling, but she knew the label would come. People wouldn't hesitate to mark her baby out as a bastard. She had asked her mother about the birth certificate. 'What will I put for her father?'

Theodosia studied her younger daughter and shook her head. 'Well, if you do not know who he is, you will have to leave it blank.'

'What will people think?'

'Do you care?'

'Don't you?'

Theodosia shrugged. 'What alternative is there?'

Margaret had lied to her mother, saying she didn't know who her baby's father was. Louis Levy wasn't suitable husband material. When the handsome, rebellious Louis with his jet-black hair and dark-brown eyes had shown an interest in her at a church hall dance, she didn't hesitate. She knew she was treading a thin line between respectability and scandal, but her desire for a different life overwhelmed her. All she saw was Louis and the promise of a better life. She fell head over heels in love and when she discovered she was pregnant, he declared they would be married.

' I will speak to my father and the arrangements will be made. I promise.'

His optimism was premature. The following weekend Margaret waited outside the church hall. Louis loved her; they were going to be married. She hadn't considered her age or his religion. She wore a pretty cornflower blue dress her mother had made, which copied the latest fashion from Paris. Dinah had styled her hair in a classic Grecian style, so her soft brown curls covered her forehead. The rest of her long hair was combed on top of her head and people turned to look at her. She smiled, imagining dancing with her handsome fiancé and cocking a snook at the common northerners. She would be the envy of the dance! When she had arrived, there were other people waiting, now she stood alone. She listened to the music and shivered. As dusk fell, she accepted Louis wasn't coming. She trudged home and climbed into bed beside Dinah.

'He didn't come?'

'No and he didn't even send a message.'

'I'm so sorry.' Dinah hugged her and Margaret cried herself to sleep.

Margaret forced herself back to reality. She would never have managed without her mother's help. Margaret and Evie had needed Theodosia and now they needed Dinah. She tapped her fingers on the windowsill, craning her neck for a better look. Where was Dinah?

Dinah

Dinah stood outside the Registrar's office, trying to steady her breathing. She pictured the People's Park; it wasn't the quickest way home, but she needed to think. As she walked, she remembered her mother saying the park was built for the benefit of everyone in Gateshead. The heavy industry polluted and spoiled the air, deaths from cholera and typhoid were common and life-expectancy was short. Dinah was grateful for the precious oasis of green space. She headed for the lake, wanting to sit, alone with memories of her beloved mother. As she approached an empty seat her heart sank. John Todd, the local postman, waved from the other side of the lake. He smiled as he reached her.

'Good day, Miss Brown. Please accept my condolences on your mother's passing.'

'Thank you, Mr Todd.'

John reached into his postbag. 'A letter arrived for you this morning and I wanted to give it to you in person. It is from your aunt.'

The lack of discretion didn't surprise her, there were few secrets in their small community.

'Thank you, Mr Todd.'

'Please, call me John.'

John was a decent man who had taken in his nephew Jack after Jack's father died, but Dinah had no intention of pursuing his attentions. She had other priorities.

'Perhaps she wants you to go and live with her now?'

Dinah smiled. 'Perhaps.'

John left and Dinah sunk onto the seat. She shivered despite the warmth of the early summer day. She pulled her thin overcoat tighter. Before Theodosia died, she made Dinah promise to look after her younger sister and niece. A chill snaked up Dinah's spine. When her sister had found herself pregnant four years earlier, their mother's support protected Margaret from the scandal. Without their mother, Dinah feared Margaret would suffer the inevitable social branding. When Evie arrived, Theodosia stayed at home with her granddaughter while Dinah and Margaret worked. The noisy, dirty jobs at the local Ropery didn't pay much, but Theodosia ensured they had decent clothes and enough to eat. Now Margaret would have to stay at home and Dinah's pitiful wage would be all they had. She rubbed her temples as bolts of pain spread across her forehead, how would they survive? Could she keep them out of the workhouse? Her hands trembled as she opened the letter. She pictured her mother and Aunt Agatha. Theodosia; kind and loving, Agatha; brittle and cold. People who sought

Theodosia's company avoided Agatha like the plague. Theodosia loved to sing and dance while Agatha called the same activities *'the devil's work.'* Dinah started reading.

'Niece,

Your circumstances are most unfortunate. As your aunt, it is my duty to help you. I will pay for your mother to be laid to rest in something other than a pauper's grave. In death she will have the dignity that escaped her in life. You and your wretched sister will no longer live in a sinful manner. I will write to you again when appropriate arrangements have been made.

Mrs Agatha Brown.'

Dinah looked into the sky, thankful for her aunt's offer to pay for her mother's burial. She could erase the image of Theodosia in an unmarked grave from her mind. Theodosia was the most dignified and beautiful woman; Agatha would never be her equal. Margaret had broken the rules in one of the worst ways, but she was still her sister. Aunt Agatha would never accept an unmarried mother as part of her family. Dinah dreaded receiving her aunt's next letter. Their options were limited; they might have little choice but to agree to their unpleasant aunt's plans. She cried, huge racking sobs that shook her whole body. A warm wind blew through the park. The change it brought would affect them all, in ways Dinah could never have imagined.

Chapter 10

Dinah

The blood pounding in Dinah's head matched the rhythm of a marching band keeping time. Her hand shook as she copied the column of figures into her mother's book-keeping ledger. The numbers blurred in front of her tired eyes; she had lost count of the number of times she had tried to make the figures match. She was starting to lose hope, realising no matter how many times she did her calculations, the result would be the same. There wasn't enough money coming in. She closed the ledger and called again for Margaret to join her.

'What are you doing? I need to talk to you!'

Dinah feared the gravity of their situation had passed Margaret by. She had tried to explain everything, spelling things out as she would to a child. Margaret's reaction made Dinah think her sister's vivid fantasy world overshadowed their grim reality.

Dinah walked towards her mother's parlour. Since Theodosia died, she hadn't set foot inside the room where they used to gather for music and cocoa. *'La musique et 'ot chocolat'* were, according to Theodosia, the perfect remedy in so many situations. Scraped knees, stuffy noses, wintery weather, they all called for music and cocoa. Theodosia had delighted in telling them about Café de Flore in her beloved Paris, licking her lips and describing the cocoa as hot, liquid chocolate. Since Theodosia's death Dinah had scrimped and saved to buy cocoa powder for Evie's bedtime drink, going without herself to make the precious brown powder last as long as possible.

She stopped; her hand shaky on the door handle. Behind the door lurked memories so sweet they would break her heart all over again.

She took a deep breath and opened the door. She stepped inside then stepped back as if she had been struck. The assault on her senses was the lingering smell of her mother's perfume, a mixture of spice, lemon, lavender and vanilla. The small house Dinah and Margaret now shared with Evie was vast without Theodosia's *'joie de vivre.'* She felt her mother's absence like a sharp, stabbing pain. Her eyes took in the full beauty and opulence of the room, and she steadied herself as her legs shook. She slipped off her shoes and stepped onto the rug. Her feet disappeared into the soft pile, the yielding, comforting wool brought a sad smile to her face. She followed the pattern of the red and green rectangular Persian rug, brushing her feet across the medallion running through the middle. In this room she had twirled Evie around in her arms, her little niece squealing with childish delight. She turned to look at the impressive oak dresser standing against the wall. Rubbing her sleeve over the large, glazed section at the top, she apologised to her mother for the thick accumulation of dust and dirt. Theodosia had polished the old dresser until it shone. Dinah studied the plate which took pride of place, positioned to perfection right in the middle of the top shelf of the dresser. Her mother's delight grew each time she added another mismatched piece of crockery to her collection. This one was no exception.

'Dinah, look! It is for the new King's coronation!'

Dinah had gazed at the two pieces of china her mother held. 'It's broken.'

Theodosia had dismissed her words with a theatrical wave. 'Easily mended, ma chérie.'

As usual, her mother was right. Theodosia had fitted the broken pieces of the decorative coronation plate together perfectly, the join running through King Edward VII's nose and his left eye was almost invisible. Queen Alexandra's dignified, unmarked face appraised Dinah from the old dresser. She smiled, hearing her mother telling them to view every day as if it held promise. Theodosia had encouraged her daughters to make the most of every day. She always laid the table with the best of her repaired china and dressed her daughters in the best clothes she could buy or make. *'Now is best, mes chéries.'* Dinah took a deep breath; she couldn't escape her mother's most precious possession any longer. The old gramophone sat gathering dust on top of a battered storage cabinet in the corner of the room. The last record Theodosia had played waited on the turntable. Dinah's hands shook as she wound the handle then lifted the arm and placed the needle on the edge of the record. Each careful action brought her closer to her mother. She closed her eyes and waited for the familiar crackle. Her spine tingled as the music surrounded her and she marvelled at the melodious tones of Hamilton Hill as he sang one of her mother's favourite songs.

'A ballroom was filled with fashions grand,
And shone with a thousand lights,
There was a woman who passed along,
The fairest of all the sights.
A girl to her lover then softly said,
She has riches at her command,
She's married for wealth,
Not for love, he cried,
And she lives in a mansion grand.'

The song was called *'A Bird in a Gilded Cage.'* Dinah's mother hadn't married for wealth and there was nothing grand about Seymour Terrace, but Theodosia was adamant, being born in Gateshead did not mean they had to stay there. They didn't have to tread the usual path expected of women, they could be different, independent. Dinah removed the needle from the record, returning the room to silence and emptiness. As she turned to leave, she pictured her niece. Dinah hoped the happy times with her family in this wonderful room had made a lasting impression on Evie's young memory. She hoped wherever life took Evie, those memories would go with her.

As Dinah left the parlour Margaret appeared, dancing into the room as if making a dramatic stage entrance, twirling her beautiful red dress. Dinah's eyes filled with tears as she pictured her mother in the dress. Theodosia's stories of '*La Belle Époque,*' the time in France after the Franco-Prussian War ended, fascinated Dinah. Theodosia had spoken about the optimism and new-found peace during a marvellous time of renewed cultural innovation. She had wanted her daughters to be educated about other cultures, music and the arts, to know a world existed beyond Gateshead.

'Is that Mother's dress?'

'I think it suits me. It's a bit big, but I am sure cousin Lizzie will alter it. Will you come to Pipewellgate and ask her? She will say yes if it comes from you.'

There, in a few sentences, Margaret's personality was laid bare. Dinah shook her head. Margaret wasn't a bad person, but she could be self-centred and unrealistic. She was also impossible to reason with, once she set her mind on something, she wouldn't budge.

'No, I'm not coming to Pipewellgate. We need to talk about what we're going to do.'

'I am going to get this dress altered and go to the dance on Saturday!'

'Please be serious, things are different now Mother isn't here.'

'You are such a worrier, Dinah! Everything will be all right, you'll see.'

'Will it? How? And what about Evie? Remember her, your daughter?'

Margaret recoiled from Dinah's unusually sharp words. Then she smiled.

'You don't need to worry. I have already thought about Evie.'

'And what conclusion have you arrived at?'

'You can still go to work, and I will stay at home to look after Evie like Mother used to do. As you say, she is my daughter.'

Dinah replied immediately. 'That won't work.'

'Why not? You haven't even considered it!'

'One wage from the Ropery only just covers the rent, never mind buying food or clothes for Evie. Look at her, she will need new shoes soon.'

Margaret studied her daughter then turned her piercing blue eyes towards Dinah.

'Something will turn up, you'll see.'

Margaret's optimism was misplaced. Dinah doubted they could stay in Seymour Terrace much longer. Soon, matters would be taken out of their hands. Dinah hadn't told Margaret about Aunt Agatha's letter, she wanted to know what their aunt intended to do first.

'Are you sure you won't come to Pipewellgate with me?'

Dinah shook her head; it was the last place she wanted to go. 'No, sorry. I will look after Evie while you're gone and make some soup. There's a small piece of bread left, as well.'

Margaret fiddled with her dress and edged towards the door.

'Wait!'

Margaret whirled around; Dinah had changed her mind.

'Aren't you forgetting something?'

Margaret frowned.

'If Lizzie agrees to alter the dress, what will you wear to walk home?'

'Oh, what a silly goose I am!'

'Here, take this.' Dinah handed her a freshly laundered dress and Margaret smiled.

'Thank you, Dinah. I won't be long.'

Margaret closed the door behind her, and Dinah returned to the ledger. She set out their expenditure, comparing it with her wages from the Ropery. She had lied to Margaret; her wages didn't cover the rent and she was dismayed to discover how much Aunt Agatha demanded. She frowned as she turned to the back of her mother's ledger. Two columns, both in her mother's neat hand. She caught her breath as she studied the first column. She pictured the mysterious packages that had arrived every so often, and Theodosia's delight as she gathered her daughters around her to open the *petites surprises.'* After their father died, the packages continued to arrive for a while, then suddenly stopped. Margaret had pestered their mother, asking when the next one would come, but Dinah held back. Not long after, a smaller, less exciting parcel arrived. As Margaret stomped off, unimpressed by the parcel's contents, Theodosia bowed her head. Dinah clutched her mother's hand.

'Don't cry, Maman.'

'I am sorry, mon amour.'

Dinah shook her head. 'It's all right, Maman. It's all right.'

Dinah's lip had trembled as Theodosia told her the truth. They had no family in Paris. Theodosia had sent the parcels herself, to create a magical world for her daughters. After Henry died, she tried to continue with the *petites surprises'* but she could no longer afford the beautiful materials, accessories, or French cologne. Dinah had squeezed her mother's hand.

'Margaret?'

'Non, mon amour.' Theodosia had put her finger to her lips. Dinah had kept her mother's secret and protected Margaret from the truth. The other figures were a mystery. They appeared to be additional payments her mother made to Aunt Agatha; Dinah had no idea what they were. She lowered her head onto the ledger, the ever-present spectre of the workhouse hovered above her.

Margaret

Margaret absorbed Dinah's words. Other than the boredom of being at home with Evie every day, she had thought it the perfect solution. She would have been pleased to rid herself of the endless hours in the hateful Ropery. When she and Dinah had started work, they were handed large heavy brooms and told to sweep. More recently they had started operating the huge clattering spinning machines; Margaret heard the noise in her sleep. She rubbed the calluses on her hands; the rough, ugly red skin would have healed once she left the Ropery.

She frowned; she didn't understand why Dinah had dismissed her suggestion so quickly. Dinah had been so serious since their mother's death. Margaret missed Theodosia too, but she was trying to get on with things. Dinah spent all her time poring over the boring numbers in their mother's ledger. Margaret was convinced her sister was keeping secrets. A few days earlier she saw Dinah slip a letter inside the ledger. Curiosity got the better of her and she sneaked it out and hid it in her dressing table. She decided it was from Paris; their mother's relatives had written to insist they go and live with them. Theodosia had taught them some French and Margaret was confident she could learn the language. She had such dreams of the rich, handsome, sophisticated Frenchmen she and Dinah would meet. She liked this new daydream, their life in Paris would be full of surprises, like the mysterious parcels their mother used to receive. The letter lay in the top drawer of her dressing table, full of Parisienne promise.

She wasn't happy about going to Pipewellgate alone, but determination spurred her on. She must get her mother's dress altered before the dance on Saturday. She turned out of Seymour Terrace and crossed the road, towards the church hall. She stood outside the hall and closed her eyes, lost in memories of Louis. She missed his arms around her and she longed for those days, full of music, dancing, laughter and love.

She forced herself to concentrate on the here and now. She quickened her step, the sooner she saw Lizzie, the sooner she could go home. She reached the top of the hill leading to Pipewellgate and hesitated. She looked towards the oily, forbidding Tyne. A dirty, grey mist hung over the river as if the sky had fallen into the dark, leaden water. Heavy industry stretched along the riverbank as far as she could see. The gloomy buildings housed works for making bottles, rope, bricks, chemicals and worst of all, manure. She covered her nose with her handkerchief. She peered down the sloping hill, regretting her decision to visit Lizzie. She took small, careful steps, desperate not to ruin her smart shoes among the filthy, stinking soil covering the street. She studied the row of tenements and the path closer to the houses. The tall, neglected buildings rose towards the sky, the ruinous brickwork and rotten timber of the external staircases linking the houses threatening imminent collapse. Dirty, foul-smelling liquid ran around her feet and down the street. Why did Lizzie live in this derelict, putrid slum? Everyone knew the houses were worse the closer to the river you got. She started to move closer to the houses when a harsh voice stopped her.

'Howay then lads, get a look at the lassie! Whe the hell does she think she is in that fancy clobber? A divvent think she's from round heor, dee ye?'

Margaret jumped at a roar of loud, rough laughter. A group of men huddled on the corner. She tried to move away from their stale smell of beer and tobacco. She stopped suddenly, almost losing her balance. She gasped, one of her pretty shoes was stuck fast in the stinking soil. She shuddered; their mother had warned them about men loitering around Pipewellgate.

'She's a bit of areet, like! Where ye gannin, pet? Wanna have a little drink in the Globe?'

She flinched at the man's rough Geordie accent. He walked towards her and his ugly smile revealed rotten, yellow teeth. He winked with his eye, the other a dark hole where the eye used to be. His beaten, drink-ravaged face and drunken gait told of a misspent life. She shuddered and turned away. She yanked her foot and to her dismay her shoe remained in the foul-smelling soil. The man roared with laughter, revelling in her discomfort.

'A can help ye pet, nee bother. Haad on, Geordie to the rescue!'

She held her breath, horrified by what she was about to do. She reached into the midden of a street and grabbed her shoe. Trying not to look at the stinking mess covering her gloves, she pushed her foot back into the ruined shoe and started to move away.

'Howay owa heor, pet.' The lecherous man smirked and she quickened her step.

'What's ye name, hinny? Think yersel too good for the likes of us? Stuck-up tart!' He snarled as he reached for her.

'No, get off! Get away from me! I'll call for the police!'

'C'mon hinny, divvent play hard to get, ye knaa ye wanna. There's nee poliss heor, anyway.'

The men continued to laugh as they drew closer. She recoiled from the man's filthy grasp as the stench from his unwashed clothes reached her. 'Get off me! I'm going to my cousin's house!'

'Whe's that when she's at yem?'

'Lizzie Brown.' The man stopped dead as Margaret stood outside Lizzie's house. Her knuckles stung as she pounded on the door, praying for Lizzie to answer.

'She lives here, my cousin.' She knocked again, harder.

'Howay, Geordie man! Hadaway from the mad bitch!' The other men shouted to their friend as they hurried away. Geordie stayed put, waiting to see if Lizzie would answer and save her cousin from his unwelcome clutches. He skulked at the side of the door, ready to pounce.

'Lizzie, are you in there? It's me, your cousin Margaret! Quick, let me in! Please, hurry up!' A shuffling noise came from behind the door and she knocked again, desperate to get inside.

'Lizzie! Please answer the door!' She screamed as a large rat ran out from under Lizzie's door, the source of the shuffling. The man seized his chance and lunged towards her.

'All right, where's the bloody fire?' Lizzie appeared outside the Globe, stumbling and swaying her way towards them, a basket over her arm.

Margaret let out a huge breath at the sight of Lizzie's ruddy face. By the time Lizzie reached her door the man had scurried away. Lizzie's broad frame filled the doorway as she shoved the door open. Margaret jumped as Lizzie bellowed at the man, grubby hands on her large hips. 'How, you, George bloody Green, what the hell do you think you're doing? Get away from my door, you scruffy one-eyed gobshite! Go on, crawl back to your stinking hovel!'

Margaret hurried inside, shaking from the encounter and cringing at her cousin's easy use of swearwords. She blinked, adjusting her eyes to the gloom. She caught her breath, hoping she wouldn't have to stay long. She took in the dirty, shabby furniture and the dusty floor. A lump grew in her throat at a memory of her mother. Theodosia always made sure they had enough to eat, she looked after Evie and kept their small house clean and warm. Margaret pinched the material of the red dress between her thumb and index finger, she wouldn't cry, not in front of hard-faced Lizzie. She reminded herself why she was there. She had to get the dress altered and go to the dance, meet a handsome man, fall in love and get married. Then all their problems would be over. She had hitched the dress up with a belt and hidden it under her long black coat. Now she removed the coat with a flourish and faced Lizzie. She jumped as Lizzie slammed the door shut. The older woman glared.

'Hello, cousin. How are you keeping?'

'What the hell was all the commotion outside? And what in the name of Christ are you doing here? Did you and your fancy bloody clothes get lost on the way to church?'

Margaret stared at her cousin; this would be more difficult than she had imagined.

Lizzie

Lizzie shook her head at her stuck-up cousin's bare-faced cheek. Margaret had turned up at her door uninvited, caused a scene in the street, pushed her way in and left her to deal with the toerags outside. Lizzie had no trouble in sending them packing, she met worse than them most nights in the Globe. She was used to looking after herself, people living in the area, men and women alike, knew not to pick an argument with her.

She had never cared much for her cousins, particularly this one. Their mother had given them airs and graces which no one living where they did should have. As young girls they had singing and ballet lessons and like their mother they spoke with a strange accent, not like Geordies at all. They worked at the Ropery, but Lizzie knew they believed themselves above such menial jobs. Lizzie accepted her situation, unmarried women had to work to survive. Dinah and Margaret went to the local dance every weekend, and their dresses matched the latest fashionable styles from London and Paris. Aunt Theodosia had once offered to make Lizzie one of the dresses.

'I wouldn't be seen dead in one of those horrible creations!'

Lizzie had jutted out her chin but caressed the silky fabric when no one was looking. When would she wear it? She was never invited to go anywhere. Margaret wore a smart black coat, good shoes and a flowery bonnet. Why had she come here dressed like that? Those clothes had no place in Pipewellgate. She smirked at Margaret's once smart shoes, now ruined and covered in filth. Margaret removed her coat and held it out. Lizzie arched an eyebrow and ignored the gesture. Margaret folded her coat across her arm. Lizzie narrowed her eyes at the bright red dress, how could Margaret wear such a colour so soon after losing her mother? Lizzie had liked Aunt Theodosia. She was kind, and kindness was in short supply in Lizzie's life. She didn't approve when Theodosia allowed Margaret to keep her bastard, but secretly she admired her aunt's independent nature and strength of mind. If her tight-lipped, bitter mother had been more like her aunt, Lizzie's life might have been very different. Margaret held a handkerchief to her nose. With a quick, furtive move Lizzie placed her basket under the table, her sherry would have to wait.

'Crikey, Lizzie! How can you live in this hovel? It is awful!'

'We don't all have family to support us, some of us just have to get on with things.'

'Well, I could never live somewhere like this.'

'What the hell do you want, anyway?'

With each insult from Margaret, a vein in Lizzie's neck throbbed a little more. She considered shoving her cousin back out into the rancid street and the rough arms of Geordie Green. Curiosity stopped her. What could be so important to make snooty Margaret come to Pipewellgate?

'Well? It must be something important! Hurry up, I've got work to do.' Lizzie gestured towards the basket she had carried inside.

Margaret shifted from foot to foot then produced her best smile.

Lizzie grinned; Margaret wanted a favour.

'I wanted to ask if you could help me with something.' Margaret stopped; the words stuck in her throat as Lizzie maintained her ferocious stare.

'Well? Help you with what?'

Margaret took a deep breath and asked the question quickly. 'Would you alter this dress for me? Please? It needs the hem taking up a few inches and the waist making a bit smaller. Please?'

Lizzie continued to stare until Margaret lowered her eyes.

'And what's in it for me? How much are you going to pay me?'

'Pay?' Margaret stood in front of her cousin, struck dumb.

'I thought as much,' Lizzie laughed. 'So, my whore of a cousin comes here, wanting something for nothing, eh?' She wanted Margaret to beg. 'Well?'

Margaret's cheeks burned, but she nodded.

Lizzie sniffed as she looked her up and down. She smiled, enjoying the power.

'Oh, for pity's sake, come over here and stand on this stool. God, I must need my head looking at to agree to do this for nothing!'

Margaret stood on the rickety stool and mumbled her thanks. Lizzie started pinning the hem.

'Ow, that hurt!' Margaret cried out as Lizzie caught her leg with a sharp pin.

'Don't be such a bloody cry-baby!'

Lizzie pulled another pin from her mouth and smiled. She would stick as many pins as possible into her childish, stuck-up cousin. She would poke and prod her and spill sherry on the dress, her payment in kind. She would enjoy doing these alterations.

Chapter 11

Dinah

Dinah's hands shook as she read her aunt's second letter. *'I do not hold with my late sister-in-law's idea of an all-female household. It is improper and unbecoming of young women from a respectable family, your behaviour is that of heathens. It is my duty to remove you from your sinful situation. In our dear Lord's words, you will not be led into temptation and you will be delivered from evil.'*

Dinah held her breath. Bitter nausea rose into her throat as she absorbed the next sentence.

'Your mother has an outstanding debt to me and I am sending my son-in-law, Mr Andrew Glass, to collect payment. He will call at noon tomorrow; I trust he will find you at home. Your mother failed to make good on her debt, now it is yours.'

The mysterious figures in the back of her mother's ledger suddenly made sense. Dinah dropped the letter and rushed to find the ledger. Her hands shook as she turned to the final page. She gasped as the numbers blurred in front of her eyes, why had her mother owed Aunt Agatha so much? Dinah hadn't understood her mother's tearful apology when she became ill, now she did. Theodosia knew her death would leave her daughters in a desperate situation. Dinah's temples throbbed as she returned to the letter. Aunt Agatha's distaste for her nieces screamed from every word. Dinah shook as she placed the letter on the table. They were already struggling, without this debt. She had nothing of value to sell, her mother's possessions were all second-hand. She closed her eyes, picturing Andrew Glass, her cousin Mary's husband. A man easily cowed by his domineering mother-in-law. She would find no sympathy there.

When Margaret had returned from seeing Lizzie, she regaled Dinah with the full horror of her visit to Pipewellgate, the rough men and their cousin's disgusting living arrangements.

'And I am sure she'd been drinking alcohol!'

'You shouldn't go around saying those things, Margaret.'

'Anyway, she agreed to alter the dress, that's what matters.'

Dinah had opened her mouth to disagree. Other things mattered a lot more; how they would pay the rent and buy food and shoes for Evie. Her shallow sister could see no further than her plans to go dancing. She had forced Margaret to face a different reality.

'Who will you go to the dance with on Saturday?'

'Why you, of course!'

'And who will look after your daughter while we are out dancing?'

Margaret was speechless.

Theodosia had encouraged her daughters to socialise, she wanted them to have opportunities to meet other young people. The church hall dance was safe and the best their local community offered. Every Saturday afternoon members of the local congregation took turns to act as chaperones to the young people. Theodosia never tired of telling her daughters about her dancing days in Paris, she was happy to stay at home with Evie while they went out.

Margaret had found her voice. 'I don't know. Can you suggest anyone?'

'Yes, me.' Dinah had no desire to socialise so soon after losing her mother.

'Who will I go to the dance with if you are here with Evie?'

'If you want to go, you will have to go on your own.'

'What would people say?'

Dinah had shrugged. Now she massaged her temples with her knuckles, but the throbbing continued. She pictured her mother; Theodosia had hidden her despair well. As the image faded, another took its place. Her mother's smiling face, free of worry. She wore the red dress Margaret had worn to Pipewellgate. Around her mother's neck was the answer to their problems. The necklace. Dinah gasped and silently thanked her mother. She could sell the necklace and repay her mother's debt. She hurried upstairs. She opened Theodosia's bedroom door and stopped. She choked back tears and entered the room. She opened her mother's dressing table; everything was neat and clean. Theodosia never had many material possessions, but she taught her daughters to value what they had. With careful fingers Dinah looked through the items in the top drawer, apologising for invading her mother's privacy. She found nothing other than underwear. She sighed as she closed the drawer, realising Theodosia might have already sold the necklace. But then why was she still in debt to Aunt Agatha? She opened the second drawer. She removed a soft cotton nightdress and held it to her face. As she breathed in her mother's sweet scent her knees gave way and she thumped onto the floor, clutching the nightdress. She brought her knees to her chest and sobbed into the soft cotton.

Dinah shivered, how long had she been on the floor? She grabbed the bed for support as she struggled to stand, the throbbing in her head persisted and black dots danced in front of her eyes. She held her mother's scrunched up nightdress, damp from her tears. As she laid it on the bed to smooth the creases, something under her mother's pillow caught her eye. She moved the pillow to one side and a wave of her mother's perfume hit her. She closed her eyes and took deep breaths of the familiar bouquet. Under her mother's pillow lay Theodosia's pretty white handkerchief, perfectly folded with the small blue flowers embroidered in one corner, surrounding a blue letter 'T.' As she stroked the delicate embroidery her finger bumped against something inside the handkerchief. She held the corner of the white square in between her thumb and index finger and lifted the cotton. She blinked as the handkerchief revealed its precious secret. Her mother's silver necklace. Her fingers trembled as she passed the silver chain between her fingers, marvelling as the small stones sparkled and shone. Her mother's beauty was reflected in every stone. Tears soaked Dinah's cheeks as she caressed the treasured solution to their problems.

She sat on her mother's bed, holding the handkerchief and the necklace. She made a silent apology to her mother. The necklace had been Theodosia's mother's and Theodosia brought it with her from Paris. It broke Dinah's heart to lose it but it was her only chance to free them from Aunt Agatha. She didn't know how she would go about selling it. All she could do was offer it to Andrew Glass when he called to collect on her mother's debt. She still hadn't told Margaret about Aunt Agatha's letters, she wanted to protect her sister and niece from their aunt's cruel judgment for as long as possible. She would wait until she had given the necklace to Andrew Glass. Once the debt was repaid, she and Margaret could find other ways to support themselves and Evie. Perhaps they could get better paid jobs in Newcastle or Margaret could work in the evenings.

A knock at the door interrupted her thoughts. She wrapped the life-changing necklace in the delicate handkerchief and placed it back under her mother's pillow. Jack Todd, the postman's nephew, had brought Margaret's dress back from Lizzie.

'Hello, Miss Dinah. Miss Lizzie asked me to bring this for Miss Margaret.' He was a pleasant, polite boy, a little older than Evie. She smiled and handed him an apple.

Margaret

Margaret's good cheer at the sight of the dress was short-lived. As she unfolded it, she stepped away from the table, wrinkling her nose. The stench wafting from the stained material transported her back to Pipewellgate. The soiled dress bore little resemblance to the beautiful creation she had left with Lizzie. The small stitches were neat, but the hem was uneven and too short. Margaret cried in anguish and ran upstairs. She closed her eyes; the visit to Pipewellgate and Lizzie's spite strengthened her resolve to get as far from Gateshead as possible. She lay on her bed, her face turned towards the window. She heard Dinah's footsteps coming into the room. Dinah sat on the bed and offered her a handkerchief.

'I'm sorry Lizzie ruined your dress.'

Margaret sniffed. 'Well, it doesn't matter. I cannot wait to get away from this awful place!'

'What do you mean?'

'Don't pretend you don't know. I saw you hiding the letter in mother's ledger.'

Dinah frowned. 'Did you take the letter?'

'Yes, and I cannot wait to leave! Paris will be so much better than here!'

'Paris? What do you mean? Have you read the letter?'

'It must be from our French relatives. We are going to Paris to live with them.'

'Margaret, I am sorry. The letter was from Aunt Agatha, and I received another from her today. She is making plans for us, and they do not involve Paris.'

'What? No, it's not true!' Margaret put her hands over her ears.

'Come on, let's have some cocoa.'

Margaret followed Dinah downstairs.

The following day, Margaret walked towards the People's Park, holding tight to Evie's small hand. She hadn't hesitated when Dinah suggested she should take Evie out. Yesterday had gone from bad to worse following Lizzie's sickening trick. Dinah had told her about Aunt Agatha's letters and their mother's debt. Margaret wished she could erase the conversation from her mind. As long as she hadn't known the awful truth, she had been able to pretend they were going to have a wonderful new life in Paris. Reality was a cruel disappointment.

Evie skipped along the path in front of her, oblivious to their predicament. Margaret's heart lurched when Evie turned and smiled, the reflection of Louis's large, dark-brown eyes in her daughter's. Margaret and Dinah had their mother's piercing blue eyes. Margaret had loved her mother, but her death and this debt to Aunt Agatha were such an inconvenience. Who would look after Evie? How would they manage? She had admired her mother's independent nature but thought they would be better off with a man looking after them now. She smiled as memories of her lost love filled her mind. She scooped her daughter into her arms and stepped onto the grass. People stared but she ignored them, she wanted to sing and dance, to forget her troubles. Evie chuckled as her mother sang. The song was one Theodosia had taught her daughters.

'Sur le pont d'Avignon,
L'on y danse, l'on y danse,
Sur le pont d'Avignon,
L'on y danse tout en rond.
Les beaux messieurs font comme ca,
Et puis encore comme ca.'

Margaret placed Evie on the grass and her daughter swirled around. She narrowed her eyes at the sight of a man in the distance. Her heart skipped a beat, could history be about to repeat itself? She closed her eyes as she remembered. She had only seen Evie's father once since their daughter's birth, her breath had quickened when he walked towards her, here in the park. She had stopped the large, heavy pram in front of him and at first there was an awkwardness between them. He had spoken first.

'I am so sorry. I told my father about us, but he refused to allow me to come and meet you. He refused us permission to ever meet again, never mind get married.'

'Why didn't you send me a message? A word to explain why you couldn't come?'

'I am sorry. I should have stood up to him. I have never stopped loving you. Can I see her?'

Her heart soared at his declaration and interest in their daughter. 'Be quiet, she's asleep.'

When he peeked under the large hood of the pram he smiled and tears pooled in his eyes.

'She's beautiful, like her mother.'

Her moment of joy was ruined by the sight of a couple in the distance. Her happiness turned to horror as they drew closer, Uncle William and Aunt Agatha.

'I must go.' She started to push the pram away, desperate to avoid the inevitable nasty scene. As she took a last look at him and her chance of a different life, Louis spoke.

'I am so sorry, my love, my Mona.'

Her lip trembled at the use of his pet-name. She longed to fall into his arms, instead she hurried away. His words had reached her as she produced a fake smile for her aunt and uncle.

'Mona, if you ever need me, I will always be here to help you. I promise.'

Now, she opened her eyes. She hadn't seen or heard anything of Louis since that day. The man she had seen in the distance tipped his hat towards her as he passed. A stranger. She managed a weak smile, but her heart ached.

'Mamma! Mamma!'

Margaret walked towards her daughter. Evie pointed at the ducks and Margaret mustered some enthusiasm. She made a silent wish for Louis to appear. Nothing happened. Evie's tiny hand found hers. Her daughter's beautiful smile should have made everything all right, but she broke out in a cold sweat as a woman spoke behind her. She turned; this was the last piece of history she wanted repeating.

'Aunt Agatha, Uncle William.'

'Have you no shame, girl?'

Margaret started to speak then stopped herself, it was pointless.

'Why are you not at home? My instructions were for him to speak to you *and* your sister.'

Now Margaret spoke. 'What instructions? Who is going to speak to us?'

Aunt Agatha's tight smile didn't reach her eyes. 'Well, well. So, you remain ignorant.'

'Ignorant of what?' Margaret's lip trembled. Uncle William studied his shoes.

'I suggest you and the brat run along home and see what news your sister has for you. I guarantee your whore's smile will be wiped clean from your face.'

Margaret grabbed Evie's hand and ran. Now she understood why Dinah had almost pushed them out of the door, but she had no idea what awaited her at Seymour Terrace.

Dinah

Aunt Agatha wasted no time in sending her son-in-law to see them. Dinah knew she wouldn't have dreamt of soiling her own hands by dealing with her nieces in person. Andrew Glass ducked as he entered the house. His beady eyes darted around the room as if searching for something, settling at a point somewhere above Dinah's head. His formal, black morning coat matched his sombre expression and his spectacles slipped as he peered down his long nose, all sharp angles and disapproval. He cleared his throat.

'In the matter of the outstanding rent...'

Dinah didn't let him finish, determined to gain the upper hand in their negotiations. 'Yes, I know my mother owed Aunt Agatha money. I can settle the debt.'

Andrew Glass raised his eyebrows, his eyes wide. 'You can? May I ask how?'

'With this.' With a flourish Dinah produced her mother's necklace. Her heart sank as a sardonic smile spread across his face. He held out his hand.

'May I?'

She handed it over. He held it to the light, turning it this way and that and inspecting the small stones through his spectacles.

'Do you know how much money your mother owed your aunt?'

She repeated the amount written in her mother's ledger.

'And you think this,' he waved the necklace in her face, 'would cover that amount?'

Her lip trembled as she retrieved the necklace. He cleared his throat again.

'All is not lost. Your aunt has a resolution to this unfortunate matter.'

She waited, knowing her aunt's resolution would serve only to benefit Aunt Agatha herself.

'Where is your sister? She also needs to hear of your aunt's plans.'

Dinah stared at the man, a stranger who was about to tell her how their future would unfold. She had made the right decision in persuading Margaret to go out.

'She isn't here. Tell me about Aunt Agatha's resolution.'

As Andrew Glass started to speak Dinah's knees gave way and she slumped to the floor.

*

Dinah sat with her back to the door. She didn't move when Margaret slammed in, pulling Evie behind her. A stream of incoherent questions flew from Margaret's mouth as Evie climbed onto Dinah's knee. Dinah closed her eyes and stroked Evie's hair. When Margaret ran out of steam she thumped into a chair. She stared open-mouthed at Dinah's tear-stained face.

'Dinah, whatever has happened?'

Dinah sat Evie on the floor and the little girl busied herself with a woollen dolly. Dinah looked at her sister and started to speak.

Margaret

Margaret paused as she packed her few belongings into her mother's ancient carpet bag. Dinah had offered it to her as if she was doing her a favour, but Margaret took no comfort from Dinah's words. 'It will be like having a part of Maman with you.'

There was no point in taking a pretty dress or dancing shoes. She closed her eyes and tried to conjure up the familiar comforting pictures. Nothing. The trapdoor trick didn't work, her treasured daydreams were lost. She tried again but her mother's wonderful images of Paris and the Seine had gone. Even precious memories of dancing with Louis had slipped from her mind since she learnt of their aunt's plans. When Dinah had started to explain, she interrupted. Dinah closed her eyes.

'I'm sorry. But I don't understand how Maman could have left us in this situation.'

Dinah spoke slowly. 'I'm sure she tried to sort this out before she died.'

'But she didn't and now it's our problem.'

'Yes, I'm afraid it is.'

Dinah had said they owed Aunt Agatha a large amount of money and had no way to repay it.

'What was so important to make her borrow money, Dinah?'

Dinah didn't answer but Margaret suspected she knew more than she was saying.

'What are we going to do?'

'We don't have a choice. We have to follow Aunt Agatha's instructions.'

Margaret stared at her sister. Had Dinah lost her mind?

'I know it's not ideal. But what alternative is there?'

'I would sooner die!'

Dinah raised her eyebrows. 'It won't be for long. We'll work hard, save as much as possible, then come back for Evie and we'll all live together again. It will be all right, you'll see.'

'Work in *service*?' Margaret spat the word. 'Work as someone's maid, Dinah? Cleaning and scrubbing from dawn 'til dusk to earn a pittance and scraping low to people no better than us! Can you do it? It's not who Maman brought us up to be! Why do we have to do what vile Aunt Agatha says, anyway? You're 20, I'm 19, we're old enough to make our own decisions!'

'We have to repay the debt, Margaret.'

Dinah had set out their aunt's plan. The debt would be repaid from the sisters' wages working as scullery maids at Hampson Hall, a large country house in Northumberland. They were to leave as soon as possible, and Evie would stay with Lizzie until the debt was repaid. Margaret continued trying to press home her point of view, reminding Dinah of her ideas to find better paid jobs in Newcastle or for Margaret to work in the evenings. Faced with the prospect of working as a scullery maid, evening work didn't seem as bad. Dinah shook her head, explaining if they didn't have a solution in place today, they had to follow Aunt Agatha's plan.

'It's too late for anything else, Margaret. I'm sorry. We have to go to Hampson Hall.'

Margaret tried once more to persuade her sister that going to Northumberland wasn't the answer, that working as scullery maids was beneath them.

'Can't we get away before he comes back?'

'Where would we go? We have no money! And what about Evie?'

Margaret bowed her head. She couldn't imagine being hidden away in the dull countryside enduring the shame of working as a maid, answerable to strangers who considered themselves better than her. She closed the carpet bag and put her head in her hands. This couldn't be her life; nothing was as she had dreamt. Set against such misery, none of her dreams seemed possible now.

Chapter 12

Dinah

Dinah considered Margaret's reaction to the news about their future. She had expected her sister's attitude, but Margaret knew only something of what had brought them to this point. Dinah hadn't told her how she begged and pleaded with Andrew Glass. She grew hot with shame as she recalled how she got on her knees to him, beseeching him not to separate them from Evie.

'She's too young to understand why she's being separated from us! She needs to be with her mother and me! She's never even met Cousin Lizzie! And Pipewellgate is a slum!'

She had demanded to speak to her aunt, the brittle, penny-pinching woman with a rock for a heart. He took pleasure in telling her Agatha refused to see Dinah or her *'errant sister.'* Margaret was unhappy about the prospect of working as a scullery maid, but she didn't know Dinah was trying to save her from the alternative. Aunt Agatha's threat was clear, if the sisters refused to take the scullery maid positions, she would see them all in the workhouse. She would ensure their indebtedness to her was known throughout Gateshead, further blackening what she described as their already tainted characters. Once in the workhouse and with no one to repay the debt for them, they would be forced to carry out hard labour until they settled the debt to their aunt's satisfaction.

When Margaret had asked what was so important to have made their mother borrow money, Dinah hadn't known what to say. She had turned away from her sister, recalling the moment she replaced her mother's necklace under the pillow. She had spotted something else. Her mother's diary. When Margaret was asleep, Dinah went back. By the flickering light of a candle, she opened the diary. The invasion of her mother's privacy was wrong, but Dinah had so many unanswered questions, she hoped the diary would fill in some of the blanks. In Margaret's world everything she needed for her baby had arrived as if by magic and she didn't give it a second thought. Dinah had lain awake at night wondering how her mother managed it. Now she knew.

By the time Dinah had finished reading, the candle had burnt out and the sun was rising. She had pushed her face into her mother's pillow. Her beautiful, exceptional mother. Everything in Theodosia's small, neat hand was written in the form of letters to her own mother. The diary answered some of Dinah's questions and she learnt something of Theodosia the woman, before she became their mother. She learnt about her father and how her parents met and fell in love. She was reminded of Jeannie, her mother's dear friend. Dinah had vague memories of a pretty, gentle woman who had spent a lot of time with them when she and Margaret were small. This, she now knew, was the woman who persuaded her mother to leave Paris. Dinah cried at Theodosia's telling of Fred's story and her heart swelled with pride at her mother's support for her friend. She gave a silent cheer when the friends left London and escaped from the sinister Solomon Zettler.

Her stomach fluttered as she read about Mrs Swann and Springbank Lane. She imagined everyone at the guest house would welcome Theodosia's daughters and granddaughter with open arms. Her hopes were dashed when Theodosia wrote of Mrs Swann's marriage to Monsieur Olivier Despereaux and the scattering of her guests. For a moment Dinah imagined finding Madame Despereaux in Paris. The hope was extinguished in Theodosia's next letter to her mother.

'Dearest Maman,

Some time has passed since I wrote anything. My life has changed, and I have found neither the time nor the inclination to write. Now, I fear I must tell you about the tragic events in my life. Your cocoa girl is bereft. My last letter was full of happiness and hope, but both were brutally extinguished the very same day.'

Dinah wept as she read about her father's death. Her beloved papa had delighted in telling her and Margaret fascinating stories. They sat wide-eyed as he regaled them with tales of maidens in distress and swashbuckling heroes. His stories always ended happily with his captive audience calling *'More, Papa, more!'* Now Dinah had learnt of the manner of his death and her girlhood love for him flourished anew. For her mother to have lost Henry, Ernie, Jeannie and the prospect of Jeannie's baby all in one day, was unimaginable. Dinah had no memory of the day; some things were so bad the mind hid them away. Theodosia lost almost everyone she held dear and was left with no way to support her young daughters.

'I tried everything I could think of, Maman. I hoped the railway would help but the accident report concluded there was uncertainty around whether the casting had been safely lashed to the truck. It stated, "with great and unpardonable neglect the fault fell on the part of those who attached the truck to the tender, without taking the necessary steps for properly securing the iron-work." With this denouement they absolved themselves of any responsibility to me or the other bereaved families.'

Dinah shivered. Theodosia must have been terrified. Worse was to come.

'I pleaded with 'Enri's brother William to speak to his wife. To enquire whether, in our reduced circumstances, Agatha would consider lowering the rent. I should have known I would find no compassion there. Agatha refused but moved us to smaller rooms in Seymour Terrace. Once there I hoped everything might be all right, but I had not counted on Agatha's next move. She charged me more for the smaller rooms, justifying this by saying 'Enri had rent arrears. I believed 'Enri always paid Agatha on time but I had no proof. Her threat for non-payment was to send us all to the workhouse. I tried to pay her, Maman. I tried so hard.'

As Dinah read, an unflattering picture of her aunt emerged. It would have gone against her mother's nature to ask for help, but Theodosia, like a lioness with her cubs, would have done anything to protect them. She contacted her friends at Springbank Lane and Central Street, but their new addresses were impossible to come by or letters went unanswered. She wrote to Mrs Swann, now Madame Desperéaux, but her letter was returned *pas à cette adresse,* not at this address. She even appealed to William. Fear of his domineering wife prevented him from daring to help. Theodosia was alone with two small children and a bitter sister-in-law whose threatening demands persisted. Dinah wept as she read Theodosia's words about Margaret's pregnancy and Evie's arrival.

'Dearest Maman,

It is a joy to me to be blessed with a beautiful granddaughter, but my own Margaret is still only a child herself. I have done everything I can to provide for them, but I live in constant fear it is not enough. I despair that in supporting my girls I have placed myself in further debt to my vindictive sister-in-law. After 'Enri died, I could not disappoint Margaret by admitting I had no relatives in Paris, I wanted to continue buying items for the surprise parcels. I also wanted to buy a second-hand crib and pram for Margaret's baby. Now I fear Agatha has grown impatient about the debt. Oh Maman, who will help me now?'

Dinah rubbed her temples, Margaret remained ignorant of the reasons for Theodosia's indebtedness to Agatha. The final, unfinished letter shattered Dinah's heart into pieces.

'Dearest Maman,

Your cocoa girl is dying. I feel it in my soul, the life is slipping from me. I have failed, Maman. Failed to protect mes filles and now my poor daughters and granddaughter will face an uncertain future. I can do nothing more, Maman. I wish with all my heart...'

The letter ended mid-sentence and Dinah's sorrow claimed her. In her final days Theodosia believed she had failed them, but she became indebted to Aunt Agatha to maintain the fiction about Paris and to help Margaret support Evie. Dinah longed to tell her mother she knew how hard she had tried, which was all she and Margaret could have asked.

Margaret

Dinah was out. Margaret didn't know where and she didn't care. The prospect of working as a scullery maid, left to become an old spinster in the bleak countryside, filled her with horror. It was her worst nightmare, far removed from the life she wanted. She dreamt of escaping from the cold, grey north and living a life full of colour, music and beauty. Why did Dinah have a quiet, easy acceptance of their fate? Margaret knew their mother wouldn't have wanted this for them. She wouldn't, what was the word she had used about the suffragettes? Catapult? No, that wasn't it. Capitulate, that was it. Theodosia had regaled her daughters with exciting stories of the suffragettes' efforts to draw attention to women's rights. This was the future, Theodosia had assured them, exclaiming proudly that the suffragettes would never capitulate. The movement fitted with Theodosia's long-held belief; women should have the same opportunities as men.

She looked around, taking in the shabby, mismatched furniture. Their mother had done her best, but Margaret wanted more from life. She recalled Louis's stories about his family. His uncle lived in a grand house in London. Grandeur and luxury were what she aspired to, she didn't want to have to count every penny and make a pan of soup last three days. She wanted to wear the newest, most fashionable clothes, go to banquets, attend the ballet and opera and drink fine wines. Louis's cousin was a dancer with the English Ballet Company and Margaret dreamt of such a position for herself. She recalled the music Dinah had played a few days earlier. She was the bird, but her cage wasn't gilded. Her suffocating cage was Gateshead. She refused to move to another cage in Northumberland, it would kill her. She must escape, whatever the cost.

Evie toddled into the room. 'Mamma, play?'

Margaret looked into her daughter's dark-brown eyes. Evie fiddled with something, and Margaret smiled. 'What do you have there, ma petit?' Evie showed her mother what she had found. Margaret gasped.

'Where did you find this?'

Evie grasped her mother's hand and led her into Theodosia's bedroom. She pointed to the bed where the pillow had a small head-shaped dent in the middle.

'Grama.' Evie put her hands together and placed them at the side of her head, next to her ear. She put her head on one side and Margaret's lip trembled, her daughter had wanted to fall asleep with her grandmother. She pulled Evie into her arms, prising the necklace from her small grip.

Louis had said if she ever needed him, he would help her. Dinah was convinced they had to follow Aunt Agatha's instructions and Margaret had started to believe her. Now she stared at the necklace and considered Louis's words. Had he meant it? She didn't know, it was years since their meeting in the park. She looked out of the window. Jack Todd played leapfrog with a couple of other scruffy boys. Evie giggled as her mother ran to the door.

'You, Jack Todd! I need you to deliver a message for me and wait for a reply. Quick, it's urgent! There's a penny in it for you if you're fast enough!'

Jack waited at the door while she scribbled her brief words. She needed to get the message to Louis as soon as possible.

Dear Louis,

In the park you said if I ever needed you, you would help me. I need you now Louis, and I have a way to get money for us. We can get away, to London. Please say you will meet me, and we can be together.

Your own, Mona.'

Jack grabbed the letter and ran like the wind. Margaret closed the door, breathing hard. Behind her, Evie's beautiful brown eyes shone.

'Mamma, play?' Evie reached out her small chubby arms and Margaret gathered her up. She held her tight, breathing in her sweet, child smell. She needed to capture this smell. Evie planted a wet kiss on her cheek. Margaret put her mouth to her daughter's ear and sang.

'I love you truly, truly dear,

life with its sorrow, life with its tear,

fades into dreams when I feel you are near,
for I love you truly, truly dear!'
'I love you, Mamma.'

Margaret whispered into her daughter's ear. 'I love you, my own sweet Eveline. Always remember your mamma loves you truly, wherever I am.'

She returned to the window, watching and waiting for Jack Todd.

Dinah

Dinah shuddered as she considered Lizzie's reaction to the news about Evie. She knew her cousin wouldn't welcome Evie into her home, there wasn't a maternal bone in her body. Lizzie was angry and unhappy with her lot. Dinah understood her cousin's loneliness, she also hoped to fall in love and get married. She loved Evie but longed for a family of her own. She wanted to feel the strength of love described in the books she read and the songs her mother had sung. Her ideal man would be a gentleman and a bohemian type, an artist, singer, writer or perhaps an actor.

She ran a hand along her bookshelf, stopping at Robert Louis Stevenson's *'Penny Whistles.'* Theodosia read to them from the book of poems and Dinah had continued the tradition with Evie. As she flicked through the well-thumbed volume, her mother's French lilt floated from the pages. She paused at *'The Lamplighter,'* recalling the vivid images Theodosia had conjured up from her favourite poem. She closed her eyes, picturing the shadowy figure climbing his ladder to illuminate the streetlamps outside their window. Her childhood comfort returned. Theodosia had given her a copy of *'Dr Jekyll and Mr Hyde'* for her sixteenth birthday. Dinah's eyes widened as she read her mother's inscription. *'Chère Dinah, here is a dark tale.'* Theodosia had shown Dinah a picture of the author and she was fascinated by his mysterious good looks. Her mother also told her about Enrico Caruso, the Italian opera singer. Thanks to Theodosia, Dinah's love of books and music ran deep. She sang one of her mother's favourite songs as she worried about their future. '*O sole mio*' translated as '*My Sunshine.*'

'What a beautiful thing is a sunny day,
The air is serene after a storm!'

Dinah longed for sunshine and serenity. She closed her eyes and used her mother's trapdoor trick. She wrapped herself in her mother's tales of the opera and the music hall, anything to remove her from reality. She knew her mother wouldn't have wanted her daughters to work in service, but their choices were limited. Andrew Glass had taken pity on Dinah, agreeing to ask Agatha to take Theodosia's necklace as a down-payment towards the debt. Dinah had offered this with a condition, if Aunt Agatha took the necklace Evie would be saved from the workhouse. Her hands shook as she opened her acerbic aunt's reply, her niece's future rested on her aunt's decision.

'The wretched child will henceforth live with my daughter Elizabeth Ann Brown at her residence in Pipewellgate. My late sister in law's wayward daughters will take up positions in service away from Gateshead. It is not too late for you to seek redemption and I believe honest, hard work will be the making of you. My son-in-law will take the girl to Pipewellgate and arrange your transport to Hampson Hall. I expect you will forever be grateful to me for ensuring the salvation of your mortal souls.'

Dinah studied the words, recalling Margaret's tale of woe when she returned from Pipewellgate. Evie would live with Lizzie at '*her residence?*' From Margaret's description, Lizzie lived in a slum. Lizzie worked hard but Dinah knew about the seedy side of her life. Theodosia had told her Lizzie was the gossips' favourite topic. They said she spent her time in the Globe Hotel with vulgar, undesirable men. Theodosia hadn't told Agatha; suspecting her sister-in-law already knew and refused to acknowledge the situation. It was convenient for Agatha not to confront Lizzie's dubious lifestyle, particularly when she wanted something. She would know Evie staying with Lizzie wasn't appropriate. Dinah had no doubt her aunt would take the alternative path with pleasure, seeing them all in the workhouse without a moment's hesitation.

Lizzie

The day had dawned, the man was calling to collect his alterations. Lizzie was ready and waiting when he knocked. She forced herself not to drink anything when she woke up, she wanted to remember every word of their conversation and his proposal. Once they were married, she would try to stop drinking. She wiped her hands on her dowdy dress and smiled as she opened the door.

'Good morning, how are you?' She mustered all the charm she could.

'My suit? Is it ready?' He barked the questions then held a handkerchief to his nose, refusing to come inside. She handed the suit over, still hopeful.

'Here you are, I hope it is to your liking.' She'd taken extra special care over the alterations, after all, this would be the first of many jobs she did for her husband. *'Husband!'* She marvelled at the word; she'd never imagined she would have a husband.

'Is it all right?' She frowned; he had been so friendly the last time he called. Or had he? Lizzie started to question her recollection of their conversation.

The man threw the money down, turned and left without another word. Lizzie stared at his retreating back. How had he been with her the last time he called? She struggled to remember their conversation. Had she imagined the whole thing? The sherry made her forgetful and confused, perhaps she had misinterpreted his words. She pictured a homeless woman who hung around outside the Globe, begging for pennies. No one knew her name, everyone referred to her as *'the Crone.'* She stumbled from street to street, muttering incoherently. How different was Lizzie? She shook herself. She held down a job and kept a roof over her head. She wasn't anything like the Crone. She reached for the sherry and drank straight from the jug. After drinking herself into a stupor, her vicious thoughts turned to Dinah and Margaret. She took some comfort from knowing that now their mother was dead, her high and mighty cousins would get their comeuppance. It wouldn't be long before they were on the street or in the workhouse. As Lizzie sat, drinking and feeling sorry for herself, there was a knock at the door. Had the man made a mistake? She tried to stand and wobbled as the room spun. She used the table for support as she made her way to the door, swaying from side to side.

'Yes, what?' She slurred and drooled, squinting at the visitor.

'Letter.' John Todd held the letter at arm's length. He hurried away from the stench and decay of the woman and Pipewellgate.

Lizzie inspected the letter, peering at the return address. She closed one eye to focus and snorted. A rare thing, a letter from her mother. As she read, she roared. The letter explained that Dinah and Margaret were to take up positions in Northumberland and would be leaving Gateshead the following week. Lizzie's day had gone from bad to worse. First the non-existent proposal and now she had discovered her vain cousins weren't being put out onto the street. After Aunt Theodosia died, she hoped they would be brought down to earth with a crash. She snarled; they would live in comfort at Hampson Hall while they worked to put food on the table for Margaret's bastard.

The letter stated her brother-in-law would be coming to explain her role in the new set of circumstances. Her role? What the hell did any of this have to do with her? She grabbed the jug and threw her head back. Hot sherry burned her throat as she gulped it down. Until a few days ago she had been hoping for good fortune and for the first time in her life, was looking forward to the future. Now she paced the floor, blind-drunk and furious.

Andrew Glass arrived unannounced the following day. She clenched her hands as she opened the door, did he think she could always be found at home? She usually could, but that wasn't the point. He should have asked when it would be convenient to call. That would have been the correct way to treat someone, particularly someone he wanted a favour from. Her head thumped from the previous day's sherry and her hands shook in anticipation of her next drink. She fidgeted, desperate to indulge her weakness. His imperious voice interrupted her thoughts.

'...so, your cousins leave for Hampson Hall next week.'

'Why should they act all superior when one of them behaved like a whore and had a child without a husband? And what about the wretched girl?'

'Good God, woman! Were you not listening? She will be coming to live with you.'

'No! Never! Over my dead body!'

'Your sister Mary and I are much too old to bring up another child.'

It was already settled, Lizzie's opinion counted for nothing.

'I will bring the girl here to stay with you and your cousins will send money from their wages to feed and clothe her.'

Lizzie sniffed; she had no choice in the matter. Her bleak future stretched out, any chance of finding a husband was disappearing with her cousins. Andrew Glass left and she reached for the sherry. As night fell, she sat in her stinking room. The fire had long since gone out, her only heat and light came from a small stump of candle flickering in the cold draught. She cradled the grimy cup and drank herself further into oblivion. As the sherry soothed her throat, her bitter, resentful soul burned. Someone would pay for this; she would make sure of it.

Chapter 13

August 1903

Margaret

When Jack returned with Louis's reply Margaret read the short letter in disbelief, pinching herself to check she wasn't dreaming. She had expected her letter, written in haste, never to reach Louis, to be intercepted by his father, or to be ignored. Instead, tears filled her eyes as she read Louis's words.

'My darling,

I will wait at the corner of Seymour Terrace and Durham Road at sunrise. We will catch the first train to London and stay with my uncle. My cousin will arrange an audition for you at the English Ballet Company. We will be happy, and all will be well.

Your love, Louis.'

Margaret didn't consider the impact of her actions. She saw the chance of a better life and grabbed it. She didn't sleep. She waited until the house was silent and slipped out of bed, dressed and picked up her mother's carpet bag. She peered through the wooden rails of Evie's cot.

'I am so sorry, my little girlie. I cannot stay. I will send for you as soon as I can, I promise.'

She paused outside Dinah's room and whispered a similar apology. She tiptoed downstairs, holding her breath until she got outside. She closed the door behind her and ran to him.

'You came. This time, you came.' Her words were lost as he kissed her.

'Yes, my darling, and our new life together starts now.'

Margaret and Louis held hands as they hurried across the Swing Bridge. The rising sun reflected off the murky water of the Tyne. Behind them the river was a hive of activity with vessels of all sizes plying their trades. Louis didn't ask about Evie or how Dinah had reacted to Margaret leaving, he only asked how she had money. She told him about her mother's necklace and didn't hesitate when he offered to look after it. He placed it in the inside pocket of his jacket. As she closed her bag, she saw her mother's diary. She'd found it under the pillow with the necklace. She decided to read it on the journey. They reached the end of the Swing Bridge, and she didn't look back.

'We need to hurry! The train is due soon!' Louis took her arm and she laughed.

Margaret's heart filled with joy as she stood beside Louis on the platform. A warm summer breeze blew through the station as they waited for the train. London! She repeated the word over and over. She had never been on a train before. Newcastle was the furthest she had ever been from Gateshead, and now she was travelling to the other end of the country. It may as well have been the other side of the world. She had learnt a little of London life from her mother. While the long journey and being away from all she knew scared her, she was excited to see how the women of London dressed and visit some of the places she had heard about. She wanted to go to the huge department store called Harrods, have afternoon tea at the Ritz Hotel and travel on the mysterious underground trains. She hoped she wouldn't stand out as a poor young woman from the north, she longed to fit in and be mistaken as a reputable, wealthy lady of London.

She grimaced as she picked at fluff on her shabby black coat. It had been her mother's. Her penny-pinching aunt had insisted on it being altered for Margaret to wear to her mother's funeral. Lizzie had snagged her wrists as she pinned the sleeves. She pushed the image away. She lifted her chin, once they were on the train she would write to Dinah at Hampson Hall. She would send what little money she had for her sister to pass on to Lizzie for Evie's upkeep. She smiled; the decision made her feel better. She stopped worrying about Evie and Lizzie and concentrated on the excitement ahead. She pictured herself dancing with the English Ballet Company. They would pay her for doing something she loved! She was thrilled when Theodosia arranged for her and Dinah to have ballet lessons. The ballet positions came easily, and she lost herself in the beautiful music and graceful rhythms of the dance routines. She would be a successful dancer; she might even become famous. When she was paid for the first time, she would treat herself to a beautiful new dress. The brightest red dress she could find, fashioned in the latest style. She would discard everything which wasn't cheerful enough for her new life. She would buy expensive jewellery and sweet-smelling cologne, or perhaps Louis would buy it for her. She would find exquisite cologne from Paris in the magnificent department stores of London. She and Louis would have a grand house, full of splendid rooms. Her house would be the envy of her neighbours and friends. People would come from miles around to attend their lavish parties, enjoying their generous hospitality, and indulging in champagne and delicious little delicacies. She didn't consider her priority should be to send money or presents home for her daughter. All her dreams of a better life were coming true. A doubt nagged but she pushed it away.

She considered her name. Margaret Brown would also be left behind. She would use Louis's pet name for her, Mona. It suited her glamorous new life in London and she would leave shabby, poor, northern Margaret behind. She tried it out in her head.

'*Good afternoon, I am pleased to make your acquaintance. My name is Miss Mona Brown.*'

Brown was too common; she would need a new surname. She jumped at the loud, shrieking whistle of the approaching train. Huge, dirty clouds of steam billowed into the station and she took deep breaths, wanting to remember the smell and the noise of her exciting new life. On the train she placed her mother's diary on her lap and folded her hands over it. She looked at Louis.

'Everything will be all right, won't it?' She whispered her nervous question.

'Of course, my darling. It will be as we have dreamt of.'

'What about your father? Did he agree to this?' A strange look crossed Louis's face.

'Shush, my love. Look, we are leaving the station. This is a wonderful journey and you should make sure you do not miss anything. You need to take it all in and stop worrying.'

Mona gazed from the window as the train took them away from the grim northern landscape. She wrote a short note to Dinah, enclosing what little money she had. She opened her mother's diary and saw the places Theodosia had written to her mother about. She would do the same, she would take notice of each station her train stopped at and write a letter about it. She paused as she considered who she could write to. There was only Dinah or Evie. She pictured her sister; resilient Dinah would be all right at Hampson Hall. An image of Lizzie's filthy room in Pipewellgate forced itself into her mind and she pushed it away. Louis squeezed her hand and she smiled. Everything would be all right. As the train gathered speed she started to write.

'Dear Diary...'

She found it difficult to concentrate on writing, preferring to dream about her new life. She decided to note one thing about each place, providing it didn't interfere with her daydreams. She quickly grew bored and her final notes didn't tell the reader much about anywhere.

'Durham – pretty flowers on the platform. Louis mentioned a cathedral and a castle, but I saw a woman board the train wearing one of the new matted hats. Its magnificence almost filled the width of the carriage, so well was it festooned with large green feathers! A red one to match my new dress will be an essential addition to my London wardrobe.

York – from the carriage window I saw a glamorous first-class lounge on the station platform. A uniformed porter opened the door for a smartly dressed couple and I saw a beautiful woman drinking champagne. She held the glass so elegantly with her little finger raised aloft. I asked Louis if we could go but he said there wasn't time.

Sheffield – I was distracted from looking at the station because a woman boarded the train with a little girl who reminded me of my Evie. My heart skipped a beat, they were so similar. The same dark brown eyes and gentle smile. The little girl caught me looking and she held up a gloved hand. I reached out but the woman pulled her away.

Peterborough – I noted nothing about the station because Louis said there were only about 76 more miles until we would reach London. This meant nothing to me but the look in his eyes when he mentioned London! Diary, I cannot remember ever being so excited!'

During the journey Mona told Louis about her change of name. He smiled, saying he was delighted she had chosen to use his pet-name for her. He agreed Brown was an unsuitable surname and promised to think of an alternative. As the train pulled into Kings Cross, he leant over and whispered in her ear.

'I have it. Your new surname should be Leighton.'

'Leighton? Why?'

'Well, we are going to live with my uncle at Leighton Mansions here in London.'

She clapped her hands, delighted with her new name and the prospect of living in a mansion. Louis had another surprise for her.

'I am changing my name as well.'

'You are? What to?' She clapped her hands again, excited to hear his new name.

'Lewis Leighton, Louis Levy is much too Jewish!'

She smiled, oblivious to the implications of them having the same surname.

'How do you do, Mr Lewis Leighton?'

They giggled at their private game. The Leightons had arrived in London, ready for their exciting new life. Lewis held out his hand to help Mona from the train. She stepped onto the platform and smiled. Her life in Gateshead, her daughter and sister, forgotten.

Dinah

Evie's piercing cries jolted Dinah awake. She hurried into Margaret's room where Evie stood crying in her cot. She rushed over and scooped Evie up. Her heart thudded as she kissed her niece's red, tear-stained face and started to remove her soaking nightgown. Where was Margaret?

'Mamma! Mamma!'

Dinah kissed Evie's forehead as she tried to soothe the distraught child. As she turned to leave the room, she noticed the small white note lying on Margaret's bed. Her stomach lurched and she swayed as she understood. She closed her eyes; grateful her mother hadn't witnessed Margaret's actions. She grabbed the note and hurried downstairs where she cleaned and dressed her niece. She lit the fire and warmed some milk. Evie sat at the table looking at a picture book, content with Dinah's explanation; her mother had left early to go to work. Evie wasn't yet aware her mother and aunt were being sent away. Dinah had waited until the day they were due to leave before delivering the upsetting news. Now the day had arrived and Margaret had disappeared, what would she tell Evie now? Her hands shook as she read the brief note.

'Dearest Sister,

Please find it in your heart to understand. It is beneath me to do the work of a scullery maid. I am going to London with Louis; he has arranged for me to join the English Ballet Company. By the time you read this we will be on the train. I must grab this chance of a better life. Tell Evie I love her and will send for her as soon as I can. Please forgive me.

Your loving sister,

Margaret.'

Dinah screwed the note into a ball and threw it on the floor. She understood Margaret's desire to leave, to escape the cold, grim northern weather and the humiliating jobs their aunt had arranged for them. She understood because she harboured the same desires. She would have liked nothing better than an opportunity to dance with the English

Ballet Company in London. But she also understood her responsibilities. Evie depended on them for everything, and Dinah accepted the responsibility more readily than her sister, the child's own mother. She knew Margaret could be selfish, as a child she was petulant and often refused to share toys and sweets. This was altogether different; she had abandoned her own child. Dinah wouldn't have believed it without the evidence screaming at her from the stark black letters on the white paper. Margaret claimed to love Evie, but love would have been taking the job at Hampson Hall and sending money to Lizzie for Evie's upkeep. Love would have been helping Dinah to repay their mother's debt to Aunt Agatha. Love would have been returning to Pipewellgate for Evie at the earliest possible opportunity.

Dinah read the note again. She knew Margaret had never stopped loving Louis. When he hadn't turned up to meet her after she told him she was pregnant, Margaret had cried for weeks. Margaret had refused to tell their mother who her baby's father was, but Dinah knew, she had been with Margaret when she met Louis. It was unheard of for someone from Gateshead's large Jewish population to be at a dance, they rarely mixed with gentiles. Dinah wasn't sure she believed in love at first sight, but when Margaret and Louis's eyes met, the room fell silent. He held his hand out to her and they danced all night. Margaret talked about him all the way home.

'He plays the violin, Dinah! He disobeyed his father and sneaked out to the dance!'

Margaret's attraction to Louis worried Dinah, their chances of a long-term relationship were slim. After the sisters' father died their mother had insisted on keeping them together. Theodosia's difference marked her out. Outspoken and independent, she was determined not to have to rely on a man to support them. Dinah knew her mother struggled to make ends meet after their father died, and they had to move to a smaller house in a less affluent part of Gateshead. Theodosia continued fighting to keep them together, even after Margaret fell pregnant at a scandalously young age. Theodosia looked after Evie, allowing the sisters to go out to work. Dinah suspected that despite their ages, Theodosia wouldn't have prevented Margaret and Louis from marrying. His family proved a very different prospect. If Louis had now done the decent thing, why hadn't they taken their daughter with them? Had Louis's family accepted Margaret as one of their own? Evie's face was a picture of innocence. How would Dinah explain this without breaking the little girl's heart?

She left Evie playing and opened the door to her mother's parlour for the last time. She hadn't wanted to ask Andrew Glass what would happen to their belongings, but now she decided to look for a keepsake. She lifted the record from the gramophone and placed it into the paper sleeve. She didn't expect to play it at Hampson Hall, but she wanted a piece of Theodosia. She made her mother a silent promise, she would return for Evie as soon as possible. She promised herself she would have a magical room like this, one day. She would fill it with beautiful things and recreate the memories she had shared with her mother here. Her reverie was interrupted by a thunderous knocking at the door. Andrew Glass had arrived to take her and Margaret to Hampson Hall and Evie was going to Pipewellgate. She gathered her strength and closed the parlour door. Evie looked up.

'My mamma?'

Dinah's heart broke for the little girl. 'No sweetheart, not yet.' She opened the door.

Andrew Glass peered at his pocket watch. He tapped the glass then his foot. He tutted.

'Are you ready?'

'Almost.'

She wanted to delay the furious scene when he learnt Margaret had gone. She picked up her suitcase and the small bag Margaret had packed for Evie the night before. She stopped, holding the bag in mid-air. Margaret had packed her daughter's bag, knowing the horror of the place her little girl was going to, then crept out of the house like a thief in the night. How could she have left Evie behind? Dinah took Evie's hand and told her niece they were going on a little adventure.

'My mamma?'

Dinah's lip trembled as she opened her mouth to deliver the lie. 'No, my pet, she has to stay at work for a while.'

Andrew Glass looked past her into the house. 'Where is your sister?'

Dinah's anger at Margaret pushed out an abrupt answer. 'She's not here.'

'What do you mean, she is not here? Where is she?'

'She's gone.'

'Gone? Gone where? You and your disgraceful sister are expected at Hampson Hall!'

'Well, she won't be going to Hampson Hall today.' Or any other day if Margaret had her way, Dinah mused. His face had turned a dangerous shade of puce.

'What am I supposed to tell your Aunt Agatha?'

'That she's gone.'

'Gone where? And who with?'

Dinah sighed, she needed to tell him something to stop his endless questions.

'She has run away with Louis Levy. It is your fault for forcing her to go to Hampson Hall.' She wanted him and her aunt to take responsibility for Margaret's abandonment of Evie, but she knew in her heart that only her sister was to blame. He stared, stuttering as he tried to form words.

'How dare you! These are good positions and you and your errant sister should be grateful to have them! Well, we will see what your aunt has to say about this!'

Dinah stayed silent. She refused to divulge any more information about Margaret's actions or whereabouts, despite her sister not deserving her loyalty.

'This is a most unsatisfactory situation. We had better go without her or you will be late to take up your position at Hampson Hall. I suppose one scullery maid is better than none! Tell your wayward sister she has not heard the last of this, not if I have my way!'

Dinah didn't know if she would be able to tell Margaret anything ever again. She had no forwarding address for her. As Andrew Glass set off towards Pipewellgate he stopped suddenly and turned back. 'With the nonsense about your sister I neglected to collect the necklace from you.'

Dinah froze. In her shock at Margaret's disappearance, she had forgotten to give him the precious necklace. Her passport to Hampson Hall and Evie's to Pipewellgate. Neither destination had been part of her plan for their future, but they were better than the alternative.

'I'll get it.'

She hurried back inside with Evie trotting behind. After Andrew Glass had reluctantly agreed to ask Aunt Agatha to accept the necklace as a down-payment towards her mother's debt, Dinah had wrapped the life-changing find in the delicate handkerchief and placed it back under her mother's pillow. As she opened Theodosia's bedroom door an icy chill raced up her spine. The contents of the dressing table were strewn around in disarray, the bedclothes ripped off, nothing was as she had left it. She pleaded and prayed as she searched the ransacked room. No necklace. No diary. She grabbed the dressing table for support and dry-retched as the implications of her sister's actions hit home. The blood thudded in her ears and her heart threatened to jump from her chest. A small voice broke through her despair. Through the blackness at the edges of her vision she looked at her niece.

'Mamma?'

Evie's refrain had continued all morning. Never was it more prescient. Yes, Evie. Your precious mamma has consigned us to the workhouse. Andrew Glass had said if Aunt Agatha took the necklace Evie would be saved from the workhouse. Now it was gone and with it any hope of saving herself and Evie from their worst nightmare. She stood among the devastation of her mother's bedroom and considered whether she could lie, or bluff her way to a more compassionate outcome, at least for Evie. She walked back with heavy steps, each one brought her closer to admitting she no longer had the necklace, her only bargaining chip. She faced him, defeated. He was there to do Aunt

Agatha's bidding and without the necklace Dinah was beaten.

'Well, do you have it?'

Her throat tightened. Her eyes provided the answer.

'Well, this is most unsatisfactory. Whatever am I to tell your aunt now?'

Dinah stood, rooted to the spot.

'Very well. You and the child will stay where you are and I will report this disappointing turn of events to your aunt.' He turned and left.

She considered the word Andrew Glass had used to describe their situation, '*disappointing.*' It wasn't any of the words she would have used. Devastating, heart-breaking, overwhelming, these were more fitting words. And fury, towards her sister. Margaret had thought only of herself and her future with Louis. She would never forgive Margaret for her selfish actions. She sat next to her niece and stroked Evie's soft curls. While she expected no leniency or compassion from her aunt, she was unaware of the depths the brutal woman would go to. Agatha Brown had one final weapon in her arsenal and she was about to use it against her niece.

Lizzie

Lizzie's body ached for a drink, but she couldn't satisfy her craving yet. Her hands shook as she tried to thread the needle of her sewing machine, she had a pair of trousers to alter for the landlord of the Globe. He would throw in a few free drinks if she did a good job. She closed one eye, trying to focus, but the thread continued to evade the eye of the needle. She tossed the trousers aside, shouting and swearing. Her head thumped and her throat scratched like dry sticks. As she reached for the jug, she heard footsteps and a fist thundered at her door. She snatched her hand back as if scalded and hid the evidence of her addiction. She couldn't be seen indulging in her secret weakness. Andrew Glass knocked again, reluctantly she opened the door.

She had hoped this day would never arrive, hoped something would happen to change things and she wouldn't have to take Margaret's brat in. The day had come, and Andrew Glass stood at her door. He was alone. No cousins and no girl. He coughed; Lizzie smirked at his discomfort.

'They are not coming. *She* is not coming here.'

Lizzie snorted, she must still be drunk, or dreaming. 'What do you mean?'

He sighed. 'Things have changed. Your mother has changed her mind.'

'Margaret's bastard isn't coming to stay with me?'

He coughed again. 'No.' He turned to walk away and she slammed the door. She leant against it, smiling. She hadn't asked why her mother had changed her mind or what had become of her cousins and the brat, because she didn't care. Her own life wasn't about to change, which was cause for celebration. She took a huge gulp of sherry and raised the jug in a toast to her mother.

Chapter 14

Dinah

When Andrew Glass returned, he crooked a finger in their direction. They headed towards Pipewellgate. Had Aunt Agatha, in a rare act of compassion, agreed to let Evie stay with Lizzie after all? They turned away from Pipewellgate and Dinah's heart sank. 'Where are we going?'

Andrew Glass rounded a corner and as Dinah followed him the large, forbidding building loomed into view. She slowed her pace; she had her answer and her heart sank. 'No, please don't send us to the workhouse. Please, I am begging you.'

He turned to face her. He shook his head.

She frowned, if they weren't being sent to the workhouse, why were they there?

'Not you. The girl. My mother-in-law was clear. You are still to take up the position at Hampson Hall. She...,' he pointed at Evie, 'is expected in there.'

Understanding hit Dinah like a giant tidal wave. This was the cruellest thing her aunt could do, to separate them and send Evie to the workhouse on her own.

'No, please. Let me go there and let Evie go to Pipewellgate. Please.'

'It is all arranged.'

Andrew Glass passed a waiting carriage as he continued walking towards Gateshead's Union Workhouse. He tipped his hat to the person inside. Dinah stumbled. Her aunt had lowered herself to check her vicious instructions were carried out, to witness their humiliation first-hand. She turned towards the carriage and hissed. 'I hate you; I will never forgive you for this.'

Her aunt's gloved hand tapped her cane on the roof inside the carriage. The coachman urged the horses into action and the carriage took Agatha Brown away. Any chance Evie and Dinah had of escaping from Gateshead disappeared with the carriage.

Evie

Evie held tight to Aunt Dinah's hand as they left their house with the tall, angry man. After breakfast her aunt had said they were going on an adventure. Aunt Dinah and Evie's mamma were going away to work so Evie could have nice dresses and shoes and the best dollies and toys. She didn't understand. She wanted her mamma. Her lip trembled and her eyes filled with tears.

'Where is my mamma?'

'Not now, ma petit, no tears.'

Evie frowned; Aunt Dinah's face was streaked with tears. The stern man shouted at them to be quiet and hurry up. Aunt Dinah hugged her; her arms were soft and comforting. Evie took a deep breath of her aunt's perfume, it smelt of the pretty flowers in the park. They walked past a carriage and the man tipped his hat towards the person inside. Evie gasped as her aunt stumbled and almost fell. Aunt Dinah turned towards the carriage and hissed.

'I hate you; I will never forgive you for this.'

Her aunt's voice sounded different. As if someone else was speaking from her mouth, someone scary, not her beautiful, kind aunt. A woman's gloved hand tapped a cane on the roof inside the carriage. The coachman urged the horses into action and the carriage took the woman away. Evie continued to hold tight to her aunt's hand as she skipped along the path.

Mona

As Mona stepped from the train at Kings Cross, Lewis waited on the platform, his hand outstretched. She met his eyes, longing to ask whether his father had given them his blessing. Instead, she repeated the question she had asked on the train.

'Everything will be all right, won't it?'

'Of course, stop worrying.'

The shaky voice betrayed him and he turned away. As she opened her mouth to ask about his father, Lewis hurried away along the platform. She took small, quick steps as she tried to catch up, pushing her way through crowds of people streaming through the station. She reached him and clung to his arm as they made their way towards the exit.

As they left the station Mona got her first sight of London. It wasn't what she expected. She had always considered Gateshead grey, everything cloaked in a miserable, depressing greyness. In London, she had expected shining bright lights and glistening shop windows displaying the latest fashions. But the word she associated with her first sight of London, outside Kings Cross, was dark. It wasn't just the lateness of the hour; she sensed an all-pervading darkness. Shadowy figures hurried past, all staring straight ahead and avoiding anyone's gaze. In Gateshead, most people were polite and greeted their neighbours and even strangers in the street. For all the poverty and hardship of her hometown, most people were kind and generous with what little they had. Here in London, people barged into her as they rushed past. She was small and invisible, a person of no consequence in this huge, busy place. Why was everyone in such a hurry? Where were they all going? She sensed London's dark cloak settling around her like a bat closing its wings. She shook the image away; it was late and she was tired.

Lewis charged along the platform, face set and silent. Outside the station he explained they were going straight to Leighton Mansions where his uncle was waiting. Questions tumbled through Mona's mind. Did this uncle know she wasn't Jewish? Did he know she and his nephew weren't married? Did he know about Evie? Lewis tilted his head to one side as he spoke.

'Please do not worry, my dear. My uncle will look after us and soon you will be a dancer with the English Ballet Company.' His words fell on deaf ears as she started to grasp the reality of her situation. She knew nothing of London or Lewis's family. What if his uncle disapproved of her?

Lewis approached the driver of a horse-drawn cab and gave him his uncle's address. Mona looked around. She had expected London's population to be smartly dressed but outside the station, dirty, dishevelled figures shuffled around. They held out grubby hands, begging for any morsel or coin. She stepped away as a figure came closer and the stench from the unwashed, toothless crone reached her. She jumped as a train's whistle shrieked inside the station and the crone shuffled away, cackling. A cacophony of noise surrounded her; the clatter of horse-drawn vehicles on cobbles, the last desperate shouts of the day from street hawkers and her own heart thudding in her ears.

Lewis helped her into the cab. Her prepared conversations, her impressive introduction to the London life she had dreamt of, were gone. The carriage jerked away, joining a row of others making their slow progress through the dirty streets. She sat mute, paying little attention to her companions or surroundings, but one aspect of the journey was unavoidable. The smell. She covered her nose with a gloved hand but couldn't escape the all-pervading stench. Fumes oozed into the carriage and crept under her hand, finding their way into her soul. She wrinkled her nose, but Lewis sat, apparently oblivious to the noxious mixture of horse manure and human sewage. As the carriage passed yet another rowdy public house, she turned to him. His expression told her the moment had passed when she could have asked him about his father. His dark face suggested he carried the weight of the world on his shoulders. The cab slowed to a halt. As Lewis helped her out, an image of Evie and Dinah in an unfamiliar room pushed its way into her mind. Her lip trembled and she took deep breaths, determined not to cry. The path sloped upwards and she followed Lewis towards a smart, three-storied London town house. A welcoming lantern blazed in the entrance. The door flew open, revealing a small, grey-haired man in orthodox Jewish dress. Her stomach lurched.

'Louis, my brother's son – you are welcome in my home!'

'Thank you, Uncle Samuel. Please may I introduce Miss Mona...er, Brown?'

Her legs shook as everything shifted. She grew hot as she felt Samuel Levy's stern gaze on her. His eyes moved past her and he led his nephew inside. She followed, uninvited. She allowed herself to relax a little in the warm hallway with its soft lighting.

'Sit.' Samuel Levy barked at her and gestured towards a single chair in the hallway before leading his nephew into a room opposite. He started to speak the moment the door closed. Hebrew. Lewis had never spoken Hebrew to her, and a shiver ran up her spine. She realised the Levy family's disapproval of her ran deep. Samuel Levy's angry voice shouted her name and the word *'goyim.'* She understood this, it was her. A non-Jew, an outsider. Her eyes darted around the hallway. She sat in the silent house, waiting to learn her fate. Lewis came out of the room and moved towards the front door. He bowed his head and his shoulders slumped. She followed him outside. He studied his shiny shoes and mumbled an apology.

'What's going on?' She tried to meet his eyes, but he kept his head bowed. 'Lewis? Why are we outside? Are we not staying here after all?' He mumbled into his chest. 'What? What did you say?' She grasped his chin and pushed it up. He tried to look away, but she held his face in her hands and looked into his eyes. 'What did you say?'

'I'm sorry my darling, but you can't stay here.'

She heard his words but didn't understand. 'What do you mean, I can't stay here?'

'It's my uncle...he...,' his words tailed off.

'Well then, where shall we go instead?'

Lewis shook his head. 'I'm so sorry, he has instructed me to stay here.'

Nausea rose into her throat. 'What? You mean to abandon me here, alone?' Suddenly he seemed small, and she realised she didn't know him at all. Blood pounded in her ears as she found her voice. 'What about the English Ballet Company? I left my daughter in a slum for the promise of a better life with you! Don't you care what happens to me?'

He had no answers. She had made the biggest mistake of her life. Louis (he was no longer Lewis, that was his name for their new life together) was a weak man, a coward, a dreamer. He had fooled himself into believing this new life could be a reality. In the same way he had failed to stand up to his father, he had been crushed under his uncle's anger and disapproval.

'You will do one thing for me.' She tempered her anger, determined to remain dignified. 'Post this letter to Dinah at Hampson Hall. I wrote it on the train. Do it tomorrow.'

As she thrust the precious envelope into Louis's hands, Samuel Levy burst out of the front door and ordered his nephew back inside. As she watched the door close behind Louis, Samuel Levy grabbed her arm and pulled her away from the house.

Dinah

Dinah put her hands over her ears, but Evie's desolate wails were seared into her memory. The deafening clang of the workhouse gates echoed around her as Andrew Glass gestured towards a waiting carriage. It would take her to a new life, away from everything and everyone she knew. She bowed her head as the carriage left industry-scarred Gateshead behind. Houses gave way to fields as the charming countryside revealed itself. Her life changed with each twist and turn of the narrow roads. The life she had dreamt of, full of entertaining people, music, dancing and fun, had been swept away. Replaced by a spiteful agreement with her vicious aunt. She shook her head to shift the images of the workhouse. Everyone dreaded a descent into poverty and admission to the heinous place. She never dreamt any of them would be brought so low, least of all her four-year old niece.

She flinched at Evie's new, humiliating label. A pauper child. Orphaned and abandoned children slept three to a bed and were hired out to work in factories or mines. An image of Evie playing danced behind Dinah's closed eyes. Evie's grandmother Theodosia looking on, smiling. Evie's innocent playing days were over. A different image crept into Dinah's mind. Evie stripped and forced to bathe in dirty, cold water then dressed in a drab uniform. Her food would contain none of the goodness a child needed. Workhouse staff boasted that they provided education, but local gossip insisted there was no reading or writing. Disobedient inmates were forced to sleep in the morgue and illness swarmed amidst the insanitary conditions. The same pots were used for cooking and to wash soiled bedclothes and linens. Inmates were denied vital medical care and often starved to the point of exhaustion. Nicknamed the 'pest house' due to rat and flea infestations, severe overcrowding and filthy water led to the easy spread of infectious diseases. Improvements in sanitation had led to a dramatic decrease in deaths from cholera and smallpox in Gateshead and Newcastle, but not in there. The enclave of decay clung to pestilence and contamination like limpets clinging to a rock. Dinah shuddered, remembering hushed conversations in the streets of Gateshead. The hubbub of rumour about smallpox returning to Newcastle. She steepled her fingers, praying the invisible killer didn't cross the Tyne and slip unnoticed into the workhouse. A phrase popped into her mind and she pushed it away. *'Abandon hope all ye who enter here.'* She slumped in her seat; she had abandoned Evie to a terrible fate.

She tried to imagine Margaret's journey to London. Had she given her daughter or sister another thought? Had she imagined Evie being taken to Pipewellgate to live with Lizzie? Had she struggled with her decision to leave? Now Margaret had abandoned Evie, Dinah was faced with an even greater responsibility to support her niece. Dinah was all Evie had and it broke her heart to leave her behind. Country roads rose and fell through a breathtaking landscape. Fields stretched as far as the eye could see, burgeoning with crops ripe for harvest. The carriage rounded a corner and Dinah slid along the seat. She righted herself then bowed her head. Summer's last flowers raised their faces for her attention, but found indifference. The landscape opened up, revealing swathes of moorland, heather blanketed the ground like a vast purple carpet. Deep dales and fast-flowing rivers guided the carriage through lush green valleys, but the dramatic scenery passed her by.

She breathed deeply. How would her mother have reacted to her elder daughter working as a scullery maid? How horrified would she have been to see her granddaughter in the workhouse? She had let her mother down. She choked back tears as the carriage turned into a long, wide driveway. She stared wide-eyed at the cherry trees lining the path, their branches bent low on both sides. Too late to see it, she imagined the sweet scent of the heavy pink and white blossoms forming an aromatic canopy over the top of the carriage. On both sides were splendid, landscaped gardens and trees. She shook herself. How could she appreciate anything when she had abandoned her niece to such a dismal existence? The horses' hooves crunched on the gravel as the coachman steered them around the side of the hall to a square courtyard at the rear. He pulled the horses to a halt at the servant's entrance. Hampson Hall's honey-coloured stone gave the large hall a welcoming look. She took in three floors and too many windows to count. The coachman lifted her suitcase down and gestured towards a doorway. She made her way along a narrow passageway. The passageway led to the kitchen, and she blinked as her eyes adjusted to the light in the large, busy room. It was a hive of activity with people shouting and hurrying around. Mouth-watering smells filled the hot air, and she pictured her niece. Evie wouldn't be eating in a warm, welcoming kitchen. Her lip trembled as she recalled stories of the back-breaking labour workhouse inmates endured, only to fight over scraps of rotting meat and cheap, foul-tasting broth.

A small, round woman bustled towards her and introduced herself as Mrs Foley, saying everyone called her Cook. She wiped her wet hands on her messy apron and shook Dinah's hand. Cook's hand was warm, although reddened and rough from years of hot, hard work.

'So, you're the young girl from Gateshead, are you?' Cook smiled kindly. Dinah nodded, struck dumb by her new surroundings.

'Welcome to Hampson Hall! I'm pleased you're here; we need the extra help what with Lord Hampson's elder son talking about making plans to come home!'

'Cook! The girl does not need to hear all that!' The sharp voice belonged to a tall, reed-thin woman who introduced herself as Mrs Jackson, the housekeeper.

'Where is the other one? Wasn't your sister coming with you?' Mrs Jackson's tight smile didn't reach her serious eyes. 'Well, girl? Have you nothing to say for yourself?'

'Will you leave her alone, woman; she's only been here five minutes.' Cook took Dinah's arm and led her through the kitchen.

'Well, she will do the work of two if the other one does not turn up.' Mrs Jackson's sharp words followed them out of the kitchen.

'Don't mind her, pet.' Cook tried to reassure Dinah as she led her out of the kitchen and up a long winding staircase. 'The first thing you need to remember, pet, is there are separate staircases. This is the staircase for household staff. This is the one you should always use, unless you're dressed for above stairs.' Dinah's head spun at her unfamiliar situation and the instructions, 'separate staircases' and 'above stairs.' Cook led her to a small attic room, explaining she would share it with two other scullery maids. 'They're working now pet; you'll meet them later. You'll also meet my husband Mr Foley, he's head gardener, and the housekeeper's hen-pecked husband Mr Jackson, Lord Hampson's butler.'

The room contained three single beds and three small sets of drawers. Cook gestured to one of the beds and Dinah placed her suitcase in front of the drawers. Cook pointed at a wardrobe and said Dinah would share it with the other scullery maids. A lump rose in Dinah's throat.

'Don't worry, pet, we were all the same when we first left home. You'll soon settle in. I'll leave you to unpack and I'll see you in the kitchen when you're ready.'

Dinah looked at the steep, sloping ceiling and the high, square window and tried not to cry. Unlike her selfish sister, she had taken this position to repay their debt to Aunt Agatha. The idea had been to send money to Lizzie to support Evie. How could she support her niece in the workhouse? She shook her head; she would work hard and send as much money as possible to her aunt. Once she started to repay the debt, perhaps Aunt Agatha would allow Evie to leave the workhouse and stay in Pipewellgate with Lizzie. She had never imagined viewing Pipewellgate as a preferred place for Evie, but anywhere was better than the workhouse. She resolved to send whatever money she could and be a thorn in her aunt's side. Persistence and industry were her only weapons in this war with her formidable aunt. She made another resolution. Once her aunt allowed Evie to leave the workhouse, she would save enough money to travel to London. She would find Margaret and confront her. She considered her own life, what would she do once she had earned enough to satisfy Aunt Agatha? She longed for somewhere to call home, with a husband who would love both Evie and her. A man like that might be hard to find, but she vowed never to abandon Evie again. Her own dreams would have to wait, she would do the opposite of her irresponsible sister. To fulfil her dreams Margaret had left behind the most precious thing she had, her daughter.

She placed her suitcase on the bed and unpacked. She held her mother's white cotton handkerchief to her nose. She had found it in Theodosia's bedroom, discarded by Margaret when she snatched their mother's necklace. Dinah picked up a second handkerchief; the white cotton and pretty lace edging were identical to her mother's other than the green 'D' embroidered in the corner. Theodosia had given her and Margaret the handkerchiefs, her sister's had a red 'M' stitched in the same position. It was only a handkerchief, but her selfish sister hadn't bothered to take Theodosia's with her. Had Margaret taken her own or did it matter so little she had left it behind? Dinah folded the handkerchiefs and placed them with her underwear in the set of drawers. She stared at her suitcase, now empty apart from Evie's bag and her mother's gramophone record. She shook her head. How ridiculous she'd been to bring it; she would never be able to listen to it here. She left the record in the suitcase and pushed it under the bed, embarrassed by her own stupidity. She sat on her bed and opened '*The Strange Case of Dr Jekyll and Mr Hyde.*' Her tears blurred Theodosia's inscription and she closed her eyes. She tried to use her mother's trapdoor trick to bring them together again, singing to gramophone records in the parlour at Seymour Terrace. It didn't work, her mother was dead and she had been separated from her sister and niece, perhaps forever. She cried then; huge sobs that shook her whole body. Her eyes flicked open as someone took the book and sat beside her. A young woman with bright red hair and a face full of freckles slowly traced Theodosia's words with her index finger. She looked up and smiled.

'Hello...er..., Dinner?' The young woman's broad Geordie accent danced. Dinah breathed deeply and managed to stop crying. 'I'm Ruby Rogers, Dinner.'

The way Ruby said her name made Dinah smile and she didn't have the heart to correct her. Ruby's hair was as red as her name and curls sprung like corkscrews from under her white maid's cap. She had a wide, happy smile and Dinah warmed to her straightaway.

'Are you ready to learn all about being a scullery maid, Dinner?'

Before Dinah could reply a loud, sharp shout caused both women to jump.

'Ruby Rogers! Why can I never find you when I need you?'

'Maybe because she never looks in the right place!' Ruby whispered, laughing as she stood. 'I'd better go before Mrs Frosty-Face Jackson catches me here with you!'

Dinah stood, but the other woman stopped her. 'Better not go together, or we'll both be in trouble. Follow the smells and sounds from the kitchen.' Ruby hurried out, wild red curls escaping from her cap. 'Comin' now, Mrs Jackson!' Dinah followed a few minutes later.

Cook stood over a huge pan. 'Sit and have some soup while I tell you everything you need to know.' When Cook had finished speaking, Dinah's soup was cold and her head spun. She had learnt the scullery maids started work at daybreak, continuing until Lord and Lady Hampson retired to bed. The scullery maids had to be in the kitchen within half an hour of waking, washed and neatly dressed in their uniforms, having made their beds and left their room clean and tidy. The scullery maids had the most physically demanding of the kitchen tasks including cleaning and scouring the floor, stoves, sinks, pots and dishes. They were the lowest ranked of the female domestic servants and the worst paid. In compensation, Cook reassured her that the hall was always warm, she would have clean sheets and plenty of good food. Cook said she should change into her maid's uniform. Lord and Lady Hampson had a large party of guests attending a seven-course dinner and there was a lot to prepare. Dinah returned to the attic bedroom; the full-length black dress was covered by a long, crisp white apron which she pinned to her bodice. She tied her hair back and pushed it under the little white cap. She stared at the unfamiliar reflection. She took a deep breath and pushed her shoulders back. This was temporary, she would rise above her humiliation and remain the person she had always been, Miss Dinah Jane Brown, daughter of Theodosia Brown.

Mona

Speech deserted Mona as Samuel Levy dragged her along the cold, dark streets. She struggled to keep up as they turned corner after corner and crossed road after road. The houses became more rundown and she saw people gathered outside taverns, singing and shouting. Wherever they were going, it wouldn't be anything like Leighton Mansions. Samuel Levy stopped outside a derelict terraced house. A rundown music hall theatre stood opposite. As her eyes took in the group of men slouched against the wall outside the theatre, Samuel gestured for her to follow him up the steps at the front of the house. She didn't move. He turned, an ugly, twisted expression on his face.

'Hurry up, I haven't got all night to waste on you.'

She found her voice. 'What is this awful place? Why have you brought me here? I have an audition with the English Ballet Company.'

He ignored her. He hammered on the door, peeling paint fell to the ground as his knuckles hit the rotten wood. The door creaked open, and a man peered out. He was bent double, and tendrils of greasy white hair escaped from his dirty skull-cap. An image of Evie danced in front of Mona's eyes. Was she warm? Had Lizzie read her a bedtime story and sung her a lullaby? Her bottom lip trembled as the consequences of her actions hit home. The men exchanged sharp words. She stumbled as Samuel pushed past her in his haste to get away. The bent man dragged her into the house and slammed the door. He grabbed a candle and she struggled to get her bearings as the weak light flickered in the foul corridor. He crooked a finger at her. Up and up they went, until she grew dizzy. He stopped and leant against the wall, wheezing and coughing. He opened a door and pointed a wizened finger at a small, dirty bed. He pushed her inside and closed the door. She blinked hard, trying to fight back tears. A hand touched hers and she jumped.

'Here doll, let me take your bag.' At the woman's soft voice and kind gesture, Mona collapsed onto the hard bed, sobbing uncontrollably. She reached for her handkerchief but found her pocket empty. Her sobs increased, where was Evie? Was she all right?

'Shush, don't cry.' The woman tried to sooth her.

'I've been such a fool,' Mona managed through her sobs.

'Haven't we all?'

The woman's soft laugh was joined by others. As Mona's tears slowed and her eyes adjusted to the dim light, she took in four small beds and three women. The woman sitting on the bed beside her was beautiful, her long black hair fell to her waist. She would have been perfect if it wasn't for her black eye, the black-blue bruising stretched to her ear on the right-hand side of her face.

'Don't worry doll, you won't see it once I'm on stage tomorrow.'

At the mention of the stage Mona's hopes soared. 'Is this the English Ballet Company?' Her words echoed in the silence of the room.

'Not exactly doll,' the woman with the black eye spoke into the dark, sad silence. 'We are all dancers though, and I'm guessing you're here because you're also a dancer?'

Mona nodded.

'I'm Violet. You should try and get some sleep. We'll talk more in the morning.'

Mona didn't intend to sleep but removed her hat, coat and shoes and sat on the hard bed. She didn't undress, she wouldn't be staying. Tomorrow she would find the English Ballet Company and audition for the job Louis had promised her. She stared at the damp ceiling. She would never tell anyone what had happened this night. She would pretend she was living the life of her dreams.

Evie

The woman slammed the huge door shut and Evie blinked, trying to adjust her eyes to the gloom and stench of the unfamiliar building. In the dark cavernous room, the only light squeezed in through tiny, dirty windows set high along the top of one wall. She squinted, there were tables and chairs as if food would be served, but she was alone with the angry woman. Where was her mamma? She focused on the woman. As she stared, the woman turned to face her. Evie averted her eyes, but the woman watched her like a hawk.

'What are you staring at, you stupid girl? Get over here!'

Terror rendered her motionless. Matron stepped towards her, and she recoiled, desperate to put distance between them. She hit the damp, mouldy wall and put out her small hands to steady herself. She cowered as Matron raised a large hand towards her. Hot wetness ran down her legs and she began to cry. Matron grabbed her and dragged her into the middle of the room. She wrinkled her nose as the woman's sour smell reached her. Matron shoved her and she sat down hard on one of the rickety chairs. She wobbled but didn't fall. Towering over her, filthy hands on podgy hips, Matron snarled. Her stinking breath turned Evie's stomach and dirty spittle hit her face.

'No food for you tonight!'

'Where is my mamma?'

'She's gone. Your slut of a mother is long gone, and you'd better get used to it, and fast.'

'Who are you?'

The quick, hard slap across Evie's cheek took her by surprise and she fell off the chair.

'I am every monster you have ever imagined, little girl.'

Chapter 15

Dinah

Dinah settled into life at Hampson Hall. Most of the household staff were friendly and Lord Hampson was a fair man. Concern for Evie nagged constantly and anger towards Margaret burned. Dinah wasn't afraid of hard work but the amount the scullery maids were expected to do shocked her. Ruby helped when she could. The other scullery maid, a quiet, serious young woman called Winnie Smith, kept to herself and Dinah hadn't learnt much about her. Winnie and Ruby were like chalk and cheese. Ruby said the tall, thin Winnie never smiled; all she knew about her was gossip.

'I don't hold with rumours meself,' Ruby whispered, 'but you know the saying, where there's smoke there's fire?' Ruby said Winnie had a baby out of wedlock. The man wasn't in a position to marry her, and no one knew what became of the child. Winnie's father packed her off to Hampson Hall as punishment. The similarity of Winnie's situation to Margaret's struck Dinah. She kept the details of Margaret's life to herself.

At first Ruby told Dinah about the scullery maid's morning duties. The first task was stoking the kitchen range to a good heat, to boil water for early morning tea. The scullery maids and the lower servants made tea for the upper servants. Dinah soon learnt the scullery maids were at the bottom of the household staff chain. Her least favourite job came next, emptying the female servants' chamber pots and washing them with vinegar-soaked rags. She remembered Margaret's horror at the idea of working as a scullery maid, she agreed with her sister where this job was concerned. At home in Seymour Terrace their family had much better lavatory arrangements than in other parts of Gateshead. Theodosia made sure they each had a clean chamber pot under the bed at night, and knew they were responsible for emptying and cleaning their own each morning. During the day they shared an outside water closet with the other residents of Seymour Terrace and each family took turns to keep it clean. Theodosia said they should be thankful everyone took this responsibility seriously, meaning their risk of infection from dirty, unsanitary conditions stayed low. Dinah's lip trembled as she pictured her niece, things would be different for Evie now. Fatal diseases were easily caught by drinking and washing in filthy water, sleeping in rooms with damp, mouldy walls, inhaling fumes from badly built chimneys and living in cramped, disease-ridden conditions. Dinah prayed Evie escaped the terrible illnesses which thrived among the filth and pestilence of the workhouse. She pushed away an image of Evie's hand reaching for hers.

The scullery maids' other responsibilities before breakfast included cleaning the kitchen and its passageways, the pantries and scullery. When Cook arrived in the kitchen at half-past seven, she expected everywhere to be scrubbed clean and polished ready for the day's cooking. Dinah, Ruby and Winnie were responsible for setting the table for breakfast in the Servant's Hall. Cook prepared regular, delicious food for the household staff as well as the Hampson family. Once Cook started her day's work, the smells made Dinah's tastebuds sing and dance. After their hearty meal the three young women cleared the table and washed the dishes. Once breakfast duties were finished, Ruby gestured for Dinah to follow her and Winnie upstairs to their room. They changed into clean aprons and made their way to the Main Hall for Monthly Prayers. The only time it was acceptable for them to be seen above stairs. Well, that's meant to be the order of things, Ruby told Dinah, a by-now familiar glint in her eyes.

'What do you mean, meant to be the order of things?'

'You must have noticed things here are different to other large houses?'

Dinah shook her head; she didn't know how this level of society conducted their lives. Ruby continued, her eyes sparkling. 'Lady Hampson is his Lordship's fourth wife, she's much younger than him and an absolute beauty. She doesn't care for the traditional rules.'

Dinah shrugged. 'What do you mean?'

'Watch. Take Monthly Prayers for example.'

When they arrived in the Main Hall, clean aprons sparkling, Dinah started to understand. The local vicar, Reverend Ash, stood at the front of the almost empty room, prayer book open waiting to call his flock to order. As well as Ruby and Winnie, only Mrs Jackson was present. Of the family, Dinah saw only Master James, Lord Hampson's younger son. Ruby had told her a little of Lord Hampson's sons, both had reputations as handsome, eligible men-about-town. While Master Walter worked as a solicitor, the younger Master Hampson led a riotous lifestyle. His brother had been called to rescue him from troublesome legal proceedings several times.

'See?' Ruby whispered, 'they don't care. They'll be sleeping off last night's champagne!'

Ruby continued, explaining how unusual it was for women to be allowed to work in service once they were married. Here, both Mrs Foley and Mrs Jackson worked alongside their husbands.

'This is the future, Dinner! Lady Hampson is involved in the fight for women's rights!'

Dinah recalled her mother's stories about women who were prepared to take drastic action to further the cause for women to obtain the vote. Encouraging her daughters to be independent, Theodosia told them they could have careers, earn their own money, and make their own choices. Dinah smiled, her judgemental, spiteful aunt had sent her here, believing it would redeem her godless soul. If she had only known, of all the country houses in Northumberland, here, the conventional rules meant little. Theodosia would have been delighted that in this most traditional of places, married women were able to have some independence. Reverend Ash recited the Lord's Prayer and Dinah spotted Ruby steal a glance at Master James. He winked, and as Dinah prayed for Evie, she wished Aunt Agatha could bear witness to this unusual gathering.

After Monthly Prayers, the scullery maids resumed their cleaning duties; pots, pans, crockery and cutlery from the family's breakfast. Mid-morning tea was served in the Servant's Hall at eleven o'clock. Dinah and the others were responsible for setting and clearing the table, followed by more washing and drying of dishes. She started her next task, helping the kitchen maid and Cook with preparations for the servants' dinner and the family's luncheon. Their dinner was served at midday after which she, Ruby and Winnie were allowed a short break. Ruby said they should take a walk in Mr Foley's gardens, and she would tell Dinah about their afternoon duties. The afternoon would continue in the same way. More meals to set out, clear away and dishes to wash and dry. After the family's dinner in the evening, the scullery maids repeated their morning cleaning duties, the kitchen and its passageways, the pantries and the scullery. Supper was the final meal of the day, served at half-past nine. Once all traces of this were cleared away and if Lord and Lady Hampson made no further demands, they could enjoy their leisure before going to bed.

As they walked, Ruby told Dinah the maids were given some time off on one Sunday every month. It wasn't a full day, they had chores to do first thing in the morning and could only consider themselves off duty once Mrs Jackson was satisfied. At first Dinah misunderstood.

'That's nice, perhaps the three of us could go for a walk together? You can show me the grounds to the hall and I can get to know Winnie better.'

'No, we don't have the same Sunday off, how would the work get done?'

Dinah knew what she would do on her first Sunday off. The knowledge that she would see Evie would get her through her first month at Hampson Hall. The visit would eat into her hard-earned wages, but she would walk to the train station and buy the cheapest third-class train ticket.

Ruby interrupted her thoughts. 'What are you so happy about?'

'Nothing.' She wasn't ready to talk about Evie.

Mona

Mona was determined not to fall asleep in the stinking, flea-ridden attic bedroom but exhaustion took over. She opened her eyes to Violet's bruised face, the black eye watched her from the bed beside hers. In daylight the eye was purple and yellow as well as black and blue.

'So, what's your name, English Ballet Girl?'

Mona flushed, in the cold light of day her question from the night before sounded ridiculous. She muttered, the prim and proper intro-duction she had practised for her new life in London forgotten. The other women introduced themselves, Nellie and May. Before they could learn any more about one another, they were interrupted by a sharp knock at the door and a boy's voice. He asked if they were decent. Mona jumped at Nellie's deep, coarse laugh, identical to Lizzie's.

'Decent? What are you talking about, kid? We've never been decent in our lives – why do you think we've ended up here?'

Mona opened her mouth to reply then closed it again. She refused to accept she had 'ended up' anywhere. She *was* decent. She frowned, if the women learnt about Evie, would she be able to cling to that notion? Her head pounded with confusion, anger, despair and, she realised, hunger. She and Louis hadn't eaten on the train, he had promised they would have something at Leighton Mansions. Her stomach churned as she pictured Louis, how wrong he had been about everything and how stupid she was to trust him.

'Where are we going, Violet?'

'Breakfast, doll – well, if you can call it that!'

Mona took a deep breath and pushed her shoulders back. She would have something to eat then leave. She would find the English Ballet Company. She would demand the audition Louis had promised her, and by nightfall she would be sleeping in warmth and comfort with a full stomach. In daylight the full dilapidation of the damp, crumbling house was evident. What little wallpaper remained clung to the filthy, greasy walls. Paint peeled from the banisters and Mona snagged her hand on the rough edges as she followed the women downstairs, a rat scampering in front of them. They reached the dark, dingy hallway. The solitary candle the bent man had carried the night before now extinguished. Mona hesitated when Nellie opened the front door.

'I thought we were having breakfast, Violet. Where are we going?'

'You don't think the old miser gives us anything, do ya?' Nellie hurried across the road towards the rundown music hall. Violet and May held back and walked on either side of Mona. Mona side-stepped the stagnant pools of disease-breeding water and piles of rubbish as she crossed the road. When she arrived at the broken pavement on the other side Violet touched her arm.

'Don't mind Nellie, doll, she acts tough as old boots, but she has a heart of gold, you'll see.' Mona wasn't convinced and resolved to keep her distance from Nellie. May took her arm and led her towards the music hall, the Diamond. Mona grimaced. Its dark, ugly brick facade gave the building an unwelcoming air and the dirty lamps outside, unlit in the daytime, had nothing of a diamond's bright sparkle. The women walked around the side of the rundown building until they reached the stage door. A long table leant precariously against the wall and a group of women, including Nellie, helped themselves to an insipid liquid from a large metal pan. Violet and May reached for dirty-looking bowls and spooned something from the pan. Mona hesitated when Violet handed her a bowl.

'I would, doll. You might get nothing else.'

Mona tried not to look at the rusty spoon and the congealed fat as she scooped a small amount of the foul-smelling, greasy liquid from the pan.

'What is it?'

'Good question, doll.' Violet peered into the pan, grimacing. 'Skilly.'

Mona stared.

'Watered-down porridge, doll. Sometimes it's flavoured with meat but usually it isn't. Occasionally there's a bit of potato skin or oatmeal thrown in, usually it's tasteless.'

Mona held her breath as she lifted the spoon to her mouth and swallowed a small amount of the cold broth. Even during their worst times, Dinah had bought fresh vegetables and cooked meals with a small piece of meat or fish. Dinah had tried hard to keep Evie healthy and strong. Dinah, not her. Her lip trembled. The women devoured the awful brew and Mona shuddered.

'We should go, doll.' Violet led her towards the stage door. As Mona walked inside, she caught her breath. The smell of the grease-paint sent her mind reeling, home, to the ballet lessons Theodosia had insisted she and Dinah took. The sisters fell in love with dancing from their first lesson in the church hall. Their elegant teacher, Miss Trudy, had allowed her pupils to see her make-up. The sisters knew about make-up from their mother. Theodosia had regaled them with glamorous stories of her theatrical life in Paris. She swore them to secrecy about make-up, whispering that it was part of a world known only to actresses and dancers. The sisters loved being part of a secret world and when Miss Trudy opened her suitcase, they stared wide-eyed at the treasures inside, delighted to see make-up laid out in full view right in front of them.

Mona stood at the stage door and pictured the delights in Miss Trudy's battered old brown suitcase. Pots of rouge as ruby red as any jewel and dusting powder with sheets of *papier poudre.*' When one of Miss Trudy's pupils asked what the papers were, the sisters smiled. Theodosia had told them the thin pieces of paper permeated with face powder fitted neatly into a lady's purse for a quick, discrete repair of a shiny nose or face. Also in the suitcase were feathers, ribbons and other adornments, worn to accompany their dances. And the colours! Mona had never seen as many different shades; the whole rainbow was captured inside Miss Trudy's suitcase.

'Hey! You! The boss doesn't pay you to stand around dreaming!'

The harsh voice cut into her thoughts like a knife. The bent man from the night before pushed his face into hers and she recoiled from his foul breath. She clasped her hands together as they started to shake. 'I'm sorry, I…,' her words were lost as the door behind her opened. The noise levels rose as a group of women rushed past.

'Off you go.' The man gestured for Mona to follow the women.

'I have a position with the English…,' she stopped.

'What? Think you're better than our dance troupe, do you, Miss English Ballet Company?'

Mona grimaced; news of her stupidity had travelled fast. 'No, I mean to say, I…'

'Hurry up, rehearsals start in five minutes.'

Mona's head spun as she followed the other women. She didn't know where she was going or what they were rehearsing for. The women disappeared into a door on the right-hand side, and she followed. At the entrance to the dressing room, she stopped. The women were semi-naked. Some crowded in front of a grainy, spotted mirror to apply garish make-up, painting their faces with heavy, mask-like strokes. There was no place for Miss Trudy's suitcase in this debauched room.

'No.' Mona started backing away.

The bent man placed a firm hand on her shoulder. 'Very well.'

She let out a huge sigh and placed her hand on her chest. She would find the English Ballet Company. They would give her a job, a decent meal and somewhere to stay.

'Thank you.' As she turned to leave, the man delivered his devastating blow.

'Pay me for your bed and breakfast then you can leave.'

Mona turned to confront him, horrified at the suggestion she should pay to stay in the rat-infested hovel and eat the foul liquid. Her heart skipped a beat, she had no money, not one penny. She had written to Dinah from the train, apologising again for running away.

She had enclosed what money she had and asked Dinah to send it to Lizzie for Evie. She had given the note to Louis, insisting he send it to Dinah at Hampson Hall. She hadn't kept anything for herself. When she wrote the note, she had trusted Louis and believed his promise of an audition with the English Ballet Company. She shuddered as if a bucket of ice-cold water had been tipped over her, realising Louis still had her mother's necklace. Vile skilly rose into her throat and she lowered her head. She vowed never to trust another man as she had trusted Louis. The bent man smirked and narrowed his eyes.

'Money?' He snarled the word, his filthy hand outstretched towards her.

Her eyes darted around.

'Or payment in kind?'

He grinned at Mona's blank stare. Nellie shouted from across the room.

'Pay up or open your legs for him, English!'

The greasy skilly rose into her mouth and her bottom lip trembled. She wouldn't cry, she refused to let them see her fear. Violet pushed her way through the throng and stood by her side. She had undressed, her modesty now covered by a few large, strategically placed feathers.

'Dance today, doll. Then you can pay him and go on your way.'

Mona's hands shook as she started to undress. Violet explained the set up as she handed Mona something to cover her embarrassment. They rehearsed every morning then put on three shows, a matinee performance and two shows each evening. The last show was the worst, Violet explained, as by then the sleazy men in the audience were drunk and they got *'handsy.'* Mona frowned and Violet whispered, 'don't get too close to the front of the stage, ever.'

On stage Mona tried to block everything out and concentrate on dancing. She tried to ignore the stench of stale tobacco and beer wafting from the dirty sawdust and lose herself in the music and dance routines. There was nothing graceful or beautiful about the dances, but the music removed her from the Diamond. She had a talent for dancing no one could take away. She silently thanked her mother for her ballet lessons, pushing away an image of Theodosia's horror at her younger daughter performing suggestive routines with this scantily clad troupe. The music ended abruptly, and the women ran off stage. Mona followed them to the small dressing room. She wanted to do the matinee performance, get paid, settle up with the odious man and use the rest of the afternoon to find the English Ballet Company. She walked to the lodging house with Violet and May.

'Where's Nellie?'

Violet and May exchanged a glance. 'She has another dancing job.' Violet reddened, caught out in her lie. Back in their room Violet suggested Mona should get some sleep before the matinee.

'I'm hungry, will there be more food later?'

'After the matinee.' Violet smiled but Mona spotted the same look between her and May.

'We need to tell her, Vi. To be honest with her.' It was the first time May had spoken and her accent surprised Mona.

'Where are you from, May?'

'Edinburgh, in Scotland.' May whispered the words.

'How did you get here from Edinburgh?'

Again, the look between them. What were they not telling her? Violet gestured for Mona to sit on the bed in between her and May. Before Violet could say anything, the door burst open and Nellie collapsed into the room, her face covered in blood and her dress ripped. The smell of hard spirits entered with her, and Mona knew she hadn't been to another dancing job.

'Ah Nellie, not again.' Violet took Nellie in her arms and helped her onto her bed. Nellie's eyelids flickered as she allowed Violet to help her.

'You need to avoid him, he's bad news.'

Mona's head spun as she tried to make sense of everything. She opened her mouth to speak but May shook her head. 'Not now doll, we need to get Nellie cleaned up.'

Violet and May tended to their friend. Once Nellie was patched up and snoring, they motioned for Mona to sit. They sat on either side of her and told their terrifyingly similar stories.

Chapter 16

Lizzie

After receiving the welcome news that Margaret's bastard wasn't coming to stay, Lizzie celebrated. For days. The knowledge that she wasn't about to get an unwanted lodger, and that her whore of a cousin had shown her true colours, made up for years of misery. Margaret wasn't such an example of goodness after all. She had abandoned her child to run off with a man, and not just any man, a Jew! She left without a chaperone, now everyone knew exactly what she was. Lizzie raised the jug and stuck out her tongue. Nothing. She groaned as she pushed herself out of her filthy chair. The room swayed and she thumped back down. She belched and closed her eyes. She would sleep for a while then go to the Globe. She hadn't worked for days and had no money, but would try and cadge a jug from the landlord. She grunted and snored as a deep sleep claimed her.

It was dark when she woke. She shivered. Her head pounded; she needed a drink. She forced herself up and staggered towards the door, pulling a moth-eaten shawl around her shoulders. Pipewellgate was silent save for the ever-present scurrying of rats and prostitutes' calls. She shuffled along the street towards the single gloomy lantern illuminating the entrance to her second home. A figure huddled in the doorway reached out a filthy, wizened hand as she passed. Lizzie pulled her arm away and snarled at the beggar, before realising she knew her. The Crone.

'Areet, Lizzie? Aye, ye think ye are, but there's news comin' for ye!'

Lizzie pushed her face into the Crone's. 'What are ye bletherin' aboot?'

The Crone tapped a filthy finger against her warty nose and grinned. Her mouth gaped open, revealing a single, pointed black tooth. Lizzie stepped away from her breath.

'She's comin'. That's aal I'll say.'

'Ye divvent knaa what ye're sayin', ye taak nonsense.' Lizzie pushed the door open. As the Globe's sweaty, raucous atmosphere claimed her, the Crone spoke again.

'Aye, ye drink yersel into a stupor, ye'll soon knaa.'

Lizzie shook her head; everyone knew the Crone wasn't all there. She glanced behind her where the Crone stood, tapping the wizened finger against her nose. Everyone also knew the sinister beggar had a gift for being the first to hear about any news around Pipewellgate, and her tittle-tattle was often true. Some said she possessed the second sight, that she was everywhere, if you turned around, she would be there, listening. Lizzie chewed her bottom lip as she arranged her face to beg a favour from the landlord. What was the news the Crone had said was coming for her?

Dinah

Dinah rolled her neck from side to side. Her first four weeks at Hampson Hall had felt more like four months. The back-breaking work; scrubbing, cleaning and polishing, seemed never-ending. As her first Sunday off approached her mood lifted, she was going to see Evie. The cost of the train would eat into her savings, but she had to see her. She had made a little rag doll from leftover pieces of material, hoping it would remind Evie of happier times. Cook gave her some bread and butter and a slice of fruitcake, all wrapped in a clean tea towel. Ruby and Cook had accepted her story, that she was visiting an ill friend in Gateshead. A friend with a little girl. She hated lying, but she wasn't ready to tell them about her family's situation. She sat on her bed. She opened one of her drawers and removed a small piece of soap. She had been on her hands and knees scrubbing the scullery floor when Ruby crept up behind her. Ruby reached around her and whispered, 'for your friend's little girl.' She flinched, alarmed by what Ruby had in her hand.

Ruby whispered. 'It's all right, they won't miss one little soap!'

Ruby had pushed the soap into Dinah's hand. Now she held it to her nose, breathing in the sweet smell. Rose, her mother's favourite. Three handkerchiefs lay in the drawer, her mother's with the blue 'T' embroidered in one corner, hers, identical apart from the green 'D' and her sister's, with the red 'M.' Margaret's had been in the bag she packed for Evie, before she fled. Dinah wrapped the soap in one of the handkerchiefs, sniffing the fragrance through the delicate material. She pictured Evie unwrapping Margaret's handkerchief and finding the soap. Margaret didn't deserve the gesture, but Dinah wanted Evie to have a reminder of her mother. Her eyes fixed on something in the drawer. She sighed as she removed the one short note she had received from Margaret.

'Dearest Sister,

I am so sorry to have left in the way I did. I will write more once Louis and I are settled at his uncle's house in London. For now, please find enclosed a small sum of money for my dear little Evie. I would be grateful if you could send it to Lizzie on my behalf.

Your loving sister, Margaret.'

The paper shook as Dinah tried to control her anger. When Margaret left for London, she had condemned Dinah and Evie to an uncertain future. Margaret hadn't known the necklace was Dinah's only bargaining chip, but she had taken it without any consideration for her sister or daughter. Margaret's actions meant Evie was now in the workhouse. Dinah couldn't send money to her there. Instead, she added the money she had saved to the small amount in Margaret's note and sent it to her aunt. After a month at Hampson Hall, she had received no more word from Margaret. She was surprised Margaret had sent less than she had managed to save from her paltry scullery maid's wage. Wouldn't Margaret be earning more money than her? After all, wasn't she now a dancer with the English Ballet Company? And didn't she have Louis to support her? Dinah had accepted her position at Hampson Hall as a temporary situation, but her heart thumped when she pictured her selfish sister living a life of luxury in London. Why had Margaret not written more and sent regular money for Evie? She shook her head, she had to concentrate on saving enough to repay Aunt Agatha and getting Evie out of the workhouse. She worked quickly, longing for permission to leave. When it came, she ran to the stairs.

'Girl! Where is your sense of decorum?'

'Sorry, Mrs Jackson.' She hated the deference but knew better than to annoy the housekeeper.

'Very well, but remember. I can call you back to your duties like this!'

The surly housekeeper snapped her fingers and Dinah apologised again. She tried to leave without speaking to anyone, but Ruby insisted on walking her to the end of the driveway. Dinah hurried in front, uncomfortable with her lies and concerned she would give herself away.

'Cheerio, Dinner! See you this evening!'

Dinah's steps quickened; she had waited four long weeks to see Evie. Each part of her journey took longer than expected, the long walk to the station meant she almost missed her train. As she ran along the platform, the guard blew his whistle as a final warning for passengers to board.

'Quickly, Miss!'

She grabbed her skirt and leapt onto the train. She vowed to leave earlier next month, Mrs Jackson's mood permitting. She took deep breaths as the train moved towards Newcastle. In her head she told Evie she was coming. At Newcastle she was one of the first to step onto the platform. As she started to run her hat slipped off her head. It bounced against her back and the ribbons cut into her neck but still she ran. A sharp pain needled her side as she ran across the Swing Bridge and started the steep climb. The dark building loomed into view, and she slowed her pace. *I'm here,* she told her niece, *I'm here.* The huge, intimidating iron gates were bolted shut. She banged on the gates until her knuckles were raw and bloodied. No one appeared. She shouted until she was hoarse. Still, no one appeared. She put her head back and craned her neck to see the top of the sheer stone walls on either side of the gates. She tried to get a foothold on the wall, but her shoe slipped on the damp, filthy stone. She shouted her niece's name. The ever-present crows took off from the dirty pools of water surrounding the workhouse. Their caws were cruel laughter and her shoulders slumped as she leant against the impenetrable gates. She knocked her fist against her head.

'Stupid woman, why would they let you visit her?'

Head bowed, she stumbled back towards the train station, dragging Evie's bag behind her.

A few minutes later a side gate opened, and a man left the workhouse. He frowned as a bedraggled young woman hurried past him, her head bowed. Matron called him back and he turned, the young woman forgotten.

The journey back to Hampson Hall passed in a blur. Dinah clutched Evie's bag to her chest as she stepped from the train. Rain fell but she dawdled. Water dripped from her hat and coat as she slipped unseen into the passageway to the kitchen. The usual welcoming noise greeted her as she reached the kitchen door and she flattened herself against the wall. She chose her moment and slid past the open door like a ghost. She crept upstairs but stopped with her hand on the bedroom door at the sound of sobs from inside. Winnie's thin frame was curled into a ball on her bed, but she didn't resist as Dinah held her. Through her sobs Winnie explained today was her baby's birthday. When Winnie stopped crying, she raised her eyebrows, gesturing towards Dinah's wet clothes and Evie's bag lying on the floor. Dinah found herself telling Winnie about Evie, and her visit to the workhouse. She ended by saying that despite the wasted money, she would go to the workhouse every month and pound her fists on the gates until they let her in.

Winnie shook her head. 'I tried that, but they don't let you visit.'

The women embraced, connected in their loss and longing. As the door crashed open, Dinah pushed Evie's bag under her bed.

'Dinner! I didn't hear you come in! How were your friend and her little girl?'

Dinah welcomed Ruby's questions; her friend's enthusiasm gave her time to compose herself. When Ruby stopped talking, Dinah delivered a convincing story about her visit to Gateshead, as she changed into a clean dress. As she followed Ruby down to the kitchen for their evening meal, she counted the cost of her futile visit. She had wasted some of her hard-earned wages getting to Gateshead, money she still owed Aunt Agatha, and she had no idea how Evie was.

Evie

Evie didn't know how long she had been in the big dark building. At the beginning she kept asking for her mamma and aunt, but no one told her when they were coming. The woman with big arms slapped anyone who asked questions, so after a while she stopped asking. She didn't know where she was or why she was there, she shivered most of the time and her tummy rumbled constantly. There were other children in the big room where she tried to sleep. They huddled together under dirty blankets and they hit, bit and scratched each other to gain an extra piece of hard, flea-ridden material. She didn't fight but took what she could get, which was often nothing.

The woman with big arms told her she had jobs to do until she started school. She didn't understand. Her mother and aunt had done jobs while she played. Why did she have to do the jobs here? Why wasn't she allowed to play? Every day started with a loud bell ringing. The woman with big arms shouted names and the children said *'yes, Matron.'* On the first day the woman slapped her for not answering. She didn't know her name was Eveline Brown. She had always been called Evie or *'ma petit.'* She answered *'yes, Matron'* after that. After the names the woman sent them into another filthy room and ordered them to wash their faces in ice-cold water. Then, the woman hurried them into the cavernous room, and they were given what passed for breakfast. On the first day she refused to eat the dirty, thin liquid and black bread, and Matron slapped her. By nightfall her stomach growled, and she would have eaten anything, even the pan of watered-down porridge.

Her lip trembled as she scrubbed floor after floor and washed pan after pan. What had she done wrong, why did she have to scrub floors and wash pans? She had always tried to be a good little girl. She tried to do what Matron said because she had seen what happened to children who didn't. She'd seen them walking round and round at night, in bare feet with baskets on their heads. The basket held their day clothes and if they dropped any, they received a beating with the birch. She had also seen children made to kneel on the wire netting that covered the hot water pipes. She tried to be good because the screams of these children were stuck in her head. She tried to speak to another little girl, but Matron shouted at them to shut up, so now she didn't speak to anyone and none of the other children spoke to her. There were lots of little flies buzzing around everywhere and they jumped and bit. She scratched at the bites until they bled. A little boy picked one of the flies off his head and ate it. He scrambled around on the floor and grabbed something in his filthy hand. He held it out towards her. She shook her head; she would die of hunger before eating a biting fly or rats' droppings.

On her first day a little boy was lifted out of the bed beside the one she shared with two other girls. The boy was straight like a statue and covered in spots. The other children stepped back and whispered as the boy was taken away. Smallpox. She didn't know the word. She tried to picture the faces of the other children but there were so many, and some were there one day and gone the next. She had nothing. No picture books, no toys. Aunt Dinah had brought a bag, but she didn't have it. Aunt Dinah had gone away to work and said something about getting her a new dolly. Her mamma had said she loved her truly, but that was so long ago. Where were they and why didn't they come and take her home?

Mona

Mona rubbed her tired, aching feet then lay on the hard bed, desperate to rest before returning to the Diamond for the first evening performance. She tried to sleep but the leering faces, grasping hands and raucous shouts from the audience filled her mind. As usual Nellie had disappeared as soon as the matinee finished. She recalled her first day, when Nellie had lain battered and bruised on the bed. As Nellie slept Violet and May had told Mona their tragic stories. As they spoke, her nerves tingled. She had arrived in London with the man she loved, looking forward to the future. Then she had found herself alone and penniless. As Violet and May's horrific stories unfolded, her resolve strengthened. She needed to escape from this hellhole and find the English Ballet Company.

May had led a charmed life in Edinburgh. Her doctor father and wealthy socialite mother entertained the cream of the middle and upper classes. Their French chef prepared the finest cuisine and champagne flowed. Tears glistened in May's eyes as she described the beautiful dresses and hats and the lyrical music drifting into her bedroom. May's life changed in an instant when she went to Waverley station with her parents to wave off some visitors. She became separated from her parents outside the station and went inside, expecting to find them on the platform. She couldn't see her parents among the throng of people. As she tried to get her bearings, she was pulled onto a train. A strong-smelling cloth was placed over her mouth, then there was only darkness.

'Did no one come looking for you?'

May turned away as her lip started to tremble. Violet continued. 'No, but she refused to accept that her parents would have abandoned her.'

147

Mona lowered her eyes. She could never tell them about Evie.

'Then one day our infamous employer appeared. He doesn't often lower himself to visit his seedy premises.' Violet said she overheard him speaking to one of his henchmen. She learnt May's parents met with tragedy the day their daughter was abducted. As they searched in desperation outside the station, May's mother stepped into the road. As her husband pulled her clear, a tram hit them. They died at the scene, and it wasn't until later, when their housekeeper told the police May had been with them, that the search for her began. The trail was cold, May had gone. The result and the sickening truth as Violet overheard it was *'no one is looking for her, she's staying here.'*

Violet's story was equally tragic. She had lived an ordinary life in London until the age of 12, when her parents contracted the fatal influenza virus and died within two days of each other. Violet escaped the virus but with no other close family, was taken in by a catholic charity. Any expectation of being safe and cared for was short-lived. She endured starvation and regular beatings before managing to escape. Her descent was swift, taking her first to the workhouse then onto the streets. One of their employer's henchmen found her, begging to survive. Violet explained their sinister employer's men scoured London in search of young women down on their luck, who would appreciate a hot meal and somewhere to stay in return for some work. Once they took the bed and food they were in debt and trapped.

Mona's stomach lurched. Samuel Levy had offered her up to this depraved enterprise. Once she had stayed in the decaying lodging house and eaten the vile skilly, she was in debt to their corrupt, anonymous employer. 'When will we get paid?'

Violet and May exchanged a glance, giving Mona her answer. Her plan to pay for her bed and breakfast and leave to find the English Ballet Company was shattered.

'Sometimes we do, doll, but most times, we don't. When we do it's not much. Some girls, like our Nellie, they find other ways of earning a shilling or two.'

'What ways? Perhaps I can do that?' She glimpsed a sliver of hope, a way out.

'No, it's much too dangerous.' As Violet spoke, Mona heard Dinah's voice.

Chapter 17

June 1904

Dinah

Ten months later, the image of Evie being dragged away remained ever-present in Dinah's mind. Following her unsuccessful visit to the workhouse she resolved to repay the debt to Aunt Agatha. Then she would stand outside the fortress holding her niece until they let her in. After telling Winnie about Evie, she had also confided in Ruby. Her friends' lack of judgement drew her closer to them.

Each day one of the scullery maids went to a nearby farm for fresh eggs, milk and butter. When her turn came, Dinah revelled in the early morning walk across the fields. Today the sky was full of fluffy clouds, like floating marshmallows. The sun's morning rays lit the edges of the clouds, turning them silver. Then the light changed, and the marshmallows were pink. The walk took her through Mr Foley's gardens, and she took in the colour and scent of each flower and plant. They hadn't had a garden at home, and at first, she didn't know what anything was. She had frowned, wishing she still had her mother's diary. Theodosia had written about visiting Le Jardin des Tuileries in Paris. Dinah had plucked up her courage and asked Mr Foley about the plants. As she closed the small wooden gate at the bottom of the gardens, she caught the familiar smell of what she now knew were the nearby gorse bushes. She moved closer, spotting delicate gossamer cobwebs hanging precariously between the blooms. She took deep breaths, tasting the buttery, nutty scent of the bright yellow flowers. She paused and rubbed a lavender leaf between her thumb and index finger, a trick Mr Foley had shown her to release the plant's delightful aroma. The path to the farm was bordered by the first of summer's wild daisies and dandelions, and to her left lay a dense wood. When she had arrived at Hampson Hall the previous year, Cook had said she was too late to see the bluebells. This year she had seen them for the first time. She had promised Cook she wouldn't dawdle, but she stopped and stared at the last of the delightful, breathtaking flowers. The vast expanse all together in one place, created a thick, blue carpet, the colour of a clear, azure sky. Her mother's favourite colour.

As she strolled back armed with fresh eggs, a warm breeze blew from the river. She moved into the cool of the wood and sat in the shade of the trees. She closed her eyes, longing to share this with Evie. She put her hand on her heart and made a promise. She would work her fingers to the bone to repay the debt to Aunt Agatha and once free, would demand Evie's release from the workhouse. She and Evie would live together in a little cottage in the countryside, whatever the gossip-mongers said. They would have the garden her mother had longed for. She stood beneath the canopy of trees and smoothed her dress. She clung to the promise, albeit unrealistic. As she turned back a branch snapped behind her and she jumped. The sound echoed through the trees, and she whirled around. Her mind had been playing tricks on her since she started visiting the workhouse. She had sensed someone watching her as she pounded on the iron gates. Now the sound grew closer, and she turned to run. Facing her in the cool shade of the wood stood the most beautiful creature she had ever seen. The deer stood motionless, watching her from beneath long, elegant lashes. She remembered Theodosia showing her and Margaret a book of beautiful animal drawings when they were small. It explained what each animal stood for, the deer was independence and regeneration. She smiled into the sky, what better sign could she have to find the strength to carry on? With a graceful nod of her beautifully sculpted head, the deer bade Dinah a majestic farewell.

As she walked through Mr Foley's gardens, she stopped to admire the array of breathtaking blooms. The brightest and tallest were the sunflowers, the plants stood proud, facing the warm sun. She admired their open, yellow faces. Mr Foley had said they were telling her to keep her face in the sunshine and out of the shadows. She passed what she had learnt was honeysuckle, jasmine and best of all, sweet peas. She breathed in the aroma of the delicate little flowers. Their pastel appearance belied a deeper strength, the sweetness took her back to life before her mother died. She imagined Theodosia's voice, the exquisite French lilt turning simple words into something magical.

'You can do this, ma chérie. Work hard then return for chère petite Evie.'

She clenched her hands into fists and shouted at the sky. Theodosia hadn't lived long enough to see the establishment of the Women's Social and Political Union, but Dinah knew she would have been delighted to learn of Emmeline Pankhurst's commitment. The union aimed to obtain the vote for women on the same terms as men. Their motto was *'Deeds Not Words.'*

Delicious, tempting aromas greeted her as she entered the kitchen. Mrs Foley was an accomplished cook and Dinah would never go hungry at Hampson Hall.

'I should know when you go for the dairy, you'll take much longer than anyone else!'

'Sorry Cook, the walk is so beautiful, I lost all track of time.'

'It's all right, pet. You have to appreciate the sunflowers now; summer will be over before we know it. Now, pass me those lovely fresh eggs for his Lordship's breakfast.'

She was fortunate, despite the hard work and long hours, life at Hampson Hall wasn't unpleasant. But guilt overwhelmed her whenever she sat at the large kitchen table. She tried not to imagine what Evie was eating. At Monthly Prayers that day she had met Lord Hampson's elder son for the first time. His work at a firm of solicitors in London meant he was rarely at home, but the kitchen was buzzing with gossip that he intended to establish a practice in Newcastle. As Mrs Jackson had made the introductions, Master Walter's kind eyes appraised Dinah.

'Where are you from?'

'Gateshead, Master Walter.'

'Your accent is different. Some Geordie accents are much harsher.'

'My mother was French sir, perhaps that is why it sounds different.' She spoke quietly, her eyes lowered. Mrs Jackson had told her in no uncertain terms how to behave with her *'betters.'*

'How interesting, I should like to hear more about your mother.' Master Walter turned away. Mrs Jackson loomed but Dinah dared to glance up. Master Walter turned back, and their eyes met. In another life, could they have had a different relationship? She shook her head; she understood her situation. Evie couldn't be left in the workhouse, and as her feckless mother seemed to have forgotten about her daughter, Dinah was all Evie had. She couldn't be distracted by Master Walter Hampson or anything else. Margaret had weaved a web of deceit to justify her actions. Dinah was shocked her sister still hadn't sent more money; she had already saved more from her scullery maid's wage. Couldn't her sister, a dancer with the English Ballet Company with Louis to support her, have sent more? She was living a grand life in London according to her recent letter, why couldn't she spare more to support her daughter? Later that day Dinah re-read the letter. It had arrived with no money and no return address.

'Dearest Sister,

I hope this finds you in good health. I am well and Louis looks after me. Dancing with the English Ballet Company is a dream come true, I only wish you could share it with me. [...]

Yours with affection, Mrs Mona Leighton. (My new name for the stage in London.)'

The letter was full of glamorous tales, Dinah grew hot as she read about splendid balls and fashionable new dresses and shoes. Her sister didn't ask about Evie or apologise for not sending any money. Instead, she wrote that they were very happy living with Louis's uncle. She read her sister's closing sentence again. Were she and Louis married? Or was it another deception? Louis's surname was Levy, not Leighton. Mona was Louis's pet-name for her sister, but there was nothing wrong with the name their parents had given her. Dinah counted her savings. Still nowhere near enough to repay Aunt Agatha and travel to London to confront Margaret (she would never get used to calling her Mona).

Mona

After hearing Violet and May's stories, Mona knew she was trapped. Almost a year later, she still had no safe way of earning money to send home. She didn't know how she would escape from her sinister, unseen employer. Violet said no one knew much about him, only that he left his henchmen to run his sordid empire of dancers and brothels. According to rumour he was Jewish, but kept his depraved businesses well away from the orthodox community. The hypocrisy didn't surprise Mona. She had been dragged there by a member of the apparently respectable Jewish community. Violet had warned her that women disappeared if they asked too many questions.

She stretched, trying to ease her aching back. Every day she longed for the final evening performance to end. The work was relentless and what little money she earned she sent to Dinah. It was never much, and her sister would be questioning why, when she wrote about her wonderful life, she didn't send more. She could never tell Dinah the truth, could never admit how stupid she had been to trust Louis. She had no right to cry when Dinah had taken the scullery maid's position. She hadn't put a return address on her letters, how could she tell Dinah she lived in poverty and danced almost naked for drunks at a rundown music hall? She yearned for home but expected never to see her daughter or sister again. She would live and die a miserable death in this excuse for a lodging house. She shook herself, resolving once again to escape and discover the London of her dreams.

'Ready, doll?' Violet smiled as she moved towards the door.

She was grateful for Violet's friendship. Violet had apologised for allowing Mona to believe she could perform once then leave. They had become closer since May disappeared. They wanted to believe she had escaped, but knew it was unlikely. There were whispers about new jobs their employer was giving some of the girls. The women were doing everything possible to make themselves invisible when the boss's henchmen came calling. Rumour had it their employer was imprisoning the women in his new brothel. The new addition to his depraved empire was worse than his other establishments. The men frequenting his new club demanded the most depraved acts of supplication and humiliation. The men paid their employer and occasionally he gave the women a paltry sum. May was there one day and gone the next, as if she had never existed.

Mona imagined her mother's reaction to her younger daughter making a living in this way, reliant on hand-outs from a sadistic employer and humiliating herself on stage. She recalled her mother's stories about the women fighting for the right to obtain the vote. Theodosia would have wanted her daughter to march for her rights and independence, not sell her body to depraved, drunk men. She sighed; it was time to go back to the Diamond for the final performance of the day. The drunks would be at their worst, staggering and vomiting in the aisles and reaching onto the stage to grope the dancers. The previous day a new dancer got too close to the front of the stage and was dragged off. They didn't see her until much later when she reappeared battered and bloodied.

Mona's bones ached like those of a much older woman. The lack of food had made her weak. Some nights, she struggled with the short walk to the grim lodging house because of intense back pain. Other than dancing, there was only one other possibility. She shuddered. She had learnt about Nellie's *other dancing job* from Violet. Nellie went to a private club and provided *services* for men. She hadn't plucked up the courage to ask Nellie about it yet. As she and Violet left, Nellie banged into the room, not beaten and bruised, but dishevelled and dirty. She crashed into the old bucket in the middle of the room, strategically placed to catch rain from the leaky roof.

'All right, English?'

'Yes, thank you.' Mona wanted to stay on the right side of the tough woman. She righted the bucket and Nellie slumped onto her bed.

'I need sleep, English.' Nellie slurred as she covered herself with a moth-eaten blanket. Nellie snored and mumbled in her sleep and Mona decided. She had to do it, despite the danger.

Dinah

Dinah used her wrist to push a stray curl back under her white cap and continued scrubbing the stove. Day to day activities had become routine and she had learnt the quickest and easiest ways to do her jobs. Winnie had fallen deeper into her sorrowful state despite Dinah and Ruby trying to help. She sat back on her heels and stretched her tired, aching back. Sometimes, in the quiet, she imagined Evie laughing as she played make believe. Today, images of Evie in the workhouse haunted her. She accepted having to work long, hard hours to have any chance of changing Evie's future. To her surprise she found she enjoyed some aspects of life at Hampson Hall. She took great pleasure from Mr Foley's gardens, and her walks to the farm filled her with joy as she basked in the beauty of nature. She had been intrigued to learn about the Hampson family's annual picnic. Cook explained it was held on the last Sunday in July and everyone attended, the family and every member of staff. She had missed the picnic the previous year; this year she was helping Cook with the preparations. As the scullery maids got into bed a few weeks earlier, Ruby revelled in setting out every detail. As usual Winnie lay silent, her face turned to the wall. Dinah frowned; it wasn't right for a young woman to be so sad all the time.

'Are you listening, Dinner? It's the best day!'

'Yes, sorry Ruby. Please carry on.'

'You'll never have seen so much delicious food! Cook prepares a feast fit for the king!'

'And we're all allowed to attend?'

'Yes, we're like one big happy family for the day!'

Ruby explained the picnic would be held by the river, beyond the bluebell woods. The men set everything up, including making a small canopy for the family to sit under. The food and drink were transported to the spot by the river and there would be music. Dinah stared at Ruby.

'Like our Sunday evenings with the gramophone?' Dinah whispered the precious words. The best surprise had come on her first Sunday at the hall. Ruby had explained that Lord and Lady Hampson retired early on Sundays, and Mrs Jackson allowed them to gather in the kitchen. Cook provided cold cuts of meat and whatever was left of the day's home-made bread. On Dinah's first Sunday evening, she watched as Mr Jackson carried bottles of beer to the table and Mrs Jackson poured each of the women a small sherry. Her jaw dropped when Mr Jackson called for help with the gramophone.

'A gramophone?'

'Yes, pet, we'll have some music tonight.' Cook smiled at Dinah's delighted expression.

'Mind, that's a pretty smile, you should use it more often!'

She blushed, there hadn't been much to smile about since her mother died and she was separated from Evie. She stared as the men assembled the bulky piece of machinery. As the scene unfolded, she pictured her mother's old gramophone in the parlour at Seymour Terrace. Theodosia's second-hand gramophone, her pride and joy, had gleamed with well-polished care and attention, but Lizzie never missed an opportunity for spite.

'Ooh, the bloody parlour!? Who do you think you are? You're no better than the rest of us.'

'Parlour is from a French word.' Dinah had tried to explain, and Lizzie smirked.

'I couldn't care less!' Lizzie shouted her parting shot as she stormed out.

Dinah suspected Lizzie did care, and what lay behind her bitter demeanour was jealousy. As she sat in the warm kitchen at Hampson Hall, a faint taste of sweet sherry warming her lips, she imagined her mother singing along to the gramophone.

'What's first, Mrs Jackson?'

She soon learnt the choice was small and the playful question was asked every week.

'Let me see, Mr Jackson. What about, *"The Boy I Love Is Up in the Gallery?"'*

'A superb choice, Mrs Jackson!'

She smiled as Mr Jackson took the fragile record from its sleeve and placed it on the turntable. He wound the handle, then carefully lifted the arm and placed the needle gently on the edge of the thin black record. As the needle made contact with the record, the scratching noise transported her back to joyful times at home. As the magical sounds were drawn from the record, the dulcet tones of Marie Lloyd filled the kitchen.

'I'm a young girl, and have just come over,
Over from the country where they do things big,
And amongst the boys I've got a lover,
And since I've got a lover, why I don't care a fig.'

When the song reached its chorus, the kitchen erupted. Dinah blinked, convinced Lord Hampson would appear and put a stop to the deafening noise. She caught Mrs Foley's eye, the cook smiled and gestured for her to join in. She didn't hesitate.

'The boy I love is up in the gallery,
The boy I love is looking now at me,
There he is, can't you see, waving his handkerchief,
As merry as a robin that sings on a tree.'

Her happiness was bittersweet. Evie was in everything she did and everything she saw. She prayed her niece had happy memories of singing with her family in Gateshead, before they were torn apart. She prayed Evie was still singing.

Chapter 18

July 1904

Mona

Mona asked Nellie about her other job before she lost her nerve. Her opportunity came as the women waited for their meagre breakfast outside the Diamond. She sidled up to Nellie. Her carefully practised conversation disappeared when Nellie spun round to face her. She blurted the question out.

'You dance for them, and they pay you, English.'

'Just for dancing?'

'Well no, they like to touch, and some like to do more.'

She caught her breath. There were places in Gateshead where men went for these services, Theodosia had warned her and Dinah to avoid them. Women waited on corners and outside public houses; Mona had seen them on Pipewellgate. She pushed the memory away. She didn't want to picture Evie there.

'I'm not sure I can do it, Nellie.'

'It's worth it, English. I'm saving to get out of here and onto a ship to New York City, in America.'

Mona stared. 'New York City? Why, what's there?'

'Broadway. The Casino Theatre is what, English. Proper jobs with proper food and wages.'

She knew nothing about Broadway, New York City or America, but the possibility of a better future hung there, tantalising, and tempting. Any extra money she earned had to be sent to Dinah. But New York City? Was it possible?

'So, English, are you one of us now?'

'I just need to earn more money.' She hung her head. She hadn't been sure about it, then. But as the days wore on in exactly the same way, she changed her mind.

Violet tried to dissuade her. 'It's much too dangerous.'

'It's all right, Nellie will find me one of the better men.' She tried to convince Violet (and herself) that Nellie's other job was acceptable.

'No, doll, it's not safe.'

'Nellie does it!'

'You are not Nellie, doll.'

She turned away; she needed the money. She had hardly sent anything home since she arrived in London and Dinah would be furious. She continued to lie when she wrote to her sister, she would never tell her the truth about this dreadful place. 'It'll only be the once.'

Violet shook her head. 'Well, be careful, and don't go on your own.'

Lizzie

Lizzie's spiteful eyes slid towards the letter lying on the old, scorched table. She jumped up from her sewing machine and grabbed it. There wasn't much left of the fire, but the few remaining embers would do the trick. She scrunched the letter into a ball and tossed it into the middle of the red glow. Dinah had put a letter for the girl inside the envelope, but Lizzie had no intention of setting foot anywhere near the stinking workhouse to hand it over. Dinah's words disintegrated.

'Please, Lizzie, I'm begging you to go to the workhouse and try to see her.'

It wasn't her fault the brat's mother had disappeared. She pursed her lips. Was her own mother's treatment of the child harsh? She wrinkled her nose. No, the girl was a bastard. Margaret had displayed her true character when she disappeared without a word. Now living a life of luxury in London without a care for the child she brought into the world, she had shown herself to be a whore. For all her own faults,

161

Lizzie had longed for a family of her own. If she had been blessed, she would have loved her children with her whole heart. She would have enjoyed spending time at home with her family. She would have lived, not existed. She drank too much and had gained a bad reputation for spending so much time in the Globe, but what was the alternative? She eked out a living. She closed her eyes; with a husband and children her life would have been very different. She despised her cousin for discarding the most precious gift of all. She heaved herself out of the chair at the sound of footsteps. She opened the door and her mouth fell open.

'Good day, Miss Brown. I have some more alterations. I realise I was rude the last time I visited you. Please forgive me, my grief over the loss of my dear wife consumed me.'

After his last visit she had pushed all thoughts of the man away, thinking her drink-addled mind had invented their earlier conversation. And yet, here he was, and once again his behaviour towards her was..., she couldn't describe it, it was new to her.

'What do you think, Miss Brown?'

'I'm sorry, what did you say?'

'Would you like to take a walk in the People's Park with me this afternoon?'

*

She pulled on gloves to hide her red hands and adjusted her hat for the umpteenth time. She smoothed her old coat and moved towards the door. Her hand shook on the handle, and she spoke to the empty room. *'It's only a walk in the park, woman!'* She could calm her jangling nerves with a drink but was determined to arrive at the park sober. This was her chance, in all likelihood her only chance, of a better future. A future with a husband and, she dared to whisper it, their child. She smiled; the Crone had got it wrong. *'She's comin'* should have been *'he's comin.'* Lizzie couldn't wait to wipe the grin off the nasty old woman's face.

The Registrar

The Registrar straightened the papers on the small desk and ticked off another Sunday, the last Sunday in July. He despised this part of his job, but someone had to come to the workhouse once a week and sign the latest batch of death certificates. He hated every aspect of it, the stench as he approached the dark building, the dank corridor leading to his office, the knowledge of the cruelty in the locked rooms beyond. The worst thing was the rising number of death certificates. Sanitation improvements in Newcastle and Gateshead should have meant the end of diseases like cholera and smallpox but here, in this foul place, they were as rife as ever. He shook his head as he put the death certificates in a folder. Again, this week, too many children. The door opened.

'You'll be off now, then?'

'Yes Matron, all done for another week.'

She wheeled round as a child cried out from somewhere deep in the bowels of the building.

'Bloody brats!'

He met her narrowed eyes. 'Tell me Matron, do you have to use such force on them?'

'It's the only thing they understand. Mind, there's one pauper girl here I can't get a sensible word out of, no matter how many times I take the birch to her! Still, someone has to do it, eh?'

He stared. The girl, one of many, deserved to be acknowledged as a person, not just a problem to be dealt with. 'This girl, Matron. What is her name?'

Matron crossed her ham-like arms over her chest and scowled. 'Why?'

He shrugged. 'I'm interested.'

'I'm not sure I should say. She's got the devil in her.'

'Between us, Matron.' He put a finger to his lips and produced his most charming smile. The blush started on her neck and rose to her fleshy chins as she divulged the girl's name.

'Eveline Brown. Been here nearly a year and hardly said two words. Don't know what I'm going to do with her.'

An icy chill ran up his spine and he averted his eyes.

'I'll open the side gate for you, shall I?'

Yes, thank you Matron.'

The gate shut behind him and he heard Matron shove the sturdy bolts into place. He walked around the corner to the front of the building. This was where he had seen the young woman several times in the last year. She had pounded her fists on the gates and craned her neck to the top of the impenetrable walls. She had trudged away, shoulders slumped. He pretended he wasn't sure; she could have been one of many desperate relatives. In the far reaches of his mind he knew who she was and why she was there. He shook his head. He had watched from the shadows as her horror unfolded, but he could have prevented it from happening. He could have risked his own reputation and protected them. He knew why he had been impotent, cowed and beaten into submission. He, better than anyone, knew how far his old adversary would go. Their long history had taught him what she would do to triumph over anyone who crossed her. Now he feared one of the death certificates he would sign in the near future would be the young woman's niece, Eveline Dinah Annie Brown. He had a choice; he could go home, closing his eyes and his mind to the inevitable tragedy or he could act. He could rid himself of the threat that had hung over him for so long.

August 1904

Dinah

Despite Winnie's warning, Dinah continued to make trips to the workhouse to try and see Evie. She woke to a bright sunny morning, full of promise and hope for the day ahead. She carried Evie's bag, one day her niece would receive the precious gifts inside. By the time she crossed the Swing Bridge a thick mist had fallen, it shrouded the grim building as if wishing to hide its mean facade. Familiar with the bleak landscape, the mist didn't trouble her. She followed her nose towards where she knew the gates to be. As she drew closer a figure came into view. A cloaked man wearing a black top hat. He wasn't alone. At his side stood a small girl. A girl she hadn't seen in twelve months. A girl in rags with a filthy face. The girl gazed into the middle distance, her eyes dull and unseeing. Dinah's heartbeat quickened; how could this be? Who was the man and how had he persuaded Matron to allow Evie to leave the workhouse? And how did he know she would be visiting today? The questions could wait. She ducked to Evie's eye level and opened her arms wide.

'Evie? It's me, Aunt Dinah.'

The girl didn't move but her eyes shifted a fraction and met Dinah's. Dead eyes. What horrors had her niece endured behind those gates? She gathered Evie into her arms. The girl didn't move, her arms hung by her sides as if pinned there. Evie smelt bad and Dinah spotted lice in her hair. She swallowed to shift the lump in her throat and stood to face the man.

'Who are you?'

'You don't remember me?'

She frowned. 'I'm sorry, I don't mean to be rude.'

'It doesn't matter, what matters now is that this child needs care.'

'I agree. But, how is this possible?' She had no desire to explain the circumstances of Evie's incarceration or her aunt's hand in things, but she needed to understand what had happened.

'All you need to know is, the child is out of the workhouse.'

'But what now? My heart's desire would be to take my niece with me, but I work in service, and it wouldn't be allowed.'

'Alternative arrangements have been made for her.'

'What arrangements?' Evie hadn't moved or spoken. Dinah reached for her small, cold hand and squeezed it. Her heart soared when the lightest of squeezes came back.

165

'Your aunt, Agatha Brown, has agreed the child may stay with her daughter Elizabeth, in Pipewellgate.'

'But how?' Dinah stopped. To pursue this further would mean divulging the matter of her indebtedness to her aunt, and she had no desire to share family business with a stranger. She studied the man. When he had said her aunt's name, she recognised a certain inflection in his speech. He pronounced Agatha the same way he had pronounced Theodosia when he asked if she was her daughter. An 'f' sound in place of the 'th.' When she registered her mother's death. The man standing in front of her was the Registrar. She pursed her lips, what was this man's interest in their family?

'I work here on Sundays. I have seen you trying to visit your niece. I made some enquiries to ascertain whether anything might be done. I sought agreement for her to leave.'

'How? My aunt was resolute.'

'I can say nothing more. Now, you should make haste to Pipewellgate before this weather suffocates us all.' He tipped his hat towards her and disappeared into the mist.

Dinah's concern for Evie outweighed any desire for an explanation. She pulled the little girl towards her. Evie raised her arms and curled them around her aunt. Her words were a whisper.

'You came back.'

'Yes, and you will never go back inside that awful place.'

Evie's brown eyes met hers. 'Do you promise, cross your heart and hope to die promise?'

Dinah drew a cross over her heart with her fingers. 'Yes, ma petit. I promise.'

She started towards Pipewellgate, holding tight to Evie's hand. Evie didn't belong there, but she couldn't take her to Hampson Hall. Evie staying with Lizzie was the only option. As they walked, she offered her niece words of comfort, saying Lizzie would look after her and she would be warm and well-fed. She prayed Lizzie understood what a little girl needed. Her heart thumped, she had no idea how Lizzie would greet them or if what she had told Evie was true. Surely her young niece would be better off staying with Lizzie than left in the workhouse? Evie didn't speak once during the short walk.

*

The Registrar waited, hidden by the thick mist. He wanted to make sure Dinah and her niece weren't tricked into being taken back into the workhouse, that they made their way to Pipewellgate while they could. He didn't know how the little girl would fare with Elizabeth Brown; everyone knew her reputation. But staying with a drunk must be a step up from incarceration behind these walls with the sadistic matron. He straightened his shoulders as he walked away. He had done the right thing this day. Now came the task he dreaded, confronting his sister.

Lizzie

Lizzie paced; her footsteps heavy in the small room. With each footfall clouds of dust flew up from the dirty floor. She stopped and swigged from the jug. Sherry dribbled onto her dress. She had been so close. She had been surprised during their first walk, to find conversation with the man came easily. She was delighted when he asked her to repeat the walk the next week. They became closer and she had convinced herself he was building up to a proposal. She dared to imagine their future. He hadn't been blessed with children with his late wife, and she hoped the news about Evie would make no difference. That being part of a family might make him even keener. She was wrong.

His expression changed when she mentioned Evie. 'A child? Living with you? Whose child?'

She spoke quickly, as if the detail was unimportant. 'My cousin's. It won't be for long.'

'The one born out of wedlock to a woman with loose morals? The pauper child?'

There it was, the brusqueness he had used with her before. He left and she hadn't seen him since. Her mother sent her obsequious son-in-law Andrew Glass, to deliver the devastating message.

'What do you mean, the brat is coming here? I thought she'd gone to the workhouse?'

Andrew Glass blew out his cheeks. 'Your mother has instructed me to tell you things have changed. The girl will be leaving the workhouse and coming here.'

'Why? What's changed?'

'What has changed is immaterial. These are your mother's instructions.'

'And if I say no?'

He smiled wryly, tipped his hat and left. Lizzie yelled; the Crone had been right. She lifted the jug and sarcastically toasted her mother. Agatha Brown enjoyed revenge. Lizzie had seen her ruin people with a bad word here or a lie there. Someone was knocking. She slammed the jug down and flung the door open.

Evie

Evie watched as Aunt Dinah knocked on a strange door. It opened and her nostrils twitched as a bad smell travelled up her nose. She hoped she would be going home soon. An angry woman with a red face stood in the doorway, scowling. She hid behind her aunt's skirt.

Aunt Dinah nodded and Evie knew she had to go to the horrible woman. Where was her mamma? Why had the man taken her outside the gates? Why had Aunt Dinah brought her to this awful place? She closed her eyes tight, praying when she opened them her mamma would be there, and she would take her away from this smelly place. She opened her eyes. The red-faced woman was shouting. Evie didn't understand, she had forgotten Aunt Dinah's explanation. Aunt Dinah knelt to meet her eyes and hugged her so hard, she thought she would break.

'This is my cousin Lizzie; you are going to stay here, and she will look after you while I go away to work. It won't be for long, I will send for you as soon as I can, I promise.'

'Where's my mamma?'

Lizzie

The girl hid behind Dinah's skirts. Lizzie screwed her eyes up, trying to remember her name. Nothing came and she didn't care. She had no intention of inviting Dinah in. She hadn't forgotten Margaret's insults when she came to beg her to alter her dress. It was bad enough having the brat to stay, she wouldn't give Dinah an opportunity to pass judgement on her living arrangements.

'Why can't she stay with you?' Lizzie imagined a faint glimmer of hope.

'I wish I could take her with me Lizzie, but I can't.'

She pursed her lips. 'Why does she have to stay with me? I know nothing about children.'

'You work at home. I can't have Evie with me at Hampson Hall.'

For the first time, Lizzie acknowledged her hatred for her work. Her eyes were ruined from long hours working by candlelight, working at home meant she hadn't met men of her own age when she was younger, and now her occupation meant she had been chosen as the brat's babysitter.

'I don't have much room. I don't know where she's going to sleep or what I've got for her to eat. I don't have money to buy extra food for her, you know.'

Lizzie stood her ground. She hadn't done anything to prepare because she had prayed the girl wouldn't come to stay with her after all.

'I suppose I can see if anyone has an old mattress and a blanket they don't want. I'll get them later on. I'll need some money, though.' She held her hand out.

Dinah handed over what little money she had. 'I'll send more as soon as I can, I promise.'

'You had better, otherwise she'll go hungry.'

'And I will visit Evie every month, on my day off.'

Lizzie turned away as Dinah made a fuss of the brat. All the hugging and kissing and whispered words, she wanted her cousin to leave so she could have a drink.

'I had better go, Lizzie. I can't afford to miss my train back to Hampson Hall. Thank you for looking after Evie. I will write soon and send what money I can for her upkeep.'

Lizzie pulled Evie into the house, slamming the door behind them. She grabbed her jug and took a huge swig. She shot a baleful glance in Evie's direction. 'I was so close!'

The girl's eyes were blank as she returned Lizzie's stare.

'So bloody close and now he's gone. And it's all your fault!' Lizzie roared and Evie cowered.

Chapter 19

Evie

Evie sat on the dirty floor, alone in the gloomy room. Aunt Dinah had left in daytime and now it was dark. After Aunt Dinah left, the woman called Lizzie stomped around muttering to herself. Evie stood beside the door, not moving or speaking. She jumped when Lizzie shouted at her, and she wet herself. Then she made a mistake by asking where her mother was. The hard slap to her leg took her by surprise and she fell onto the filthy floor. Lizzie grabbed a dirty jug and drank from it, closing her eyes as she swallowed. Evie licked her dry lips.

'What are you staring at, you little brat?' Lizzie's angry words dripped onto her head.

'Nothing.' She whispered the word and averted her eyes.

'Well, you better not, you hear me? I don't want you here, understand?'

Her lip trembled and she sniffed. Aunt Dinah had said there were to be no tears.

'And now I have to find you a bloody mattress!' Lizzie stormed out, slamming the door.

Evie opened the bag Aunt Dinah had given her. Inside she found a dolly and a picture book. She spotted something else. Her little fingers closed around the small, white square. A pretty handkerchief with a sweet-smelling soap hidden inside. It had lace around the edges and pretty stitching in one corner. She brought the soft cotton to her face and breathed in the soap's scent. The soothing smell filled her nostrils. She hoped her mamma would come soon and take her home. There was something else in the bag. As she unwrapped the brown paper package, her eyes widened. She put it back and looked at her book. She pictured her mamma and aunt, laughing and smiling. And her grama. She missed her grama's warm cuddles and lullabies. Another picture crept into her mind, the dark prison and the small, suffocating cupboard. She didn't know which girl or boy was in the cupboard tonight, just that it wasn't her. Hunger gnawed at her empty stomach. She jumped as the door flew open. A strange man backed into the room, carrying one end of a dirty mattress. She clutched her bag and leapt out of the way as the man on the other end hollered.

'Quick man, put it down, I canna hold it any longer!'

Huge clouds of dust flew up as the old mattress hit the floor. The men took deep breaths then rubbed their hands together to rid themselves of the dirt and dust.

'Right, Lizzie. Now for the drink you promised us, eh?'

Lizzie stood in the doorway, staring. 'There, you've got a bed.' She left, slamming the door behind her. Evie sat on the edge of the thin mattress. It had a strange, damp smell and she fingered the dirty, rough blanket. She opened her bag and unwrapped the brown paper package. She took out the bread and the apple, whispering thanks to her aunt. After her meagre supper she lay on the mattress and wrapped herself in the scratchy blanket. Under her breath she sang one of her grama's lullabies.

'Petite fille Evie, petite fille Evie,
Dormez-vous? Dormez-vous?
Sonnez les matines, sonnez les matines,
Ding ding dong, ding ding dong.'

She didn't know what the words meant but her memory told her they were sung with love, like a caress. She sang the words without making a sound as her tears fell. She had to escape from this dreadful place, even if the escape was only in her mind. She turned her face to the damp wall and cried herself to sleep.

September 1904

Evie

Evie's teeth chattered and her scrawny body shook as she dipped her hands in the freezing cold water. She washed quickly, avoiding the chipped edges of the old enamel basin sitting precariously on the small table next to her thin mattress. She reached for the small piece of hard soap, pushing away a memory of Grama washing her with a soft face-cloth. She used the soap as gently as possible, being careful not to make the red, itchy patches on her skin any worse. Her eyes filled with tears as she remembered the sweet-smelling soap she'd found in the pretty handkerchief. Lizzie had taken it, saying it was too good for her. She patted herself dry with the harsh towel and got dressed. She had few clothes to choose from but took her time despite the cold, putting off having to speak to Lizzie for as long as possible. She shivered as she smoothed her threadbare dress, painfully aware of her shabby appearance.

Something in her memory told her it was important to be neat and clean and she tried, but it was hard without help. She didn't ask Lizzie for anything, everything led to an argument. She existed in a small, miserable space but kept her few possessions and what little room she had clean and tidy. It was something she could control, a sense of order amidst the chaos of life with Lizzie. An image formed at the corners of her mind. She tried to push it away, but it wormed its way in. The tiny dark cupboard at the prison. She'd only been in it once for answering back to Matron. She stopped speaking after that. She was small, so her time spent in the cupboard had no lasting physical effects. But the tall girl couldn't straighten up after being left in there for two days. Matron's face grew redder and redder as she shouted at the poor girl to walk with a straight back.

Lizzie moaned and swore as she made their meagre fire. Evie opened the dirty curtain separating her mattress from the rest of the small room. Lizzie's bed was beside her sewing machine, but Evie suspected the disgusting woman slept in her moth-eaten chair.

'Oh, you're up, are you? Well, make yourself useful and sweep the floor! Then there's dishes need washing!' Lizzie's large podgy hands gestured towards the dustpan and brush.

Evie set about her task. Her stomach growled with hunger, but what little there would be in the way of breakfast would only be offered once the floor was clear of dust and ash.

'And don't miss anything this time!'

She had vague memories of a warm house, of beautiful, happy women and hugs and kisses. The women sang and they ate hot porridge for breakfast. They had a delicious warm, sweet drink, but she wouldn't dare to ask Lizzie for it. She didn't know if the memories were real, or images her mind conjured up to stop her thinking about the dark prison. She didn't know why she was taken there, or why the man in the cloak had brought her outside the gates. When Aunt Dinah appeared, her chest had fluttered, like a baby bird trying to fly. She hadn't dared to hope but as the woman drew closer, she knew her smell. A sweet smell, of new, clean things. She wanted to hug her aunt, but her arms wouldn't move. Her aunt's bright blue eyes had glistened with tears. Then she came here, and the woman called Lizzie gave her jobs, like she had to do in the dark prison. This was another prison. Was she taken away and left in this dirty place with the awful woman because she did something bad? If she knew what, she would put it right and her mamma and aunt would come and take her home. She carried on sweeping but turned away so Lizzie wouldn't see her tears.

She didn't know when her birthday was, but she knew her fifth one had come and gone. Not because of a new dress or a cake. Because Lizzie told her she would be out from under her feet. When Evie asked what she meant, Lizzie said she was going to South Street Infants School.

'School?'

'Yes, school.'

'When?'

'Tomorrow. And in a few years, you'll go out to work to earn your keep.'

There was little Evie liked about school. On the first day her difference became obvious. Who would want to make friends with the scruffy, dirty-looking girl? She did her best, but her threadbare dress and shoes let her down. Lizzie had cut holes in the shoes *'to make them last'* and the holes were stuffed with newspaper, but her feet stuck out.

'Your whore of a mother hasn't sent any money for new shoes, so these will have to do.'

She shivered and her heart raced as she stood in the schoolyard. One by one the other children moved away from her. A teacher appeared and called them in with a large, loud bell. Evie entered the classroom last and saw two empty desks, right at the back. She stared straight ahead, trying to ignore the spiteful glances and the girl who held her nose as she walked past. She had never seen as many children, but she refused to acknowledge them. Aunt Dinah had said something Evie didn't understand at the time, but it made her feel better now. She smiled to herself; she had a trick her classmates knew nothing about. She could make herself invisible and go somewhere else in her head. She whispered to her aunt.

'I am a pretty flower growing in the stinking mud of Gateshead.'

She wasn't walking the gauntlet of sly looks and whispered jibes in Miss Kinghorn's classroom any longer, she was strolling in a beautiful garden with her aunt.

'Hurry up, girl! We don't have all day!' The teacher's voice interrupted her daydream.

She quickened her step. She stared at the empty desks, which horrible girl or boy would sit beside her? She took the desk on the end, leaving a space between her and the next pupil, a little boy with a dirty face and a trembling lip. She smiled and her heart soared when he smiled back, revealing yellow, rotting teeth. As she took her seat she glanced at the boy's dirty, bare feet. The teacher closed the door and Evie breathed a sigh of relief, grateful for her tatty shoes and the realisation no one would be sitting next to her. The teacher sat at a high desk at the front, positioned where she could see right to the back of the room.

'Good morning, girls and boys. Welcome to South Street Infants School. My name is Miss Kinghorn, and you will address me as such. We are still waiting for one pupil to join us.'

Evie's heart sank and her eyes bored into the door, willing it to remain closed. Miss Kinghorn was dressed in black; her full-length skirt covered her shoes, and her high-necked blouse was held in place at the neck by a white cameo brooch. As Evie studied her, Miss Kinghorn turned towards the opening door.

'You must be Nancy Glover. There is one seat left, right at the back of the class, next to...?'

The teacher stared at Evie and pointed. The new girl's eyes followed Miss Kinghorn's finger along with the rest of the class. Evie froze, she had no choice but to speak. She stood.

'Eveline Brown, Miss Kinghorn.' Her cheeks flamed at the stifled giggles around the room.

'Well Eveline Brown, move along and make room for Nancy Glover.'

Nancy made her way to the back of the room. She received the same stares and whispers as Evie, until Miss Kinghorn grabbed the hand bell on her desk. She rang it three times and shouted.

'Class! Desist this instant!'

Nancy sat next to the boy with the bad teeth and bare feet. She said nothing.

Miss Kinghorn called the class to attention and reeled off the school rules and regulations. They were not to interrupt when she was speaking unless she asked them a direct question. If they needed to attract her attention, they were to raise their hands and wait for her to notice before speaking. They school bell boomed out from its tower for miles around each morning. They were to listen for it and she would accept no excuses for lateness. They were required to be in school from 9 o'clock in the morning until 4 o'clock in the afternoon. They had morning and afternoon breaks and dinner time was from midday until 1 o'clock. No food or drink was provided, pupils were required to bring their own. Evie's classmates looked around, the lucky ones clutched their precious rations or hid them inside their desks. Others knew they would have nothing to eat all day. Evie tried to work out which category Nancy fell into, but the girl stared straight ahead.

Miss Kinghorn finished her introduction with a warning.

'Remember, you are here to learn. I will not tolerate insubordination or bad behaviour. Any misdemeanour will be punished.'

She gestured towards a wooden cane resting at the side of her desk. Evie didn't know what insubordination or misdemeanour meant and she didn't want to find out. She had enough trouble with Lizzie, she didn't need any more at school.

'The first lesson is spelling. I will write a word on the blackboard, and you will copy it onto your slates. There are ten words, and I will test you on them tomorrow.'

Miss Kinghorn wrote something on the blackboard. Evie's classmates picked up their chalks, bowed their heads and wrote. She continued to stare at the blackboard. The letters danced around in front of her eyes. She tried squinting, closing first one eye then the other, but it made no difference. The letters wouldn't stay still, and the word made no sense. Sweat stood out on her forehead and her hand shook as she put the chalk to her slate. She didn't know what to write and expected to be the first pupil to feel the brunt of Miss Kinghorn's cane. Something caught her attention; Nancy had tilted her slate. The words were still blurred but by closing one eye and concentrating hard, she made out the word 'hat' in small, neat letters. She copied the letters onto her slate as best she could and mouthed 'thank you.' Nancy made a strange gesture and smiled. The spelling lesson continued in the same way with Evie's blurred vision and Nancy's help. After a lifetime Miss Kinghorn announced there would be a short break, for pupils to *'answer the call of nature.'* Nancy and the boy with rotten teeth and no shoes stayed where they were. Evie did the same.

'I'm Evie.'

Nancy stared straight ahead. Evie didn't know what to do. 'Are you all right?'

Nancy remained silent. Evie tugged the sleeve of Nancy's dress and repeated her name. Nancy turned towards her and smiled, but still said nothing.

'Attention class, the next lesson is arithmetic.'

Evie struggled to make out the numbers Miss Kinghorn wrote on the blackboard, but she found once she copied them from Nancy's slate, they were easy to add or subtract, depending on the instruction. So far, she liked sums and she liked Nancy. Dinnertime arrived and Miss Kinghorn's pupils moved from her classroom to the school yard, the lucky ones clutched their food parcels. Evie tried not to look at the precious pieces of bread and the apples, but her stomach rumbled. Something touched her arm, and she turned to see Nancy holding a small piece of apple out towards her. She devoured it and thanked Nancy. Nancy made another strange gesture. Evie shrugged. They stared at each other, then Nancy pointed at her ears and shook her head from side to side.

'You can't hear?' Nancy nodded then pointed at her lips and shook her head again.

'You can't speak either?' Nancy nodded again.

'How do you know what I'm saying?'

Nancy made strange movements with her hands then pointed at Evie's lips. Evie frowned and shook her head. Then an image pushed its way into her mind, a woman who had brought some alterations to Lizzie. Lizzie had pushed Evie into the back lane, but she peered through the window. The woman was gesturing to Lizzie with her hands. When she was allowed back in, she plucked up her courage and asked Lizzie about the woman and their strange communication.

'She's deaf and dumb!' Lizzie cackled.

'But what was she doing with her hands all the time?'

'She reads your lips when you talk and answers with signs. And here's a clip for being nosy!'

The conversation meant Evie understood that Nancy was deaf and dumb. She decided to learn how to make the strange signs. Her stomach still rumbled but she raised her chin and pushed her shoulders back. Perhaps with Nancy by her side she could withstand her miserable life.

Chapter 20

Six years later
July 1910

Dinah

The day of the picnic dawned bright and fair. As if the weather understood the importance of the occasion, there wasn't a cloud in the sky.

'Dinner? Are you listening?' Dinah blinked; Ruby was telling her about the picnic. 'Sorry, Ruby.'

'Lord Hampson has invited a singer from London, we get to listen to her as well!'

Dinah jumped at Mrs Jackson's sharp shout. 'Girl, Cook needs you. Now!'

She tried to stay on the right side of Mrs Jackson, unlike Ruby. Her friend often found herself in trouble with the stern housekeeper, but she laughed it off.

'Dinah pet, run and get me some mint and parsley from Mr Foley's kitchen garden.'

Her cheeks burned; she still didn't know which herbs were which. Cook smiled.

'Lad, show Dinah. Hurry up now, the pair of you!'

The trees at the bottom of the beautifully landscaped flower garden were heavy with blossom. It fell like soft, scented snow in the gentle breeze. She smiled, once she was settled in a little country cottage, she would have a garden. She pictured Evie planting flowers. The lad, a young man of about 18, helped Mr Foley. Rumour had it, he was Lord

180

Hampson's son, but Lady Hampson wasn't his mother. He was known as *'Edward'* or *'the lad,'* no one talked openly about his dubious parentage. She frowned. Did people whisper about Evie? Did they call her a bastard? She was saving hard, but once the debt was repaid, would Aunt Agatha keep her word and allow Evie to leave Pipewellgate? As Edward pointed out different herbs, she pictured Gateshead's drab streets. She had to be reunited with her niece and together they would build a better life.

When Dinah handed over the herbs, Cook said there were extra reasons to celebrate this year. She lifted her floured hands from the large mixing bowl and said the words slowly, explaining that Lady Hampson was part of the National Union of Women's Suffrage Societies. Dinah knew about the NUWSS but didn't understand its significance to the family. Cook told her about Lady Hampson's efforts to further the cause for women's rights. Three months earlier Lady Hampson had attended an NUWSS rally. Over 1,000 women from trades and professions including actresses, journalists, teachers and doctors marched to the Royal Albert Hall in London, carrying banners and lanterns to light their way. At the same time the Suffragist International Congress was being held in London with a British woman, Millicent Fawcett, as one of the speakers. Lady Hampson was lucky enough to meet her and hear the inspirational speech. Unusually, Lord Hampson had accompanied his wife. Dinah imagined Theodosia's delight at their conversation.

'To his credit pet, because it's unheard of, His Lordship supports his wife in everything she does, including celebrating her involvement with the…er,'

'The National Union of Women's Suffrage Societies, founded in 1897 under the leadership of Millicent Fawcett.'

'That's it, pet! Mind, you're clever, aren't you?'

Dinah blushed, anything she learnt about developments in womens' independence stayed with her. She smiled, daring to hope for a better future. Cook said the other reason for celebration was the picnic marked Master Walter's return. He'd been there off and on since Dinah arrived, but would now be staying in rooms at his Newcastle club during the week and at the hall at weekends.

'It'll be like the old days, when both boys were young.' Cook had worked at Hampson Hall for years, a constant presence to Lord Hampson throughout his marriages. Only one of his wives had taken against her, but she wasn't long in His Lordship's affections.

'He's like Henry VIII! Died, went missing, divorced, survived!'

'Mr Foley! Don't let Mrs Jackson catch you making fun of his Lordship! She'll hide the gramophone and you know how much you enjoy your Sunday evening sing-a-longs!'

Dinah smiled as Mr and Mrs Foley joked. She hoped to find a husband to laugh with, one day. For now, she had to focus on repaying Aunt Agatha and getting Evie away from Pipewellgate.

Later, Dinah and Ruby carried blankets and parasols to the river. 'Where's Winnie, Ruby?'

'I don't know, she should be here. I saw her earlier, she'd been crying.'

'I feel sorry for her, she always looks so sad.'

'What can we do? She can't seem to help herself.'

Once everything was laid out, the band arrived and set up their instruments. The singer from London, a friend of Master Walter's, accompanied the family to church before joining them for light refreshments at the hall. It was one of the few occasions when Lord Hampson insisted the whole family attend church and give thanks for their good fortune. The other was Christmas Day. Lady Hampson dressed up for these rare days of piety, to the consternation of some members of the local congregation, who attended church every Sunday without fail. Lady Hampson stood out like a bright sunflower among the regular, drab devotees.

The table groaned under the weight of Cook's feast. A magnificent cake provided the centrepiece, surrounded by meat, game, ham and fish, pies and pastries. There was champagne, fruit punch, home-made lemonade and beer. The band struck up The National Anthem and Dinah stood. She sensed Master Walter watching her and she looked away. The musicians played a piece she remembered from the church hall dances in Gateshead. A lifetime ago. She told Ruby what each of the instruments were, a flute, a violin, an accordion and a cello. Once the family had eaten, the staff were off-duty and she wandered towards the river. She stared, mesmerised by streams meandering over small pebbles and around larger rocks, until the shade of an old oak tree tempted her. A bird landed in the tree and blossom fell around her, sweet and gentle. She kicked off her shoes. She smiled at the bird's melodic phrases. A song thrush, the beautiful, speckled bird her mother had called 'le Mauvis,' the Mavis. She closed her eyes as her mother's words drifted back.

'I have heard The Mavis singing,
His love song to the morn,
I have seen the dewdrop clinging,
To the rose just newly born.'

She daydreamed. If she ever had the precious gift of a baby girl, she would call her Mavis. For all Margaret's faults, she had been Dinah's best friend. If she had a second daughter, Dinah would take Margaret's middle name, Patricia. She breathed deeply, appreciating the birdsong and the aroma of wild garlic on the gentle breeze blowing from the riverbank. Music drifted from the bandstand; it had been an almost perfect day. When she was reunited with Evie, she would prepare a magnificent picnic. She hoped Evie's Sundays were pleasant, that she was playing with friends while Lizzie cooked something tasty. In the distance she saw Winnie walking towards the river. She resolved to ask if she could help her. The sweet strains of the violin lulled her into a gentle slumber and in the cool shade of the ancient tree, she dozed. In her dream people splashed and shouted as they swam in the river. A sharp cry forced her eyes open.

'Help! Someone, help me, please!'

She jumped up and ran towards the river.

Evie

Evie scrubbed the fireplace, sobbing silently. Lizzie had yelled she was 'old enough to earn her keep.' She bit her bottom lip; she wouldn't cry. Aunt Dinah visited, but Lizzie warned Evie to keep her mouth shut. She knew better than to disobey Lizzie, but she choked back tears when her aunt asked if they could take a walk together. She longed to say that Lizzie didn't look after her, but visits came and went, and nothing changed. She stole a glance at overweight, grumpy Lizzie, who bore no resemblance to Evie's mother and aunt. Her memory of their clean, pressed clothes was in stark contrast to Lizzie's stained, ragged dress. At first, she hadn't understood Lizzie's harsh Geordie accent, because she had spent much of her first four years with her French grandmother. She couldn't remember Theodosia, but she knew words from songs, sung in a different language. Dancing, rhyming words. Lizzie caught her looking.

'Get on with it, and when you've finished there's coal to fetch.'

She didn't talk back to Lizzie, not since she had said she wouldn't always be there to do the chores. Lizzie had thrown back her head and cackled.

'Everyone knows nobody wanted you! You and them sisters think you're a cut above! Well, they left you and now you have to work for your keep!'

Lizzie's words cut through her like a knife. It wasn't true. Her aunt had said she and Evie's mother were going away to earn money so they could have a better life. Aunt Dinah had promised to send for her as soon as she could and Evie clung to this, her only hope. She soon discovered Lizzie spent most of her time in the Globe. At home, her reluctant guardian sewed and drank from her filthy cup. When her customers called, she pushed Evie into the back lane, whatever the weather. Evie had become firm friends with Nancy. She had learnt the signs Nancy used to communicate, giving them a secret language. Nancy was Evie's eyes when she struggled with her vision and Evie was Nancy's ears and mouth. The other children kept their distance. In their own little world, Evie and Nancy talked about the teachers and other pupils. They met every morning and walked to school together and Nancy's presence made life bearable for Evie.

She cleared up after eating the stale bread Lizzie called supper. She couldn't wait to close the dirty curtain separating her mattress from the rest of the room. She took a deep breath and washed her face in the cold water. She dried herself on the small towel and shivered. The coarse, threadbare towel scratched her skin and she longed for comfort and warmth. She lay on the thin mattress and closed her eyes. The grating sound of Lizzie's sewing machine vibrated through the worn floorboards, as the heavy woman pushed the foot pedal back and forth. She covered her ears and sang to herself to try and drown out the noise. The jarring vibrations implanted themselves in her mind, the sound would haunt her forever, reminding her of these cold, dark, loveless days. She tried to remember things from before, sometimes inventing memories. A favourite was of her grandmother, Theodosia. Evie had called her Grama, but Lizzie mocked her French accent, so she only said it to herself now. She recalled the dancing lilt of Theodosia's voice. On her lips *'Evie'* was glamorous and exotic. She used the trick to drown out the hateful sewing machine and disgusting Lizzie slurping sherry from her filthy cup. She escaped to a happy time, spent with her grama. She conjured up precious memories, false or otherwise, she didn't care.

Dinah

'Help!'

Winnie struggled to keep her head above water. As she disappeared once more Dinah plunged into the river, gasping as she hit the icy water. She reached out but the riverbank shelved suddenly, and Winnie was in much deeper water. She dived under and stretched out her arms. She flayed about in the dark, murky water but found nothing. She came up for air and was submerged again by the force of someone else diving into the unforgiving water. She knelt at the edge, shaking. Master Walter removed his morning coat and wrapped it around her shoulders.

'It's Winnie, Master Walter, she's in the water!'

'Try not to worry, he'll get her.'

'Who went in?'

Before he could reply, a figure emerged from the murky depths, carrying Winnie in his arms. Edward, *'the lad,'* the young man who said little. Master Walter rushed forward and took Winnie. He laid her on the riverbank and the crowd waited anxiously. Dinah trembled, Winnie couldn't be dead, not in this beautiful place, on the day of the wonderful picnic. Suddenly Winnie coughed and dirty river water gushed from her mouth. Dinah saw Edward kneeling at the water's edge.

'Is she all right?' He whispered, then cleared his throat. 'My Winnie? Is she alive?'

Dinah smiled. The quiet lad and the melancholy woman were in love.

'She's all right. She's over here with Master Walter.'

Edward sobbed as he knelt beside Winnie. They touched hands, then lips.

Master Walter approached Dinah. 'Come. Cook will find you some dry clothes.'

'Thank you, Master Walter.'

'Once you have changed and warmed up, please come to the library.'

Dinah was speechless as they reached Mrs Foley. Back in the attic bedroom she quickly changed into dry clothes. She tidied her hair, wondering why Master Walter had asked her to go to the library. She hoped she wasn't in trouble for falling asleep under the tree, she couldn't afford to lose her job. In the years since she had taken Evie to Pipewellgate, she had only managed to see her niece a few times. Each time she left Gateshead feeling uneasy, as if everything about the visit had been false. Evie hardly spoke in front of Lizzie, and during what little time aunt and niece were alone, the girl was silent. She couldn't persuade Evie to leave Lizzie's dismal room. If she suggested a walk, Evie shook her head. She asked Lizzie what Evie ate and how she was doing in school, but her cousin's mumbled answers provided no reassurance. She wanted to ask Lizzie what she did with the money she sent, but Evie's eyes stopped her. She couldn't risk making life any worse for her niece. After the Registrar had intervened and secured Evie's release from the workhouse, Dinah believed she had an ally. She didn't understand the man's connection to their family, why he had bothered himself with one child over any other. She wrote to him at the Registry Office, but her letter came back marked *'return to sender.'* She couldn't risk raising her concerns with anyone else in authority. If Aunt Agatha found out, and she would, she had spies everywhere, she would send Evie back to the workhouse. All Dinah could do was continue to repay the debt, but it never decreased. She made her way to the library, crossing her fingers behind her back. Her hand shook as she knocked at the ornate door.

'Enter!'

'Master Walter, you asked me to come and see you.'

'Ah, Miss Brown. What a strange turn of events at the picnic.'

'Yes, Sir.'

'Hopefully Miss Smith will be all right thanks to you and young Edward.'

'Yes, Sir. It is a blessing he was there. I couldn't reach Miss Smith.'

'But you tried. It was most courageous of you.'

'Thank you, Master Walter.'

'Now, I wanted to speak to you about something else.'

She braced herself. Whatever she had done wrong, she would beg him to reconsider.

'Don't look so worried. I only wanted to ask where you learnt to sing?'

Her mouth fell open. 'To sing, Master Walter?'

'Yes, have you taken singing lessons?'

She smiled, her mother had insisted she and Margaret would be cultured. Ballet and singing lessons were part of her plan for them to rise above their low beginnings and escape from the poverty of Gateshead. *'Mes filles chéries, you will have every opportunity your maman can give you.'* She knew Theodosia had struggled to pay for the lessons and she whispered her thanks.

'Yes, Master Walter. My mother sent my sister and me to singing and ballet lessons.'

'I thought as much. I heard you singing at the picnic and once or twice on a Sunday evening.'

She blushed; her Sunday evening singing wasn't meant to be heard outside the kitchen.

'It is all right. You are not in trouble. You mentioned your sister, where is she now?'

She bowed her head. How could she tell Master Walter about Margaret?

'Don't be afraid. If your sister has met with some misfortune, I may be able to help.'

If it hadn't been for Evie, she would have told Master Walter her sister had a good job with the English Ballet Company in London. Instead, she found herself telling him almost the whole story. She stopped short of mentioning her concerns about Evie, confident Aunt Agatha wouldn't hesitate to see her niece back in the workhouse, if she heard of Dinah's complaint.

'What a tale, Miss Brown. Now, how can I help?'

Her head spun, she had expected shock or outrage, but he wanted to help.

'Should I try and discover where your sister is living? Perhaps then you could write to her?'

'Thank you, Master Walter. I'm afraid I have very little information about my sister's whereabouts. All I know is she and Louis Levy went to London to stay with Louis's uncle. His name is Samuel Levy but London is such a big place, where would you look?'

'Don't worry, Miss Brown. With my contacts in London, I am sure it will be possible to locate this Louis Levy and his uncle. And they should lead us to your sister.'

'Thank you, Master Walter. I'm very grateful.'

The door opened and the singer from the picnic floated into the room. Her shimmering, summery dress shone as it caught the light from the late afternoon sun.

'Ah, Grace, there you are. Please meet Miss Dinah Brown.'

'Oh, the songbird from the picnic! I'm pleased to meet you, I'm Grace Opal.'

Dinah had heard Cook talking about Grace Opal's career the previous day.

'And the singer this year, you'll never guess who it is!'

'No Cook, and I'm not sure I want to know.' Mrs Jackson feigned disinterest.

'Grace Opal!'

'Am I meant to be impressed?'

Cook pulled herself up to her full, short height. 'She's an opera singer and an actress and she's only 22! A few years ago, she played the title role in *'The Merry Widow!'*

The crowd at the picnic had fallen silent when Grace sang. Dinah imagined her mother watching, how delighted she would have been to see her elder daughter listening to such an accomplished young woman. She realised Grace's elegant hand remained outstretched.

'I am so sorry, Miss Opal. You must think me rude.'

'Please, call me Grace.'

Dinah stifled a giggle at the thought of her hateful aunt witnessing this exchange. She pictured Aunt Agatha's pursed lips and sour countenance, on full display at the sight of her low-born niece keeping company with a star of the stage and Lord Hampson's elder son.

'Have you discovered where your songbird learnt to sing, Walter?'

'I have, my dear.'

Master Walter relayed Dinah's story, saying he planned to enquire about Margaret's whereabouts. He said it was the least he could do after Dinah's valiant efforts at the picnic. She thanked him again and returned to the kitchen. Cook was making cocoa. Like Theodosia and her mother before her, it was Cook's cure-all remedy. Dinah warmed her hands on the comforting cup. If Master Walter found Margaret perhaps their fortunes would take a better turn. She sipped her cocoa and dared to hope.

Evie

Evie hated Sundays. School had been bearable since she met Nancy, and it got her away from Lizzie. Saturdays weren't too bad, Lizzie's customers called to collect their alterations. Evie was pushed into the back lane, but she used her time well. She looked in through the dirty window, inventing stories about the different visitors. Her favourite was a woman known to everyone as the Crone. Rumoured to be a witch with sinister powers, the gossips said she had poisoned someone. Evie imagined Lizzie making a mess of the woman's alterations and the Crone poisoning her. One day the Crone handed Lizzie an apple. Evie watched hopefully as Lizzie munched, but nothing happened. Lizzie yelled, interrupting her daydream.

'Come here, I need to measure you for a new dress.'

Evie stopped, scrubbing brush in mid-air. She risked a slap by asking Lizzie to repeat herself. She had never had a new dress. Her clothes were patched and extended, anything to avoid Lizzie spending money on new material. She held her nose as she moved towards Lizzie. She took a deep breath; she wouldn't dream of getting this close if it wasn't for the possibility of a new dress.

'We need to get your feet measured as well.'

'New shoes?'

Lizzie turned at Evie's high-pitched question. 'Aye.'

Lizzie said nothing more and Evie didn't ask. Her eyes were out on stalks as Lizzie helped with the cleaning and tidying. The only other times Lizzie did any cleaning were when Aunt Dinah visited. As much as Evie wanted to see her aunt, the visits were torture. Lizzie warned Evie not to speak, and she never got to keep anything Aunt Dinah brought. She knew better than to disobey Lizzie and during Aunt Dinah's visits she was mute, muzzled by fear. Little could be done about the black mould on the walls, but by the end of the week the room looked cleaner than Evie had ever seen it. She discovered the reason for the change in lazy, dirty Lizzie on Sunday morning.

'Here, put these on.'

Evie wouldn't have chosen the material. The thick, dark brown wool made for a dowdy garment. The dress was much too big, and the shapeless covering hung around her thin frame.

'I made it to last. You'll grow into it. And these.'

The shoes were also too big but at least the toes weren't cut out.

'Beggars can't be choosers.'

Evie dared to tut. She would never consider herself a beggar.

'Aren't you going to thank me, you ungrateful brat?'

'Thank you.' Evie murmured, not wanting to question the sudden change in her fortunes.

'When he gets here you say nothing. Understand me?'

'When who gets here?'

'My stuck-up brother-in-law. He tried to catch me out, but the Crone told me he was coming.'

Evie smiled, everything made sense. The new dress and shoes were part of an act, along with the cleaning, to convince Andrew Glass she was well cared for. She shook her head, at least she had some new clothes. She would stay quiet; she wouldn't risk losing her new wardrobe. When Andrew Glass arrived, Evie stared. He seemed familiar but she didn't know why.

'Doesn't she speak?'

'Girl, answer Mr Glass when he talks to you.'

Evie's brow furrowed. 'Hello, Mr Glass. How do you do?'

'What time does she go to Sunday School?'

Evie saw a flash of fury on Lizzie's face before she delivered her lie. 'After dinner.' Evie stared; Lizzie never fed her in the middle of the day.

'Right well, I had better let you prepare her dinner. I will call at the church hall to see she arrives on time. Your mother gave specific instructions to ensure she has regular attendance.'

He left and Lizzie reached for her jug. Evie took a chance. 'What's for dinner?'

Lizzie slapped her but Evie continued to stare, eyes blazing.

'How dare you! Never mind dinner, you'll get nothing else to eat today!'

Evie's cheek stung but she didn't care. Lizzie marched her out of the house, displeasure all over her red face. She left her outside the church hall, instructing her to wait and make sure Andrew Glass saw her go in. Evie had no intention of moving, anything was preferable to spending time in Pipewellgate. After a while other children started to arrive. She recognised some of them from school, but Nancy wasn't among them. Her friend lived on the other side of the railway lines and Evie knew little of her home life. She had recognised some of the same signs of neglect from her own experience, Nancy was sometimes barefoot and often bruised. One day Evie had tried to ask about her injuries. She gently touched Nancy's arm and pointed to a fresh, angry bruise, her eyes questioning. Nancy's lower lip trembled, and Evie regretted her curiosity. She signed *I'm sorry* and Nancy nodded. Evie never mentioned it again.

She recognised an older boy, one of the few pupils who didn't avoid her. He smiled as they waited for the Sunday School teacher to open the door.

'I'm Jack Todd. You're Eveline Brown, aren't you?'

'Yes, I'm Evie.'

She saw Andrew Glass approaching. As she moved towards the door, he spotted her, tipped his hat and carried on walking. She hurried inside. She wanted to make the most of what was likely to be her one and only day at Sunday School.

Chapter 21

December 1910

Mona

Mona trudged towards what passed for breakfast, her steps those of a woman twice her age. She had no idea how long she'd been at the Diamond and things were worse than ever. Two weeks earlier, as she and Violet were leaving the music hall after another exhausting day, one of their employer's henchmen told Violet to wait. Mona protested but the man batted her away like an irritating insect.

Since then, Mona had mostly been alone in the cold, damp attic room. Sleep eluded her and she spent her nights staring at Violet and May's empty beds. A bitter winter wind snaked in through the broken window and she hugged herself for warmth. The silence deafened her, and she pushed images of her friends from her mind. Images of them in one of their employer's brothels. As she approached the women waiting to be fed outside the Diamond, she scanned the group for Violet. She had appeared once or twice but was never alone. Her every move was scrutinised by their employer's nameless thugs. Violet wasn't there but Mona spotted Nellie, holding court amidst the emaciated group. Nellie gathered the women around her before telling one of her bawdy stories. The women threw back their heads and shrieked. One of them called for Nellie to '*do it again.*'

'Do what again, girl?'

'You know, Nell. Your impression of him, it's that good you've got us terrified!'

The women shrieked again, and Mona stopped dead as Nellie accepted the request from her bedraggled admirers. Nellie hunched over, her back bent. She produced a short, wheezy cough. She grabbed the ladle from the greasy skilly pan and used it as a walking cane. Now the cough was accompanied by the tap tap of the ladle as Nellie made slow, faltering steps towards her. The women chanted *tap, tap* as Nellie came closer. The ice in Mona's veins rooted her to the spot.

'All right English, how do you like the entertainment this morning?'

Mona stepped away from Nellie's stale breath and the women shrieked. After the matinee, Mona returned to the lodging house alone. She stretched her aching bones. She closed her eyes and saw Nellie, coughing and tapping. She reached under the bed and pulled out her mother's battered carpet bag. One last vestige of her mother remained, safe in the bottom of the bag. It had been her salvation since Violet disappeared, a longed-for link to family. She removed her mother's diary and hugged it to her chest. As she opened it, she longed to be wrong about Nellie's impression of their menacing, invisible employer. She read her mother's words; her knuckles were white as she gripped the diary. She put her head in her hands and rocked from side to side. She wasn't wrong.

Since Mona had discovered what Nellie did at the private club, she had come close to asking if she could go with her, but each time she lost her nerve. Despite everything, she hadn't forgotten whose daughter she was. She clung to the little pride she had left. Her narrow world revolved around the rundown lodging house and the Diamond. Violet had been her anchor, the one bearable aspect of her pitiful, empty existence. Things were changing for women in Great Britain, so Violet had said, but the changes made no difference to Mona's world. She didn't doubt Violet, but she questioned how the changes could reach women like them. When Violet had enthused about Emmeline Pankhurst's Women's Social and Political Union, Mona mumbled that it was a great achievement. But the significant national events passed her by, as she slid further into a life of debauchery. She buckled under the pressure of life at the Diamond and lay curled in a pit of shame. How were women like them, hidden away in the worst parts of London, doing unthinkable things to survive, meant to make those changes? She shook herself. Where was the strong, independent woman? The one who had refused to go to Hampson Hall, who defied her heartless aunt and Andrew Glass and ran away to London with Louis?

Mona wished her mother had lived to see Emmeline Pankhurst and the other members of the WSPU, fighting despite the odds being stacked against them. She tried to picture Theodosia in the rat-infested lodging house where she lay her head. She stopped; her mother had no place there. Mona clenched her hands, neither did she. She had to find the strength to change things. She had to speak to Nellie about working at the private club or risk dying in this vile place.

'Will you take me? Please.'

Nellie frowned.

'Just once; I must earn some money.' Mona was adamant. Christmas was only a few weeks away and she was determined to send Evie something. She had learnt Christmas meant additional shows and even rowdier, more disgusting audiences, but no more money for the dancers.

'I'll take you after the matinee today. When we get there, you're on your own.' Nellie said Billy's club wasn't for the likes of soft, gentle women, you needed a thick skin to work there. Mona knew it was dangerous, but she had no choice. She couldn't rid herself of the debt to her employer. There was always something to pay for, garish outfits and feathers which failed to cover her modesty. She had less and less as the years passed. Nellie told her to stay close. Mona's heart pounded hard in her chest, but determination spurred her on. She started a rhythm in her head which she repeated with each step, *'only once, only once.'* A mid-afternoon darkness was gathering as winter tightened its grip on London. She took small, careful steps as they made their way along the icy streets. She shivered as she repeated her refrain, *'only once, only once.'* As they rounded a corner, she bumped into something on the path. She mistook the bundle for rags until it cried out. A boy of about Evie's age, selling matches. His dirty, icy hand gripped hers. She took in his filthy, ripped clothes and bare feet. Dark-brown eyes with long lashes sparkled from his grimy face. Her stomach lurched as she pictured Evie. Was she safe? Was she warm and well-fed? Or like this unfortunate boy, was she selling matches in the slums of Pipewellgate?

'Buy some matches, lady? Please help me.'

'Oh, I...,' She patted her coat, desperate to help, but she had no money. 'I'm sorry, I can't.' Her eyes beseeched Nellie. Nellie shook her head and pulled Mona away.

'Oh Nellie, can't you help him? He looked desperate.'

'Listen, English. You can't help all the beggars and street urchins. Besides, after today I'll have enough to get away. I've booked my passage.'

Mona breathed deeply. She had planned to do this awful thing once, earn as much money as possible and send it to Dinah. Now, having seen the little beggar-boy, a different plan was forming.

'How much can I earn at this club, Nellie?'

'It depends what you're prepared to do, English.'

Mona frowned. Could she do whatever it took to earn enough to go home and be reunited with Evie? She tried to push away an image of Evie, begging. They arrived at a black door and Nellie stopped. There was nothing to indicate what sort of establishment it was, but Nellie pushed the heavy door. Mona followed, blinking as her eyes adjusted to the gloom. Hot, smoky air caught the back of her throat. She wrinkled her nose, the club reeked of cigar smoke and stale alcohol. Nellie led her down a set of steep stairs, into the bowels of the club. At the bottom, a large, suited man stood outside another door. He nodded at Nellie then raised an eyebrow in Mona's direction.

'She's with me, all right?'

The muscled man smirked and pushed the door. Nellie pulled the beaded curtain to one side and walked into a large room. The thick smoke made Mona cough. Drinks were being prepared at a bar to their left, served by semi-naked waitresses to men sitting at round tables. The men drank, smoked and leered. A small stage provided a dancing platform for a naked, emaciated, dead-eyed woman. Mona had seen enough to realise the place was worse than she had expected. She started to say she had changed her mind, but they had been spotted. She swallowed a knot of fear. Billy Shaw, the manager, gestured to Nellie from the bar. 'All right Nellie girl, how are you?'

'All right Billy, this is my friend Mona.'

Billy looked her up and down. 'Good to meet you, Mona. Are you looking for business?'

'Mona wants to do one dance, Billy. With someone safe.'

'All right, ladies. Let's see who's around.'

A waiter approached them and whispered in Billy's ear.

'I'm needed elsewhere, ladies. Wait here. I'll find someone half-decent for delightful Mona.'

Mona's palms grew sweaty, and her head pounded. She was about to tell Nellie she had changed her mind when a short, wheezy cough and the tap tap of a walking cane filtered through the smoke. The tapping stopped and she sensed someone standing behind her. The hairs on the back of her neck bristled as stale breath reached her nostrils. She turned to face the man and her throat contracted at the acidic smell. She had worked at the Diamond long enough to recognise opium. The stooped old man was almost bald and what little hair remained stood in wiry, grey tufts on top of his head.

'Well, well, who have we here?' He leant on his silver walking cane, peering at them through narrowed eyes. His suit oozed money and arrogance. He grinned, his piercing eyes fixing on Nellie as he jabbed a long dirty fingernail towards her.

'I heard you were cheating me by working here, but…' he switched his gaze to Mona, 'I didn't know you were here. The last time I saw you was…' He stopped suddenly and frowned. 'But it can't be you.' He scratched his head and flakes of dead skin fell to his shoulders. He moved closer and Mona stepped back.

'How old are you?'

Mona didn't reply. Instead, she shrugged.

'Mon Dieu! That shrug! Those eyes! I see it now. I've waited a long time for this.'

The man grabbed Mona and pulled her away. Nellie's feet were rooted to the filthy floor.

Dinah

Life changed for the scullery maids after the picnic. Following the incident at the river, Dinah and Ruby insisted on helping Winnie. She was still very shaken, but they tried to persuade her to talk about her troubles. On the fateful Sunday, they talked long into the night.

'It all became too much.' Dinah moved closer to hear Winnie's whispered, tearful words.

'Nothing can be so bad, surely?' Winnie shook her head at Ruby's gentle reply. Winnie's eyes filled with tears and Dinah and Ruby held out their hands, a friend on either side.

'Thank you, you are both being so kind to me.' Winnie's lip trembled as she tried to smile.

'You need to thank Edward, he jumped in and saved you.'

Winnie's cheeks reddened at the mention of the lad.

'Yes, he is a good man.'

'That should give you some hope. You've had a horrible time, but you have the chance of a happy future with Edward.' Ruby was matter of fact about Winnie's situation.

'What about my baby? Edward says he will accept another man's child, but I don't know where my baby is.'

Winnie's words hung in the air. Dinah frowned; Master Walter had been kind to her. Perhaps he could find Winnie's child? She would wait until Winnie recovered before broaching the subject.

Nellie

Fear rendered Nellie motionless. She had based her impersonation of their sadistic employer on gossip but had never seen him in the flesh before. Now she knew the ghastly descriptions were true she feared for Mona's safety. His vile reputation had led the dancers to speculate he could be responsible for the horrific murders in Whitechapel. Nellie had intended to do business herself or leave once Mona met someone, but now she waited. She knew what people thought of her, but she wasn't all bad. She would do the decent thing by Mona, then the others might change their opinion of her. She looked towards the room where their employer had taken Mona. Nellie had been in the room many times, with lots of different men; some gentle, some violent, some desperate for comfort from a stranger. But she was much tougher than Mona. And the man with Mona was rumoured to be a murderer. She leapt up and ran towards the room. She flung the door open and took in the horrific scene. Mona lay naked on the bed, her ripped, bloodied clothes strewn on the floor. The glint of a knife in his hand, the man shouted obscenities as he jabbed the knife towards Mona's white throat. Nellie screamed and launched herself at him. She jumped on his back, and he dropped the knife.

'Dirty whores! I'll kill you!' He tried to throw Nellie off, but his next words were lost as she grabbed the knife and plunged it into his chest. He hit the floor, blood pooling around his body.

'Quick, English! Grab your clothes and run!'

Mona's shaking body thumped onto the floor. Nellie rifled through the man's pockets.

'What are you doing, Nellie? We need to leave! Now!'

'I'm getting your wages English, and something extra. Then we can escape to New York City!'

Mona

Mona arranged her ruined clothes around her emaciated frame. Blood pounded through her veins, and something shifted. She had been deceived, humiliated and attacked. She gritted her teeth, her determination to survive overwhelmed everything else. She slid her trembling hand across the bloody floor. In one quick move she grabbed the knife and shoved it into Solomon Zettler's neck.

'That's for my mother! For Fred, Kitty, Jeannie and all the other women, you bastard!'

Nellie stared wide-eyed as Mona's fury filled the room. Mona turned, her head full of all the put-downs and insults she had endured. She knew Nellie thought her too nice to work at Billy's, too weak to stand up for herself. She would always be grateful to Nellie for saving her from Solomon Zettler but now, picturing her mother, Mona knew it was time to fight. She held the knife, dripping with Solomon Zettler's blood, to Nellie's throat. 'Give me the money, now!'

Their eyes locked and Nellie smiled; a sad, bitter smile.

'What? You think I won't?' Mona pushed the knife into Nellie's throat and drew blood.

Nellie handed the money over.

'Now your clothes!'

Nellie shook as she undressed.

'Hurry up!' Mona expected Billy to appear at any moment.

'Why, English? I tried to help you.'

'I'm sorry, Nellie. But you taught me we have to help ourselves in this life.'

Mona swapped her ripped, blood-stained clothes for Nellie's. 'You'll be all right, Nellie. You're a survivor.'

Nellie's words reached her as she ran. 'Well beggar me English, so are you!'

Chapter 22

Dinah

Dinah longed for news of Evie. She wrote to Lizzie, placing a letter for Evie inside the one addressed to her cousin. She didn't know what Lizzie did with the money, she prayed it wasn't spent in the Globe. She wrote to Aunt Agatha and sent what she could towards the debt. Her aunt sent a regular reminder of the outstanding amount and Dinah's eyes rested on the words, '*interest accrued.*'

After the picnic, Winnie's melancholia started to lessen. Her baby wasn't mentioned again. Dinah saw her and Edward walking in the gardens, heads close together. A few months later, they were married. Winnie moved out of the attic and into a little cottage in the grounds with Edward.

Mrs Jackson had instructed everyone to attend Monthly Prayers because Lord Hampson was going to make an important announcement. The kitchen buzzed with speculation, but Mrs Jackson hushed them, saying she had an announcement of her own. Dinah watched Ruby shift from foot to foot, looking anywhere other than at her nemesis. Dinah's cheeks burned as she remembered the little soaps. Winnie turned to look behind her, a smile playing around her lips. Dinah's eyes followed Winnie's to Edward. Winnie was pregnant. What Mrs Jackson added was that Lord Hampson wouldn't engage another scullery maid when Winnie entered her confinement.

'I have assured him we are more than up to the task of achieving the same level of efficiency.' Her pointed look invited no argument, but Ruby's question burst out.

'What about our Sunday off? How will Dinah or I manage when the other one isn't here?'

'You will henceforth have either a morning or an afternoon off, once a month.'

Dinah went cold. That wasn't long enough to visit Evie. She had tried to see her niece many times but was thwarted at every turn. She had lost count of the number of times Lizzie *'sent Evie on an errand,'* claiming to have forgotten about Dinah's visit. She tried to get an earlier train and catch Lizzie out, but Mrs Jackson's beady eyes spotted every speck of dust and every unpolished piece of crockery. Severe weather and cancelled trains added to her problems, but she never lost hope. On the few occasions she had seen her, she was deeply concerned about Evie's welfare. She couldn't ask anyone to check, no one would dare to challenge Lizzie. She considered writing to Evie's teacher but was worried Lizzie would find out and make Evie's life even more miserable.

Reverend Ash raised his eyebrows as they all trooped in. Dinah looked around; as well as the family and their household staff, Grace Opal stood next to Master Walter. Lord Hampson approached Reverend Ash and Dinah heard him ask to make an announcement.

'Good morning, everyone. Thank you for your attendance. We all appreciate Reverend Ash finding time to deliver a personal sermon for us.'

Ruby stifled a giggle and nudged Dinah, 'His Lordship is usually still in bed!' Dinah shushed her. She was watching Master Walter and Grace Opal.

'Without further ado I would like to announce that my elder son, Walter Hampson, is betrothed in marriage to the delightful Miss Grace Opal. I hope you will join me in congratulating the happy couple!' Lord Hampson said something to Reverend Ash and the bemused vicar nodded.

'Let's give three cheers for Walter and Grace!' The cheers rang out and Lord Hampson shook Reverend Ash's hand before taking his seat.

After the service Dinah started to follow the other staff downstairs but stopped as a hand touched her arm. Master Walter. 'Miss Brown, might I speak to you in the library?'

Dinah crossed her fingers behind her back, praying Mrs Jackson wouldn't stop her. The housekeeper sniffed but nodded. Master Walter and Grace Opal were sitting in the library when Dinah arrived. 'Miss Brown. How are you?'

'I am very well, thank you, Master Walter. Please accept my congratulations.'

'Thank you. We are very happy, aren't we, my dear?' Walter reached for Grace's hand and Dinah's heart ached. Would she ever experience a love like theirs?

'Now, to business. I am sorry it has taken me this long to bring word of your sister.'

Dinah wasn't surprised; Margaret would go to extreme lengths to cover her tracks.

'I am also sorry to tell you I do not have good news.'

Dinah froze. She cleared her throat. 'Has she had an accident? Is she ill? Is she…?'

'No, not that I am aware of. However, I am afraid I have been unable to find your sister.'

Dinah frowned. Master Walter was well-connected, why hadn't he found Louis's uncle?

'She went to London with Louis Levy, there must be some trace of them.'

'Of Louis Levy and his family, yes. And of Samuel Levy. They live at Leighton Mansions in Maida Vale. But there is no record of your sister ever having lived at the address.'

Dinah's head spun. She reached for her handkerchief. If Margaret wasn't with Louis, where was she? And what about her letters? In each one she regaled stories of her life in London with Louis. Her life at Leighton Mansions. Her job with the English Ballet Company. Was it all lies?

'But where is she? That is the only information I have about her.'

'I am sorry. I know you are desperate for news, but I am afraid I don't know where she is.'

'Wait. You said Louis Levy and his family live at Leighton Mansions. What family?'

'I am so sorry. Louis Levy lives there with his wife, Esther. And their baby son, Jacob.' Dinah swayed and the floor rose to meet her.

Mona

Mona tore from the club in a blind panic, all thoughts of Evie and Gateshead gone from her mind. She had no idea of the way back to the Diamond or the rundown lodging house. She ducked into an alleyway and counted the money she had taken from Nellie and Solomon Zettler. She breathed deeply to steady her nerves. She cocked her head at a familiar sound.

'Matches for sale, please buy my matches.'

Mona crept out of the alley. The boy was hunched against the wall, shivering. He jumped when she touched his arm. She smiled, hoping he would see she meant him no harm. He moved away and she smiled again. He frowned, unused to kindness. She held out her hand and his eyes opened wide at the shiny new shilling in her palm. 'This and more are yours if you help me.'

The boy led Mona through the Soho streets. She would have preferred not to go anywhere near the rat-infested lodging house ever again, but she wouldn't leave without her last link to her mother. Nellie's plan had been to buy her passage to New York and work at the Casino Theatre on Broadway. Mona ran through her options: go to New York, return to Gateshead for Evie, apologise to Nellie and beg forgiveness. She wanted to see her daughter, but she couldn't face Dinah or Lizzie. She was terrified of seeing Nellie again. Her only option was to go to New York. Once she was settled there and dancing at the Casino Theatre, she would send money home for Evie.

Rain fell as she followed the boy. Big fat drops, soaking her to the skin. When the streets began to look familiar, she kept her promise and the boy fled, clutching his reward. She stood around the corner from the Diamond as slobbering, staggering men waited to be admitted for the first evening performance. The dancers would be wearing the garish make-up and revealing outfits she despised. Nellie would have returned, and they would be hanging on her every word as she regaled them with the story of Mona's transformation. She stepped back as the stage door banged open and two of Mr Zettler's henchmen burst out carrying blazing lanterns and sharpened sticks. As they charged in the direction of Billy's club, she ran into the lodging house. Her breath came in rapid, shallow bursts by the time she reached the attic bedroom. As she reached for the handle she froze. She cocked her head, the familiar tap, tap sound came from behind the door. Solomon Zettler was there, tapping his cane as he waited. Tap, tap, tap. Why wasn't he dead? She opened the door.

Rain dripped from the decrepit ceiling into a metal bucket. Tap, tap, tap. Mona grabbed her carpet bag. She checked the diary was inside and ran, not stopping until her lungs were ready to burst. She slipped into an alleyway and leant against the wall. She took deep breaths, what had Nellie said when she regaled the dancers with tales of her journey to America? She had said she would board the ship somewhere called Southampton and the journey to New York would take five or six days, depending on the weather. Mona didn't know what the train or ship's passage would cost. Her breathing had calmed. This had been Nellie's escape plan, now it was hers.

Before leaving, she was determined to confront Louis and his uncle and show them she had survived, despite the dire circumstances they left her in. As she pictured Leighton Mansions and Samuel Levy, her heart beat faster and nausea rose. She crept out of the alleyway. She was prepared to use some of her precious money on a carriage. She looked left and right, the street was quiet, and she hurried towards a waiting cab. The driver looked her up and down and sniffed. She jutted her chin out, hoping her good looks hadn't faded too much.

'You have money for the cab, Miss?'

She ignored the insult and handed him the fare. The horses set off and the cab jerked as it took her towards Leighton Mansions.

Lizzie

Lizzie slouched, her head lolling towards the Globe's beer-sodden bar, the last of her money gone. She shook her head, anything she received for the wretched girl came from Dinah, the brat's whore of a mother hadn't sent a penny. Lizzie's mother had sent Andrew Glass to make sure the girl went to Sunday School. What good was Sunday School to a bastard? Lizzie spent precious money on a new dress and shoes for her, making sure they were big enough to last. She shook her empty glass. Things would be better after another drink. The landlord raised an eyebrow, he knew Lizzie had no money. A man squeezed in beside her. He leant over and she recoiled at his stale, beery breath.

'All right, Lizzie? How's the scamp of a girl? Not be long before you'll be able to make some money out of her, know what I mean?'

Lizzie closed one eye and tried to focus. Harry Campbell winked. He was a creep, but a creep with plenty of money.

'Get lost, Harry. She's only a girl.'

'She won't always be. Think of it as a business opportunity. You'll have another drink?'

Darkness fell as Lizzie and Harry drank. When the Globe closed Lizzie stumbled back to Pipewellgate, Harry's words ringing in her ears. She shoved her shoulder against the rotting door, thumping onto the stone floor. She pushed the door closed with her foot and lay there, drunk and repellent. She tried to focus as the room swayed. Before she passed out her eyes settled on the grimy curtain separating Evie's mattress from the rest of the room. What had Harry said? A sly smile crept across her face.

'You'll make your fortune with that girl, Lizzie Brown.'

Mona

Mona's memory of Leighton Mansions was vague, but as the streets started to improve, she knew her destination was close. She asked the cab to stop. She stood at the corner, looking towards Samuel Levy's house. The lamplighters had started their work and a welcoming lantern blazed outside the house. She blew on her fingers; she wasn't dressed for winter. A cab stopped in front of the house and a man stepped out. She stepped back into the shadows. Louis. Her love. Evie's father. She caught her breath at his familiar good looks. He entered the house and gave a cheerful greeting.

'Hello! I'm home!'

He shut the door and Mona closed her eyes. Now. She would go and knock on the door. She stepped out of the shadows but before she could cross the street, a deep voice startled her.

'Move along Miss, you can't do business here. This is a respectable street.'

She stopped dead. 'How dare you! I am not..., I am here to see...,'

Her cheeks burned as she pictured herself through the policeman's eyes. Her threadbare clothes and dishevelled appearance. How could she explain she was visiting the Levy Family? She shuddered; they might make the same mistake. She hung her head. Louis's stupidity and his uncle's cruelty had led to her downfall, but the shame was all hers. She started to walk away. After a few steps she turned. The policeman motioned for her to carry on. She rounded a corner and leant against the wall, breathing hard. Louis had said he was home. His home, his life. He wasn't losing sleep over a lost love. She pictured the little beggar-boy. After she had seen him, she was determined to go home for Evie. Now, she knew she couldn't. Dinah would despise her for abandoning her daughter. There was only one option. She would make her fortune as a Broadway dancer then stand on Louis's doorstep wearing the best clothes New York had to offer. Then she would return to Gateshead for her daughter. She would be the respectable lady her mother had brought her up to be.

Chapter 23

Evie

Since meeting at Sunday School, Evie and Jack had become good friends. He always looked for her in the school yard to offer her some of his dinner. He never mentioned her shabby clothes and second-hand shoes. The following weekend, she told Lizzie she was going back to Sunday School.

'If you say no, I will write to Andrew Glass and tell him things.'

Lizzie turned, her gaze thunderous, and Evie stepped back. She started to regret her plan, but Lizzie didn't strike her. Instead, Lizzie stared; her bloated face screwed up in a grotesque mask.

'All right but tidy up before you go. I divvent knaa, I must be gettin' soft in me old age!'

Lizzie was unaware that even if Evie had known Andrew Glass's address, she couldn't write to him. She struggled to read without the letters moving around on the page. Nancy helped her at school and Jack had helped during her one visit to Sunday School. Evie was surprised Lizzie hadn't put up more of a fight. She had expected at least a slap for threatening to write to Andrew Glass. It would have been worth it. Before long, Lizzie was snoring like a fat pig in her filthy chair. Evie put her hand in her dress pocket and checked. It was still there. She knew Aunt Dinah's letters arrived regularly because Lizzie always had something to say when she opened them.

'Does she expect me to feed the brat and put clothes on her back with this?'

If Jack was at Sunday School Evie hoped he would read the letter for her. Usually, Lizzie took the money then crumpled Aunt Dinah's letters and threw them on the fire, but Evie was in luck when this one arrived. As Lizzie started reading the letter, she was interrupted by a knock at the door. Evie grabbed it and stuck it in her dress pocket.

Lizzie belched and pushed herself up. 'What are you doing still here, girl? Why haven't you gone to bloody Sunday School? You better go now, before I change my mind.'

Evie spotted Jack walking towards the church hall, and she crossed her fingers, hoping he wouldn't go inside before she reached him.

'Hello, Evie.'

'Hello, Jack. Are you going inside?'

'Do you want to?'

'No.'

'Should we go for a walk instead?'

Evie's spirits soared. She felt for the letter in her pocket, desperate to ask Jack to read it. They walked to the People's Park and Evie smiled. A friend and a trip to the park all in one day.

'Should we sit under this tree?'

Evie nodded; she would have sat anywhere with Jack Todd.

'Now, Miss Eveline Brown. Tell me all about you.'

'I live in Pipewellgate, and I go to South Street Infants School.'

'No, tell me what you like to do.'

'Do?'

'Yes, when you're not at school. How do you pass your time?'

Evie's cheeks flamed and she studied her dress. Should she be honest with her new friend? Jack smiled and waited for her to answer. She decided to trust him.

'I have to do jobs then I'm tired and I go to sleep.'

Jack's expression changed. 'What? That awful woman makes you do her cleaning?' Evie nodded.

'It must be miserable.'

She nodded again. Her lip trembled. 'Jack, I hope you don't mind me asking…,'

'What is it, Evie?'

'I can't read very well. I think something is wrong with my eyes. I have this letter. I need to know what it says.' Her words came out in a rush, tumbling over each other.

'Of course, let's have a look.'

'I know I shouldn't have taken it, it's Lizzie's, but I need to know. Is it from my aunt?'

Jack frowned. 'This isn't Lizzie's letter. Look.'

The letters danced in front of her eyes, but Jack said her name was on the envelope.

'There are two letters. One is for Lizzie, but the other is yours. Did Lizzie not give it to you?'

'No.' Evie whispered the word, aghast at Lizzie's deception.

'My uncle is a postman. I'm sure he would say this is against the law. People are meant to receive their own letters, anything addressed to you should only be given to you.'

This was a revelation to Evie. How many more letters had Lizzie kept from her? Had her mother written to her? Her head spun.

'Who is it from, Jack? What does it say?'

As Jack started to read, Evie closed her eyes.

'My darling niece,

I worry I receive so little word of you. I hope Lizzie is looking after you and you like school. I hope you have made lots of friends. Life at Hampson Hall is pleasant enough, but I miss you very much. I hope we will soon be together again. I promise once I am married you can come and live with me. I know you will still be learning your letters, but I hope before long you will be able to write back to me. I long to hear from you. I will write again soon.

Your loving aunt, Dinah.'

Evie pictured her aunt. This wasn't the first letter she had sent, what had happened to the others? Lizzie must have kept them, or worse, destroyed them. How dare she? It was one thing to destroy her own letters, but how many of Evie's had she burnt? She sniffed and Jack patted her arm.

'What does the other letter say, Jack?'

Jack hesitated. 'You can't tell anyone we read this; it's not addressed to you.'

'I know, but she kept my letters so I'm going to read this one!'

'All right.' Jack smiled at his young friend's determination.

'*Dear Lizzie,*

I hope this letter finds you and dear Evie in good health. I wish you would send some word, cousin. I would be glad to know how Evie is progressing in school. Is she growing fast? I have enclosed a small sum from my wages again, I hope you can buy some fresh fruit and vegetables, to keep Evie strong. I wish I could send more but my wages do not amount to much. The staff have been promised a small bonus at Christmas. I will send more for Evie then. Please use it to buy her a nice present, a dolly or a book to help with her reading. Please do write soon with news.

Your cousin, Dinah Jane Brown.'

Evie stared into the distance; her eyes dry. She turned; grief etched into her face.

'All this time, I thought no one cared about me. Lizzie has never given me a letter, or any word of my aunt and she doesn't spend anything on me. Look at me!' Jack shook his head as Evie pulled at the sleeves of her tatty, second-hand dress.

'What about my mother? Has she written to me?'

'I don't know, Evie. But my uncle can make sure you get letters that are addressed to you.'

'But the letter for me was smaller, it was inside the bigger letter addressed to Lizzie.'

'Oh. I don't know what to do about that.'

Evie took a deep breath. 'Can you help me with my reading?'

'Yes, of course.'

Now her tears came. Tears of despair at Lizzie's deceit and tears of gratitude for Jack's help. As dusk fell, they walked home, a new, deeper understanding and affection between them.

Dinah

Dinah came round to find herself lying on the chaise lounge. Grace Opal held smelling salts under her nose and wafted her face with a fan. Dinah sat up; she couldn't be seen being so familiar with the family. Her lip trembled. Master Walter had said Louis had a wife and a baby.

'Please forgive me, Master Walter. I don't know what came over me.'

'I have a suggestion, Miss Brown. If you are willing?'

Dinah would consider anything, if it meant she found Margaret. Master Walter set out his plan. A few days later Dinah was packing her belongings when Ruby burst into their room.

'I thought I'd missed you!'

Dinah smiled. 'I wouldn't have left without saying goodbye. I'll write.'

'Promise?'

'Promise.'

Winnie also said goodbye, more quietly than Ruby, but as heartfelt. Dinah suspected she and Edward would stay at Hampson Hall, would perhaps be the next Mr and Mrs Jackson. Winnie's baby was never mentioned again, but Dinah sensed Winnie had found some peace since the terrible events at the picnic. As Dinah climbed into the cab she looked back. She had never imagined she would make so many friends in service, but a strong bond existed between the household staff. They had gathered to wave her off and even Mrs Jackson had wished her good luck. Cook blew her nose on her apron and Mr Foley put a protective arm around her. Winnie and Edward stood close together, Winnie's hand on her belly, cherishing their precious unborn child. The driver stirred the horses into action. As their hooves crunched on the gravel Dinah heard a shout.

'Dinner! Dinner!' Dinah laughed; she had never had the heart to correct Ruby. She looked out of the cab. Ruby hung onto the side for dear life. Mrs Jackson's reproach reached them.

'Stupid girl! I won't pick up the pieces when you go under the hooves!'

The driver slowed the horses and Ruby climbed inside. The friends embraced.

'Take me with you, please!'

'I would love to, Ruby. But I can't, I'm sorry. I must find my sister. I have no idea what has happened to her or what awaits me in London.'

'But I don't want to stay here without you. I don't want to work with someone new.'Dinah smiled; she would always be grateful to Master Walter. He had persuaded Lord Hampson to employ another scullery maid so Dinah could leave.

'I'll send for you to come and stay with me as soon as I can. And I'll write.'

'All right. But I hope it's soon.'

The friends embraced once more before Ruby climbed out of the cab.

'Cheerio, my dear Dinner!'

'Cheerio, dear Ruby!'

As the cab turned out of the driveway Dinah counted off the promises on her fingers. First, find her errant sister. Next, get Evie away from Pipewellgate. Then, send for Ruby. As usual, Dinah's last consideration was for herself. When she reflected on her own situation, she smiled. She could sing. Grace Opal, the famous singer and actress, had said she could sing. She could have a career and a life of her own, as her mother had always wanted for her daughters.

Mona

Once Mona had set her mind on getting to New York she didn't waste any time. She found a cab and asked to go to the train station for Southampton. It used more of her precious money, but she had to put some distance between herself and Leighton Mansions. When the cab

213

left her at the station, she hesitated. Where would she catch the train? She examined her scruffy clothes and shuddered; the policeman had mistaken her for a prostitute. Did she have time to buy a new dress or coat? She dismissed the idea, the fewer people she met, the better. She wheeled round as rancid breath warmed the back of her neck. She came face to face with a rough-looking man. He smirked.

'Got a penny for a fella down on his luck, Miss?'

'I'm sorry, no.' As she hurried away, she bumped into a woman laden with packages.

'Oh, please excuse me.' The woman's accented voice was soft.

'No, I'm sorry, it was my fault.'

'I say, are you all right my dear? You look as if you've seen a ghost.'

Mona stared. The immaculate woman was perfectly coordinated, her light blue jacket and full-length skirt matched her wide hat, artfully adorned with osprey feathers.

'Let me help you, Madam.' The station porter started collecting the woman's packages and loading them onto a trolley. 'Where are you travelling to, Madam?'

'Southampton. I am meeting my husband on the train.'

'Of course, Madam. First class, is it?'

'Yes, thank you.'

Mona backed away into the shadows. To herself she thanked the woman, she was in the right place. She made her way to the opposite end of the train. As she paid for her ticket she glanced along the platform. The train guard helped the beautiful woman into the first-class carriage. Mona promised herself that she would be the smartest woman on the train one day, travelling in style in first-class. It grew dark as the train made its way towards Southampton. At Southampton station she stood, surrounded by people and noise. She forced herself to concentrate, she had to find out how to get on the ship to New York. A man stopped right in front of her, blocking her path.

'And you, Miss? Are you with the dancers?'

Mona stared. He was about her age and wore a cheap but smart suit. He carried a small notebook and she noticed ticks against names. She hesitated, was it a trick?

'Yes, I dance.'

'And you're sailing to America? What's your name?'

She took a deep breath. It was a chance, and she had to take it. 'Nellie. Nellie Pilkington.'

The man laughed and she froze. She turned, ready to flee.

'I don't mean any offence. But it's your name.'

She kept her back to him, guarded.

'Pilkington isn't exactly a stage name, is it? We'll have to think of something different before you start work at the Casino. There's the matter of the outstanding balance to pay, Miss Pilkington?'

She fished in her bag and handed him the money, her hands shaking.

'Right, we're all here. Come on Nellie, let's get you into the cab with the others.'

She breathed a sigh of relief. Outside the station she saw a group of women gathered beside a cab. The man waved to them. 'Here she is, Nellie Pilkington. The last of our little group.'

She tried to hide her face, what if one of the women knew Nellie and knew what Mona had done? She kept her eyes lowered, she couldn't be found out, not now when she was so close.

'Next stop Southampton docks!' The man's cheer rubbed off and the women clapped their hands. Mona held her breath as the cab moved. As she relaxed a strong, bony hand gripped her leg. She turned to the woman sitting beside her. The woman hissed in Mona's ear, her breath stale.

'Hello, English Ballet Girl.'

Chapter 24

Dinah

Dinah longed to ask the cab to travel through Gateshead so she could visit Evie. But the last time she had tried to see her niece, Lizzie had once again contrived to keep them apart. Dinah had arrived in Pipewellgate only to find Evie missing. Lizzie said she was at Sunday School, but Dinah found no sign of her at the church hall. Before leaving Hampson Hall, she had written to Lizzie with money from her Christmas bonus, asking her to buy something special for Evie. Terrified Aunt Agatha would find a way to thwart her plans and return her to a life of service, Dinah didn't tell Lizzie she was leaving Hampson Hall. Instead, Ruby agreed to look out for letters and forward them to Dinah's new address. Dinah didn't expect Lizzie would notice her letters now came from London, as long as they contained money. Snow fell heavily now, and she yearned to be with Evie, to tie her scarf tight against the biting cold wind. But first, she needed to discover what had become of her sister. Once she found Margaret, they would come back for Evie together.

Master Walter had organised Dinah's journey to London, and Grace had arranged for her to stay in a guest house that welcomed women travelling alone. Grace agreed with the suffragettes, that women should have the same opportunities as men. Master Walter had paid Dinah's first month's rent and she had her wages from the hall to live on until she found a job. Master Walter had given her Samuel Levy's address, suggesting she could start looking for her sister there. He warned her about the undesirable parts of London, in particular some of the less reputable music halls and clubs. He reassured her he didn't imagine her sister would be anywhere like that but said she must keep her wits about her. Grace had arranged an audition for her at a small theatre close to the guest house. With her voice, Grace was confident Dinah would get the first job she auditioned for.

'But how will I repay you?'

'That won't be necessary. Remember how courageous you were on the day of the picnic? This is my way of repaying you for risking your life, Miss Brown.'

Dinah pictured Winnie outside Hampson Hall and smiled. She had only done what anyone else would have by jumping into the river, but she wasn't about to refuse their generosity. Cook had tried to persuade her to stay for the festive celebrations, but Dinah was determined to reach London before Christmas Eve. As the train took her towards London, she considered Margaret's journey. Was she excited by the prospect of starting a new life with Louis? Did she give any thought to her daughter and sister? What went wrong when she arrived in London? Dinah's head spun with unanswered questions as the train moved through the dark. After a while the train slowed and pulled into York station. Dinah closed her eyes, what had Theodosia said about York? She had written that it was the most beautiful of all the train stations she had seen since leaving France. Dinah craned her neck to see the copper lanterns. The old lamps, polished until they shone, illuminated the charming station with a soft orange light. She longed to tell her mother she was at York station, on her way to London. She leant her head against the window as the train departed.

When the train pulled into Kings Cross, Dinah yawned and gathered her belongings. She stepped onto the platform and stood, as people streamed around her. A man tutted as he barged past, nudging her elbow. Everyone was in such a hurry! Porters pushed trolleys full to the brim with shiny luggage and boxes of various sizes. People from all walks of life hurried towards the exit and she joined them, quickening her pace. Outside the station she hesitated, it was late, and the streets were dark. She held her handkerchief to her nose. Beneath the clean, natural smell of horse manure lurked a nastier, fetid aroma. She pushed away an image of the Union Workhouse. Several hunched, shuffling figures came into view. The more she looked, the more she saw, hands outstretched for whatever they could get. A tall, well-dressed gentleman shooed a bare-footed woman away as he would a fly. He walked towards a row of neat carriages; the horses hooded as they waited. Small lanterns shone at the front of each carriage and Dinah remembered Master Walter saying she should ask to be taken to Parkview Guest House on Chestnut Tree Avenue. The coachman took her luggage and helped her into the carriage. She smiled and nodded to the other passengers.

'Good evening, I am Miss Dinah Jane Brown.'

The carriage jerked and turned away from Kings Cross. The horses' hooves clattered on the cobbles as they travelled along the dark streets. Dinah's eyes moved from one side of the carriage to the other as she tried to make out famous landmarks, but the gloom obscured her view. Until they passed Queen's Hall on Langham Place. There, despite the late hour, a small group of women were gathered. They stood beneath a banner, the words *'No Surrender'* illuminated by the flickering lamplight. The woman sitting next to Dinah cheered and a man opposite looked towards the banner and sniffed. The woman smiled and nodded at Dinah. Dinah nodded back, acknowledging the banner's significance. For some years The Women's Social and Political Union had held rallies at Queen's Hall, and the women's suffrage societies used it for their public meetings. Dinah turned to catch another glimpse of the women. As the carriage turned out of Langham Place a bell started to chime. Dinah smiled; Theodosia had sung about the bells of London.

'Oranges and lemons,
Say the bells of St. Clement's.
You owe me five farthings,
Say the bells of St. Martin's.
When will you pay me?

Say the bells of Old Bailey.
When I grow rich,
Say the bells of Shoreditch.'

Dinah didn't know which bells the deep, mellifluous tones belonged to but in her head, she told her mother she was in London. She was repaying the debt to Aunt Agatha; once she found Margaret they would return to Gateshead for Evie. Like the suffragettes, she wouldn't surrender.

*

A pretty young woman wearing a smart maid's uniform answered the door to Mrs Newbold's guest house. She wore a small pin on her bodice. Dinah recognised the purple, white and green colours of the suffrage movement. She introduced herself and asked the girl's name.

'I'm Clara, Miss.'

'How do you do, Clara? I'm Dinah. I'm pleased to meet you.'

'This way please, Miss.' Clara led her along a bright passageway. The walls were covered in pictures of singers, dancers and actors. Clara knocked on a door and presented Dinah to her landlady. Mrs Newbold's parlour sparkled with Edwardian splendour and Dinah's heart ached for her mother, she would have adored this room. Mrs Newbold's welcoming hand was warm but firm.

'I'm pleased to make your acquaintance, Miss Brown. I hope you will enjoy your stay. Walter explained you hope to be engaged at the West London Theatre. I have many actresses and music hall artistes staying here, you will fit in very well. My colourful, entertaining guests have kept me in good company since Mr Newbold took his final breath.'

'Oh. Please accept my condolences, Mrs Newbold. I was unaware of your loss.'

'Thank you. The dear man passed several years ago but I feel his absence as if he left me only yesterday. Now, come into the dining room, Clara has prepared supper for you. My other guests are all at work, but you will meet them tomorrow night. I am sure you will wish to retire after supper, and they are unlikely to be up early for breakfast.'

Dinah followed Mrs Newbold into the dining room, admiring the splendour of the elegant woman's silk gown. The simple design belied the intricacy of the garment and Dinah knew the flowing silvery fabric must have come from Paris. She was relieved at Master Walter's discretion, he couldn't have said anything about the other purpose of her visit, to discover what had become of her sister. She had Samuel Levy's address, and she intended to make it her priority to pay the family a visit the following morning, before her audition in the afternoon.

*

There was snow on the ground when Dinah woke. Over breakfast she asked Mrs Newbold how she would arrange a cab to visit a friend who was recovering from an illness. She hated lying but couldn't tell Mrs Newbold the truth. She was soon stepping into the cab with a promise of cocoa on her return. When they arrived at Leighton Mansions, she asked the driver to wait. She fought back tears at her sister's descriptions of the grand house. Her sister hadn't ever lived here. As she walked towards the door she hesitated. Louis was married and had a son. As much as she needed to find her sister, she wasn't so cruel as to bring heartbreak to an innocent woman and child. The path sloped upwards, and she could see in through the front window. The room was lit with candles and a slight, dark-haired woman, her back to the window, picked up a small child and pointed at an elaborate candelabra. The candles signified Hanukkah, the Festival of Lights. Louis walked towards his wife and child. He kissed the boy's forehead, then he kissed his wife. Dinah knocked at the door and waited. It was answered by a man whom she took to be Louis's uncle, Samuel Levy.

'Yes?' He looked her up and down, making no attempt to disguise his disapproval. Dinah refused to be intimidated and she stared back, unassailable in her determination.

'Good morning. I am Miss Dinah Jane Brown. May I please speak to Mr Louis Levy?'

'There is no one of that name here.'

He started to close the door, but she placed her foot on the jamb.

'What are you doing? Get away from my door or I will call for the constabulary.'

'No, not until I have spoken to Louis. I know he lives here. Or should I speak to his wife?'

At the mention of his nephew's wife, Samuel Levy bristled.

'This is most irregular. Wait there!'

He pushed the door to but didn't close it. She waited. She heard hushed voices in the entrance lobby then the door opened wide. Louis blanched. 'Dinah! Whatever brings you here?'

'What do you suppose brings me here, Louis? Or should I say who?'

Louis glanced behind him.

'I have no interest in upsetting your family. But I need to find my sister.'

'But she isn't here. I don't know where she is.'

'She came to London with you, didn't she?'

'Yes, but...'

Dinah refused to put him out of his misery. 'But what, Louis? You abandoned her in a strange city? You should be ashamed of yourself!'

'I'm sorry, Dinah.' He glanced behind him again. His uncle hovered in the hallway.

Dinah snapped. 'You! Samuel Levy!'

Louis jumped at Dinah's sharp, yet quiet words. He was weak, a coward of a man.

'I am not my sister! You don't scare me! Now, tell me where she is, or I will ask Esther what she knows about this sorry situation!' The threat worked and Samuel Levy said Dinah should go to the Diamond Music Hall on Warwick Street. As she moved away, she turned and regarded the men with cool eyes. 'If your information is incorrect, I will come back, rest assured.'

'Dinah, wait. I have something for you.' Louis disappeared into the house. When he returned, he pushed something into her hands and apologised, over and over. Dinah shook her head as she turned away.

She climbed into the cab and gave the driver her destination.

'Are you sure, Miss? That area isn't very respectable.'

'I'm sure.' As the cab retraced Mona's late-night walk, Dinah's lip trembled. Her sister must have been terrified. She clutched the precious item Louis had given her, her mother's necklace. The cab pulled to a halt, and she looked out, frowning.

'There you are, Miss. I'll wait here.'

'This is it?'

'Yes, Miss. This is Warwick Street and the Diamond Music Hall.'

Dinah gazed at the building. How could her sister have worked here? The theatre doors were shut but a group of women huddled together around the corner. Dinah started to approach them but stopped, terrified she would find her younger sister among the dirty, desperate-looking women. They were serving themselves from a filthy pan. The food resembled nothing Dinah recognised. She recalled the warmth of the kitchen and the delicious food at Hampson Hall. Her sister would have been better off there, despite the lowly positions their aunt had arranged. Dinah tried to hide her fear as a tall, emaciated woman approached her.

'Can I help you?' The kind voice caught Dinah off-guard, and she stumbled over her words.

'I..., em..., I'm looking for my sister, I've been told she works here.'

'What's her name, this sister?' Dinah recoiled from the smaller woman's rough accent.

'Margaret. My sister is called Margaret Patricia Brown.'

The tall woman furrowed her brow and shook her head. 'No, I'm sorry, I don't know her. You had better go now, before he sees you talking to us.'

'Are you sure? I understood she had been here for a number of years.'

The smaller woman mimicked Dinah and the others laughed as she made a theatrical bow. Dinah looked away. Samuel Levy had lied. She hadn't wanted to upset Louis's wife but now she had no choice. She would return to Leighton Mansions and do whatever it took to get the truth. She turned to leave but stopped as the taller woman moved away from the group.

'Your sister, did she ever go by any other name?'

Dinah stared. The woman had an air of grace about her, yet she cut a forlorn figure. What terrible experiences had brought such a woman to this low place?

'Sometimes, as dancers, we prefer to use a different name. It's part of the act I suppose.'

The woman's voice dripped sadness and a memory tugged at Dinah. What was the name in her sister's letters? At the time she had refused to acknowledge her sister's latest fanciful idea.

'Yes! Mona! She called herself Mona Leighton!'

The silence was thick and immediate. The tall woman stared. Dinah sensed the smaller woman moving towards her and she stepped back. The woman's filthy hand grabbed Dinah's arm.

'Here, look at this! This is what your precious sister did to me!' She yanked a scarf away from her neck to reveal an angry, red weal. 'She cut me with a knife, your little Miss English Ballet Company! What do you think of your precious sister now?'

Dinah's mind spun. Gentle, dreamy Margaret? Could she have attacked another woman?

'I..., em..., I'm sorry but I don't think...,'

'What? Your snooty sister wouldn't stoop so low? Lady, the things I could tell you about how low your sister fell! This wasn't even the worst of it! I don't think you know her at all!'

'Nellie, you've said enough. I'm Violet, I shared a room with Mona before she left.'

Dinah bit her lip. 'Left? Left for where?'

'She did this,' the angry woman gestured to her throat, 'after she stabbed him and before she robbed me. Stole every penny I had.' Despite her tough exterior, tears welled in the woman's eyes.

'I am sorry, I didn't know what she had done. Do you know where she is now?'

'She stole my money for passage on the ship and she's gone.'

'What? Where?' Dinah whispered the word. 'Ship?'

Nellie spat. 'America. New York City to be precise. You've missed her. By two days.'

Mona

'It's all right, your secret's safe with me. I never liked that Nellie much anyway. Good for you, I say.'

The woman patted Mona's leg and a memory surfaced. She was a dancer at the Diamond.

'It was an accident.' Mona started to explain but the woman placed a finger on her lips.

'Shush, it's done. Haven't we all done things we regret?'

Mona nodded; she did regret betraying Nellie. She clutched her mother's carpet bag, the diary safe inside. She had been working for the man who terrorised her mother, Jeannie and so many others. When she came face to face with him at Billy's club his opium-addled mind mistook her for Theodosia. Then she had shrugged, and he understood. He attacked her and she defended herself, plain and simple. But when she recalled how her rage had surged, she shook. She hadn't imagined herself capable of such behaviour, but life had taught her to defend herself, to fight.

As *RMS Matilda* set sail, Mona stood on the deck, her face in the cold breeze. Crowds had gathered to wave farewell to relatives and friends. She picked out a couple who would have been about the same age as her parents and waved, tears in her eyes. She had escaped from the horror of dancing for Solomon Zettler. She had been betrayed and left heart-broken by the man she loved, starved, forced to dance almost naked for drunk, disgusting men and attacked. She refused to be defined by having a child out of wedlock or selling her body in order to eat. She had defended herself against a sadistic man, a man with blood on his hands. She moved away from the rail and walked to the other side of the ship. She looked at the wide-open sea. She swore she would never again depend on a man for anything. She let out a wail, Evie was better off without her.

As the ship made its way across the ocean people moved around the deck. Some sat, their coats pulled tight against the wind. Others walked from side to side, marvelling at the steely water as the vessel ploughed its furrow through the waves. A young man leant over the rail; his skin sallow as he succumbed to seasickness. Mona opened her battered carpet bag and took out her mother's diary. She wanted to write to Dinah, and she wanted to do it now, in case she became ill with seasickness. She turned to the last page of the diary. She wrote quickly, her words scrawling and uneven as the waves grew higher and the ship's passage rougher. When she had finished, she ripped the page out and folded it across the middle. She slotted the page into the pocket fixed to the back cover of the diary. She didn't notice the other folded page already hidden inside the pocket.

She set off along the deck to explore her new surroundings, ignoring the sly looks and stares. She brushed the sleeves of her coat and tried to smooth her dress. She frowned. What would happen when they arrived in New York? If she managed to avoid her travelling companions on the ship, she would have to reunite with them to travel to the theatre. Where would she go if her true identity was uncovered? In her desperation to escape she had grabbed the chance without thinking. When she bought her ticket, she wasn't given a choice of class, looking at her shabby clothes she understood why. She was travelling as a steerage passenger. She walked along the deck; her eyes lowered. She caught snippets of conversation, soon realising steerage passengers had the least comfortable conditions. Too many people were packed into small spaces, leading to dangerous overcrowding. The food was poor and steerage passengers had to cook it themselves. A woman talked of disease ripping through steerage on a friend's journey. The woman crossed herself, her friend hadn't survived. Mona jumped at a loud shout. She flattened herself against the rail, looking around for better cover. She heard another shout then a cheer. A group of men playing quoits. She sighed and carried on along the deck. A snatch of music reached her on the breeze, and she moved towards it. She leant against the rail and closed her eyes. The music came from a small group gathered on deck with their instruments. The musicians were playing '*The Entertainer.*' She smiled, she had first heard it in 1902, the year before her mother died. She lost herself in the music and happy memories. Her eyes opened wide, and her head whipped round as someone collided into her.

'Oh! I'm so sorry! Please, excuse me!'

The petite woman's blond hair curled across her forehead, her large tricorne-shaped hat emphasised her stature and elfin features. She wore a smart, tightly fitting navy travelling suit. Mona recoiled as she compared her own baggy, shapeless outfit, stolen from Nellie, with this pretty, elegant woman's attire. She started to move away but the woman stopped her.

'Sorry to trouble you, but could you help me back to my cabin? I suffer from seasickness, and I shouldn't have come on deck. The music tempted me, but I'm not sure I can get back. Please?'

Mona understood the woman's plight, but she hesitated. The woman's eyes pleaded.

'All right.'

'Oh, thank you. I'm so grateful. I'm Peggy Willow, I'm pleased to meet you, Miss?'

Mona swallowed. 'I'm Nellie Pilkington.'

They made their unsteady way along the deck until Peggy gestured towards a set of steps.

'My cabin is down there, in second class. Is your cabin in the same area, Miss Pilkington?' Mona shook her head; her accommodation wouldn't be at the same level as Miss Willow's.

'I don't know, I haven't found it yet.'

'Oh well, I hope it is as comfortable as mine, when you do locate it.'

Mona helped Peggy down the steps, leading to a bright, narrow corridor with doors on both sides. Peggy peered at each numbered door from under her hat, stopping at the end of the corridor.

'This is it. Thank you again. I wouldn't have managed without your help.'

'You're welcome, Miss Willow.' Mona started to move away. Peggy put her head on one side and regarded the other woman, narrowing her pretty eyes at Mona.

'How can I repay your kindness?'

'There's no need. It was nothing.'

'Why don't you come inside, and I'll fix us a drink? I would like the company.'

Mona's mind raced but produced no justifiable reason to refuse.

Peggy opened the door to her small cabin. It was comfortably furnished, warm and well-lit, a direct contrast to what Mona expected to find in steerage.

Peggy met her eyes. 'What is it?'

Mona flushed and looked away. 'I'm sorry.'

'You're wondering how I can afford this.'

Mona's flush deepened.

'It's all right, I understand your curiosity. Don't worry, it's nothing bad. Well, not unless you view dancing on the stage to make a living as bad?'

'Oh, you're a dancer? Whereabouts?'

'I'm engaged at the Paradise Theatre on Broadway in New York. Do you know it?'

'No, but I'm hoping to find a position at the Casino Theatre.'

'Well, what a fine coincidence this is!' Peggy stopped, looking Mona up and down.

Mona flushed again, her scruffy appearance at odds with her story. Peggy waited.

227

'I've got myself into a bit of a scrape, you see.'

'Well, let's have a drink and you can tell me all about it. Pink gin all right, darling?'

Peggy gestured towards a pretty upholstered chair and Mona sank into its softness. The drink was presented in a crystal glass with a conical top and a slender stem. She sipped the drink and grimaced at the strong, sour taste. Peggy laughed.

'Angostura Bitters, darling! You get used to it after a few! Now, what's your story?'

Mona didn't know if it was the comfort of Peggy's cabin, the gin, or the young woman herself. Perhaps it was a combination, but her story poured out. Nellie and the Diamond, Louis, her abandonment of Evie. Every shameful detail including attacking Solomon Zettler and stealing Nellie's name, money and passage. She didn't go as far as admitting to murder. For all she knew, Solomon Zettler could still be alive. She ended her tale by telling Peggy her real name. She chewed the inside of her cheek, waiting for Peggy's reaction. She drained her glass and peered at Peggy, expecting immediate eviction from the warm cocoon. Instead, Peggy took Mona's glass and refilled it. Peggy smiled, her pretty eyes glinting, the edge evident for the first time.

'Lord, love a duck, Mona! Your tale is even better than mine!'

'You're not shocked by my disgraceful behaviour?'

'Circumstances, darling. Circumstances can lead us to do things we never thought possible.'

'What about your life, Peggy? How did you become a dancer?'

Peggy hesitated and averted her eyes. She said her mother had died in childbirth and she was brought up by her father. She lived above one theatre or another, and her father took her with him to his jobs as a stage manager in London. She was brought up around the music, personalities and excitement of the theatre. There was never any doubt she would be a dancer or an actress, she had never known any other life. She worked in London and in repertory theatre on the south coast before learning about the opportunities in New York. Her father had died a few years earlier and now she was her own woman, not answerable to anyone other than her current employer.

As Mona sipped her drink, she sensed Peggy watching her.

'I know we don't know each other very well, but I'm sure there would be enough room for two of us in the bunk. Unless you want to join the great unwashed in steerage? And in the morning, we'll visit the hairdresser and I'll find you something decent to wear!'

Mona stuttered her thanks as Peggy poured them another drink. Suddenly Peggy shrieked.

'I've got it! Don't go to the Casino! Come to the Paradise! I'll get you a position there. The Paradise is a superior theatre, the Casino is Off-Broadway, darling!'

Mona stared; Peggy had lifted a weight from her shoulders. She wouldn't have to see her travelling companions again. Peggy turned away; her eyes narrowed. She turned back with their drinks, her beautiful smile and false face in place once more.

Chapter 25

Dinah

As Dinah hurried away from the Diamond, Nellie made to follow her, but Violet placed a firm hand on the smaller woman's arm. Violet had urged Dinah to leave in case anyone saw them talking. Who was she so afraid of? Dinah felt eyes boring into her back, but she didn't turn round. Her whole body shook as she reached the cab.

'Come on now, Miss. I need to get you back to Mrs Newbold right away. She will get the doctor to come and check you over.'

'No, I am all right, thank you.'

'You don't look it, Miss. You look as though you've had the fright of your life!'

'Please, take me back to Mrs Newbold. Thank you.'

Dinah rested against the comfortable seat and closed her eyes. She struggled to take in what Violet and Nellie had said about Margaret. Had her sister done those things? Margaret was wilful but would she have attacked Nellie and stolen her money? And who had she stabbed? Dinah knew she needed to face facts. Her sister wasn't at Leighton Mansions, and she wasn't at the Diamond. Where was she? She suspected Violet and Nellie were telling the truth and her sister was already on her way to America. '*America!*' She repeated the word over and over.

As promised, Clara had made cocoa and Mrs Newbold was waiting.

'Your friend, Miss Brown? I hope all was well?'

'I am afraid my friend is still unwell, Mrs Newbold.' Dinah lowered her eyes as she lied.

'Oh, I am so sorry, my dear. Now, after your cocoa you must prepare for your audition.'

Dinah stared. She had forgotten about the precious opportunity Grace had arranged. She wasn't sure she could go through with it. She needed to discover what had happened to her sister.

'What is it, Miss Brown? Your pallor is most alarming! Should I call for the doctor?'

'No, thank you. I...'

'Nerves. I have seen it many times, my dear. Let me tell you a story.'

Mrs Newbold left the room but returned quickly, clutching something to her chest. A photograph, taken from the wall outside the parlour. 'Now, do you recognise this young woman?'

Dinah peered at the photograph then smiled. 'It's you, isn't it?'

Mrs Newbold clapped her hands. 'Yes, my dear. You see, I too was young and nervous once. When I arrived in London, I didn't know anyone or anything. Mr Newbold's sister befriended me; she was a dancer at the theatre where I had my first audition. That was how I came to meet my wonderful Mr Newbold. I was very lucky.'

Dinah smiled; she knew how fortunate she was to have this opportunity. She pulled herself together. 'I'm sorry, Mrs Newbold. I was troubled by my friend's illness.'

'Very well, my dear. Now, are you ready?'

'Yes, I think so.' Dinah stood and smoothed her skirt.

As she turned to leave Mrs Newbold stopped her. 'Have you decided on your stage name?'

'Oh, can I not use my own name?'

'Sorry, my dear, I mean no offence. Dinah is a good, strong name. Isn't its meaning something to do with vindication? An admirable aspect of one's character, but a stage name should be gay and memorable, it should conjure up images of entertainment and joy.'

Dinah was grateful to her parents for giving her a strong name, one she was proud of. She pictured Grace Opal. Mrs Newbold was right,

Grace's beautiful name made Dinah smile.

'Yes, I understand. I will think about it on my way to the theatre. Thank you.'

Mrs Newbold clapped her hands again. Dinah's stage name came to her during the short cab ride to the West London Theatre on Shaftesbury Avenue. Mrs Newbold had been kind and Dinah wanted to please her. With her permission, she would borrow her Christian name, Ivy. She thought about her sister's change of name. She had struggled to understand it before, but now it was clear her sister had transformed herself when she arrived in London. Dinah yearned to know her sister was safe, but until she found her there was a way she could feel close to her. Her stage name would be Ivy Leighton. She and Mona would have the same surname again. Mrs Newbold had talked about the significance of a name, saying it could be chosen to set something right or in memory of someone. The cab drew to a halt outside the West London Theatre and Miss Ivy Leighton stepped out, ready for her audition.

Mona

The following morning, Peggy produced another travelling suit, identical to the one she had worn the previous day other than the colour. Peggy said the light grey made for a nice contrast with Mona's brown hair. The problem was the length, Peggy was a good deal shorter than Mona.

'I know! You need a long petticoat! I've got some wardrobe props with me from my last show in London, I'm sure you'll find something in there to pair with the suit.'

Peggy had her back to Mona as she rifled through her trunk but some of the contents were visible. Mona spotted glamorous dance costumes and adornments but frowned when she saw other less attractive garments. Why would Peggy have such a dowdy, ragged coat and dress? Peggy turned round, a pretty petticoat in her hand. Mona thanked her and shook her head to shift her suspicions. She saw shadows every-where. Peggy explained that soap and towels were provided each day, along with fresh water. Mona's new ensemble was an improvement on Nellie's cast-offs, but she wanted to earn her own money and go shop-ping for her own wardrobe. Her dream of owning brightly coloured dresses had been forgotten while she was in London, now she could make it real. There were lots of other purchases she would make once she had some money. Peggy had shown her a document from the ship-ping company, Peggy's voyage having been planned, not embarked upon at the last minute. Paid for, not stolen.

Mona smiled wryly as she read the document. Peggy explained it came from a set of information entitled *'What To Pack For Your Ocean Voyage.'* Warm clothing and rugs were recommended for ladies, along with two cloth suits, flannel waists, one or more silk waists and several shirt waists with necessary changes of underclothing. Also suggested, space permitting, was a gown for dinner and evening wear. The *'Ladies List Of Things Not To Be Forgotten'* included gowns, underclothing, a bathrobe, bath slippers, extra shoes and an umbrella. Mona grimaced, she had the clothes she wore, and they weren't even hers. The *'Ladies List Of Toilet Articles'* was equally alarming. It included a brush, hair-pins, toothbrush and powder, cold cream, cologne, powder, safety pins, needles and thread, buttons, hooks and eyes, manicure articles, a foun-tain pen, writing material and address book. Mona frowned. When had she last sent money home for Evie? She made a promise. As soon as she was settled in New York, she would write to Dinah. She would make up for neglecting her daughter.

After washing and dressing they made their way to the dining room. As they walked Peggy mentioned the other places they could use, the music rooms, gymnasium and lounges.

'Won't anyone question who I am? My ticket states steerage class.'

'Don't worry. Let's see if anyone wants to question me, shall we?'

No one did and Mona relaxed a little as they took their seats for breakfast. As she read the list of dishes she salivated. She couldn't remember her last decent meal. The menu included apples, oranges and grapefruit, oatmeal, salted codfish, kippered herring, beefsteak, French mutton, sausage with mustard sauce, fried Yorkshire ham, fried Wiltshire bacon, sautéed and baked potatoes, cerealine and buckwheat griddle cakes, new-laid eggs, banana pancake, coffee and tea with fresh milk or cream. Mona's head spun; she had taught herself not to think about food. Now she didn't know what to have first. Peggy took a plate full, but Mona rationed herself, worried her empty stomach wouldn't react well to a sudden influx of good food. She allowed herself some fruit, a small piece of codfish and some sautéed potatoes, all washed down with good, strong tea.

After breakfast Peggy led her to the hairdresser. Mona hesitated before removing her hat, she hadn't visited a hairdresser for years. In London, the women had helped each other with their hair, keeping it long to use as additional covering for their exposed bodies. The longer the better.

'Mona!'

'Sorry, Peggy. What did you say?'

'Your hair, darling. What are we going to do with it?'

Mona removed her hat to silence. The hairdresser busied herself with brushes and scissors before speaking. 'I think we need to tidy this up, Madam. Perhaps a style more like Miss Willow's?'

Mona kept her eyes lowered. When the hairdresser had finished, she handed Mona a mirror and Peggy smiled. Mona's hand shook as she stared at her reflection. Her bright blue eyes stared back but she didn't recognise herself. The years at the Diamond had taken their toll, her prominent cheekbones gave her face a sunken look. Her hair, now shorter and styled, was out of place beside her ravaged face. Her lip trembled and Peggy removed the mirror. 'Next step, make-up!'

Back in Peggy's warm cabin Mona's transformation continued. As well as her travelling wardrobe complete with costumes and props, Peggy had a small make-up case. She helped Mona choose colours to suit her pale skin, a rouge to emphasise what Peggy said were *'marvel-*

lous cheek-bones, darling!' a light lipstick and dusting powder to finish. 'Now, time for lunch!'

Mona hesitated. She had survived on one meagre meal a day in London.

'What is it? You look wonderful, let's go and show you off!'

'It's..., everything I've done and here I am, carrying on as if nothing happened. It's not right.'

'You were in danger. What if you hadn't escaped? We do what we need to, to survive.'

Mona frowned. What had Peggy done to survive? She tried to accept Peggy's reassurance, but images persisted. Evie in Pipewellgate. Dinah at Hampson Hall. Nellie on the floor at the club.

'Now come on, lunch is waiting.'

By the time *RMS Matilda* made her majestic way into New York Harbor five days later, 1910 was over and they had welcomed 1911. As she prepared to disembark Mona took a deep breath, the new year brought the promise of a new life in an exciting new country.

Ivy

The imposing entrance of the West London Theatre came into view. Mrs Newbold had told her to enter by the stage door at the side of the building. A group of young women were walking in front of the the-atre, and she followed them. At the stage door one of them held the door open.

'Thank you.'

'You're welcome. Are you here for the auditions?'

'Yes, are you?'

'We are!' The women chattered and giggled until a pompous voice called them to order.

'Ladies, some decorum, s'il vous plaît!' The smart man stood in front of them, hands on hips, a monocle in his left eye and a multi-col-oured cravat tied neatly at his throat. He peered down his short beak-like nose, reminding Ivy of a fledgling bird as he waved his hands around theatrically.

'Merci. I am Monsieur le Grand, your director. You may call me Monsieur. You are here to audition for my delightful production of *"Olympic Contests,"* non?' The women nodded, the irony of his name and mismatched stature threatening to reduce them to giggles once more.

'Which of you is Mees Brown?' The women giggled again at his pronunciation of *'Miss.'*

Ivy blushed and raised her hand.

'Mees Brown! Non, non, non!'

'Non, Monsieur. Maintenant je m'appelle Miss Ivy Leighton.'

Monsieur clapped his hands, apparently delighted by his newest recruit's ability to speak French and her choice of stage name. He asked Ivy to perform a short routine from a scene in '*Olympic Contests,'* to enable him to assess her skill as an actress, dancer and singer. Ivy took a deep breath and pointed her toes as she danced onto the stage using *'dainty steps with sprightly humour'* as per Monsieur's instructions. Her role was to stop a downcast man who had been rebuffed by the leading lady Miss Wilhelmina Ponsonby-Smythe, and persuade him to try again. The song was appropriate. Ivy took the man's arm and turned him back towards his intended as she started to sing.

'I am dreaming Dear of you, day by day,
Dreaming when the skies are blue. When they're grey,
When the silv'ry moonlight gleams, still I wander on in dreams,
In a land of love, it seems. Just with you.'

Monsieur clapped his hands and told her to stop. She stared; her audition was over. She returned to Chestnut Tree Avenue. As she hurried up the front steps Clara opened the door.

'Mrs Newbold is waiting for you in the parlour, Miss.'

'Thank you, Clara.'

As Ivy opened the parlour door Mrs Newbold jumped out of her chair and grabbed her hands. Her questions came out in a rush.

'It was splendid, Mrs Newbold. Monsieur was very kind. He said the range of my voice is unusual, being somewhere between contralto and mezzo-soprano. He was confident he could cast me as a singer and an actress. We start rehearsals for *"Olympic Contests"* tomorrow.'

'My dear, what marvellous news! Let's have a cocktail to celebrate!' As Mrs Newbold walked towards her drinks cabinet she turned round. 'Did you decide on a stage name? I cannot imagine Monsieur le Grand was very impressed by the notion of a Miss Brown on his bill!'

When Ivy told Mrs Newbold about her stage name her landlady gasped. She took Ivy's hands. Mrs Newbold's hands were soft and warm, and tears glistened in her eyes.

'Thank you, what a compliment. You have made me so happy!'

Ivy retired to her room to change for dinner and as she sat on her soft bed, she considered her new situation. With her position secured at the West London Theatre she could repay more of her mother's debt and continue to send money to Lizzie for Evie. She closed her eyes, she needed to know what had happened to her sister. Margaret. Mona. Were the things Violet and Nellie said true? Was Mona on her way to America? Ivy's head spun as she tried to take in everything she had learnt. She had to prove herself to Monsieur, then she could work out how to find her sister.

Mrs Newbold's guest house was geared towards accommodation for theatrical types. As a dancer herself, Mrs Newbold took great pleasure from the fun and entertainment her artistic guests brought into her home. Mrs Newbold had said that they gathered in the parlour for pre-dinner drinks. The first person Ivy met was Harold Barnes, a small man with tufty dark hair standing straight up on top of his head. He introduced himself with a bow, smiling to reveal a mouth devoid of teeth. Ivy gasped and he laughed, explaining broken teeth were an occupational hazard because his act involved catching plates in his mouth. He also juggled joints of meat, miming the act before accepting Mrs Newbold's proffered drink. Harold was regaling Ivy with a tale of a misjudged side of beef when an almighty crash came from the hallway.

Mrs Newbold laughed, and Harold spurted gin from his toothless mouth, 'it sounds as though our favourite trick cyclists are home!' A young couple fell into the parlour, laughing hysterically. Clara struggled to help them lift a large bicycle with a broken wheel. Mrs Newbold stopped laughing and sought an explanation.

'My dear Mrs Newbold, I beg your pardon most sincerely. A mishap befell Mrs Stratton and I on our way home from the theatre!'

'It looks as though you had a mishap in a hostelry to me, old chap!' Ivy thought Harold's playful comment was accurate, Mr and Mrs Stratton did appear inebriated.

'My dears, please leave the bicycle in the passageway and meet our new guest. Celia and Lawrence Stratton, please meet Miss Ivy Leighton, new and upcoming star of *"Olympic Contests"* at the West London Theatre.' Ivy blushed; it was much too early in her career to be referred to as a star. The couple came towards her, smiling and pleasantly effusive. Ivy smelt the next guest before she saw her, the well-known stage actress Bessie Bentley wafted in on a cloud of cologne.

'Miss Leighton, I am pleased to make your acquaintance. Monsieur tells me your dulcet tones will be a welcome addition to our little production. I look forward to working with you.'

Ivy was starstruck to meet the lead actress in *'Olympic Contests.'*

'Oh, Mrs Newbold, I hope you don't mind me bringing someone this evening?'

'My dear Miss Bentley, you know my rules, the more the merrier as long as they are merry!'

Bessie's dinner guest entered the parlour and Ivy's prepared greeting stuck in her throat. Ralph Lynn. Mrs Newbold made the introductions and as he approached, Ivy put down her martini and clasped her hands together to stop them shaking. This man was one of her mother's favourite actors. Theodosia had been fortunate enough to see him performing in a comedy production at a small theatre in Newcastle, and she always compared any new comedy actors to his outstanding performance. Theodosia's words to her daughters after their father died were etched into Ivy's mind.

'Mes belles, sometimes life will be hard, it will seem cruel and unfair, like now. You did not deserve to lose your papa. But remember, even in sadness you can find joy. You must look around you and search for the joy in life. You must laugh whenever you can and of course, you must sing!'

Theodosia had proceeded to sing something from *'The Mikado,'* the last show she saw with their father. The song was *'Three Little Maids From School Are We.'* As a girl, Ivy didn't understand the words, but one line stuck in her mind. It was *'filled to the brim with girlish glee'* and whenever Ivy recalled her mother's advice to search for the joy in life, she heard this line. The man standing in front of Ivy was a sensation in comedy acting and someone her mother had greatly admired. His presence reminded Ivy of the need to laugh, even in dire circumstances. Bessie explained Mr Lynn was visiting her in London after they became friends while appearing together in the British provinces. Ivy smiled to herself. The man responsible for making her mother laugh was standing in front of her with his hand outstretched, ready and waiting to make her acquaintance. As 1910 became 1911 Ivy settled into her new theatre family, at Mrs Newbold's guest house and at work.

Chapter 26

January 1911

Evie

Evie poked her shoe at the icy puddles in the back lane. As usual on Saturdays when Lizzie's customers called, Evie had been shoved outside. She peered in through the window, shivering. She knew Lizzie's routine, once all her customers had been, she would start drinking. First at home, then she would drink her wages in the Globe. Evie shuddered, she had scars from Lizzie's beating the year before, when she had taken a letter and asked Jack to read it. It was worth the bruises to know Aunt Dinah sent money for her, although she never benefited from any of it. Lizzie still received letters, but it hadn't been worth taking another one. As far as Evie knew there had never been a letter from her mother. Could Lizzie's cruel accusation that her mother had forgotten all about her be true?

Aunt Dinah's letter had stirred Evie's imagination and she disappeared into daydreams when despair threatened to overwhelm her. In her favourite she was in a beautiful house with Aunt Dinah, playing the piano and singing. She had a full tummy, clean clothes and she felt safe. She had been preparing to lose herself in this daydream the previous evening, when Lizzie and a strange man fell into the room, shouting and swearing. A smell of stale beer arrived with them, and Evie gagged.

The bright sparks in Evie's miserable existence were Nancy and Jack. In addition to sign language, Nancy had taught Evie how to read lips. This made Evie's time outside more entertaining. As well as inventing stories about Lizzie's visitors, she could sometimes make out their conversations. Most were boring and Evie could invent better herself. There was one exception, whenever the Crone called. She always had something interesting to say. Evie watched as Lizzie opened the door and the sinister woman crept inside. They pulled their shawls tighter and sat close to the meagre fire. Evie blew on her hands. The Crone faced Evie, making it easy to watch her lips. Lizzie sat with her back to the window, but Evie's interest lay in the latest gossip from Pipewellgate.

'Aye, she's knocked up again!'

Lizzie shook her head as the Crone delivered her tittle-tattle. Evie stared at her guardian's hunched back. How dare she judge anyone?

'Another little bastard in the workhouse!'

Lizzie gestured towards the window and Evie guessed she would be saying something nasty about her. As Evie started to turn away, she caught something on the Crone's cracked lips. Her name. She turned back and paid closer attention.

'Aye, he'll have her.' The Crone's malevolent lips moved as Lizzie nodded.

'Name your price, he says.'

Lizzie sniggered and the Crone cackled. Both women started to cough, and Lizzie poured the sherry. Evie moved away from the window; she had seen enough.

The following day she waited for Jack in their usual meeting place. From reading the Crone's lips she knew Lizzie was planning something bad. She bit her lip, her desperation to get away had never been stronger. She refused to buckle under the pressure of life with Lizzie and her tiny frame belied a hidden strength, but she was vulnerable to the unspoken threat against her. Where were the people who claimed to love her? Aunt Dinah had promised to come back for her, had she and Evie's mother forgotten about her and left her to rot in this slum? She bowed her head and wept as she waited in the cold street. It grew dark but she continued to wait.

Mona

As they prepared to disembark, Peggy gripped Mona's arm and pointed towards a huge sculpture on a nearby island. 'Isn't it amazing? I never tire of seeing it.'

To herself, Mona thanked her mother. Theodosia had told her daughters the story; the statue was a gift from the people of France to the people of America. Mona had never imagined she would see it and now, as the Roman goddess of liberty held her torch aloft, her heart thudded in her chest. The Statue of Liberty. Her liberty. She was free. Free from being degraded at the Diamond, free from men who took pleasure in humiliating women, free from the desolation of Gateshead. She looked at Peggy, imagining how her crossing might have been if they hadn't met. Now Peggy had given her the opportunity of a life-time, the chance of a job at the Paradise Theatre.

'Look. Do you want to have your picture taken?' The photographer was positioned to capture passengers as they disembarked.

'I'm not sure, Peggy.' Mona had eaten well during the journey and her new shorter hairstyle and make-up had improved her appearance, but she hesitated. Peggy handed her a small compact.

'You're beautiful. A bit scrawny, but beautiful. Go on, send a pic-ture to your girl.'

Mona opened the compact. The Diamond was reflected in her bright blue eyes.

'Be a dancer and an actress! Look straight into the camera, pose like a ballerina, raise your hand and wave! Wave as if your girl is standing on the dock waiting to meet you!'

Peggy pushed Mona towards the photographer. She took a deep breath. She had to do this, for Evie. She spotted a young girl, waiting on the dock with an elderly couple. She waved as the photographer pre-pared his camera. The girl raised her eyebrows but waved back. Mona smiled. Peggy paid the photographer and gave the man her address in New York.

'When it arrives, you can sign it and send it to your girl.'

Mona murmured; she would see what it looked like first.

As they prepared to disembark Mona's eyes darted around. Peggy touched her arm.

'Just remember what I said.'

Mona knew Peggy's tiny frame belied a fierce nature, but she hesitated. She didn't want to discover whether Peggy could protect her, if they met the people she had joined the ship with. What if they saw the woman who had recognised her, and she gave Mona's secret away? And what about the other story Peggy had told her? Mona had arrived in America with no previous experience of travelling to another country and no knowledge of immigration procedures. A few days earlier Peggy had explained what happened to steerage passengers. She said they were separated from the other passengers and taken by small steamboats to somewhere called Ellis Island. They underwent a medical examination where doctors checked for signs of illness including eye disease, skin disorders and heart trouble. If they passed the examination, they were filtered into long lines to be interviewed by immigration inspectors. Peggy regaled a story of a passenger who answered the inspector's questions only to learn information about her had been sent to Ellis Island. As a result, she was detained and denied entry to America. Mona was horrified.

'That will happen to me! They will discover I'm not Nellie Pilkington!'

'No, they won't. Sorry, Mona. I didn't mean to frighten you.'

'But I will have to disembark as a steerage passenger! I'll be sent to Ellis Island!' Mona knew the questions would result in her being sent back to England.

'No, you won't. Follow me and don't speak to anyone.'

Mona's legs shook as she followed Peggy down the gangplank. A uniformed man stopped each passenger at the bottom. He inspected their tickets and, in some cases, looked through their bags. Mona clutched Theodosia's carpet bag to her chest. Peggy tipped her pretty tricorne hat in the man's direction, and he nodded. Peggy moved past him, and Mona followed.

'This way.' Peggy hurried away from the ship towards a horse-drawn trolley car. She handed their bags to an attendant and helped Mona inside.

'We're here, Mona. You've arrived in New York!'

Mona frowned as images from the voyage flashed in her mind. Peggy talking to a man in an immaculate dinner suit, heads close together then the man shrugging Peggy's hand away as if her touch had burned him. The ragged clothes in her trunk. And Peggy's mysterious ability to allow them to disembark from the ship, no questions asked. Why were they allowed to walk off the ship without having their documents checked? During the voyage Peggy had been a regular in the cocktail bar, how often did those visits involve furtive conversations with wealthy gentlemen? Peggy also hung around outside the smoking room where men travelling in first class retired after dinner to drink, talk and play games. Peggy stank of cigar smoke when she returned to their cabin.

Another memory surfaced. Her mother's story of her ferry crossing from Calais to Dover. Theodosia had written about Solomon Zettler's medical bag and his exchange with the man when they left the ferry. He had bribed the man to allow them to disembark without question or inspection. Had Peggy bribed someone in the same way?

Peggy drew close and whispered.

'Don't worry, Mona. Let's put it this way, I know things about important people. Things those people wouldn't want other people to know. Secrets are valuable.' Mona smiled to hide her disappointment. Her new friend wasn't everything she seemed.

Ivy

Ivy lay in bed, stretching. She smiled. She longed to tell her mother about her conversations with Bessie Bentley and Ralph Lynn. The kind actress had insisted Ivy sit between them, given she didn't know anyone at dinner very well. The table was a hive of activity and entertainment,

Mrs Newbold's residents never forgot they were performers. They tried to out-do one another with comic tales and antics throughout each delicious course and numerous bottles of wine.

At first, she found it difficult to adjust to her new routine. But as she settled into life at Mrs Newbold's, that changed. It suited her to eat a leisurely breakfast, then be busy from late morning until whatever time Mrs Newbold decreed dinner was over. One thing tempered her happiness, images of her niece. London grew colder in January, and she hoped Lizzie was keeping a good fire and feeding Evie properly. As for her sister, Ivy had no idea about the weather in New York.

The West London Theatre wasn't the biggest theatre on Shaftesbury Avenue, but it had a reputation as one of the best. When Ivy had arrived for her audition, she hurried inside, wanting it to be over. Following their auditions Monsieur had allowed his performers to familiarise themselves with the inside of the building. She gasped as she stepped into the large foyer. Cherubs and angels gazed at her from the ornate ceiling. The exuberant design flowed with an abundance of curves and undulations, like waves on the ocean. The centrepiece was a grand staircase leading to the upper levels. She smiled as she looked down from the elegant balcony hanging out over the dress circle. When she left, she stood on the opposite side of the street, marvelling at the splendour of the entrance. The stone portico facade had six huge temple-style pillars and ornate stonework, forming a formidable entrance for theatregoers. Once rehearsals for 'Olympic Contests' began, her nerves disappeared. She learnt her lyrics easily and made friends among the other performers. She should have been happy but dark images of Evie and Mona arrived at all hours of the day and night. She woke in a cold sweat, disorientated and fearful, until her night terrors abated. During rehearsals she was beset by images of her sister at the Diamond. And something one of the women there had said continued to niggle. She tried to push it away, but it refused to leave, '...after she stabbed him.' Who had her sister stabbed? She needed to get to America and find out what had happened.

245

'Mees Leighton? Are you ready?'

'Oh, excusez-moi, Monsieur!'

'Quick, quick! We open tomorrow! Mon Dieu! This is our final rehearsal and our first performance of my *"Olympic Contests"* production is tomorrow! Positions everyone, please!'

Weeks of rehearsals had passed by in the blink of an eye. Now Ivy took her position and prepared to sing in their final rehearsal. The story behind the production concentrated on the 1908 Summer Olympics in London, when Britain topped the medals table. Politicians, authors, artists and performers wasted no time in putting their capital centre-stage however they could. Monsieur had recognised that interest in Britain's achievements remained strong. The foundation of his story had nothing to do with sport and everything to do with love. The contest in question sought to discover which of her many suitors would win the hand of Bessie's formidable character, Miss Wilhelmina Ponsonby-Smythe. Ivy had a relatively small part, but Monsieur had promised there would be further productions and greater parts for her, if *'Olympic Contests'* was well received.

The following evening, she waited for her cue. She positioned her parasol at right-angles to her pretty bonnet, festooned with summer flowers, as she tapped her foot to the music. As the previous number ended and Bessie's character brushed off yet another suitor, Ivy made her entrance. She held her head high and pointed her toes as she danced onto the stage. As she reached the chorus, she handed the man over to Wilhelmina, encouraging him to sing.

'Let me call you Sweetheart, I'm in love with you,
Let me hear you whisper that you love me too.'

Ivy's light-hearted dance steps took her slowly backwards as the man serenaded Wilhelmina. She covered her face with the parasol as she discreetly left the stage, smiling at the ripple of applause. Adrenaline flowed through her veins. At the end of the show, the curtain flew open to thunderous applause, and she bowed with her fellow performers. Monsieur joined them for their second encore and as she glanced along the row, she made eye contact with the funny little Frenchman. His tears made her heart swell with pride. As the company took their well-deserved bows, she spotted Mrs Newbold in the audience. The previous day she had confided in her landlady that she was nervous about her first real stage performance.

'A little nervousness can be a good thing, my dear. You have worked hard at rehearsals, and I have heard you practising in your room many times. I am sure you will be fine.'

Mrs Newbold waited backstage.

'My dear, you sang beautifully, like a nightingale!'

'Thank you. I'm pleased the first performance is over, but I did enjoy it.'

'I should think so Mees Leighton, you were an absolute triumph! Bravo tout le monde! Well done everyone!' Monsieur strode around like a small, preening French peacock. Ivy beamed, delighted to have played a small part in his successful production. Mrs Newbold clapped her hands.

'Let's all go back to Chestnut Tree Avenue for a celebration!'

Ivy smiled; every evening was a celebration at Mrs Newbold's.

Mona

Mona looked out of the trolley car and smiled. At last, her horizons were expanding. She pictured Gateshead and Newcastle. Both were relatively small, and it hadn't taken them long, even when she and Dinah were little, to see everywhere. Despite London's size, she hadn't seen much of the capital beyond the Diamond and the flea-ridden excuse for a lodging house Solomon Zettler used for his dancers. Here in New York, she wanted to see everything. She stared open-mouthed at the rows of straight narrow streets, bordered on both sides by buildings reaching into the sky. She had expected bright lights and music but as the trolley-car made its way to Broadway, snow blanketed everything. Fat flakes fell onto the icy streets. The horses' breath blew into the cold air as they ploughed on through the freezing conditions. A cacophony of noise accompanied them, the clang of trolley-cars in front and behind, the ding of the bell when people got off and the shouts of street sellers trying to catch the last of the day's business. Peggy put her gloved hand through Mona's arm.

'Don't worry, it isn't always this cold!' Peggy's breath floated around them like icy clouds.

Mona's teeth chattered a tune. She stamped her frozen feet on the damp floor. 'But it *is* cold, Peggy. Gateshead is cold in the winter, but this is colder than anything I ever knew at home.'

Peggy reassured her they would arrive at Broadway soon. Peggy hadn't said anything about where she stayed when she worked in New York and Mona frowned as the trolley-car moved through the dark streets. What if Peggy stayed somewhere like Solomon Zettler's lodging house? She shook herself. Did she imagine immaculately groomed Peggy, resplendent in her fur coat, muffler, hat and high heeled ankle boots, would stay anywhere like that? She bit her bottom lip as she considered Peggy's situation. Peggy turned and she flushed. Peggy had helped her more than anyone else in her life, was this how she repaid her? She hoped the smile hid her suspicions.

Peggy had done her best to clothe Mona, but her slight build meant Mona's clothes were barely big enough. She had given her two pairs of embroidered silk stockings and lent her a travelling coat which afforded some extra warmth. Peggy said their first outing would be to buy Mona a new wardrobe, suitable for a New York winter. Mona objected, saying she couldn't repay Peggy, but the other woman waved her concerns away with a manicured hand.

'Hush. When you're as wealthy as me, then you can repay me!'

Mona promised she would. Without Peggy, her duplicity would have been discovered and she would be on her way back to England and an uncertain fate.

'Look, we're almost there! The next block is Broadway!'

She stared out at the snow-covered street, identical to many other snow-covered streets they had already passed. As dusk fell the gloom obscured the view. Until Peggy pointed.

'Look, Mona! The Paradise! The most wonderful, majestic theatre in the world!'

She craned her neck for a better look and despite the falling snow made out the outline of a building and an expanse of dazzling bright lights. She blinked as the trolley car drew to a halt in front of the theatre and the Paradise came into full view. She gasped; it wasn't anything like the Diamond. It sparkled, and unlike the Diamond, this theatre was well-named. Peggy was in full-flow and Mona caught snippets as she gazed at the theatre. The Paradise was built in the Beaux Arts French style, the classical design demanded perfect symmetry, arched windows and doors and a grand entrance. Mona's eyes sought the sculptures. The Paradise was adorned with the most beautiful sculptural decoration, all coordinated along a particular theme. Stonework images of the Roman goddesses Venus and Diana sat proudly above the theatre's grand entrance. Diana – the goddess of the hunt and nature. How like Dinah. With a heavy heart Mona pictured her sister. She lowered her head, realising how little thought she had given to Dinah's situation at Hampson Hall. All she had thought about in London was survival. An image of Solomon Zettler and Nellie pushed its way past the beauty of the Paradise. With everything she had done to get to America, she wasn't sure she could face Dinah again. She returned her attention to the theatre.

'Oh, Peggy. What a majestic building!'

'Isn't it? I wanted you to see it. Now we need to go to my apartment and get warmed up.'

'You have an apartment?' Mona knew a little of Parisian apartments from her mother but had never imagined she would set foot in one, in Paris or anywhere else.

'Yes! And it's not far!'

Peggy rapped on the wooden trolley car and gave the address to the attendant. The horses took off through the snow. They drew to a halt outside an elegant apartment building. Peggy said the intricate facade was glazed terracotta and the delicate Gothic details and French Renaissance styling, all light grey, were the height of New York fashion. It was, Peggy stated, a most desirous place to live. Mona smiled, until recently she had lived in a flea-ridden lodging house. Now she was about to enter a most desirous New York apartment building. They stepped onto the snowy street and the attendant helped with their luggage. Mona had her mother's carpet bag, inside were clothes Peggy had lent or given her. She jumped as a plume of hot steam rose from a grate in the path.

Peggy laughed. 'You'll get used to it! Come on, you'll catch your death out here!' Peggy hurried to the front entrance of the apartment building where a smart, liveried doorman stepped out.

'Miss Willow! Welcome back! It sure is great to see you again!'

'Thank you, Alberto. This is my friend, Miss Leighton. She will be staying with me.'

'Of course, Miss Willow. You ladies let me know if you need anything.'

Mona smiled at the man's American drawl. It was nothing like the Geordie accents of home or the cut-glass English Dinah would hear at Hampson Hall. Alberto's swarthy, weather-beaten good looks told of long hours outside in New York's extreme seasons. He held the door open, and the thick warmth hit her as she entered the building. Peggy took her arm and Alberto hurried past them.

'Let me call the elevator for you, Miss Willow.'

Mona raised her eyebrows as Alberto pressed a button on the wall next to a metal door.

'You'll see, it's the most fabulous thing! Especially after a hard night at the theatre!' Peggy laughed and Alberto stood to one side as the mysterious button set a noisy mechanism in motion.

'Whatever is it?'

Peggy laughed again. 'An electric elevator!'

'A what?'

Alberto smiled and looked towards the source of the noise.

'Miss Leighton, let me explain. The noise you hear is an electric motor which powers the elevator car. I press the button to call the car to our floor and when it arrives it knows to stop here.'

'How on earth does an electric mechanism know where we are?'

Alberto pointed towards the button on the wall. 'There is a button on each floor, Miss Leighton. The elevator recognises each one as belonging to a particular floor in the building.'

'Isn't it amazing?' Peggy clapped her hands as the noise grew louder.

Mona jumped as a loud clang signalled the arrival of the mysterious elevator. Alberto moved forward and pulled the metal handle sideways to open the door.

'Ladies, your elevator awaits.'

Peggy stepped inside the strange metal box, but Mona hesitated.

'It's all right, my dear. It's not dangerous.'

She followed nervously, jumping as Alberto closed the door. Peggy's petite gloved finger pressed one of several buttons set into the inside wall of the elevator. Mona jumped again when the mysterious contraption started to move upwards.

'Peggy, whatever in the world is this?'

'The future my dear Mona, this is the future.' Peggy smiled as the elevator made its clunky, noisy way towards her apartment. As much as Peggy reassured her, Mona gripped the rail inside the elevator and held her breath until they clanged to a halt on the tenth floor.

Chapter 27

Ivy

The morning after Ivy's first performance in '*Olympic Contests*,' breakfast at Mrs Newbold's was later than usual. She smiled as she made her way downstairs, recalling the fabulous celebrations when they returned from the theatre. She and Bessie had reprised their roles, over and over again, until Harold fell asleep at the table and Mrs Newbold suggested it was time for bed.

Clara had done a marvellous job tidying up, all traces of the party were gone. Ivy admired the young maid, she worked tirelessly behind the scenes to ensure Mrs Newbold's residents were well-fed and she kept the large town house as clean as a whistle. She also volunteered at a nearby mission for the homeless, helping to gather second-hand clothes and shoes for needy children. Mrs Newbold had mentioned that Clara was walking out with a young coachman and Ivy decided to buy her something to wear on one such occasion, to show her appreciation for everything she did. Clara didn't follow the latest fashions and she kept her sleek dark hair unfashionably short, the skilful cut reaching to the nape of her neck. Ivy admired Clara's commitment to the suffrage cause and women's struggle for the vote, the young woman proudly wore a small tricoloured rosette on her outdoor coat. She eschewed the popular fashion of over-sized hats staked with plumes of feathers, bows, flowers, birds, lace and tulle. Not for Clara the fussy '*bird's nests*,' instead she favoured the small Tudor beret as an evening hat. Ivy decided to buy Clara a beret in plush black velvet and silk and adorn it with purple, white and green ribbons, the colours of the suffrage movement. As she pictured Clara in the beret, an image of Ruby's freckled face appeared. She smiled, resolving to write to her friend. Mrs Newbold greeted Ivy with her usual enthusiasm.

'Good morning my dear, or is it good afternoon? Come, you need coffee and breakfast!'

Ivy ate everything Clara put in front of her.

'Now, my dear, you must read your marvellous reviews!'

The magazines and newspapers were spread out in front of Mrs Newbold. Ivy had been so busy rehearsing she had forgotten about the possibility of anyone writing about Monsieur's new production. Mrs Newbold pointed towards a copy of the '*Play Pictorial*,' a specialist magazine which reviewed and published illustrated features about West End plays and musicals.

'See what they say about you in here, my dear! There's a delightful little sketch too!'

Ivy hesitated. It was one thing to perform, but another to have a stranger review the performance. She wasn't sure she would ever become accustomed to the scrutiny. Mrs Newbold pushed the '*Play Pictorial*' towards her. Ivy read the few short lines.

'Miss Bessie Bentley provoked uproarious laughter, dancing and singing in her character of Miss Wilhelmina Ponsonby-Smythe. Miss Ivy Leighton also had some attractive numbers and is a girl new to the West End stage to take close notice of.'

In the tiny sketch, Ivy made out the figure of Bessie. She was just visible behind Bessie; mouth open wide and singing. As Mrs Newbold placed the other magazines and newspapers in front of her and Clara poured more coffee, Ivy considered her new situation. She would always be grateful to Master Walter and Grace Opal for arranging her journey to London, her audition at the West London Theatre and her introduction to Mrs Newbold. She could have relaxed if not for the dark clouds hovering on the horizon. She longed to visit Evie, but Monsieur had advised his performers they wouldn't have a day off for quite some time.

'My dear, what is it? I thought you would be happy, but you look close to tears.'

'Oh Mrs Newbold, I am sorry. The reviews are most welcome, I assure you.'

'Then what is troubling you?'

Ivy liked Mrs Newbold, but she wasn't ready to unburden herself. She had to focus on repaying Aunt Agatha and sending whatever money she could to Lizzie. On her first day off she would visit Evie. Then, she would work out how to find her sister in America.

'Oh, I'm just a little tired and overwhelmed by everything. I'm sorry.'

'No need to apologise, my dear. A little nervous exhaustion is understandable. As long as you are all right. Now, you had better get ready. Don't you have a matinee performance?'

'Yes, I do!'

She thanked Clara for her meal and headed to her room to prepare for her second performance of *'Olympic Contests.'* Anything else would have to wait, for now. Over the following months *'Olympic Contests'* continued to play to sell-out audiences and the reviews were for the most part very favourable. She settled into life at Chestnut Tree Avenue and soon learnt Mrs Newbold celebrated both happy and sad occasions with equal amounts of enthusiasm and martini. The death and funeral of Edward VII, the succession of George V and, after a telegram was sent to the ship's captain, the arrest of the notorious wife murderer Dr Crippen aboard the *SS Montrose*.

Mona

When the elevator arrived at the tenth floor Mona stepped out, her legs shaking from the unfamiliar mode of transport. Peggy walked ahead and stopped at the door to her apartment.

'I want you to make yourself comfortable here. This is a new start for you.'

'Thank you, Peggy.' She would never forget Louis's betrayal, the Diamond or the manner of her leaving London. But she intended to make the most of the opportunity Peggy had given her. Inside the apartment Peggy clapped her hands. 'Do you like it?'

'It's beautiful. Was it like this when you moved in?'

'Oh no, I've had it decorated. And each room is different, come and see!'

Peggy led her through the apartment, revelling in the layout. There were two bedrooms, a bathroom, a small entertaining space, a living room, dining room and kitchen. She explained her use of a variety of different styles to decorate and furnish each room.

'I'd never had a place to call home before and I didn't know what I liked best!'

Peggy's joy rubbed off as she showed Mona the living room. Mona's feet sank into the deep pile of the soft wool carpet, and she admired the velvet upholstery, perfectly coordinated with the opulent curtains and luxurious tapestries on the walls. She trailed a gloved hand over the shining lacquer finish on an elegant dresser, stopping suddenly at her reflection. The woman bore no resemblance to Margaret Patricia Brown, the poor unmarried mother from Gateshead. This woman was Miss Mona Leighton, the dancer, of New York City. She smiled as she stepped onto the black and white geometric floor tiles in the dining room. The room's centrepiece was a walnut dining set with a large, rectangular table and six dining chairs. She ran her hand along one of the chairs, admiring the sleek lines and carved floral finials. Peggy stroked one of the cushioned chairs.

'It's called *'The 'Strawberry Thief.'*

Against a blue background, green strawberry plants with bright red berries were adorned by beautiful gold thrushes. Peggy said the artist took inspiration from song thrushes he found stealing fruit in his Oxfordshire garden. As Peggy spoke, an image of Theodosia's parlour pushed its way into Mona's mind. There was one stark difference. Every piece of sparkling china and glass in Peggy's dining room was new.

Peggy would never repair a broken plate or cup and saucer. Peggy said she had chosen the china set for its name, *'English Rose.'* Each delicate item was a gentle speckled grey, painted with small pink roses and green leaves. As they left the dining room, Peggy reached towards a small stained leaded glass lamp at the end of the dresser. Tiny blue dragonflies decorated the beautiful Tiffany lamp and when Peggy pulled the ornate metal cord a gentle, muted light bathed the room.

Peggy opened another door. The elegant oak bed matched the wardrobe and dressing table. Mona stroked the white lace bedspread embroidered with small pink roses, longing to be wrapped in the comforting embrace of the luxurious fabric. A small stool sat in front of the dressing table. She imagined using all three mirrors to examine her hair from every angle. Peggy opened an adjoining door; the smaller bedroom was identical.

'You can make yourself comfortable soon, but I have one more room to show you!'

Peggy flung a door open, exclaiming, 'this is my small entertaining space!'

While the space was small compared to the other rooms, its character was anything but. Peggy clapped her hands.

'I modelled it on a music hall, isn't it fabulous?'

Mona's eyes darted around the room. Her heart thumped.

'Whatever is it? Don't you like my music room?'

'I'm sorry, Peggy.'

Peggy moved closer. 'We'll have fun here, I promise.'

Mona nodded but the dread persisted.

'Don't you think you could enjoy yourself in this delightful room?'

Mona's eyes scanned the room, noticing the small faux stage and elaborate beaded curtains. A baby grand piano sat to the side of the stage and several chairs were laid out, ready for an audience. She shook her head; it wasn't anything like the Diamond. She changed the subject.

'Where did you get your ideas for the designs? I wouldn't know where to start.'

'Wait until you get to the Paradise, then you'll understand. You'll meet dancers, singers and performers from all over the world! There's a French actress on the bill. She's one of the most beautiful women I've ever met, and she knows all about French design.'

'But how does it all get here?'

Peggy tapped a finger against her nose.

'Your apartment is beautiful, Peggy.' Mona stopped, unable to ask the burning question.

'You want to know how I afford it all, don't you?'

Mona's cheeks reddened. Peggy explained that after her father died, she resolved to earn as much as possible, to have the best of everything. Never again would anyone look down at her.

'Now, we need to get cleaned up before I ask one of the building's maids to bring us a light supper. Tomorrow we're going shopping for your new wardrobe!'

Peggy gave a quick nod before leading her back to the living room. As she turned away, Mona caught something in Peggy's face. If her time at the Diamond had taught her anything, it was to know when someone was hiding something.

Chapter 28

Ivy

Soon after Ivy arrived in London, Bessie took her to Oxford Street. They visited the large department store that had taken London by storm when it opened in March 1909. Standing outside Selfridges, Ivy hesitated. She licked her lips, but her mouth was dry. She inspected her coat and shoes. Bessie grabbed her arm. As she followed her friend through the doors she stopped and stared, picturing the Gateshead shops she had visited with her mother. She went there after Theodosia died, searching for the cheapest pieces of meat or fish and fruit and vegetables. And now she was in Selfridges of Oxford Street. As they passed gleaming glass drawers displaying ladies leather gloves a hum of excitement and hushed whispers started up.

'Look Ivy, it's him!' Bessie grabbed her arm.

'Who?' Ivy looked around, frowning.

'Him! Harry Gordon Selfridge! Oh Ivy, he's as handsome as his picture!'

Amidst the crowd, Ivy spotted the good-looking, debonair man causing the commotion. She was impressed by what Clara had said about his attitude towards the suffrage movement. He advertised in publications run by the activists and flew the WSPU flag above his store. Bessie insisted on visiting each floor and Ivy was surprised to find the staff were helpful, not intimidating. No one sniffed or looked down their nose at her and with this realisation she relaxed and enjoyed choosing her new wardrobe. To Bessie's consternation Ivy bought practical items. A day dress, an overcoat, a pair of shoes, a hat, a pair of gloves, stockings and undergarments. As they made their way towards the cafe Bessie pointed at a particularly colourful part of the store.

'Look Ivy, evening gowns!'

Ivy spotted satins and silks and for a moment, was tempted. Right at the front of the display hung a full-length evening gown of delicate French silk. Its burnished gold shades, the perfect colour for her complexion, shimmered in the light streaming in through the windows. She shook her head as a picture formed in her mind. Evie in Pipewellgate. How could she waste money on a dress when her niece needed every penny she could spare?

'No, Bessie. I don't think so.'

Bessie pursed her lips but shrugged. They made their way to the elegant roof terrace cafe. As the waiter showed them to their table, Bessie pointed out the mini golf course and all-girl gun club.

'We should try it next time we visit, don't you think?'

Ivy wasn't sure but agreed, not wishing to dampen her new friend's enthusiasm any further.

After a few months Monsieur started preparing for his next production. He advised his performers it would be his London swansong, because he intended to return to Paris. As he described the premise of the production, they stood in silence, aghast at the scale of the diminutive Frenchman's vision. The production, based on writings of a Parisian friend of Monsieur's, concentrated on a period during *'La Belle Époque.'* It brought to life the optimism of the era through elaborate dance routines and uplifting, colourful songs. There was much to celebrate about *'La Belle Époque,'* Monsieur enthused. Not least the peace and cultural developments but more than anything else, the love and beauty of the time. The cheerful story celebrated love and beauty in all its forms. Ivy knew a little of *'La Belle Époque,'* and the idea of a stage production celebrating everything her mother adored about Paris was perfect. She closed her eyes, hoping she would be cast in the masterpiece. Someone asked Monsieur what the new production would be called.

'Ah, bien sûr. Our new theatrical delight will be entitled "*Toujours Belle!*"'

Ivy smiled, *'always beautiful'* was a fitting tribute to the city her mother adored. The months passed quickly with a gruelling schedule of performances and little time off. Each week Ivy sent money to Lizzie and Aunt Agatha. She also tried to save for her trip to America. She didn't need much for herself. Her performance schedule left little time or energy for socialising. The loss of her family never left her, and she yearned for her mother, wishing she had lived long enough to see her elder daughter performing on the London stage. There was so much she longed to tell her mother, including the activities of the suffrage movement. Clara had told her about the Mud March, the demonstration in 1907 where more than three thousand women marched from Hyde Park Corner to the Strand in support of the women's suffrage movement. Clara said she returned to Chestnut Tree Avenue drenched to the skin from the day's incessant rain, but delirious with excitement. Ivy smiled sadly; Theodosia would have loved Clara.

Mona

Mona slept a dreamless sleep, only waking when Peggy tapped on her bedroom door.

'Wakey, wakey!'

She stretched and yawned, taking in her surroundings. It was real, she was in New York, in her own bedroom in Peggy's spectacular apartment.

'What time is it?'

'Gone ten. We need to get a move on, we've got things to do after breakfast!'

She dressed quickly. A maid had set the table for breakfast, and she stared at the array of delicious food, realising she was ravenous.

Peggy laughed, 'would Madam like some English breakfast tea or some coffee, or "*corfee*," as the Americans call it?' Mona joined in with her laughter, relaxing. 'I'll have "*corfee*," please!'

As Peggy poured the hot, brown liquid from an ornate silver jug she whispered, 'and after breakfast, I've got a surprise for you!' After a short trolley-car journey, they arrived at the Paradise. 'But I thought my audition wasn't until tomorrow?' Nerves gripped Mona, she wasn't prepared for her audition, and she wasn't dressed for it. Peggy had promised to take her shopping for a new wardrobe before introducing her to the director. Had her friend forgotten?

'No, it is tomorrow but I want you to see the inside of where you'll be working. Last night you saw the outside of the Paradise. You need to see this, trust me.'

Mona's concern persisted. 'You said where I'll be working. You're assuming they'll hire me.'

'Of course they'll hire you! Come on, let's look around, then we're going shopping.'

Peggy walked around to the side of the building, and they entered the theatre by the stage door. Inside she took Mona's hand and led her along a bright corridor, explaining she was taking her to the entrance hall, but from the inside. Peggy stopped when she reached a door at the end of the corridor. She touched the door handle then paused.

'Ready?'

'Yes, I think so.' But Mona wasn't prepared for the sight awaiting her when Peggy turned the door handle. Like the outside of the theatre, the interior of the Paradise took her breath away. The door they exited the corridor through was to the side and underneath an elaborate staircase, hidden to audience members as they entered the magnificent lobby. Peggy told Mona to close her eyes then led her to the doors at the front entrance of the theatre. She put her hands on her friend's shoulders and turned her around to face the impressive staircase.

'Imagine you've come up the steps and in through the grand entrance. This is the view you see on entering the Paradise. Now, open your eyes.'

Mona gasped. Paintings and plants adorned the marble lobby. She blinked at the sparkled mosaic pattern on the floor and ran her hand along the sleek walnut and cherry-wood staircase. She reached out towards the wall but stopped, her hand hanging in mid-air. Peggy nodded and she caressed the silk wallpaper. Her eyes ascended the ornate staircase, following the beautifully sculpted images of Venus and Diana. Peggy said there were three levels, each as beautiful.

'You'll see more of it when you come for your audition tomorrow but now, we need to take you shopping. You're in desperate need of a new wardrobe!'

As soon as they were inside a trolley-car, Peggy started talking.

'You'll be amazed by the stores here! I know you didn't make it to Oxford Street or Selfridges in London, but New York is so much better!'

Peggy told her about the first store in New York to employ a female executive. Margaret Getchell started work as an entry-level clerk but due to her hard work and quick mathematical mind, soon gained promotion to be the store's bookkeeper. Before long she was training new cash girls and recommending trends to Rowland H. Macy, the store's founder. On her recommendations the store's range of goods expanded to draw in more customers. She was the inspiration behind the installation of a marble and nickel-plated soda fountain at the back of the store, meaning thirsty customers had to walk past aisles of merchandise before quenching their thirst.

'A genius idea,' according to Peggy.

The woman's innovations earned her promotion to store superintendent at just 26. Her influence, Peggy stated, transformed Macy's into the first modern department store in America.

'And then there's Ladies Mile, where we're going!'

Mona's head spun as Peggy talked about New York's chic emporiums and boutiques. Ladies Mile was *the* place to shop, with a choice of places to eat or drink, where unaccompanied ladies were welcome. Peggy's favourite was Mallard's Luncheon Restaurant and Bonbon Store. They used the best vanilla cocoa beans; it was like nothing Peggy had ever tasted before. Mona licked her lips, remembering the cocoa at home. She found her voice.

'Peggy, where are we going for my new wardrobe?'

'Bloomingdale's! They sell all the latest European fashions!'

As the trolley-car bumped along the Manhattan streets Mona pictured Gateshead. Theodosia had bartered with shopkeepers and stallholders in the grim streets to ensure they ate decent food. Thanks to her skills as a seamstress, they always had beautiful hand-made clothes. Mona prayed Lizzie was doing right by Evie, feeding and clothing her well.

'Look Mona, this is Bloomingdale's!'

Mona stepped from the trolley-car. Without Peggy, she wouldn't have dared to set foot inside the huge, imposing building. She would be singled out as an imposter, someone with no business in a place like Bloomingdale's. Peggy walked confidently towards the entrance. Mona straightened her shoulders and followed. Later, they giggled as they carried their purchases back to Peggy's apartment. They were balancing their various bags and boxes when Alberto appeared.

'Ladies, let me help you with those bags.'

'Thank you, Alberto, we got a bit carried away!' Peggy handed her bags over and Mona copied her friend, eager to be rid of a cumbersome hatbox.

'You should have caught a trolley-car Miss, it's cold on the streets.'

'We did, but I asked to be dropped before our block. I wanted to show Mona more of New York! Silly me, we're freezing!' Peggy blew on her gloved hands as Alberto juggled their bags and held the door open. Mona rushed to the elevator, eager to demonstrate her new-found confidence in the contraption. Inside Peggy's apartment Mona kicked off her shoes and collapsed into an armchair.

'I'm not sure I'll ever get used to the weather here, Peggy.'

'Oh, like you weren't sure you'd ever get used to the elevator? Look at you now! It's as if you've lived here for months, not a couple of days!'

The next day Peggy took Mona for her audition. Following their shopping trip to Bloomingdale's and a delicious afternoon tea with vanilla cocoa at Mallard's, Mona was a different person when she arrived at the Paradise. As she entered the stage door, she adjusted her new hat and smoothed her smart new coat. She glanced at Peggy, suddenly nervous.

'You look fabulous, darling!'

She took a deep breath, telling herself it wasn't anything like the Diamond. She walked into the Paradise with her head high. Peggy led her to the director's office. She knocked and a deep booming voice with the familiar American drawl shouted.

'Enter if you dare!'

Mona took a step back and Peggy laughed. 'Don't worry darling, he doesn't bite!'

Mona froze, picturing Solomon Zettler and his henchmen. If she had been alone, she would have fled. But Peggy was already in the room and a huge, bear-like man had emerged from behind an equally large desk. He removed a fat cigar from his lips and laughed as he threw his massive arms around Peggy. Mona's petite friend almost disappeared in the man's massive bear-hug.

'Peggy Willow, as I live and breathe! Where the hell have you been, girl?'

'London, darling! You know I've been in London!'

'And have you been up to your usual tricks?'

Mona pretended not to notice the exchange between Peggy and the man, but there was no mistaking her friend's expression. Peggy put a finger to her lips and Marv was silenced. His eyes settled on Mona. She shrunk back towards the wall, trying to get as close to the door as possible.

'And who's this delightful young lady you've found on your travels?'

'Miss Mona Leighton, meet Mr Marvin Marvel, director extraordinaire of the Paradise!'

'Well, I'm mighty pleased to make your acquaintance, Miss Mona Leighton.'

'How do you do, Mr Marvel?'

Mona jumped at the man's booming laugh. 'That accent! It gets me every time! Now, what is it you do, Miss Leighton? Do you sing, dance or act? Or all three like Peggy here?'

'Well, I...'

'Mona had ballet tuition, Marv. She knows all the traditional ballet positions and has a fabulous ear for music. Pick any piece and ask her to dance, you'll soon see what she can do.'

'Ok, let's do it. Follow me, Mona.'

'What, now?'

'Yup, no time like the present!'

Peggy rushed her into a dressing room, found a tunic and ballet shoes and hurried her towards the stage. Mona held back, hidden behind the curtain. The dramatic music started, and she stirred. Marv had asked the pianist to play something Mona could demonstrate traditional ballet positions to, he chose a piece from 'Swan Lake.' She breathed a huge sigh of relief; she could dance to this music in her sleep. She could tell this story with her body. She glided out onto the stage, arms outstretched, toes pointed, the embodiment of Odette, the Black Swan. Her brisk, allegro steps were smooth and precise. Her elegant pirouette was followed by an elaborate jeté and as she lowered her front leg, she extended her arms and lifted her elbows. Her graceful swan arms took her higher and higher until the last one when she affected a demi-pointe. On the downward wing beat of her arms she bent low and ended with her arms outstretched in front, her head prone. Marv nodded as she left the stage, saying she had a place in the chorus of his current production and to return for rehearsals the next day. Mona laughed as she embraced Peggy.

'I'm so grateful, Peggy. I have a beautiful room in your splendid apartment and now I have a job. A proper job, with proper wages, dancing on the stage in New York!'

'You're a good dancer, you deserve it!'

'But without you, I don't know where I would be.'

'Well, the next time we go shopping, you're paying for the cocoa!'

'It's a deal!'

Later, Peggy explained that she split her time between New York and London. She invited Mona to travel with her and stay with her. Mona put her head on one side. She had thought Peggy fiercely independent and hadn't imagined she would want a companion.

'Are you sure? Won't I be in the way?'

'The truth is, I would appreciate the company. My father worked hard to bring me up, it was us against the world. After he died, I threw myself into the one thing I knew, the theatre. Living above theatres and spending all my time with my father meant I never made any real friends.'

'Didn't you make friends at school?'

'I didn't spend much time at school. There was always something more interesting and exciting happening at the theatre.'

'But you're so clever, you know so much about everything!'

Peggy laughed. 'My father taught me to read and write and I read anything and everything! He also made sure I had the knowledge I needed to be independent. I've worked hard and furnished two beautiful apartments, but sometimes I get lonely.'

As Mona considered Peggy's offer, she asked another question.

'Have you ever been in love, Peggy?'

Peggy smiled wryly. 'I can't say I have. Men have been interested, but in my experience, they fall into two categories. Ones who want to control you by making you their wife and the mother of their children and ones who want to ruin your reputation, if you know what I mean? I want an equal, someone who doesn't only see me as a vessel for his offspring, is it too much to ask?'

Mona shook her head. 'Not at all. My mother said women don't need a man to be independent. Since my experience with Louis, I haven't been interested in falling in love.'

'Is it a yes, then? Will you travel with me?'

Mona pushed the doubts about her friend to the back of her mind and nodded. A few weeks later Alberto stopped her as she returned to the apartment. A letter had arrived. Her hands shook as she took the envelope. Beads of sweat formed on her forehead as she considered who it might be from. Had Aunt Agatha tracked her down, intending to return her to Gateshead or send her to Hampson Hall? Or was it from someone in London who knew where she was and what she had done? Peggy took the envelope.

'It's the picture you had taken before we left the ship, you silly goose!'

Peggy handed the envelope back and Mona smiled. Later, she examined the picture. The woman waved and smiled as though she hadn't a care in the world. She had told Peggy she would send the picture to Evie but now she hesitated. If Lizzie got her grubby hands on it, Mona knew her spiteful cousin would refuse to give it to Evie. She would have to send it straight to her daughter. She studied the picture again and tried to imagine her little girl, she would be 11 now. Her heart ached, she longed to sign it *from your loving mother'* and remind Evie she still loved her truly, but she couldn't risk revealing her identity. Her hand shook as she wrote, *'To my little girlie, with fond thoughts, yours lovingly, Mona.'* She sealed the envelope and Alberto arranged for it to be posted. After a few weeks she settled into the routine of rising late and working until it grew dark. She impressed Marv with her dance skills thanks to regular, decent food and the absence of fear. She slept well and her body was supple, other than her back. Each persistent, painful ache was accompanied by hideous memories of the Diamond and her miserable existence in the rundown lodging house. She tried to put those images, along with ones of Nellie, out of her mind. She had a new life in New York.

Chapter 29

Summer 1911

Ivy

Despite his performers being desperate for rest, Monsieur insisted auditions for *'Toujours Belle'* would be held before the final performance of *'Olympic Contests.'* Ivy was delighted to be cast in a more prominent role, with lines and songs. Her character has endured serious hardship before the new golden age of *'La Belle Époque'* is ushered in. The opening scene finds her being serenaded by the leading man, the renowned French actor Rémy Sand. As the heavy crimson curtains open, it is spring and Rémy finds Ivy sitting in La Jardin des Tuileries dreaming of better times. Her instructions from Monsieur were to face away from Rémy, to glance into the distance as if unaware of his approach. Her costume, a plain dress and nondescript hat would be replaced later in the show when she embraced the opportunities of *'La Belle Époque.'* Her character sits mute as Rémy approaches but she can't help smiling as his pitch perfect baritone begins.

'Beautiful dreamer, wake unto me,
Starlight and dewdrops are waiting for thee,
Sounds of the rude world, heard in the day,
Lull'd by the moonlight have all passed away!'

Butterflies fluttered in Ivy's stomach at the idea of rehearsing the scene with the handsome Rémy Sand. Monsieur promised that once the run of *'Olympic Contests'* ended they would have two days' rest, before continuing with rehearsals for *'Toujours Belle.'* He kept his word and on her first day off since arriving in London, Ivy caught the early morning train from Kings Cross to Newcastle. She hadn't told Lizzie about her visit; she didn't want to give her cousin time to arrange for Evie not to be there. Their gruelling performance schedule had taken its toll and as soon as she took her seat, she fell asleep. She dreamt fitful, restless dreams and only came fully awake as the train pulled into York. Yawning, she pushed herself up. She grabbed her bag and hurried to change trains. Plumes of black smoke rose from the dirty Tyne, signalling her arrival in Newcastle. She hurried from the station, over the Swing Bridge and up towards the workhouse, averting her eyes as she passed the grim building. Turning into the street leading to Pipewellgate, she grimaced at the uproar from the Globe. She walked up the other side of the street and stopped. Lizzie leant against the wall, coughing and belching. Ivy strode across the street but stopped short as the smell of stale beer and tobacco hit her.

'I've come to see Evie, is she at home?'

Lizzie lurched towards her, and Ivy stepped back as her cousin slurred, 'Sunday School.'

'She's at Sunday School? The last time you said that she wasn't there.'

Lizzie shrugged and staggered backwards before disappearing into the hot stench of the Globe. Ivy hurried to the church hall, but the doors were locked. She turned towards Pipewellgate, hoping Evie was at Lizzie's. She held her breath and lifted her skirts away from the stinking filth beneath her feet. Outside Lizzie's she shielded her eyes and peered through the dark window. The glass, broken and encrusted with black grime, afforded no sight of the room. She called Evie's name, but her words fell into silence. She pounded on the decaying door until her fists throbbed. She walked the streets, knocking on doors, but no one had seen her niece. She tried the vicarage, but the housekeeper said the vicar had been called out to a dying parishioner. She asked the housekeeper for an address for the Sunday School teacher and the woman's eyes narrowed. She wanted to scream. Instead, she squared her shoulders and smiled.

'I'm just trying to find my niece.'

The housekeeper relented and provided instructions to a house *'right at the top of the hill.'* Ivy sighed, she couldn't get there and back in time for the last train. She trudged away.

At breakfast the next day, everything stuck in Ivy's throat. Mrs Newbold suggested she could take a walk. Ivy breathed deeply as the fresh air and warm breeze caressed her face. Mrs Newbold had said Henry VIII created Hyde Park for hunting deer, and over the years it had held duels, demonstrations and summer parades. Speakers' Corner was a focal point for free speech and debate and recently, the park had come alive with suffrage demonstrations. Ivy stood at the side of the path as people walked and rode horses beside the lake. Following the footpath as it bent to the shape of the Serpentine, she spotted tall oak trees and elegant silver birch. She pictured her mother standing there. She longed to tell Theodosia about the developments in women's suffrage activities. In April that year thousands of women had hidden from the authorities during a country-wide census. Their reasoning: if women couldn't vote they wouldn't cooperate with the Government by being counted. Women gathered in secret *'safe houses'* and a group of suffragettes hired the Aldwych skating rink and skated through the night. Some women in Wimbledon took secret night-time treks and hundreds of others defaced their census returns. The most audacious act was carried out by Emily Wilding Davidson. She hid in a cupboard in the crypt of the Palace of Westminster to be recorded as resident at the House of Commons on census night. Ivy knew Theodosia would have hidden them. Evie's giggles rang in her ears as she pictured courageous Theodosia squeezing them into a hiding place.

Her eyes followed the flow of the Serpentine, named for its snaking, curved shape according to Mrs Newbold. She had related a notorious story and as Ivy looked into the water, she wished she didn't know about the unfortunate Harriet Westbrook. The heavily pregnant wife of the poet Percy Bysshe Shelley had drowned herself in the lake in December 1816. Icy fingers caressed Ivy's spine as she imagined how cold the water would be in winter. The poor woman left a suicide note but Mrs Newbold said, *'not that he cared, her cad of a husband, he married Mary Wollstonecraft Godwin less than two weeks later!'* As Ivy walked, her mother's favourite Shelley poem sprung into her mind. She imagined a skylark high in the cloudless blue, singing its *'unpremeditated art,'* unmatched by *'rainbow clouds.'* Shelley's graceful bird ascended *'higher still and higher,'* soaring across the descending sun like *'an unbodied joy.'* She turned to retrace her steps. When she arrived at Chestnut Tree Avenue Mrs Newbold was waiting. As Clara poured coffee Mrs Newbold leant towards Ivy and whispered.

'Did you meet anyone from the theatre?'

'No, why?'

'Oh, nothing, I just thought you might have bumped into someone you knew.'

Ivy knew Mrs Newbold was eager for her to meet eligible bachelors. If she had known about Evie, she would have understood Ivy's reluctance. Since starting work at the theatre she had been approached by several admirers. Men waited at the stage door, hoping for autographs. Bessie assured her they were potential suitors, but Ivy knew her circumstances would be a deterrent. If she never found her sister, she would have to marry a very special man. One prepared to offer both her and Evie a home. As she wrote to Lizzie, she tried to picture Evie. She didn't know whether Lizzie spent the money she sent on Evie or wasted it in the Globe. She hadn't told Lizzie she was in London, terrified her whereabouts would be passed on and Aunt Agatha would order her back into service. Her life and work were reputable, but her aunt would continue to view her as sinful. She bit her bottom lip as she tried again to picture Evie. She started writing another letter, smiling as she imagined her friend.

'Dear Ruby,

I do hope this letter finds you in good health and you are not causing too much trouble for Mrs Jackson!'

Mona

Manhattan's seasons presented themselves as Mona settled into life in New York. Winter's icy tentacles were replaced overnight by the verdant greenery of spring, and summer, without warning, brought with it a breath-stealing, overpowering cloak of heat. On a rare day off Peggy took Mona to Central Park, everyone's garden in the city of skyscrapers. As they approached the vast green space Peggy said that in 1853, more than 750 acres of Manhattan land had been set aside to create the park. Officials hoped it would contribute to a more civilised society and improve public health. The landscapers favoured sweeping meadows and vast bodies of water, reflected by the park's long narrow rectangle running through the centre of Manhattan. Mona stood open-mouthed as Peggy said she found the picturesque woodlands and meandering streams a calming antidote to the unforgiving pace of work at the Paradise. Peggy led her towards the Mall, a grand promenade lined with vase-like elm trees. She pointed out Bethesda Terrace. The grand sculpted terrace overlooking the lake had magnificent carvings representing the four seasons and, on the side, facing the Mall, the times of day. Mona sniffed; Gateshead's People's Park could never rival Central Park.

She hadn't revealed her whereabouts but had been sending Lizzie money. Memories haunted her. She had abandoned her daughter without a second thought. For a weak, deceitful man. She pictured Louis outside Leighton Mansions, his sheepish, coward's look. The rough way his uncle had dragged her through the London streets and dumped her at the rat-infested lodging house was seared into her memory. One day she would return to Leighton Mansions. She would stand at their door, dressed in her best New York City clothes. She would show them they hadn't defeated her.

Ivy

Ivy closed the front door and leant against it, her feet and head pounding. Rehearsals for *'Toujours Belle'* were relentless. Clara appeared from the dining room.

'A letter arrived for you, Miss Ivy.'

'Thank you, Clara.'

She took the small white envelope. She didn't recognise the child-like hand, but her heart soared. Her niece had written to her! She shook her head; how could it be from Evie? She hadn't given Lizzie her address. Before she could open the letter Mrs Newbold flew out of the parlour.

'Have you heard the news, my dear?'

'No, what has pleased you so much?'

'Miss Grace Opal is joining the cast of "*Toujours Belle!*" She has agreed to perform one or two specially arranged numbers as a favour to Monsieur le Grand. Isn't it wonderful news?'

Ivy agreed it was and joined Mrs Newbold for a martini. She looked forward to seeing Master Walter again, if he accompanied Grace on her return to London. After her martini she went to her room to rest before dinner. In her excitement at Mrs Newbold's news, she had forgotten about the mysterious letter. She opened the envelope and unfolded the small sheet of white notepaper. Her eyes shot to the end of the letter and the mystery was solved. It was signed, in the same child-like hand, *'Always your friend Ruby Rogers (Miss).'* Ivy smiled and returned her eyes to the beginning of the letter.

'To my dear friend Dinner,

You said your name is Ivy and Cook said I should put that on the envelope but you are always Dinner to me. Thank you I was smiling when I read it. I am still trouble for Mrs Jackson it is a lot of fun. I am glad it is happy in London the people at your guest house are funny. Winnie and Edward have a little baby her name is Rose. Winnie smiles more but not when Rose cries all night and she is too tired. Master James is still in trouble he was drunk in Newcastle and Master Walter had to speak to the police-

man to sort it out. Do you know Master Walter and Grace Opal are coming to London? I think she is singing at a beautiful theatre. I wish I could go and see you my dear Dinner. I miss you a lot. I have to go because Mrs Jackson is shouting and I am not where I am supposed to be.

Always your friend Ruby Rogers (Miss).'

Ivy conjured up Ruby's cheerful smile and freckled face. Ruby had started work at 13 and hadn't spent much time at school. Ivy appreciated the effort she had taken in her letter. Rehearsals continued unabated and a few weeks later Monsieur appeared in the dressing room, even more animated than usual. He clapped his small hands.

'Attention, tout le monde!'

The room fell silent, and all eyes turned towards him.

'I have splendid news! The delightful, beautiful, incomparable Miss Grace Opal has agreed

to join our production for a limited number of shows!'

Monsieur clapped his hands again and the room exploded with chatter. Ivy feigned surprise and joined in; she wouldn't spoil Monsieur's moment of glory by saying she already knew. Grace Opal was all anyone talked about for the rest of the day. What a coup to have secured such a star to take centre-stage in their show. They would be the toast of the West End. The theatre was a hubbub of excitement when Grace arrived. Monsieur made sure she had her own dressing room and whatever she needed, but her list of demands was short. For all her success, Grace remained down to earth. Ivy was delighted to receive a message to visit Miss Opal in her dressing room. She knocked and the familiar voice rang out.

'Please, do come in!'

'Miss Opal, how wonderful to see you again.'

'My dear, I've told you before, call me Grace! And I hear you have a new name for the stage. What news of your sister? Did you find her? Oh, my dear, I'm sorry, whatever is wrong?'

At the memory of her visit to the Diamond, Ivy's grief was undammed. Here, with this kind woman, her tears flowed until she could cry no more.

'Now, tell me what happened.'

Grace placed a delicate arm around Ivy's shoulders. Through sobs she told Grace about her visit to Leighton Mansions and the Diamond.

'But she wasn't there?'

'No, and the women said she had gone to New York City in America. So that's that.'

'Whatever do you mean?'

'Well, even if I knew where she was, how would I get to America? Isn't it a big place?'

Grace smiled. 'Yes, but I know some people who work in New York theatres. I can ask around to see if anyone knows of her performing anywhere.'

'You would do that for me?'

'Yes of course, and I'm sure with his contacts, Walter will be able to help us. Leave it with me, my dear. Now, we had better get to our rehearsal or Monsieur will be in a French flap!'

As they left Grace's dressing room Ivy smiled. At last, she might find her sister.

Evie

Miss Kinghorn rang the dinner time bell, and her class ran into the schoolyard. Evie followed slowly. She frowned as the other children played. She had been forced to grow up too quickly and had missed the joy of a proper childhood. Nancy wasn't at school, and she had struggled to read anything Miss Kinghorn wrote. She wanted school to be over, but she had nothing to look forward to at Lizzie's. She stood as far away from the other children as possible and lip-read their conversations. She stopped, most of them were talking about what they were eating. Her stomach growled, there hadn't been much in the way of breakfast at Lizzie's. She closed her eyes and tried to conjure up images of her grama. She frowned, the pictures were becoming harder to recall, even her pretend memories escaped her. A lump rose in her throat as she walked towards the school gates. Would anyone miss her if she wasn't there? Someone touched her arm and she jumped.

Jack laughed. 'Sorry, Evie! I didn't mean to startle you.'

She turned towards her friend, wiping away the tears.

'What's wrong?'

'Oh, nothing. I'm being silly. Nancy isn't at school today, and I miss her.'

'Are you hungry? I don't have much but I'm happy to share.'

Her heart swelled; Jack knew she was always hungry. She took the piece of bread.

'Thank you, Jack.'

'I've got something else for you. Look.' He held a small white envelope out towards her. 'Uncle John is meant to hand this to you in person, but I asked if I could bring it. Otherwise, he would have had to take it to Pipewellgate and risk bumping into Lizzie.'

'What is it?'

'I don't know, you'll have to open it.'

'Is it addressed to me?' Her nerves prickled. Jack's uncle had said if a letter arrived addressed to her, he would hand it to her in person. Jack held the first such letter.

'Yes, it's addressed to you. It's yours.'

Evie wiped her hands on her dress, she didn't want to get the precious letter dirty. Her hands shook as she took the envelope from Jack. The letters blurred but Jack pointed out her name and Lizzie's address. She turned it over, examining it carefully.

'There's nothing to say who it's from.'

'Not everyone writes a return address on the envelope. It'll be inside, at the top of the letter.'

She opened the envelope as carefully as possible, desperate not to damage the letter and equally desperate to know who had sent it. She expected to find a sheet of writing paper inside but instead found a piece of thin card.

'It's not a letter, Jack.'

'What is it?'

As she withdrew the item from the envelope, she caught her breath. She held a picture of a woman. The woman stood on a ship with her hand raised in a friendly wave. The beautiful woman had a cheery smile but sad eyes.

'It's a picture.'

'A picture? Who of?'

'I don't know. It's a woman but I don't know who she is. Why has it been sent to me?'

'Let me see.'

As she handed the picture to Jack, she spotted some writing on the back.

'What does it say on the other side, Jack?' He turned the picture over and frowned.

'It says, "*To my little girlie, with fond thoughts, yours lovingly, Mona.*"' Evie knitted her brows together.

'I don't know anyone called Mona. Why has she sent it to me and why does she call me her little girlie?'

Jack hesitated. 'Could it be your mother? Do you remember what she looked like?'

Evie held the picture closer then further away, closing one eye then the other to focus on the woman's features. She had no memory of her mother's face, only a woman singing to her. But she didn't know if that was a fake memory she had created to ease her misery. She blushed, embarrassed to admit she didn't know if this was her mother. But why would a stranger send their picture and sign it *to my little girlie?*' Her head spun as the bell rang to signal the end of dinner time. She decided to trust Jack but bend the truth a little.

'Yes, I think it's my mother. I can't ask Lizzie and risk her destroying it, but would you ask your uncle? He remembers my mother, doesn't he?'

'Yes, I think so. Give it to me and I'll ask. We had better get inside or we'll be in trouble.'

The rest of the school day passed in a blur and Miss Kinghorn shouted at her more than once to concentrate and stop daydreaming. She bolted from the classroom the moment the bell rang, wanting to catch Jack before he went home. She waited outside the school gates until he appeared.

'You'll ask your uncle about my picture? Will you see him this evening?'

She had waited years for word of her mother, and she didn't want to wait a moment longer.

Jack smiled. 'Yes, I'll ask him this evening. I'll meet you here in the morning, before school. I'll return it to you then and will tell you what my uncle remembers about your mother.'

Evie didn't sleep. She arrived at school long before the gates opened. She waited for Jack. When she spotted him in the distance, she ran towards him.

'What did he say? Is it her? Is it my mother?'

Jack smiled. 'Yes, Evie, he says it is her.'

Her lip trembled; she had a picture of her mother. 'What does he remember about her?'

Jack hesitated. 'There were lots of rumours at the time she left Gateshead.'

'Rumours? What about?'

'People say she went to London with your father.'

'My father?' Evie's mouth fell open, no one had ever mentioned her father before. She held her breath. 'Does your uncle know him, my father?'

'His name is Louis Levy, he's a musician. He played the violin and your mother met him at a dance at the church hall.'

Evie's head spun. She had a father. She had a mother *and* a father.

'But why did they leave me behind? Why didn't they take me with them to London?'

'I'm sorry, Evie. My uncle said it caused such a scandal because they weren't married. Your father is Jewish.'

The school bell rang. They needed to go inside, but she had more questions.

'Did your uncle remember anything else about my mother? I wish I knew more about her, what she liked to do, what her interests were?'

'There was something else.'

'Yes, what?'

'When they left, people said she had a job with the English Ballet Company. She was rumoured to be an accomplished dancer. I have to go now Evie, but I'll see you tomorrow.'

Jack handed her the precious picture and she clutched it to her chest. For the first time, she had a sense of her identity. She was a ballet dancer's daughter! Her mother was a dancer with the English Ballet Company! She grinned as she made her way to her seat. She couldn't wait to tell Nancy. She didn't understand why her mother and father hadn't taken her with them to London, but she wasn't angry. She grinned, delighted to finally know something of her background.

Chapter 30

Autumn 1911

Ivy

Rehearsals continued with Grace Opal on the cast of *'Toujours Belle'* and Ivy had a new-found sense of optimism. She revelled in the new production. By now her character has embraced the opportunities offered by *'La Belle Époque,'* she has found a job and made new friends. The scene opens in summertime, and she sits outside Café de Flore with two other women. They wear bright and fascinating costumes, a direct contrast to hers in the opening scene. Her line is to order martinis. She read her directions from Monsieur and looked up.

'Monsieur, could my character order hot chocolates instead of martinis?'

He sniffed and raised his hands. 'Non, non, Mees Leighton. It is too 'ot for 'ot chocolat!'

She smiled. 'Très bien, Monsieur. Martinis it is!'

As the elegant women approach Café de Flore swirling their pretty parasols, a waiter flourishes napkins and wipes tables before leading them to a luxurious seating area. He waits with his notepad until one of them, a beauty with auburn hair and striking blue eyes, orders martinis.

'Martinis pour tout le monde, s'il vous plaît, Monsieur.'

As the women enjoy their drinks, Rémy Sand and two other actors spot them from across the street and start singing, shimmying their way towards them.

'Tell me pretty maiden,
Are there any more at home like you?'

The women look up and realise the men are waiting for an answer. They reply in song.

'There are a few, kind sir,
But simple girls and proper too.'

The women stand and face the men and the song continues as a sextette.

'Then tell me, pretty maiden,
What these very simple girlies do.
'Tell me gentle stranger,
Are there more at home like you?'

At the end of the song the couples pair off and walk towards the corner of Boulevard Saint-Germain and Rue Saint-Benoît. Ivy beamed when Rémy Sand took her arm.

They had worked hard and expected the production to be a resounding success. Ivy dared to feel happy. Her wages meant she could regularly send money home, and with Grace and Master Walter's help she hoped to have word of Mona's whereabouts in America before long. Grace joined her for dinner at Mrs Newbold's several times. Ivy delighted in introducing Grace to Mrs Newbold's other residents who immediately took her to their hearts. On one such evening, as she enjoyed pre-dinner drinks with Grace, Bessie and Ralph Lynn, Ivy was reacquainted with Master Walter. '*Toujours Belle*' was opening the following day and Grace said he had come to attend their premiere. Clara answered the front door and Ivy smiled at Master Walter's deep tones. She frowned when she heard a woman's voice, who was with him? Clara opened the door and Master Walter's tall, handsome frame filled the entrance, hiding the person behind him. Grace flew into Master Walter's arms. As they walked into the room together the woman in the doorway was revealed.

'Ruby! My dear friend! What on earth are you doing here?'

'Dinner!' Ruby flung herself across the room as Mrs Newbold's residents looked on, bemused at this powerful bundle of ginger energy bursting into the house. Ruby's words flew out in a torrent. Master Walter had asked if she would like to visit Ivy and attend the opening performance of '*Toujours Belle.*' Ivy asked Ruby how Mrs Jackson had reacted, and her friend laughed her glorious, unashamed laugh. Master Walter had told the stern housekeeper in no uncertain terms that Ruby would be accompanying him to London for a few days, daring her to question him. Cook hadn't been a problem; she happily accepted the news. They had a new scullery maid, so could manage without Ruby for a few days. Grace had asked Mrs Newbold if Ruby could stay at the guest house during her visit. Ruby had saved her wages for weeks to buy some new clothes for her trip. Ivy admired Ruby's smart, dark green travelling suit. Ruby pushed back her shoulders and said she had also brought a gown for her trip to the theatre the following evening.

'I didn't want to let you down by looking like a scullery maid.'

'You could never let me down, Ruby. You could have come to London dressed in your nightgown and I would still have been delighted to see you!'

Ruby laughed and Ivy recalled something her friend had told her years before, about the Hampson family. Ruby had said they conducted themselves differently to other landed gentry and here was the proof. The son of a Lord had invited a scullery maid to accompany him to London and attend the theatre with him. Lord Hampson had brought his sons up to treat people of all classes with respect and dignity, and Ivy knew from personal experience that Master Walter was a kind and gracious benefactor. She tried to think about Aunt Agatha as little as possible, but smiled as she imagined how vehemently her strait-laced aunt would disapprove of the Hampson family.

Mrs Newbold's eyes glistened but she smiled at the noisy gathering in her dining room. Ivy wished Mr Newbold could see this spectacle, but she hoped by filling the house with laughter and entertainment they brought his widow a measure of happiness. The evening turned into a riotous affair, and it was late when Master Walter and Grace left, and everyone retired to bed. Ruby had unpacked in the room next to Ivy's, but she came to say goodnight. As they sat side by side on Ivy's bed, they rested their heads on each other.

'I'm so happy you're here, Ruby.'

'Oh, me too, Dinner.'

Ruby knew about Ivy's new name but had stated she wouldn't ever call her anything but *'Dinner!'* This caused raucous laughter around the dining table, much to Ruby's bewilderment, but everything was meant and taken in good humour.

'Now, I must get some sleep. It's our first performance tomorrow.'

'Of course, I'll go to my own room now.'

Ruby moved towards the door then stopped. 'Did you find out what happened to your sister? You never mentioned her in your letters.'

'Oh. No, not yet, but I'm hoping Master Walter and Grace might bring me some news of her before long. I'll tell you more about it tomorrow. Good night, dear Ruby.'

'Good night, dear Dinner.'

Ivy smiled as Ruby closed the door behind her. She washed and changed for bed and tried to picture her sister. Was Mona in New York? Was she safe? Ivy prayed she hadn't swapped one seedy music hall for another in a different country. Despite everything Mona had done, Ivy still loved her. She whispered into her pillow. 'Goodnight my dear sister. I pray we will be reunited soon.'

Mona

Mona joined one of Marv's numerous dance troupes and quickly became an invaluable member of his company. She learnt new dances, routines and positions with ease. Marv and Peggy watched from the wings as the dancers completed their final rehearsal of the afternoon.

'She's a natural, your pretty English friend.'

'I know Marv, she's very talented.'

'She's got a job here for as long as she wants it.'

'Thanks Marv, that's great.'

'Well, we have to look after each other, don't we? Knowing what we know.' Marv winked and Peggy looked away.

They were reaching the end of a run of Marv's popular Broadway production, *'The Night Of The Season.'* The premise of the story rested on the success or otherwise of a theatre group. It followed their trials and tribulations, romances and rivalries throughout a season, and their efforts to continue performing despite losing their most famous star to a rival theatre. It culminated in the triumphant return of their favourite and the final performance being hailed as *'The Night Of The Season.'* Peggy was the star of the show. Mona joined a chorus line with various numbers throughout the show. Her favourite was a bright, cheerful song where the chorus line entered the stage on roller skates. She never failed to smile at the jingle of the bells as the line set off from the wings. They dance around Peggy's character, Lottie Linton, as the actor playing the director of the rival theatre, Chuck Chancer, tries to persuade Lottie to leave on the pretext of his theatre having the better band. On this cue Marv's orchestra strikes up and Chuck starts singing.

'Come on and hear, come on and hear Alexander's Ragtime Band,
Come on and hear, come on and hear 'bout the best band in the land...'

The chorus line forms a circle around Lottie and Chuck, their exhilarating one-foot spins and jumps creating a dizzy acrobatic display. Lottie pulls away from Chuck as he tries to get her attention and the chorus line moves backwards, splitting in two to create an exit for their star. Mona left the stage breathless but delighted, blood pumping through her veins. This was her favourite routine because there wasn't a lewd move or revealing costume in sight. They opened to outstanding reviews and audience numbers soared as the show's popularity grew. People queued around the block to buy tickets, desperate to catch the show before the run ended.

As summer turned to autumn Alberto said *'the colours of the Central Park trees in the fall are a sight for sore eyes, Miss!'* The friends fell into an easy routine of rehearsals, shopping and eating out. They received invitations to dine with men who had attended the show but declined, staying true to their intention to pursue independent lives. Mona reflected on the success of the last few months. New York was everything Peggy had promised, and she had escaped from Solomon Zettler and the Diamond. But images of Evie haunted her, with the threat of being returned to London by force never far from her mind. She continued to send Lizzie money, providing no clue as to her whereabouts. She had sent her picture to Evie but signed it *'To my little girlie, with fond thoughts, yours lovingly, Mona.'* She didn't know if Evie had received it or if she would recognise her. She prayed Lizzie hadn't got her grubby hands on it. She bowed her head; she didn't even know what Evie looked like. There was a gentle knock at her bedroom door and Peggy's pretty blond head appeared.

'Are you decent, my darling girl?'

Mona shuddered, the boy at the Diamond had said the same thing when he knocked on the dancers' door. Would she ever rid herself of those awful memories and their long shadow?

'Mona? You're miles away.'

'I'm sorry, Peggy. Yes, what is it?'

'Well, you know we'll be coming to the end of a run of *"The Night Of The Season"* soon?'

'Yes, is Marv happy with everything?'

'Oh yes, he's delighted with us. That's not the problem.'

'What do you mean, what problem?'

'You remember I told you I spend half of each year here and half in London?'

'Yes, I remember.'

'I'm getting itchy feet. I'm going to make arrangements to return to London.'

Mona gulped. She had promised to travel with Peggy but now she wasn't sure she was ready to leave.

'What is it, darling? You look close to tears.'

She wanted to be honest. She explained she wasn't ready to face London.

'It's all right, stay here if you prefer. Marv will be pleased; he's planning a new production and will need good dancers. He told me you've got a job with him for as long as you want.'

'You don't mind if I don't come back to London with you?'

'You had an awful experience there. I don't blame you for not wanting to go back yet.'

'Are you sure?'

'Yes, it's settled. Alberto and the maids will look after you here, we'll tell Marv tomorrow and I'll make plans for my journey to London.'

Peggy closed the door and Mona lay on her bed. Her lip trembled as she questioned whether she had made the right decision. Perhaps she needed to face the terrible events in her past. If she didn't, would she spend her whole life running from the horrors that continued to haunt her?

Ivy

'*Toujours Belle*' proved such a success that Monsieur didn't return to Paris and Grace Opal extended her stay. By now the company was exhausted and everyone was relieved they were coming to the end of the extended run. Tonight would be the penultimate show. Ivy re-read Ruby's latest letter. She had enjoyed her friend's visit when the show opened, and they had written regularly since Ruby returned to Hampson Hall. Ruby's short letters made her laugh; her friend always had something funny to report. In this letter she regaled her latest episode involving Mrs Jackson. Ruby never tired of hiding from the serious housekeeper and found ever-more ingenious ways to irritate the woman. At a knock on her bedroom door, Ivy put the letter down

'Yes, come in.'

Clara popped her head around the door. 'Miss Opal is here to see you, Miss Ivy.'

She thanked Clara and hurried downstairs to find Grace in the parlour with Mrs Newbold. Grace fanned herself against the warmth of the autumn day and smiled as Ivy entered the room.

'My dear Ivy, I do hope I'm not disturbing you.'

'Not at all. I was reading Ruby's latest letter before preparing to return to the theatre.'

'Ah, the delightful Ruby. Your friend who came for *"Dinner!"'* The women laughed; Ruby would always be remembered for this at Mrs Newbold's.

'What can I do for you, Grace?'

'It's more what I can do for you. I have an invitation for you. Walter is in town this evening and he intends to attend the theatre for our penultimate show. I would have expected he had seen enough of it, but he has a friend staying from out of town and he hasn't seen it, so there you are.'

'I see, but what does it have to do with me?'

'Well, Walter asked if you would like to accompany us to dinner after the performance?'

'Oh, thank you, Grace.'

'Excellent. Now there are two conditions, my dear. From now on you must agree to call Walter Walter, and not Master Walter!'

'Very well, Grace. What is the second condition?'

'You must bring an evening gown to the theatre. We'll get changed in my dressing room after the show. We might even have a bottle of champagne to celebrate!'

'Wonderful! What is Walter's friend called?'

'We call him Bertie, but his full name is Mr Herbert Joseph Primavesi. He's from Bournemouth. He's an absolute gentleman and I expect the two of you will get along very well.'

Mrs Newbold smiled at the young women. 'It sounds like the perfect evening.'

Ivy didn't seriously consider the dinner invitation until after Grace left. She was comfortable in Walter and Grace's company, and she trusted the restaurant would be high class and the food delicious. That wasn't what worried her. The man, Mr Herbert Joseph Primavesi, he worried her. She had avoided any involvement with men since leaving Gateshead. Until she met Rémy Sand. The handsome French actor had insisted on taking her to a cafe after their first rehearsal, and she found herself blushing as he showered her with compliments. They had met three times but there wouldn't be a fourth. At their last liaison Rémy had reached across the small table and taken her hand. He looked deep into her eyes, parted his lips a fraction and made to kiss her fingers. She blushed and looked away as a waiter approached. She froze when the waiter spoke.

'Bonjour, Monsieur et Madame Sand. Rémy, you did not tell me your wife was so beautiful.'

Ivy snatched her hand away and slapped Rémy's face. He was married! She left the cafe, shaking her head. He had taken her for a fool. She flushed, why had she fallen for his lies? The incident strengthened her resolve to avoid further involvement with men. She needed to focus on saving money to send home for Evie, repaying her mother's debt and trying to find her sister. But if Mona was never found, Ivy knew she would have to marry a very special man. One prepared to offer both her and Evie a home. This wasn't the right time to have dinner with a man, even a friend of Walter's. She would thank Grace but decline the invitation.

She returned to her room to prepare for the theatre. She sat on her bed and put her head in her hands. How could she decline such a generous invitation without appearing rude and ungrateful? She opened her wardrobe and it hung there, daring her to reach out and remove it. The beautiful, burnished gold evening gown. Bessie had insisted she return to Selfridges and buy it. She hadn't worn it yet, there hadn't been an appropriate occasion. She had an idea. It didn't sit well, but if she *forgot* to take her evening gown to the theatre, she wouldn't be able to accompany Walter and Grace to dinner. It would appear to be a simple mistake. She washed and styled her hair before changing into a dark pink light-weight tunic, one of a number Bessie had helped her to find in Selfridges. She popped her head around the parlour door as she left and bid Mrs Newbold goodbye.

'I won't wait up for you tonight, my dear. I suspect you will be late, and I trust Walter will ensure you arrive home safely. I do hope you enjoy Mr Primavesi's company.'

She didn't meet Mrs Newbold's eyes as she said goodbye. As she hurried away, Mrs Newbold watched from the window. The theatre was a hive of activity, the atmosphere building towards their penultimate performance. She entered by the now-familiar stage door and made her way to the dressing room she shared with the other female performers. Other than Grace, who as the star of the show, had her own private dressing room. She hurried past Grace's door, not yet ready to deliver the lie about her dress. She wasn't used to lying and hoped her honest nature wouldn't give her away. She wasn't ready to be introduced to Mr Herbert Joseph Primavesi or any other potential suitor. Her friends meant well, but they didn't know how much of a commitment any potential husband would have to make, to her and to Evie. She pushed the problem away. She needed to concentrate on preparing to deliver a performance worthy of Monsieur's spectacular production.

'Toujours Belle' had become the latest must-see West End show. Crowds flocked from all over the country, queuing for hours. Advertising hoardings encouraged audience members to dress in their best finery, to be, as the production demanded, 'Toujours Belle.' Ivy gasped as she peeked at the audience through the heavy curtains. Not one of the 2,000 luxuriously upholstered seats sat empty. A riot of colour exploded throughout the theatre as audience members tried to out-do one another with their beautiful dresses and hats, all adorned with elaborate feathers and ribbons. The men shone in their pristine white suits and straw boaters. Ivy knew her mother would have insisted on taking her daughters and granddaughter to see this show. She hung her head, how she wished Theodosia had lived to see such joyful stories of her beloved Paris brought so vividly to life. And to watch her elder daughter in the production. She raised her head and pushed her shoulders back, determined to make her mother proud. The curtains opened to deafening applause and by Ivy's first scene Monsieur couldn't contain his excitement. He ran around backstage, clapping his hands and exclaiming it was their best performance yet. Ivy delivered both her opening scene and the scene outside Café de Flore with polished professionalism, as she had done ever since her unfortunate encounter with Rémy Sand. He had tried to apologise several times, but she waved him away like an annoying insect. As the show reached its magnificent finale she hurried towards the wings, butterflies fluttering in her stomach. Excitement had reached fever pitch backstage.

The grand finale brought the story together in majestic conclusion. Beginning with a scene in front of the crimson curtains, Rémy and Grace's characters marvel at the dramatic browns and golds of the autumn trees along the banks of the Seine. He serenades her as the curtains open to reveal a winter scene. Rémy and Grace gasp at the frozen river as the rest of the cast flock on stage, accompanied by the musical tinkle of bells attached to their ice skates. Rémy and Grace join the skaters and the cast dance and sing to celebrate the changes wrought by *'La Belle Époque.'* The lively vocal ensemble transitions through the highs and lows of the story as the skaters go round and round, their bright white costumes shimmering. As the final number, reprising parts of songs from earlier in the show reaches its crescendo, children bring baskets of roses onto the stage. The cast take armfuls of roses and throw them into the audience. The scent of roses and the sound of rapturous applause filled the theatre as the curtain fell. Monsieur signalled to them to stay on stage. The curtains flew open, not once, not twice, but three times. The performers hurried to their dressing rooms, adrenaline racing through their veins. Grace walked ahead and Ivy tried to hang back, but Grace turned and crooked a finger in her direction. Ivy hung her head as she walked towards Grace.

'Ivy, quick, let's get out of the crowd! What a show!'

Grace pushed open the door to her dressing room and Ivy opened her mouth to deliver her lie. She stopped, her mouth hanging open. In Grace's dressing room, right in front of her eyes, hung her evening gown.

'You silly goose! Mrs Newbold noticed you left without it and Clara brought it to the theatre. Champagne, darling?'

Ivy flushed as she stared at the evening gown. Now she had no excuse not to join Walter and Grace for dinner, no excuse not to meet Mr Herbert Joseph Primavesi.

Evie

The day after she received the picture of her mother Evie ran to school, longing to tell Nancy her news. For the first time in her life, she knew something of her background, she had an identity. With the knowledge came confidence. If Nancy asked her to describe how she felt she would sign she wanted to burst. Her habit of imagining happy scenarios had helped her to survive the misery of living in Pipewellgate. In her day-dreams her mother hadn't abandoned her. She had married Evie's father and they had lived happily together. But the picture was real. And Evie had decided. She wouldn't let Lizzie bully her any longer, not now she knew her mother loved her. In a few more years, when she left school and started work, she would save every penny she could and go to London to find her mother. She waited for Nancy outside the school gates. She looked from one side of the street to the other, watching as children gathered in groups in the yard. Nancy was her group, her only friend apart from Jack. The bell rang. She needed to go inside or risk Miss Kinghorn's wrath, but Nancy still wasn't there. She walked backwards into the schoolyard, watching for her friend.

'Eveline Brown, turn yourself around and walk properly! And don't dawdle!'

'Yes, Miss Kinghorn.'

Evie sat at her desk; her excitement extinguished. No one else at school would be interested in her news, no one else listened to anything she said.

'Good morning, class. We will start with sums.'

Evie picked up her chalk, dreading another day without Nancy's helpful eyes. As Miss Kinghorn started to write on the blackboard, the door opened slowly. Children gasped as Nancy hobbled into the room. Even Miss Kinghorn's flinty expression crumpled at the sight of her unfortunate pupil. Nancy had a black eye and the bruises on her face, neck, arms and legs were horribly visible. With her damaged eyes fixed on Evie, Nancy limped to the back of the classroom and took her seat. Miss Kinghorn said nothing and the lesson began. At morning break Nancy and Evie didn't move. Miss Kinghorn left the room. Evie held out her arms and gently lifted Nancy's chin. 'What happened?' Tears flowed down Nancy's face, mingling with dirt and dry blood. As she signed, Evie cried too. She rubbed her friend's face with the sleeve of her dress. The gesture made Nancy cry harder, and the girls continued to hold each other until Miss Kinghorn reappeared.

She bent to talk to them. 'Nancy, we need to get you cleaned up then you should go home.'

'No!'

Miss Kinghorn stepped back at Evie's sharp outburst.

'I'm sorry Miss Kinghorn, but Nancy can't go home.'

Nancy shook her head from side to side.

'Then I don't know what we are going to do. She cannot stay here looking like that.'

'I will look after her, Miss Kinghorn.'

'And how do you propose to do that, Eveline Brown?'

'My guardian will help, Miss Kinghorn. I will take Nancy home and we will look after her.'

'It is most irregular, but I will allow it.' Miss Kinghorn stood, absolved of the problem.

Evie shook her head; Lizzie was the last person who would help. She would take Nancy back to Pipewellgate and clean her up. Her usual route took her past the Globe, but Lizzie might be there, so she steered Nancy through the graveyard. She normally avoided the creepy shortcut but today she was invincible, her new confidence bolstered by her mother's image. She had wrapped the picture in her only other possession from her mother, the pretty handkerchief with the red letter '*M*' stitched into the corner. She hid it in the space under the loose floorboard, under the small table next to her rotten mattress. These two precious items provided her with the strength she needed.

When they reached Lizzie's door, Evie paused. She signed to Nancy to wait while she checked Lizzie wasn't home. Sure enough, the old soak wasn't there. She hurried Nancy inside. The girls' friendship was strengthened further by Nancy's indifference to Evie's living conditions. Evie smiled at Nancy, poverty and abuse had brought them together and created a bond nothing could break. She sat Nancy on the dirty mattress and signed to say she wouldn't be long. She hurried outside and collected water from the shared pump in the street. She shuddered at the filth encrusted on the pump. Back inside she searched for something to use as a cloth to wipe Nancy's wounds. She grinned as she spotted a skirt the Crone had left for Lizzie to alter. She grabbed it, revenge spurring her on. Slowly and gently, she cleaned Nancy's cuts and bruises. Her friend asked about Lizzie and Evie signed she shouldn't worry. Lizzie would be drunk when she arrived home, the chances of her even noticing Nancy were slim. Once she had done her best to clean Nancy up, Evie signed to her friend to try and sleep. She covered her in the scratchy, moth-eaten blanket and pulled the curtain.

Evie sat in the dark as Lizzie's drunken bulk fell through the door. Lizzie stumbled then collapsed into her chair and started snoring. Evie curled up next to Nancy, but sleep wouldn't come. She replayed what Nancy had signed about her injuries. Her father was a violent drunk and while beatings were common, his most recent rage was worse than anything Nancy had suffered before. He had beaten Nancy's mother and when Nancy tried to stop him, he beat her. Nancy whimpered in her sleep and Evie put a skinny arm around her friend. While she was waiting for Lizzie to come back, she had studied her mother's picture. She knew what to do, she and Nancy would run away. They would go to London and find her mother. She would look after them and Nancy's mother could come and join them. They wouldn't wait any longer, they would do it now. She frowned; they had no money. She narrowed her eyes; she knew how to get her hands on some money. Lizzie's money, some of it was rightfully hers and she had never seen much of it, so now she would take it. Lizzie usually got paid by her customers on Saturdays. All she had to do was distract Lizzie, grab what she could, then escape with Nancy. She loved Nancy and she had to do this, for her sake.

Chapter 31

Ivy

Ivy sat in Grace's dressing room; her hands shook as she fastened the last of the tiny pearl buttons on her dress. One of the theatre's make-up artistes had offered to help with their make-up and Grace poured champagne as the young woman worked. Tonight, they would celebrate with Walter and Bertie. They had one more show of *'Toujours Belle'* and tomorrow Monsieur was throwing a party for his overworked, exhausted company. The make-up artiste finished, and Grace told Ivy to stand.

'Now, look at yourself in this mirror and tell me what you see!'

Ivy's cheeks reddened.

'All right, I'll tell you what *I* see. Miss Ivy Leighton, beautiful star of the London stage. Born in Gateshead but now an invaluable part of the glamorous London theatre set!'

Ivy blushed again but admitted she liked what she saw. The silk evening gown fitted perfectly, and the burnished gold colour complemented her hair and complexion. Grace had helped to style her hair in a soft, loose coiffure. She brushed Ivy's long, wavy auburn hair up and away from her face then helped her to pin it into pompadours and puffs. The overall effect, a cluster of soft, graceful curls and coils, framed Ivy's beautiful face. She completed the style with a large barrette ornament fastened through the coils to hold her hair in place. Sparkling gold sequins decorated the barrette, matching the colour of her gown.

Ivy and Grace giggled like schoolgirls as they left the theatre. As the driver helped them into the cab and Grace told him their destination, Ivy almost tripped on the hem of her gown. The Langham had been open for almost 50 years and she knew something of the hotel's history. The Prince of Wales and much of Victorian high society at the time were present at the spectacular opening ceremony. The favourite venue for royalty, artists and musicians from around the world, she had never expected to set foot inside such a grand building. Charles Dickens wrote about it in his London Guide, describing the Langham as '*the most expensive hotel meal to be had in London, but for large dinner parties there was nowhere else to go.*' The hotel was also immortalised in writing by Sir Arthur Conan Doyle, a regular guest who used the hotel as the setting for several of his Sherlock Holmes stories. As Ivy stepped through the doors, she took a deep breath. This world had only ever existed in her daydreams.

Walter and Bertie were waiting, immaculately dressed for dinner in smart white tie and tails. As the women walked into the elaborate marble entrance hall, the men moved towards them, and Walter embraced Grace. A tall, dark-haired man stood beside Walter.

'Miss Leighton, please may I introduce my dear friend, Mr Herbert Joseph Primavesi?'

The man reached out and lifted Ivy's gloved hand to his lips. He brushed a kiss against her fingertips then dropped her hand. His deep, dark blue eyes looked into hers and he held her gaze.

'I am pleased to make your acquaintance, Miss Leighton. I have heard a lot about you.'

Ivy hesitated, what had Walter told Bertie? 'I am pleased to meet you too, Mr Primavesi.'

She took in their tailcoats, waistcoats and bow ties as Walter led Grace into dinner. Bertie offered her his arm and she allowed herself to relax a little. She stopped and stared when they reached the dining room. Each table was laid with a crisp white linen tablecloth and each place setting sparkled with polished cutlery and crystal glasses. The discreet lighting offered privacy while creating a relaxed, intimate atmosphere. As the waiter showed them to their table, Walter and Bertie walked ahead and pulled chairs out in readiness for the ladies. As

Ivy took her seat the waiter picked up her white linen napkin and placed it on her lap with a theatrical flourish. He handed her a heavy, leather-bound menu embossed with the name of the restaurant and she hesitated, her forehead prickling. She had never eaten in such a high-class restaurant; how would she know what to order? As she opened the menu, she breathed a sigh of relief and silently thanked her mother. She stole a glance around the room. Theodosia had wanted this for her daughters. For them to rise above the low place of their birth and escape to situations such as this, dinner at The Langham Hotel in London. Ivy smiled and perused the menu. The men flicked through the wine list, discussing the merits of some good French wines over the less superior choices from Germany. They settled on a bottle of the best champagne with Walter declaring it could be their only choice tonight.

While Ivy understood the French menu, some dishes held no appeal. Her eyes skimmed over the *'Huîtres au Citron'* and while Grace ordered the oysters, Ivy chose *'Croûte au pot,'* a clear soup of carrots, turnip and cabbage made with a rich beef stock. It came with small pieces of toasted bread and Ivy smiled as she pictured Cook in The Langham's restaurant. Bertie raised his eyebrows and as he smiled the corners of his mouth crinkled. The fish dish, a small fillet of sole, came with a Remoulade sauce. Ivy beamed, delighted to know what it consisted of. Theodosia had made the sauce at home. Different herbs and spices were used in the chilled sauce and here, Ivy knew, the strong flavour would be anchovies. At home they sometimes had small fish, but never anchovies. Walter and Bertie chose *'Côte de Mouton grilée'* with *'petits pois au beurre,'* Grace and Ivy chose the *'Poulet rôti au cresson and salade.'* The men tucked into their grilled mutton chops with relish while the mouth-watering roast chicken with watercress and salad satisfied the ladies' appetites. For dessert they all enjoyed the fruit salad, *'Macédoine de fruits Langham'* as it appeared on the menu. The final dish was a vast presentation of fromage. Ivy tried to commit each variety of cheese to memory, planning to report every detail of the meal in her next letter to Ruby.

During the meal she learnt that Bertie's father's family were Italian immigrants who had arrived in England around the same time as Theodosia. She found Bertie an easy person to like, a gentle, caring man who worked hard and made an honest living as a jeweller. Bertie had one thing in common with the deceitful Rémy Sand, his good looks. Bertie talked about his brothers, all happily married with children. Ivy lowered her eyes, the last thing a gentleman like Bertie would want was to be lumbered with someone else's child. The idea of Evie living with her once she was married was impossible. Why should any man accept her niece? Picturing Evie, she raised her head and squared her shoulders. There would be a man and he would be the right man. Perhaps it wouldn't be Herbert Joseph Primavesi. As they finished the cheese, Walter's expression changed, and Ivy's heart started to race.

'Ivy, I hope you are not upset, but I took the liberty of telling Bertie about your sister's predicament. He has contacts in London and America, and I thought he might be able to help.'

She wanted to be angry at Walter for sharing personal details of her sister's life with a stranger, but Bertie coughed politely, and his voice was gentle.

'Miss Leighton, I assure you I have your sister's best interests at heart.'

Bertie tilted his head towards her, and she looked into his kind, compassionate eyes. He might not be husband material, but he might help to find Evie's wayward mother.

'Thank you, Mr Primavesi. I would be grateful for your help in locating my sister.'

'Excellent. Now, shall we have another bottle of this excellent champagne?'

Evie

Evie and Nancy left Lizzie's early the next morning, before the old drunk was awake. Evie explained her plan and Nancy signed that she would go on one condition. She wanted to tell her mother and send for her when they were settled with Evie's mother in London. Evie agreed and they arranged to catch the train from Newcastle to London on Saturday, as soon as Evie got her hands on Lizzie's wages. That night Evie tossed and turned, trying to work out how to distract Lizzie long enough to grab her wages and flee. Lizzie guarded her money like a hawk guards its prey. Evie knew she needed to wait until enough of Lizzie's customers had collected their alterations and paid. Saturday arrived and Evie couldn't wait to escape. Lizzie shuffled around the ramshackle room.

'What are you looking at, gutter-snipe? Here, make yourself useful and sweep the floor!' Lizzie snarled as she threw the broom at Evie. Evie caught it, smiling.

'Yes, of course.' She could be generous; it was the last time she would do Lizzie's dirty work.

By dinnertime she had been shoved outside while Lizzie entertained her customers. She walked back and forth and drummed her fingers on the window sill. She cupped her hand around her face and peered in as Lizzie collected her wages and put them on the table next to her sewing machine. Evie knew as soon as her last visitor left Lizzie would take the money and head to the Globe. The Crone was the last of Lizzie's visitors and Evie needed to be patient, this visit would be the longest. The old gossips swapped tittle-tattle and drank sherry, sometimes for hours. Today was different and as the scene unfolded Evie smiled. The Crone crept inside, and her familiar cackle reached Evie as the women sat, ready to engage in their usual chin-wagging. After a while Evie caught something on the Crone's lips. The Crone asked Lizzie to fetch the skirt she had left for alteration and Lizzie pushed herself out of her chair. Evie gasped, she had used the Crone's skirt to wipe Nancy's cuts and bruises. She had stuffed the ruined garment in the corner, not knowing or caring what happened to it. It was behind the coal scuttle, and she giggled as Lizzie fumbled around, searching in vain for the piece of clothing. The women became more agitated until Lizzie reached behind the coal scuttle. The Crone screeched. Evie didn't need to lip-read to know she was swearing and cursing like a Tyne navvy. The Crone grabbed the ruined skirt. She delivered a hard punch to Lizzie's face before heading to the door. Lizzie stumbled. She reached for the Crone and grabbed a handful of filthy hair, pulling her back into the room. As they fought Evie ran inside, grabbed the money and her small bag of belongings and ran.

Her lungs were ready to burst when she arrived at the Swing Bridge. She leant against the wall and tilted her head back. She yelled, big loud yells. People stared but she didn't care, she was free. She looked around. She hadn't been able to give Nancy a specific meeting time, but she was happy to wait. She had waited years to escape, a few more hours were nothing. She found a spot on the riverbank with a vantage point of their meeting place, and she waited. Once Nancy arrived, they would walk over the bridge to Newcastle and make their way to the train station. They would catch the train to London and find her mother. It grew dark as she waited and still there was no sign of Nancy. She walked to the Newcastle side of the bridge, but the street was deserted. She walked back; her steps heavy. She could cross the bridge and catch the train to London on her own, but she wouldn't abandon Nancy. She needed to know her friend was all right. She trudged back to Pipewellgate, anticipating Lizzie's reaction. Lizzie sat, hunched and fuming in the dark as Evie slowly pushed the door open. Despite her drunken state, Lizzie's fury propelled her across the room to deliver the first forceful blow. Sometime later Evie crawled towards her mattress, battered and bruised. She was beaten, vile Lizzie and disgusting Pipewellgate had beaten her, physically and emotionally, into submission. She curled into a ball and closed her bruised eyes. She howled in silence as she waited for sleep to come, wishing it could be death.

Ivy

Mrs Newbold had gone to bed when Bertie returned Ivy to the guest house after dinner. At breakfast the next morning her questions began the moment Ivy entered the room. Ivy lowered her eyes as she regaled the details of their evening, hoping Mrs Newbold wouldn't notice her blushes. She took a deep breath, wanting to explain why she had been reluctant to meet Bertie. Clara brought more coffee as Ivy slowly told Mrs Newbold about her life, skipping over the part about the debt. When she had finished, their coffee was cold and Mrs Newbold's eyes were wide.

'My dear, how awful for you! Your poor sister, whatever can have become of her?'

'That's what Walter and Bertie hope to discover, with the help of a private detective. I still hope my sister will face her responsibilities as a mother and come back to Gateshead with me.'

'And then what will you do? Where will your niece live?'

Ivy ran a hand across her forehead. She longed for a society where an unmarried, working woman could have a child living with her.

'I don't know, but I need to get her away from Gateshead.'

Mrs Newbold patted her arm. 'Please let me know if I can help in any way, my dear.'

*

A few months later Ivy and Bertie sauntered through Hyde Park in between Ivy's busy performance schedule. A schedule which didn't allow her time to travel to Gateshead to try and see Evie. Winter had brought an icy chill to London, but they didn't hurry, wanting to enjoy each other's company before Bertie returned to Bournemouth that evening. Ivy stole a glance at Bertie as he slowed his stride to match hers. He was perfectly attired, today he wore a light brown wool over-coat over his suit, with a stiff white shirt and a smart bowler hat. She sensed his eyes on her and looked up from beneath her stylish velvet turban. He smiled; his eyes wide. She wore an ankle length coat with fox fur trim and matching muff. Her elegant hat, trimmed with purple satin ribbon and decorated with embroidered silk roses, matched her tailored jacket and fashionable purple hobble skirt. They drew admiring glances as they walked. Ivy recalled their first meeting at the dinner with Walter and Grace. They had met as often as possible since then, with Bertie staying in London and attending her performances at weekends, then returning to Bournemouth each Sunday evening. They spoke of small things at first, as if trying to hold back an irrepressible tide, but Ivy missed him more each time he left and he assured her he felt the same. Conversation came easily and her admiration for him grew when he told her about his sister's involvement with the suffrage movement. Like Lord Hampson, Bertie had accompanied his sister to a suffragist rally. In addition to their shared love of the theatre and music, she had learnt more about his large, jovial family. They lived close to one another in Bournemouth and his face lit up when he talked about them. He had followed his father into the jewellery business and was regaling a story about one of his brothers who mistook an extremely valuable necklace for a paste imitation. Describing his father sending the brother running along the street after the customer, Bertie laughed. A deep, delicious laugh.

The magnificent autumn colours had been replaced by cold winter winds, but Ivy asked Bertie to sit for a while beside The Serpentine. She looked out across the lake before taking a deep breath. 'I want to tell you about my family.'

When she stopped talking Bertie took her gloved hand. She flushed, waiting for the judgement but Bertie said he prayed the private detective would bring news of Mona. Ivy explained she took her responsibility to her niece seriously and if she never found her sister, she would want Evie to live with her. She kept one aspect of the story to herself, the debt to her aunt. She continued to send money to repay the debt and Ruby forwarded the *'interest accrued'* notes. Ivy pushed back her shoulders as she stood, the ever-increasing debt was her problem to solve.

Mona

When *'The Night Of The Season'* ended Marv insisted they all took a few days off to rest. Peggy used the time to finish her packing and put her affairs in order before leaving. Peggy reassured Mona she would be safe staying in New York alone and reminded her of Marv's promise to give her work for as long as she wanted. Mona mustered a cheery smile and a wave for her friend.

She wandered around Peggy's apartment, picking things up and putting them back down. She trailed her hand along the polished dresser and majestic dining table. Her lip trembled. She opened the door to Peggy's *'small entertaining space.'* In here Peggy had hosted champagne evenings with performers from the Paradise. It was fun, but Mona preferred it when she and Peggy were alone. She wrapped her arms around her body, the apartment was empty without Peggy. She tapped her forehead hard. How could she rid herself of the fear that haunted her? She buried her head in her hands. Why hadn't she mustered the courage to confront her fears by returning to London with Peggy? She shook her head; she couldn't continue to allow the awful events in her past to dictate her choices. She jumped at a knock at the door. She hadn't slept well since Peggy left, she heard noises during the night and anything unexpected startled her. She stood behind the door.

'Yes, who is it?'

'Maid, Miss. I've brought your supper.'

Mona put a hand to her chest and opened the door.

'Thank you, bring it through to the dining room, please.'

She sat in one of Peggy's William Morris chairs as the maid delivered her supper. After the maid left, she uncovered the plate. She stared at the delicious-looking meal before recovering the plate. True to his word, Marv ensured Mona had regular work. The rest of the company were pleasant enough but there was no one like Peggy.

Marv called the company to the Paradise to inform them of plans for his next production. They assembled on stage and Marv held court, cigar in hand. He cleared his throat and his deep American drawl reached Mona at the back of the group without any difficulty.

'First, I know I threw you all a huge party to say thank you for your hard work in *"The Night Of The Season,"'* Jeez! I'm still paying for it and some of you are still recovering!'

Everyone laughed and Marv raised his massive bear-like hands.

'But I wanted to say thank you once more, you did me proud! Now, I hope you're all well-rested because our next production will be even bigger and even better! Are you all ready?'

Everyone clapped and shouted, they were ready.

'So, what is the production? Well, I'm sure many of you are aware of the cabaret music hall in Paris, the Folies Bergère?'

There was general agreement along with some whistles and cheers, everyone in their line of work knew about the Folies Bergère.

'Well Marv here, that's me, folks, is about to put on a show to rival anything anyone has ever seen at that there Folies Bergère!'

A thunderous stamping of feet started up and the cheers, whistles and catcalls became louder still. One member of the company called out.

'What's it called, Marv?'

'You wanna know what it's called, young man? Do ya?'

Mona put her hands over her ears as the noise level increased even further. All around her the other performers were in a hysterical frenzy of excitement.

'I'll tell ya! It's called *"Marv's Fabulous Femme Fatales!"* How about that for a title?'

Mona went cold as Marv told them about the new production. She had never been to the Folies Bergère but knew all about it from her mother. Theodosia had told her daughters the cabaret music hall was a bustling but scandalous entertainment venue, hosting popular song and dance shows, comic opera and gymnastics. Its revues featured extravagant costumes, sets and effects and, she had leant in close to them for this bit, often the female dancers were naked. Mona shuffled her feet as Marv explained one of the attractions of his new production, especially to men, would be some nudity and erotic dancing. Mona froze as an image of a different stage wormed its way into her mind. The Diamond.

'No time like the present! Let's get started! No costumes yet but the sooner you learn your new dance routines, the better!'

Marv moved to the wings and the choreographer clapped his hands for attention.

'Quiet, quiet! Now, we, that is you, need to learn the cancan!'

Jeers and shouts went up all around her, but Mona didn't move. The choreographer, a wiry little man, pointed and gestured and people shifted their positions on the stage but still she didn't move. A woman pushed in beside her, nudging her with a bony elbow.

'The cancan, eh?'

Mona flexed her fingers and toes and stretched her aching limbs. Then the music started. The choreographer demonstrated the moves but the pounding in her head and shrieks of laughter from the other dancers drowned out the music. The choreographer indicated for them to replicate his moves and the music started again from the beginning. Mona winced as she lifted her leg. Tears sprung to her eyes. She moved sideways and collided with another dancer. The woman scowled and high-kicked towards her. The choreographer's yell hit her like a punch in the face.

'English woman, what are you doing? Get back in your line!'

She ran from the stage, pushing past Marv as he revelled in every high-kick from his position in the wings. She reached the toilet moments before being sick. The choreographer had called her *'English.'* She was back at the Diamond. She washed her face then sat in the dressing room. She covered her face with her hands, her whole body shook. As her shakes subsided, she took deep breaths in and out, in and out. When her breathing calmed, she cocked her head towards the sound of the music. The galloping, frenetic 2/4 time beat out along with the choreographer's shouts. She stood and waited for the music to end. She watched her reflection in the mirror. She told herself she was at the Paradise Theatre in New York, a reputable Broadway theatre. Not at the seedy Diamond Music Hall in London. She placed her arms straight down by her sides and when the music began again, she danced. She danced the cancan alone in the dressing room. She pushed past her body's screams of pain as she high-kicked and cartwheeled, stopping at the choreographer's loud instruction.

'Lift and shake those skirts! Now, bend over and throw those skirts over your backs, the audience are paying to see your derrières!'

She turned, startled by the sound of applause from the doorway. Marv.

'How long have you been there?'

'Long enough. What's going on? Why the private rehearsal?'

Any explanation she could have given was lost as the dancers returned. Marv frowned but moved out of the doorway. She caught his words as he walked away. 'You can dance.'

Chapter 32

Mona

Back at Peggy's apartment Mona tried to relax, but images swirled in front of her eyes. Gruesome images of the cancan. She tried to focus on Marv's words. She could dance but for the first time in her life, questioned whether she wanted to. Sleep wouldn't come, she lay awake as the sun rose. The delicious breakfast stuck in her throat and her shoulders heaved as she pictured sitting there with Peggy, laughing about *'corfee.'* She smiled an apology as the maid took her untouched plate away. She pushed her chair back and took a deep breath. She wouldn't be beaten. She would go back to the Paradise and rehearse the cancan.

Excitement buzzed around her in the dressing room. She sensed eyes on her, but no one mentioned her swift exit the previous day. When the shortness of breath came, she swallowed her fears and concentrated on her make-up. Her hand shook as she applied bright red lipstick and rouge. People started leaving the dressing room. She waited, busying herself in front of the mirror, until the last dancer left. She took a deep breath and followed the sweet, waxy smell of the greasepaint. Marv raised his eyebrows as she passed. She took a position in the last row, but the choreographer moved them according to height and she found herself close to the front. The music started and she counted the high-pitched staccato beats, three slow ones then eight faster ones. The choreographer reminded them this music heralded their grand entrance onto the stage, with their skirts held high.

'Show them everything the Good Lord gave you, girls! Remember, they haven't paid to see your faces!'

Mona winced. In the past, she would have delighted in being part of a chorus line performing such a physical, high-energy dance. Not now. As they high-kicked and cartwheeled their way through the dance, a man in elegant black top hat and tails joined them. He came on at the rear and sauntered towards the front of the stage. He removed his top hat with a flourish and Mona stopped dead and stared. She had missed this section of the routine the previous day. The dancers took turns sashaying towards the man, then high-kicking his top hat as he held it out towards them. Mona hesitated when her turn came, but the relentless choreographer motioned for her to move forward. She swished her skirts in time to the gallop and lifted her leg to kick the man's top hat. He moved the hat, inch by inch, until it was above his head. Too high for her to reach. She looked up, his smug expression unleashed her fury, and she lifted her leg again and kicked him hard in the face. He collapsed and chaos ensued. As she left the stage pain seared through her leg to her hip, but she walked with her head held high. She slipped away before the other dancers left the stage. As she closed the stage door behind her a dancer called to her, grinning, her eyes bright.

'Gee, Mona! We all wanted to do that, but you did! You're some girl!'

Mona wasn't sure whether to laugh or cry when she spotted Marv lurking behind the woman. She didn't expect to have a job the following day. Her misgivings about '*Marv's Fabulous Femme Fatales*' ran deep but she needed the work, she couldn't pick and choose her shows.

'You're on a warning but only because you're good. But you need to control your temper, poor Frankie's lost his front teeth! Dress rehearsal tomorrow, don't be late!'

Mona stared open-mouthed as Marv barked his instructions. She still had a job. The next morning, she slowly pushed the door open and entered the hot, noisy dressing room. The chatter stopped. The dancers turned and stared. Then clapped and cheered. Mona flushed, for a moment she forgot about her aching limbs. Until she saw the costumes. What had Marv said it was for? To thrill and titillate the audience, particularly the men. Men in all their horror. She covered herself as best she could and made her way to the stage. When the music started, she tried to lose herself in the rhythms but all she saw was Nellie, the Diamond, Billy's club and Solomon Zettler.

Later, as she stepped out of the elevator in the apartment building, she hesitated. The corridor was in complete darkness. Her hands shook as she felt her way along the wall towards Peggy's apartment. She counted each door and fumbled in her bag for the key once she reached Peggy's door. The darkness enveloped her; the key wasn't there. She dropped her bag and as she reached to retrieve it a sweat broke out, a thousand tiny needles pricking her skin. Blood pounded in her ears as the panic rose. A strong hand gripped her shoulder. Solomon Zettler was alive. He had come for her. She screamed and leapt away from the sinister hand.

'Gee, I'm sorry Miss, are you all right?'

She slumped against the wall as relief flooded through her body.

'Oh Alberto, you gave me such a fright. I couldn't see anything in the dark.'

'I know, Miss. I came to check you were all right when the lights went out. Let me help you.'

Once he had seen her into the apartment Alberto went to the basement to fix the lights, assuring her they would be back on 'pronto.' Mona's legs shook as she walked to the window. The man was there, standing under the streetlamp opposite the building, looking straight up at her. She ducked beneath the window and thumped onto the floor, struggling to breathe. He had been there every day for over a week. She had seen him in other places. Outside the theatre and at Mallard's when she called in for vanilla cocoa. The one time in her life cocoa hadn't worked its soothing magic, because she knew he was outside. She tried to steady her breathing and reached up from her position on the floor. Grasping the window frame, she pushed herself up a fraction and peeked out. He had gone. Had she imagined it?

Peggy's letters were packed with cheerful details of her latest adventures in London. How could Mona tell her what was happening in New York? She started to question what was real. Sleep evaded her and the more sleep she lost the more she saw the sinister man. She curled into a ball on the floor and wept. When she left the apartment building the next day, she asked Alberto if he had seen the man standing under the streetlamp the previous evening.

'He's tall and slim and he wears a dark coat and a black bowler hat.'

'No Miss, I can't say I did. But after I left you, I went to the basement to fix the lights.'

'Oh yes, of course. Never mind, it must have been a trick of the light.'

'Are you all right, Miss? You don't look too well, if you don't mind me saying so.'

'Oh yes thank you, Alberto. I'm missing Miss Willow, that's all.'

'Ah now I understand. Miss Willow is a bundle of joy!'

Mona left Alberto and headed to the Paradise. Since they had started rehearsing for Marv's Folies Bergère production, she had found it difficult to concentrate. For the first time, she forgot her steps in the new routines. Marv glowered from the wings. After her third attempt he took her aside.

'What's troubling you, Mona? You haven't been the same since Peggy left. You look washed out and tired and as much as I like my dancers thin, you've lost too much weight.'

'I'm sorry, Marv. I'm not sleeping very well. Can we try it again, please?'

Marv frowned; he worked his company hard but deep down he cared. 'All right, but you need to promise me you'll eat a proper meal this evening.'

'I promise. And thank you.'

'All right, everyone. Once more from the top!'

When rehearsals finished a group of dancers invited Mona to join them for dinner at a nearby restaurant. She hesitated; she didn't want to snub them, but she wasn't hungry. As they left the Paradise by the stage door she looked up and down the street.

'Mona? Come on, the restaurant is this way!'

'I'm coming.' She hurried to join them. Someone linked her arm and she smiled. Perhaps it would be all right after all. As the cheerful group strolled along Broadway the tall man stepped unnoticed from the shadows. Mona surprised herself by enjoying the evening and warming to some of the other dancers. She resolved to give New York another chance. She walked the last block to Peggy's apartment building with more of a spring in her step. Unseen, the man walked behind her.

Mona woke refreshed. She went to the window and looked out. There was no one there. She ate a decent breakfast and greeted Alberto as she left the building.

'You look better this morning, Miss.'

'Thank you, Alberto. I feel better today.'

Mona arrived at the Paradise, resolute in her intention to make a success of life on her own in New York. As she entered the theatre, Marv motioned for her to follow him into his office. She did as instructed, all optimistic thoughts of the future wiped from her mind.

'What is it, Marv? What's wrong?'

'That's what I would like to know.'

She stepped back and lowered her eyes. He knew she had abandoned her daughter, knew about her sleezy music hall career, the attack at Billy's club and her flight to New York with Nellie's money and identity. He knew everything.

'I run a decent ship here, I don't want any trouble at my door, do you understand?'

'Yes Marv, of course.'

'So can you tell me why someone has been here asking questions about you?'

'What? Who? What did they say?'

'I only know what I've been told. A man came to the stage door and asked if a Miss Mona Leighton was engaged here.'

'What man?' Mona whispered the question, terrified of the answer.

'I don't know but he was very keen to know your whereabouts. Now, what have you got yourself involved in, young lady?'

Mona looked into Marv's eyes. Could she trust him? She had been wrong too many times; she had trusted Louis and his uncle, but they had betrayed her. Perhaps Marv would be different, he had told Peggy Mona had a job with him for as long as she wanted. She took a chance.

'A man has been following me and standing outside the apartment building watching me.'

Marv raised his eyebrows and gestured for her to continue. Mona looked at the floor. How could she tell him about her past? She hung her head and stood in silence.

'If you don't tell me, I can't help you. If you want to work here, you need to be honest with me. Then I can protect you.'

'I can't Marv, I'm sorry.'

'Well I'm sorry, but I can't keep you on. I can't risk my reputation, do you understand?'

Tears blinded her as she ran from the Paradise, all dreams of her independent life in New York crushed under the weight of Marv's suspicion. Alberto gasped when he saw her back at the apartment building so soon.

'What is it, Miss? You look as though you've had the fright of your life. Are you all right?'

She shook her head.

'Is there anything I can do to help, Miss?'

'No, thank you, I need to get inside.'

'Let me call the elevator for you, Miss.'

Mona's whole body shook as Alberto pushed the button. The first time she had travelled in the elevator Peggy had reassured her. She longed for Peggy now, she would tell her what to do, she would sort things out with Marv, and everything would be all right. But Peggy wasn't here. Mona was alone. The elevator clunked to a halt and

Alberto opened the door.

'There you are, Miss. I hope you feel better soon, let me know if you need anything.'

'Thank you.'

Alberto started closing the elevator door then stopped.

'Oh Miss, I almost forgot. A man came to the building this morning asking if you lived here. Of course, I didn't tell him you did, or you didn't.'

Her wails echoed throughout the apartments as the elevator took her to the tenth floor.

Evie

Evie hobbled to school the day after her failed escape attempt. One of her eyes was swollen shut following Lizzie's beating, the other was open but bruised black and blue. She'd had nothing to eat since Saturday morning but her empty stomach didn't rumble. She waited for Nancy in their usual meeting place but there was no sign of her friend. Eventually she limped into school, too weak to withstand a beating from Miss Kinghorn as well.

She ignored the stares as she made her way to her desk. Nancy's seat was empty. Miss Kinghorn called the class to order and wrote some words on the blackboard. Everything blurred in front of Evie's bloodshot eyes, and she prayed for Nancy to appear. The door opened. The headmaster walked quickly to Miss Kinghorn and whispered in her ear. Evie caught the teacher's shocked look before she hurried out, closing the door behind her. She left in such a hurry that she didn't give them a task. The class erupted into whispers and giggles, but Evie didn't move. She sat at her desk, her head pounding as bile rose from her empty stomach. After a lifetime Miss Kinghorn returned. The room fell silent. A shiver ran up Evie's spine.

'Class, I have some tragic news. Our friend and classmate Nancy Glover is dead.'

There was a collective gasp, but Evie stayed silent. There must be some mistake. Someone asked what had happened and Miss Kinghorn continued.

'She was hit by a train on Saturday afternoon. It is such a tragedy. Now please clasp your hands and join me in saying a prayer for Nancy in heaven.'

The classroom filled with screams. All eyes turned on Evie as the screaming continued. She had no recollection of going to the school-yard but found herself there with Miss Kinghorn.

'I asked if you would like me to walk home with you, Eveline?'

Evie shook her head. Miss Kinghorn wanted her to scream at home, not in her classroom.

'No, thank you Miss Kinghorn. I can walk home alone.'

'As you choose, Eveline. But tell me, will your guardian be at home to look after you?'

Evie stared. Miss Kinghorn must be blind, stupid, or both. Hadn't she noticed her bruises? She smiled. 'Yes, Miss Kinghorn. Miss Brown will be there to look after me.'

'Very well. You should stay at home tomorrow; I know you and Nancy were good friends.'

At the mention of her friend's name Evie's tears welled up again. She needed to get away.

'Yes, Miss Kinghorn. Thank you.'

She ran as fast as her bruised legs would allow but instead of heading to Pipewellgate she turned towards the railway. Drops of rain pelted her face like sharp needles and as she made her strange, ungainly way along the cobbled streets she shouted to Nancy.

'You walked along the railway lines all the time, you knew the exact times of the trains because you couldn't hear them coming. Why were you there at the wrong time?'

Evie knew the answer and it was all her fault. Nancy had been going to tell her mother about their plan to run away, her father must have overheard their conversation and beaten her. Evie pictured Nancy running from the house, terrified, heading for the railway lines with no idea of the time. Miss Kinghorn said it had happened on Saturday afternoon. Nancy was on her way to their meeting place. Nancy was her best friend, her only friend apart from Jack. Evie trudged through the rain, feeling nothing. She longed for one last secret conversation with Nancy. Her pain at the loss of her friend and their chance of a better future, one she had glimpsed so briefly, clawed at her empty insides. The train rumbled towards her. She felt nothing as she stepped onto the lines.

Mona

After Mona returned from the Paradise, Alberto followed her to Peggy's apartment. She wouldn't answer the door until she knew he was alone. She opened it a fraction. He promised to help her with whatever she needed. Her hands shook as she wrote to Peggy, the one person she trusted. She didn't know who had come to New York looking for her, but she wasn't safe. She couldn't stand up to Andrew Glass or Solomon Zettler's henchmen. She needed to be with Peggy, despite returning to the place she feared more than anywhere else. She shuddered, London wasn't the problem, she was. Wherever she went, her fears would go with her. Marv sent her final wages, and she wasted no time in asking Alberto for help in arranging her passage to Southampton. Alberto leapt into action. A few days later her belongings were packed, and she closed the door to Peggy's apartment for the final time. As Alberto helped her into the trolley-car, she took a long, sad look at New York.

'Don't worry, Miss. You'll be taken safely to the dock for your voyage home.'

Mona frowned; England wasn't home. New York had been close to it, until it all went wrong. She thanked Alberto, without him she would be cowering in Peggy's apartment, terrified the next knock on the door would mark a swift return to the life that haunted her. During the long voyage the constant nausea of seasickness confined her to her cabin.

Two days before her ship was due to arrive in Southampton the nausea abated enough for her to feel hungry. She opened the trunk she had taken from Peggy's apartment. She pushed her mother's old carpet bag to one side; she had considered leaving it behind but jammed it in at the last minute. She pulled out a dress, one Peggy had persuaded her to buy on one of their shopping trips. She shook the dress out and held it against her thin frame. She looked in the mirror, admiring the different shades of red running through the delicate material. During her stay in New York, she had half-filled her wardrobe in Peggy's apartment with clothes like this, in her favourite red and other striking, bright colours. She dressed for dinner and made her way to the restaurant. As she walked along the bright corridor, she sensed someone behind her. She turned but the corridor was empty. She entered the restaurant and the maître d asked if she would be dining alone. The familiar panic stirred, and bile rose into her throat. What was the appropriate answer? Would '*yes*' make her improper? '*No*' meant waiting for a fictitious companion who would never arrive. Blood pounded in her ears as she stood mute.

'Miss?' The maître d stared.

She thought he could see into the depths of her tortured soul, that he knew she didn't belong there. As she apologised and turned to leave, she was stopped by a gloved hand on her arm. An American voice boomed into the silence, 'she's with me, aren't you, dear?'

Mona turned and looked into the ruddy face of a well-powdered, well-proportioned, middle-aged woman. She had never seen the woman before but muttered her agreement. Satisfied, the maître d led them to a table where the woman eased her considerable bulk into a chair.

'Now, I think introductions and drinks are in order, don't you?' The woman's booming laugh travelled around the room and Mona smiled.

'Thank you for helping me, I am Miss Mona Leighton.'

'It's all right, Miss Mona Leighton. I don't like eating alone so I am delighted to have your company. I am Mrs Isabella Holliday of Denver, Colorado. Bella to my friends!'

Mona relaxed. By the end of the meal, she knew all about Bella's father's successful real estate business. She told Bella something about herself but didn't mention Evie or the Diamond.

'So, what brings you back to dear old Blighty, Mona? Is it a young man, by any chance?'

Mona blushed. 'No, I'm coming back to see my friend.'

'Did you not like New York City?'

'Oh yes, it was the most wonderful place I've ever seen!'

Bella frowned. Mona blushed and looked away.

'I didn't like being there without my friend Peggy.'

Bella raised her eyebrows and Mona took a deep breath before continuing. She told Bella about the man who had followed her. She also told her about the Folies Bergère production and how uncomfortable she was dancing almost naked. Bella reached across the table and took her hand.

'You know, Miss Mona Leighton, I think we have a lot in common, you and I.'

Mona frowned, she didn't see the similarities, Bella was rich, she dressed like a film star and knew a thing or two about life. Mona, for all her recent experiences, remained a naive young woman from the north-east of England. She had earned some money in New York but was returning to England a nervous wreck, devoid of self-confidence.

'You do?'

'Yes, I wasn't always the successful, wealthy woman you see in front of you, oh no.'

Bella explained about her humble beginnings in Denver, her father hadn't always been a successful businessman and for many years their family struggled to survive. A lucky investment led to an unexpected expansion in his business and their fortunes changed overnight.

Mona spilt her wine as a commotion stirred on the other side of the restaurant. Bella turned towards the ruckus and shook her head as two stewards wrestled a woman away from a table.

'Not again!' Bella pursed her lips then took a generous gulp of wine.

The woman wailed as the stewards dragged her from the restaurant.

Mona stared. 'Whatever is happening? Why are they treating that woman so harshly?'

'She is a *"Charlotte!"* There is at least one on every voyage these days.'

Mona shrugged.

'Oh my dear, you are green, aren't you?'

Bella explained. A few years earlier a Thames pleasure cruiser named the '*Prince Charles*' was headed back to London, filled with day trippers, when it collided with an 890-ton iron-clad coal freighter. By the time the vessels realised they were about to collide, it was too late. The sharp point of the freighter's bow plunged through the '*Prince Charles,*' tearing the pleasure cruiser in half. The two halves were immediately sucked into the depths of the sewage-filled Thames, the heads of panic-stricken passengers bobbed in the filthy water as rescuers tried to pull them to safety. More than 500 people died in the tragedy and the few survivors faced the grim task of identifying family members. In the wake of the disaster a significant sum of money was raised as part of a relief fund.

'I did my bit, Miss Leighton. I was generous in my donation to the genuine fund. I may not have been if I had known the dark behaviour that would follow.'

Bella went on to tell Mona about *'The Charlottes.'* These women boarded ships with the express intention of approaching well-to-do passengers with their sorrowful tales of woe, claiming they had lost family members and livelihoods in the disaster and were now crippled by debt.

'But surely their identities were easy to verify, the authorities must know who died?'

Bella smiled wryly and shook her head. 'There was no passenger list or headcount, so the door was wide open to any charlatan or *"Charlotte"* who wanted to take their chances.'

'But how do they board the ships without raising suspicion?'

'Ah, there you have it, my dear. You will find the woman who was removed from this restaurant not ten minutes since will by now have contrived to escape from the stewards, often through an act of bribery. She will as we speak have divested herself of her vagrant's costume and will be relaxing in her second or even first-class cabin on this very vessel.'

Mona stared; her mouth open. 'You mean it's all faked?'

'Indeed it is, my dear.'

Mona shuddered as an image pushed its way into her mind. The dowdy, ragged coat and dress in Peggy's trunk. After Peggy had told her about the men who *paid her to keep their secrets safe,'* Mona refused to accept her friend's dishonesty. Now, she realised how far Peggy might go, to maintain her expensive lifestyle. Bella had returned to her previous topic, her father's lucky break.

'In short, we make our own luck in this life, my dear. You will need to work to regain your confidence, but you are a beautiful and talented young woman, don't waste your life being afraid and running from shadows. There are ways, my dear. Many ways for a woman to improve her position. After all, you don't want to travel in third class all your life, do you?'

Before they parted Bella gave Mona her card and an invitation to look her up if she ever found herself in Denver, Colorado. Mona leant against her cabin door and turned Bella's card over in her hands. It all made perfect sense. By joining Bella for dinner, she had learnt more about Peggy than she wanted to believe. Bella's address in Denver, Colorado was typed on one side of the card. On the reverse, she had written one line. 'Remember, you need to make your own luck.'

Mona slept fitfully. The following morning her nausea returned, and she confined herself to her cabin. As dusk fell, she sat on her bed, turning Bella's card over in her hands. What had she said about *'The Charlottes?'* Her legs shook as she opened her trunk, could she do it? She rifled through her trunk, burgeoning with beautiful dresses from her New York shopping trips. She pictured the woman at Southampton train station, the one travelling in first class. She squared her shoulders and chose a dress. She reached for her nail scissors, part of the manicure articles she had packed for the voyage. She punctured the dress in several places then grabbed the material in both hands and ripped with all her might. She heard shouting. As she ripped, the shouts turned to roars. The roars turned to wails and her wet cheeks told her the noise was hers. She threw the ripped dress on the floor and jumped on it, grinding the heel of her shoe into the ruined material. Her heart kicked against her ribs as she retrieved what remained of the once beautiful dress and pulled it over her head. She stared in the mirror then reached for her make-up. She applied too much lipstick and rouge, gasping at the image, the dressing room at the Diamond. She pulled her hair pins out, howling as she ran her fingers through her coiffured style. First class, first class, she repeated the mantra as she paced. She left her cabin, grabbing the door jamb for support as she turned the key in the lock. She swayed as she passed the restaurant and made her way towards the elegant cocktail bar. She covered her ears as she approached the busy bar. When she removed them the sound of jazz music transported her back to Peggy's apartment in New York. She shook as she made her way towards a group of cocktail-drinking, white-suited gentlemen. She ignored the stares and sniffs of disapproval as she reached out a hand to one of the men. He flinched at her touch.

'Excuse me sir, but can you help a woman down on her luck? My husband you see, was killed on the "*Prince Charles.*" Me and the children were left penniless!'

Eyes turned on her like daggers and she lowered her gaze. She pressed her palm against her mouth and stepped back. She turned to walk away, her breathing rapid and irregular. She pushed through the crowds; her eyes downcast. She ran out onto the deck and took huge gulps of cold, salty air. She leant against the rail and looked up. The moon reflected off the ocean and a snatch of music reached her from the cocktail bar. She looked into the unforgiving water. A gale blew and the ocean rose like mountains, breaking over the ship in all directions.

Her body shook as she lifted one foot onto the lower rail. The ship crashed through a huge wave and salt water sprayed into her face. She lifted her other foot onto the rail, her hands grabbed the higher rail for support. She pulled up her skirt and heaved herself over the higher rail. One of her hands slipped and she rubbed it on her ruined dress. She heaved herself up a second time but blinked hard as another wave caught her and knocked her off balance. Her dress billowed in the salty air as she fell. She pictured her body plummeting into the icy water. She held her breath, waiting for the splash. Her head bounced off the deck and everything went black. She heard a muffled voice as footsteps approached. She had to get away. She inched up onto her knees, but black spots danced in front of her eyes.

'What a miracle it knocked you this way!'

Mona blinked away salt water and tears as the white-suited man helped her up. He held her at arm's length, looking her up and down. He reached into his jacket and handed her something.

'I don't know how much truth there is in your story, but I won't stand by and see children starve. Now hurry back to your cabin before the stewards come for you.'

She stared as he walked away. She looked at her hands and gasped. Enough money for a first-class train ticket from Southampton to Euston. She crept back to her cabin, breathing hard. She was packed long before sunrise. She pushed her unwashed hair under her hat and pulled her coat tight as she left her cabin. She was one of the first to disembark and as she hurried along the dock, she angled her hat to hide her bruised face. Gulls flew around the dock, their cries laughter in her ears. She found an empty coach and asked to be taken to Southampton train station. At the station a porter took her luggage and led her to the platform. He stopped straightaway; first class passengers weren't expected to walk far. He helped her onto the train before loading her luggage on board. She lowered her eyes as she took her comfortable seat in her private, first-class carriage. She rested her hands in her lap then squeezed hard, digging her sharp fingernails into her skin. Blood seeped through her fingers. She had promised herself, that one day she would travel first class. She leant back in her seat, closed her eyes and wept. The only thing first class about her was the carriage.

Chapter 33

Ivy

Ivy shielded her eyes against the bright winter sun and craned her neck. The building went on forever, reaching into the clear blue sky. She couldn't believe she was here, in New York City. A few weeks earlier Bertie had called at Mrs Newbold's with news that changed everything.

'The private detective looking for Mona in New York has found her.'

Ivy was stunned. After London, she had expected Mona would make herself impossible to find. She had started to believe she would never see her again. Within a few days Bertie had arranged passage to New York for her and Grace. Because they didn't know how long they would stay, he bought one-way tickets. The timing was perfect, the final run of '*Toujours Belle*' had finished and the women hadn't yet been engaged on other productions. Ivy was torn, she longed to see Evie, but she needed to find her sister before she moved on again. The private detective advised that in his experience, it paid not to waste time once an individual had been found. She took his advice, hoping that within a week she and Mona would be sailing back to England together and catching the train to Newcastle, to finally be reunited with Evie. The private detective had found Mona working at the Paradise Theatre and staying with an English actress called Peggy Willow.

Ivy waved at a trolley-car and explained where she needed to go. On the way she pictured the bedraggled women at the music hall in London, she hoped Mona had found better fortune in New York. Before long the trolley drew to a halt outside the Paradise's grand entrance. Her eyes followed the symmetry of the architecture and like her sister, she spotted the stonework image of Diana, the Roman goddess of the hunt. She smiled as she stepped from the trolley car, praying now, finally, that the hunt for her sister was over. She made her way to the stage door and went inside. She saw a group of dancers hurrying from their dressing room. She heard an orchestra tuning up, the dancers headed in the direction of the music, and she made to follow them. She stepped back as a huge, bear-like man appeared from nowhere and barred her way with his considerable bulk.

'You! What are you doing back here?'

'I beg your pardon, who are you?'

Marv squinted. 'Gee Miss, I'm sorry. But you look so much like a dancer I had here. She was English as well. That's an English accent you have, right?'

'Yes. I am Miss Ivy Leighton. How do you do, Mr...?'

'Marvel, Marv Marvel. Did you say Leighton?'

'Yes, Mr Marvel, Miss Ivy Leighton. Why?'

'Well gee, now I understand. She's your sister, isn't she? Mona?'

'Yes! Where is she? Could I see her, please?' As she spoke, she digested Marv's words. He had spoken about Mona in the past tense. Her heart sank. Not again, please, not again.

'I'm sorry Miss Leighton, but she left. She doesn't work here anymore.'

Ivy stood outside the Paradise; her head bowed. She took a deep breath and looked both ways along the unfamiliar street. She tried to concentrate; what other information had the private detective given them? She stopped a trolley-car and gave the attendant her destination. They set off towards Peggy's apartment building. As the trolley slowed, she took in the striking, fashionable facade. Ivy smiled, her sister was staying somewhere much better than Seymour Terrace and the awful area of London she had visited. She walked towards the entrance. A weather-beaten man stood at the door, smiling proudly in his smart uniform.

'Hello, Miss. How can I help you?'

'I am here to visit my sister, Miss Mona Leighton.'

The man furrowed his brow and stared. 'Gee, but you look like her! Those eyes!'

'Is she at home? I understand she is staying with Miss Peggy Willow.'

'She was, Miss. But she's gone.'

Stunned, Ivy glared at the man. 'Gone? Gone where?'

'Back to London, Miss.'

Ivy hung her head. She had travelled for days, come thousands of miles, to discover she had missed her sister. Again. She was no closer to finding Mona or rescuing Evie. She walked the few blocks in a trance and relayed her tale to Grace. She got into bed and closed her eyes. It was dark when she woke, she had dreamt she and Mona were in a cafe with their mother. Theodosia ordered *'ot chocolat'* for her cocoa girls and they all laughed. Ivy blinked, adjusting her eyes to the light from the window as the New York night blazed, alive with music, traffic and people. There were theatres and restaurants as far as she could see, and she pictured her sister here. Mona would have loved New York. Neither Marv nor Alberto could explain Mona's sudden departure. Alberto had said Mona followed Peggy Willow to London, but what was Mona running from? She abandoned her daughter and ran away from Gateshead, she ran from the seedy music hall in London, injuring Nellie, attacking a man and stealing in her desperation to get away. Now she had left New York in uncertain circumstances. Ivy would never understand how Mona could have abandoned Evie, but she understood her desire to escape from Gateshead. Why did she continue to run?

The next morning Ivy returned to the Paradise to see if Marv knew any more about Mona's sudden departure. Members of Marv's company were making their way inside. She followed them to the stage door and headed to Marv's office. The door was open, but she knocked before entering, hoping to make a good impression so that Marv might be more disposed to help her.

'You again! What can I do for you, Miss Leighton?'

'I'm sorry to trouble you, Mr Marvel...'

'Jeez! Call me Marv, everyone does!'

'The thing is Marv; do you know anything more about the nature of my sister's departure from your company? I haven't been in New York long, but I feel sure she would have been happy here. Do you know what happened?'

'I do, Miss Leighton. And since you appear to care about your sister, I'll tell you what I know. But tell me something.'

'Yes, what is it?'

'Are you in the same line of work as your sister?'

Ivy chose her words carefully, remembering the dead eyes of the women at the Diamond.

'I have recently been engaged at the West London Theatre as a singer and an actress in two successful productions. I am not a dancer like Mona.'

'I see. I might have an opening for a singer, if you're interested?'

She hesitated, she wanted to stay in Marv's good books until she knew more about Mona.

'Possibly. Perhaps you can tell me about Mona before we discuss the contract?'

'You're smart, Miss Leighton. Ok, let's talk about your sister. You're different, aren't you?'

'What do you mean?'

'Well, your sister is a talented dancer and she's easy on the eye, if you know what I mean? But she had problems with her nerves, if you don't mind me saying.'

Ivy froze. Mona had never been nervous or lacking in self-confidence.

'I don't understand, my sister isn't the nervous type.'

'She wasn't at first. But soon after Peggy left, she went to pieces. Then a man came to the stage door asking questions about her. When

I asked her about it, she said she was being followed. That someone was standing outside the apartment building watching her.'

'What else did she say?'

'I asked your sister to tell me what trouble had followed her to my theatre, and she refused. Without knowing what she was involved in, I couldn't help.'

'So, you fired her? You sent her away knowing she was terrified and alone?'

Marv shuffled his feet. 'I'm sorry, Miss Leighton, but I have to think of my theatre's reputation. Sometimes dancers get mixed up with dangerous people.'

Ivy opened her mouth to retort with a comment about Marv's scantily clad dancers when a cold realisation hit her. Her bottom lip trembled as she asked her next question.

'The man who came here looking for her, what did he look like?'

Ivy blinked as Marv repeated the description he had been given. She didn't know what the private detective employed by Walter and Bertie looked like, but knew she had to accept some responsibility for driving her sister away from the first place of safety she had known in years.

'Miss Leighton, what is it? Please sit, I'll get you a glass of water.'

When Marv returned Ivy explained about the private detective. They agreed that between them they had driven Mona away. Marv asked what she would do next.

'I need to return to London and find Peggy Willow. Hopefully Mona is still with her.'

'I can give you Peggy's London address. And while you're here, will you consider singing with my company? I'll pay you well, I owe you and Mona that much.'

Ivy didn't need the money but the theatre and what she had seen of New York fascinated her. 'I'll make one appearance.'

They shook hands, connected in their desire to find Mona before any further harm befell her.

Mona

'Mona! My darling girl! I've missed you!'

Peggy's shout from the window of her sixth-floor flat floated down as Mona stepped from the cab, the final step of her long, exhausting journey. As they embraced, Mona's tears fell. She sobbed in Peggy's arms, giving in to the fear and paranoia that had consumed her in New York.

'Come on, let's get you inside.' Peggy placed a protective arm around Mona's shaking shoulders and led her into the building.

Peggy's London flat was similar to her New York apartment. Each room was fashionably decorated and furnished, and a luxurious bedroom was ready and waiting for Mona.

'Now, unpack and freshen up then we'll have a proper conversation. All right?'

Mona nodded, she felt better already now she and Peggy were reunited. Alone in her bedroom she berated herself. Why hadn't she been able to settle on her own in New York? What was wrong with her? What had happened to the independent young woman, the one who had left Gateshead with such exciting hopes and dreams? She considered her suspicions about Peggy. Could her friend afford to live in luxury because she used bribery, dishonesty and blackmail to extort money? Mona shrugged, even if it was all true, who was she to judge?

They made themselves comfortable with a pot of good, strong tea and Peggy reassured her she hadn't lost her independence, not permanently anyway. Peggy said she would have been terrified if someone had followed her. Mona shook her head, convinced Peggy would have confronted the man and demanded an explanation. Peggy said Mona just needed some rest, then she would get back to feeling like her normal self. Peggy smiled as she poured more tea. 'What are you going to do once you feel better, now you're back in London?'

Mona's mouth fell open, she hadn't thought any further ahead than this moment.

'It's all right darling, you don't have to decide anything now. We'll eat a tasty supper then you need a good night's sleep. Any decisions can wait until tomorrow.'

Mona smiled her gratitude. She stretched her aching limbs and yawned. She was safe. She slept until Peggy knocked on her bedroom door the following morning, to say she was leaving for the theatre. The previous evening Peggy had explained she was engaged in a production at the West London Theatre on Shaftesbury Avenue. It was a long-running production of a show called '*Toujours Belle*' which had originally ended earlier in the year, but there was a public outcry when it closed. This led to the producer, an odd little Frenchman called Monsieur Maurice le Grand, being asked to return from retirement in his beloved Paris, to re-open the show. One of their principal performers had left and Peggy learnt about the opportunity on the theatre grapevine. She suggested Mona should come and meet her at the theatre after breakfast. 'You never know, there might be an opportunity for you, too.'

Mona lay in bed, her fingers scratched at the sheets as she replayed Peggy's words in her head. She couldn't face an audition. She closed her eyes and tried to use her mother's trapdoor trick. She tried to picture her mother's beautiful face and happy, smiling Evie, but nothing came. Theodosia's innocent trick was lost to her. Her lip trembled; Louis had looked so happy when he returned home to Leighton Mansions. She pictured Dinah working hard at Hampson Hall and she buried her face in her hands. She didn't think she had any tears left but now they came to prove her wrong. Huge, fat tears rolled down her cheeks and soaked her nightgown. Eventually her sobs subsided, and she forced herself to sit up. Bella had said she needed to work to regain her confidence. She had also said she wasn't to waste her life being afraid and running from shadows. Mona sniffed and wiped her eyes with the sleeve of her nightgown. She took a deep breath.

She washed and dressed and after eating a little breakfast, started to feel a bit better. She wandered around Peggy's flat, smiling at her friend's talent for interior design and decoration. This flat was almost as splendid as Peggy's New York apartment. She stood at the window. The street was quiet compared to New York, a few people walked in one direction or the other and a cab or trolley-car passed by every so often. There was no one standing under a streetlamp watching her. She turned away from the window. She missed the excitement of New York but knew what had driven her back to Peggy. She shivered at the memory of her final conversation with Marv and the image of the man following her. Who was it? What did he want? She shook herself, she needed to do something productive. Peggy had suggested she might be able to find a position for her at the West London Theatre, but Mona wasn't ready for that. She sat at Peggy's beautiful mahogany writing desk. She would send Lizzie some money for Evie. She wouldn't reveal her whereabouts, but she suspected Lizzie paid little attention to the detail of her letters, that her interest lay solely on the money inside.

Ivy

Despite Marv insisting he was to blame for driving Mona away, Ivy acknowledged her part. If she hadn't agreed to Walter and Bertie employing a private detective, Mona would still be in New York. At the Paradise, Ivy insisted on performing as herself and singing numbers of her own choice. Marv sniffed but he knew Ivy held the cards. The songs were two of her mother's favourites, one in French, the other in English. The first, *'Le temps des cerises,'* was associated with the Paris Commune, a radical socialist and revolutionary government that ruled Paris for a short time in 1871. Ivy had never known her grandparents, but Theodosia told her daughters they were strong supporters of the revolution, particularly her grandfather. Theodosia's mother had sung the song to her husband.

'When we sing of cherry time,
And the happy nightingale and the mockingbird,
Will all be celebrating,

Pretty girls will have foolish ideas in their heads,
And lovers will have sunshine in their hearts.'

Ivy's second song, sung in English, was *'Plaisir d'amour.'* Pleasure of love.

'The pleasure of love lasts only a moment,
The grief of love lasts a lifetime.
As long as this water will run gently,
Towards this brook which borders the meadow,
I will love you.'

The song was about love. Ivy had loved her father although her memories of him were blurred. She had adored her mother, not a day passed when she didn't think of her. She pictured her foolish, flighty sister. She loved her too, despite everything she had done, and she adored her niece. And she had a new love, Bertie. This song was for all of them. Marv watched from the wings, puffing on his cigar. As Ivy left the stage, he stopped her, not wanting to miss the possibility of a more permanent arrangement.

'Would you consider staying on, Miss Leighton?'

Ivy declined. At a different time, it would have been an excellent opportunity. Singing at an elegant Broadway theatre was a dream come true. In the short time she and Grace stayed, winter claimed the city. The beautiful fall colours and gentle breezes disappeared, replaced by icy winds and snow showers blowing up the streets and avenues. Ivy beamed when Grace said their tickets had arrived. Her time at the Paradise passed without incident and her wages reflected Marv's guilt at his treatment of Mona. Ivy wrote to Lizzie and sent money for Evie, careful as always to conceal her whereabouts. She also sent money to Aunt Agatha but whether she was now paying the extortionate *'interest accrued'* or the actual debt, she didn't know. She sent them the same amount as she had from her wages at Hampson Hall, despite having earned a lot more at the Paradise. She didn't want to arouse their suspicions and risk them learning about her change in fortune.

Marv gave her Peggy's London address. After two failed attempts to find her sister, Ivy decided not to risk just turning up at Peggy's flat. If she wrote to Mona, her sister might disappear again. She knew Mona would find it difficult to face her. Mona would never be able to make Ivy understand her abandonment of Evie. But she needed to see her sister, to know she had survived. She picked up her pen. Her letter was addressed to Mr Louis Levy at Leighton Mansions in Maida Vale, London. She demanded Louis write to Mona at Peggy's London address, saying he wanted to meet her at a cafe on Shaftesbury Avenue. If he didn't, Ivy would have no choice but to tell his wife about Mona and Evie. She instructed him as to the precise date and time of the meeting, saying he must wait until then or the threat to speak to Esther would be the same. She sealed the envelope and posted the letter on her way to the theatre. This must work, it simply must.

Mona

Despite Peggy's encouragement, Mona didn't go back to work. The West London Theatre was a tempting opportunity, but her shakes returned at the prospect of an audition. Peggy asked if she was afraid of anything in particular and eventually, Mona explained about the last production at the Paradise. She shook as she recalled her first rehearsal for 'Marv's Fabulous Femme Fatales.'

Peggy handed her a glass. 'Here, drink this. It'll make you feel better.'

Mona shuddered as the strong brandy warmed her throat. She continued, her shoulders heaving as she sobbed. 'I went cold when he said what the dance was.'

Peggy's brow furrowed. 'What was so terrible?' She leant closer to hear Mona's whisper.

'The cancan, Peggy.'

Peggy poured more brandy and Mona cradled the glass in her palm as she spoke.

'When Marv told us about the production, I felt sick. He stood in the wings, salivating at our humiliation. I closed my eyes and tried to dance, but in my mind, I was back at the Diamond. For the first time in my life, I didn't know whether I wanted to dance. And the vile choreographer had us lifting our skirts and petticoats while doing high-kicks, splits and cartwheels.'

When Mona told Peggy about the man with the top hat and the missing teeth, Peggy screamed with laughter and replenished their drinks. Mona managed to smile but before she could tell her about the man outside the apartment building, Peggy spoke.

'But you've done it before, Mona. Why was it different this time?'

Mona bit her lip. This was the sadness, the acceptance that her dancing days were over. She took a deep breath.

'The furious rhythms were too much for me and I forgot my steps and cues. I left every rehearsal exhausted and racked with pain. The years of malnutrition at the Diamond have taken their toll and damaged my bones, I have permanent back ache. I'm not strong enough for such a show. I hated every minute of it.'

Peggy raised her eyebrows then took Mona's hands. 'My dear Mona, you do know every show won't be like that, don't you? "*Toujours Belle*" is a delightful production with not a whiff of scandal! Apart from everything going on between the performers backstage, of course!'

Mona smiled, it made little difference. The dark shadow of the Diamond loomed large in her mind, she feared it always would. On the one occasion she gathered enough strength to leave the flat with Peggy, she only made it as far as the front door of the building. As she stepped over the threshold panic gripped her. It started in her feet and shot up her spine then into her temples. She shook as hot then cold waves of nausea engulfed her. The familiar blackness closed in, and she leant against the door. Peggy said to match her gasping breaths to her own calm rhythm, then she led her back to the flat and told her to sleep. When Peggy returned after rehearsals, she wasn't alone. She had asked a doctor to examine Mona. Mona objected, saying it was just a fever, but Peggy insisted. Reluctantly, Mona allowed the doctor to hold her hand and ask his questions. When he had finished, he advised her to try and get some sleep. She put her ear to the door to hear his hushed diagnosis.

'Nervous, fast pulse, exhaustion…'

'What would you advise to help her?'

Mona missed his reply. After he left, she opened the bedroom door. 'Did he say I'm mad?'

Peggy rushed to reassure her. 'No, of course not.'

'What then? A lunatic who's only fit for the asylum?'

An image of Gateshead's asylum snaked into Mona's mind. Women were confined for a lot less than being too nervous to go out. She'd heard tales of women imprisoned for hysteria or laziness, women described as having vicious vices or being infected with smallpox. Some of it was rumour but she knew of women who were at home one day then never seen again.

Peggy took her hands. 'No, not a lunatic. Someone who has been through a series of terrible ordeals, and who needs to rest.'

'But when will I feel better? When will I be able to go out without panicking? When will these awful feelings leave me?'

Peggy embraced her. 'I don't know, darling. But you know you're safe here, don't you?'

Mona managed a small, sad smile. 'Yes, Peggy. I do.'

Over the next few weeks, the women fell into an easy routine. Peggy went to work, and Mona stayed in the flat. Peggy had a vast collection of books and magazines on all sorts of subjects and Mona worked her way through them. Each evening Peggy regaled Mona with stories of the different personalities at the theatre, particularly Monsieur le Grand, her dramatic French director. Part of Mona longed for that world, but a bigger part remained too afraid to leave Peggy's flat. One evening when Peggy returned, she said the director had granted them a rare day off. It would soon be Christmas and he had suggested they could all use some time to go shopping, before their already hectic performance schedule became all-consuming over the festive period.

'And, I have a suggestion. We need to get you out of this flat.'

Mona stiffened.

'I know you're anxious, but we'll get a cab right outside and it will drop us at Selfridges. I'll be with you the whole time. You need to try at some point. You can't stay inside forever.'

Mona knew Peggy was right and that she would be in safe hands, but still she hesitated. She had allowed the crippling anxiety to control her for too long and she wasn't sure she could overcome it.

'Sleep on it, darling. But remember I only have one day off.'

The next day Mona woke to snow. Soft gentle flakes fell past the window. She remembered a snowy winter in Gateshead. Theodosia had taken her and Dinah to the People's Park and they made a snowman. Back at Seymour Terrace, freezing cold and wet through, Theodosia made cocoa. Mona was comforted now by the memory of warming her small hands around the cup. Peggy knocked gently on her door, interrupting her thoughts.

'Well? What's the verdict? Selfridges? Their cocoa is delicious!'

Mona took a deep breath. 'All right. Selfridges it is.'

It was mid-afternoon by the time they stepped out of the cab back at Peggy's flat. They hurried inside as the snow continued to fall. As Peggy closed the door Mona shook her wet coat and hung it up. She turned, her cheeks glowing red with cold.

'Thank you, Peggy. I couldn't have done that without your help.'

'Was it as bad as you expected?'

Mona considered the question. She had been shaking like a leaf in the wind when they left the flat, but Peggy held her arm until they were in the cab. It happened again when they arrived at Selfridges, but she relaxed once they were inside. She was distracted by the array of beautiful goods Peggy delighted in pointing out. Once or twice, she sensed someone watching her but there was no sign of the man who had followed her in New York. The cocoa was as delicious as Peggy had promised and Mona said the trip hadn't been as bad as she expected. She yawned, her first venture outside in weeks had exhausted her. As she headed towards her bedroom, Peggy called her back.

'A letter came for you while we were out.'

Mona stopped dead, gripped by the now familiar paranoia. Every nerve in her body jangled.

'A letter? For me? But who knows I'm here? Who is it from?'

Peggy held the letter out towards her and spoke softly. 'I'm sure it's nothing to worry about but you won't know who it's from unless you open it.'

Mona's hand shook as she took the envelope. The writing looked familiar, but blood pounded in her temples as she tried to concentrate. She turned the envelope over, inspecting it from every angle. Peggy handed her an ornate letter-opener and Mona slit the envelope open with a single swift slice. She took out the sheet of crisp white notepaper and an array of emotions played across her face. Disbelief, anger, despair, delight. Then she uttered a name. 'Louis.' She sank into a chair, still clutching the letter. She relinquished her grip as Peggy reached for it.

'Why now? Why has he found his conscience and written to you after all this time?'

'I have no idea.'

'Will you meet him?'

Mona stared at Peggy. Their trip to Selfridges had proved she wasn't insane; she could find the confidence to rebuild her life. Confronting Louis and demanding an explanation for his behaviour was part of her recovery. She needed to deal with his betrayal once and for all.

'Yes, it's about time I gave him a piece of my mind!'

Peggy smiled. She handed the letter over and Mona read it again. *Dear Mona,*

I know this letter will be a surprise. I am so sorry for my behaviour; you did not deserve such poor treatment. I hope we can meet and put the past behind us. If you can find it in your heart to forgive me, please meet me at the Lyons Cafe on Shaftesbury Avenue at 11 o'clock on the 2nd of January. I hope all will be well between us once more.

Yours faithfully,

Louis.'

Ivy

Mrs Newbold's arms were outstretched to welcome Ivy back and she learnt Bertie had returned to London. Mrs Newbold said he had sent her a note, Clara had placed it in her room. Ivy smiled as she walked into her bedroom. She took Bertie's note from the dressing table and kissed it.

'My Darling,

I wanted this letter to be waiting for you on your return to London. I have missed you with all my heart and I love you dearly. I long to see you and I will call at Mrs Newbold's this evening. There is much for us to catch up on. I am truly sorry there was not better news for you in New York. I hope that together we will be able to find your dear sister in London.

Yours affectionately,

Bertie.'

Ivy lay down and pulled her knees into her chest. She jumped when Clara knocked on her bedroom door. She had fallen asleep holding Bertie's letter.

'Miss Ivy, Mr Primavesi is here to see you. He's in the parlour with Mrs Newbold.'

'Thank you, Clara. Please tell them I will be downstairs directly.'

She washed her face and tidied her hair. She opened her wardrobe. Each beautiful dress evoked a happy memory. She chose a green day dress; Bertie had said the colour complemented her auburn hair. She hurried to the parlour and tore the door open. Bertie stood in front of the fireplace; his wide, handsome smile welcomed her home. She flew into his open arms.

Mrs Newbold poured generous martinis as Ivy explained the misunderstanding about the private detective. When she had finished, Bertie took her hand and spoke in his soothing manner.

'The responsibility rests with Walter and me, my dear. I regret using a private detective, Mona must have been terrified to think someone was following her.'

'Well, I agreed to your suggestion, so I must also take some responsibility, Bertie.'

'The question is what we do next. How do we find her now she has returned to London?'

Ivy smiled as she explained about the letter she had written to Louis from New York. If he followed her instructions, Ivy would be meeting her sister in a few weeks' time. She had told Louis to say he wanted to meet Mona at the Lyons Cafe on Shaftesbury Avenue, at 11 o'clock on the 2nd of January. She prayed her plan would work, that the temptation of being reunited with her lost love would be too great for Mona to resist. The 2nd of January 1912 would be Ivy's 29th birthday and the best present she could have would be a reunion with her sister.

Chapter 34

Ivy

Mrs Newbold's house brimmed with bonhomie during Christmas and New Year and Bertie visited often. But as midnight came and went on the 31st of December 1911, all Ivy could think about was being reunited with her sister and then her niece. Two days later she waited in the Lyons Cafe on Shaftesbury Avenue. She was early but wanted to be there when Mona arrived. The young waitress approached her but she explained that she wanted to wait for her companion.

It was almost 11 o'clock, Ivy's eyes were fixed on the door. Each time it opened a small bell chimed and she jumped. Today was her 29th birthday and at breakfast Mrs Newbold and Clara had presented her with gifts. A beautiful green silk scarf from Clara and from Mrs Newbold, knowing Ivy didn't favour the popular large-brimmed hats festooned with flora, rosettes or plumage, a new style '*Tam*' hat. It was made from a deep green velvet with a brim of woven straw braids, untrimmed apart from a delicate gold cord and tassel, tied around the crown. She waited in her new green hat and scarf, listening to the beats of her heart. She breathed in and out, trying to calm her nerves.

It was precisely 11 o'clock. Bertie had offered to accompany her, but Ivy declined, worried Mona would spot her waiting with a stranger and run away again.

It was five minutes after 11 o'clock. Although Bertie had agreed not to accompany her, he had insisted on coming to Mrs Newbold's that afternoon with her birthday gift. Should she leave?

It was ten minutes after 11 o'clock. Mona wasn't coming. Ivy decided to order something and wait a little longer. As she turned to get the waitress's attention her head jerked back towards the door as the tinny chime of the bell rang out once more.

Sisters

Mona woke in a cold sweat, panic prickling her skin. She couldn't leave the flat. What if it was a trick and the letter was from one of Solomon Zettler's henchmen or Andrew Glass? The letter had arrived unexpectedly but had her lost love's conscience really got the better of him after all these years? Was he ready to do the decent thing by her and Evie? Was it possible he still loved her? She swayed as a wave of nausea rose. If the letter was from Louis, how did he know where she was?

Peggy had offered to go with her, but she refused. She needed to face Louis alone and confront the ghosts of her past. She forced herself to remember the day she went to Leighton Mansions, determined to have her say before she left London. Her down-trodden appearance had led a policeman to mistake her for a prostitute. She shuddered. She remembered the promise she had made to herself. To make her fortune as a dancer on Broadway then return to confront Louis. To stand on his doorstep dressed in her best New York wardrobe. To return as the respectable lady her mother had brought her up to be. As she stood outside the Lyons Cafe on Shaftesbury Avenue, she stroked her deep red wool coat and her new hat. If he didn't look too closely, Louis might not notice her crippling anxiety. He would see the woman Mona had fought so hard to become.

Mona pushed the cafe door open, looking up as the tinny bell chimed. Her gaze shifted as the woman stood and moved towards her. Mona met the woman's eyes, her own piercing blue eyes. She swayed as emotions flooded her body. Guilt, fear, sadness and relief. But the emotion that triumphed was love, as Mona fell into her sister's open, welcoming arms.

They asked the waitress for cocoa and sat in silence, holding hands across the table. Eventually Ivy gently pulled her hand away and picked up her cocoa. Ivy smiled, this was her sister, yet she was changed. What had Marv said about Mona's nerves? The woman opposite Ivy tapped her fingernails on the table and jiggled her leg. There was an edge to Mona, a sharpness that hadn't existed in her younger sister before. Ivy chose her words carefully. 'I wasn't sure you would come.'

'I thought it was Louis.'

'I'm sorry. I didn't know how else to persuade you to come. Are you disappointed?'

Mona smiled over her cocoa. 'No, I'm glad it was you. I've missed you.'

'I've missed you too.'

They touched hands and Ivy saw Mona's softness flicker, under the surface of her sharp edges. Once Mona started speaking, she couldn't stop. She spoke quickly, her words tumbling out like water over stones in a babbling brook. Throughout Mona's story, something nagged at Ivy, but she couldn't pin it down. When Mona had finished, she sat back in her chair and puffed out her cheeks. Her tired eyes told Ivy how much effort her speech had taken.

'It's all right. Everything will be all right now, I promise. I have a lot to tell you too, but the most important thing is for us to go to Gateshead and bring Evie to London. I have tried to see her many times over the years, but Lizzie has always contrived to keep us apart. When I have seen her, I've been worried...' Ivy stopped; it was too soon to voice her concerns to Mona. 'I'll book train tickets for tomorrow; we'll meet here and travel to Kings Cross together.'

Mona nodded. The fight she had mustered for her confrontation with Louis was gone. The sisters gathered their coats, hats and bags and left the cafe, arm in arm. After she had seen Mona into a cab, Ivy allowed her concern to take shape. Other than saying Evie could stay with her at Peggy's flat, Mona hadn't mentioned her daughter. Ivy shook her head; she was seeing problems where they didn't exist. She made her way back to Mrs Newbold's.

The Waitress

She stared open-mouthed when the second woman arrived. They were so alike yet so different. She waited until they were settled before approaching the table to take their order. Her pencil hovered over her pad, but she wrote nothing, unable to tear her eyes away. Those eyes, they must be sisters.

When she returned with their cocoa, she stole glances at them. She guessed that the one who had arrived first was the elder. The other, less polished one was younger, but an air of despair hung around her. They were both beautiful and dressed in the latest fashionable styles. When they spoke, she struggled to place their accents. They weren't from London, but both had a lilt to their accents she didn't recognise. She hovered and contrived to pass their table more than was necessary until her boss pointed towards the sink of unwashed dishes. She set about her task, but her eyes were fixed on the women, her neck craned towards their table. The boss said the broken cup and saucer would be taken from her wages. Later, she said it was a small price to pay as she regaled the juicy snippets to her flatmate. Her friend's eyes were out on stalks by the time she had finished.

She said their conversation was hushed but they had talked about such scandalous matters, *'an abandoned girl, a seedy music hall, an attack, a voyage to New York City in America, a woman called Peggy, a private detective and a man called Bertie.'*

Her flatmate asked how the womens' conversation had ended and the waitress cleared her throat before making her pronouncement, *'they are meeting at the cafe again tomorrow, then they are going somewhere called Gateshead to rescue a little girl called Evie.'* Her flatmate showered her with questions until she raised her hands.

'That's all I know; I'll tell you what happens tomorrow.'

Chapter 35

Lizzie

Lizzie lay slumped against the bar in the Globe. The room swayed and she moaned as she lifted her head and tried to focus. Harry Campbell leered as he grabbed her arm and pushed her towards the door. She tried to clutch the bar, but his firm grip held her as her feet slid across the floor.

'Ah no, Harry, one more drink, eh?'

'No. It's time for you to make good on your promise!'

Lizzie stared, a vague recollection of another conversation played at the corners of her mind, something about the girl. When had she last seen her? She had lost all track of time. As she stumbled outside, she stopped. It was dark. It had been light when she went into the Globe, but was that today or yesterday? Christmas had come and gone but had the new year started? Was it 1912 yet? She closed one eye, trying to focus. Harry had asked her to do something and offered her money, she remembered her hand in his pocket and her fingers closing around a shilling. And he had said there would be a lot more if she did something, but what? She tried to remember but as soon as a coherent thought formed it slipped away again. A terrible doubt pricked at her conscience; she had agreed to do something horrific. Harry pawed at her as they turned the corner. He pulled her into a doorway. Despite her bulk he was stronger, and he pinned her against the door.

'C'mon, give us a kiss.'

The warm stench of stale beer and tobacco reached her nostrils and she heaved. 'No!' She tried to push him away. He held her arms roughly and found her lips with his. He pushed his swollen, sour-tasting tongue in between her lips and into her mouth.

'C'mon you dirty whore, you know you want to.' He continued pushing his tongue down her throat and started squeezing her breasts with his grubby hands. She gagged, she had to stop this.

'All right, but let's go inside.'

'That's more like it.' Harry ran a dirty knuckle down her cheek and smiled lasciviously.

'Then I'll have the afters you promised me. This is the start of better things for you, Lizzie Brown. You'll never have to borrow money for your precious sherry ever again, think about that.'

Lizzie froze as if he had thrown a bucket of icy water at her. Harry pushed her against the door and the memory of what she had agreed to do returned with sickening, horrific clarity. She hesitated. Could she do this appalling thing? Harry grabbed her chin and yelled into her face.

'Not having second thoughts, I hope. We made a deal, remember?' He grabbed her arm and reached past her to open the door. He shoved her hard and she hit the cold stone floor.

'Get her, now!'

Lizzie wept; dirty, snotty sobs. How could she have agreed to prostitute her cousin's daughter and sell her to this brute? She had accepted Harry's offer after Evie stole her money and tried to run away. She had flown into a furious rage, wanting rid of her once and for all. Her bitterness at being the spinster cousin forced to look after Evie had consumed her, driving her to this shameful point. Her hopes of marriage and children had disappeared when Evie arrived. The man who was interested in her hadn't been near since the day she told him about Evie. She always intended to spend some of the money Dinah sent on Evie, but the lure of the Globe was always stronger than any desire to care for a child. Her comfort came in the form of oblivion and there was never enough money left for good food or decent clothes for Evie. After she had taught the brat a lesson she calmed down, but her memory was ravaged by drink and the conversation with Harry had been lost from her mind.

Harry's boot connected with her cheek. The cold stone sobered her up and she managed to turn her head. Harry towered over her, smirking lecherously. She pulled herself into a seating position, blinking as blood pounded in her temples. She turned her yellowed, rheumy eyes on him. 'All right, let's find her.'

Harry didn't hesitate. As he pulled her towards the curtain separating Evie's rotten mattress from the rest of the room, Lizzie grabbed the old enamel wash basin and swung it at his head. He staggered but didn't fall. She grabbed the curtain and he followed, yanking at her hair. She pulled back the curtain. Evie wasn't there. She smelt Harry's hot, fetid breath on the back of her neck.

'If she's not here I'll have you instead, then I'll have her when she comes back,' he snarled the drunken words into her face.

'Not in this lifetime, you won't!'

She pushed him and he staggered back towards the door. He roared and came towards her again. He pounced, pushing her onto the dirty mattress. Blood poured from the gash on his head and as he pushed her skirt up, she raised her foot and kicked him hard in-between his legs. He bellowed and rolled onto the floor. She tried to stand but the room tilted sharply, blood thumped in her ears and waves of nausea crashed around her. As she fell her foot twisted and snagged on something. The rough edge of the loose floorboard dug deep into her flesh. She looked down. A beautiful, haunted face looked up from under the floorboard. A picture of her cousin Margaret, Evie's mother. As she looked into Margaret's piercing blue eyes, heavy footsteps stomped towards her. Harry towered over her, clutching the bloody enamel basin. He swore and swung it towards her head.

Ivy

Before returning to Mrs Newbold's, Ivy sent a telegram. She had wanted Mona to send it, but her sister hesitated. Ivy knew it would take time for Mona and Evie to be reconciled. She smiled as she pictured Evie receiving word that she and her mother would be with her the next day.

Mrs Newbold and Bertie listened as Ivy related Mona's sorry tale. Ivy spoke of Mona's relief when she discovered the man following her in New York was a private detective. Mona said she understood why Walter and Bertie had employed him. Ivy told Mrs Newbold and Bertie that she and Mona were catching the train north the next day, to bring Evie to London. They had agreed to introduce one another to the new people in their lives, once Evie was safe. After a while Ivy excused herself to go to the bathroom. When she returned, Bertie was alone. Ivy smiled. She had fallen in love and now she had been reunited with her sister. All that remained was for them to bring Evie to London. Bertie cleared his throat. He reached into the inside pocket of his jacket before kneeling on the rug in Mrs Newbold's parlour. He produced a small, velvet box and Ivy gasped.

'Miss Ivy Dinah Jane Leighton, would you do me the great honour of becoming my wife?'

Ivy looked into Bertie's kind eyes and smiled with delight. 'Yes! Yes, of course I would!' Bertie stood and embraced her. They turned at the sound of applause and cheers from the doorway. Clara and Mrs Newbold entered the room, chilled champagne and crystal glasses at the ready.

'I took the liberty of asking Mrs Newbold's permission to make my proposal here and she insisted on providing the champagne! I hope you don't object?'

Ivy laughed as Mrs Newbold enveloped her.

'Object? I am delighted!'

Mona

After Mona told Peggy about the reunion with Ivy, Peggy said she had two questions.

'I thought your sister was called Dinah?'

Mona explained about her sister's name, telling Peggy Ivy's choice of surname meant she had never forgotten her. Despite everything Mona had done, Ivy had never stopped loving her.

'What was your second question, Peggy?'

'Were you disappointed it wasn't Louis?'

Mona considered the question. She was shocked to realise that from the moment she set eyes on Ivy, she hadn't given Louis another thought, other than in the telling of her story.

'No. It was my sister and that's so much more important.'

'Has she heard from your cousin, the one who's looking after your little girl?'

'No, although she has continued to send money to Lizzie for Evie. Now we're back together, we have a plan, and everything is going to be all right again!' Mona smiled.

'So, what is this plan?'

'We have agreed to travel back to Gateshead together. We're going to get Evie from Pipewellgate and bring her to London. She will live here, with me and you. We're going tomorrow.'

A shadow crossed Peggy's face.

'Peggy, what's wrong?'

Evie

'Evie! Where are you?' Jack's shouts reached her as the train came into view. She tried to turn towards his voice, but her neck refused to move.

'Quick! Get off the lines! There's a train!'

The train's whistle jolted Evie back to reality. Through the heavy rain the outline of the huge, thundering train was unmistakable. As the high-pitched whistle shrieked again, she scrambled on all fours towards

Jack. Needles of hot pain shot through her body as she forced her reluctant limbs to move. She tried to stand but slipped on the wet lines. Her head hit the cold metal of the track and she lay, stunned and unmoving. The whistle shrieked again, and everything went black.

'Evie! Can you hear me?'

She and Nancy were running along a beach, holding hands. Then they were in a bedroom drinking cocoa. Then a train was speeding towards her, and everything went black again.

'Evie! It's me, Jack. Please wake up!'

Her heavy limbs refused to move. A wave of dizziness hit her as she tried to move her head. Rain splashed her face and something heavy pressed on her chest. When she tried to open her eyes, pain shot through her face, she was still black and blue from Lizzie's beating. Her head thumped and nausea rose into her throat as the memories of her failed escape attempt and Nancy's death returned. She turned onto her side and the bile from her stomach threatened to choke her as she retched onto the grass at the side of the railway line. The pain in her head exploded like a firework and she put her hand to her temple. Thick, red blood.

'It's all right. Come home with me. Uncle John will clean you up.'

Evie struggled to walk but with Jack's help they made their ungainly way to his uncle's house on Cross Street. Jack's parents died when he was a baby and his uncle and aunt had taken him in. Unlike Evie, he was well cared for, had enough to eat and a comfortable, warm bed. Sadly, Jack's aunt died not long after they took him in, but his uncle didn't abandon him. As John Todd helped his nephew to get her inside, Evie bowed her head to hide her tears. This was how family should be. Jack's uncle didn't speak until Evie was cleaned up and he had applied a thick bandage to her forehead. She stayed silent as he spoke.

'Did you know you were born near here?'

She shook her head; she knew almost nothing of her life before Lizzie.

'Your mother, grandmother and aunt lived in Seymour Terrace after your grandfather died. It's only a few streets away.'

At the mention of her grandmother Evie spoke. 'I think I remember her. I called her Grama. She was beautiful and she sang lullabies to me.' Everything spilled out in a rush in Evie's desperation to show them someone had loved her, once.

John smiled. 'She loved you very much, she was so proud showing you off in your pram.'

Evie's lip trembled but she swallowed hard. She mustn't cry, not now when she was about to learn about her mother. She whispered the question, terrified but determined to hear the answer.

'My mother. Do you know what happened to her?'

John nodded, tears in his eyes. 'I'm sorry, pet. She must have been desperate to do it.'

'To do what? What did she do?'

John took a deep breath and said the words quickly. 'She abandoned you. She left you, thinking you were going to stay with Lizzie in Pipewellgate.'

'Where did she go?'

'She went to London with your father, Louis Levy.'

The rumour Jack had told her was true. Her parents had run off to London without her. They had left her to rot in a slum with a drunk for a guardian. Why had she mattered so little to them? What had she done to deserve that? She looked at Jack's uncle, suddenly cold as another memory tried to snake its way into her mind. 'What do you mean, she *thought* I was going to stay with Lizzie in Pipewellgate? I did stay there; I've got the bruises to show for it.'

John pursed his lips and shook his head.

'I'm sorry pet, before you were taken to Pipewellgate you were somewhere else.'

Evie's head spun as the memory forced itself upon her. A woman with big arms. Biting, nipping flies, a small dark cupboard. The memories had never dissipated, they had always lurked at the corners of her mind, waiting to pounce. Jack's uncle was speaking.

'I'm sorry, where did you say I was?'

'The Union Workhouse, pet. I'm so sorry you were sent there.'

Evie took a deep breath. She had come this far, she needed to know everything.

'What about my aunt? Did she go to London with my parents?'

'No, pet. She had to go and work as a scullery maid at a country house in Northumberland.'

Evie tried to picture Aunt Dinah. Her aunt had visited her in Pipewellgate, but Lizzie made sure Evie and her aunt were rarely alone. Lizzie warned Evie against *speaking out of turn,'* in other words, telling her aunt the truth about her life in Pipewellgate. Evie did as she was told.

Jack's uncle gestured towards a table where he had set out a bowl of steaming soup.

'You need some decent food inside you, then you need to sleep.'

After Evie had eaten, she lay down in bed and closed her eyes. Sleep came swiftly.

Chapter 36

The 3rd of January 1912

The Waitress

The waitress averted her eyes, trying to hide her excitement, as the more polished of the sisters arrived. The woman, her only customer that morning, watched the door. Her eyes didn't move even as she sipped her cocoa. The woman waited, but her sister was late. The woman waited for half an hour; she finished her drink. The waitress approached, intending to ask if she would like anything else. The woman stood, pushed her chair in and left the money for her cocoa on the table. The woman left without speaking, the tinny chime of the bell echoed around the now empty cafe.

Evie

Safe at Cross Street, Evie fell into a deep, dreamless sleep. The next morning, she told Jack she was going back to Pipewellgate. He frowned and repeated his uncle's offer for her to stay. She shook her head. She hobbled away and stood out of sight on the corner. She waited until Lizzie left, not yet ready for the confrontation. She entered the ramshackle house and sat on her threadbare mattress.

When she woke dusk was falling, casting sinister shadows around the room. She groped for a stub of candle Lizzie kept under her chair. As its dim glow illuminated the room, she considered Jack's uncle's words. Why had she meant so little to her parents? Why did she deserve to be sitting in this freezing cold room waiting for her reluctant guardian? She reached down to the loose floorboard under the small table next to her mattress. Her hand stopped in mid-air, there were red spots on the floor. Red like blood. She touched her forehead, but the bandage Jack's uncle had applied was dry. She looked more closely. The spots were dull, not new. As she inspected the blood her mother's face stared up at her. The handkerchief lay to one side, the picture no longer wrapped inside. Evie stood and looked around Lizzie's room, noticing the chaos for the first time. An overturned chair and dry blood on the old enamel wash basin from the sink told her there had been trouble here. Who had Lizzie been fighting with? She retrieved her mother's picture and wrapped it inside the handkerchief. She replaced it under the floorboard, she had little that was precious in her life and having lost Nancy, she wanted to keep these possessions safe.

She licked her lips; she could still taste the soup she had at Cross Street. She sighed, how many more nights would she go to bed cold and hungry? She dug her fingernails into her palms. It was time Lizzie faced her responsibilities. She smoothed her ragged dress and hobbled along the stinking sewer of Pipewellgate. The Globe's flickering lights illuminated the dark street. She stood on tiptoe and rubbed the dirty glass with the sleeve of her dress, peering through the window. It was payday and the pub was full. Women and children huddled in nearby slums would be hoping for food, money, perhaps comfort, from these men tonight. She saw women like Lizzie, women with no morals drinking and dancing with loud, rough men. Her mouth fell open at the sight of Harry Campbell. Harry had never done an honest day's work in his life, yet he always had money. Harry spotted Evie and grinning maliciously, he spun Lizzie round to face her. He pointed towards Evie and said something. Evie had seen enough; Lizzie wasn't coming home anytime soon.

She trudged away, hunger gnawing at her empty stomach. The night grew colder, and her teeth chattered. Lowering her head against the biting wind and thickening fog, she fought back tears. As she approached Pipewellgate, a shadowy figure loomed into view, near

Lizzie's tenement. Evie screwed her eyes up, but the figure disappeared into the fog. She stopped dead and squeezed back against the wall. Her heart thudded. Harry had followed her, taking the shortcut through the graveyard. A hand reached out of the fog. She didn't know what would be the death of her, a knife, a hammer, a gun? She closed her eyes and waited for the fatal blow.

Ivy

Ivy waited nearly half an hour. Mona couldn't have forgotten; they had arranged it only the day before. She left the cafe and hailed a cab. She jumped out at Peggy's flat, anger spurring her on. She had spent enough time chasing her sister's shadow, she refused to do it any longer. A man was leaving the building and she hurried up the steps as he waited to hold the door open.

'Thank you.'

He frowned. 'Excuse me, Miss. You look very familiar. Have we met before?'

Ivy tutted. 'No. You are mistaking me for my sister, Miss Mona Leighton. She is staying here with Miss Willow.'

The man raised his eyebrows. 'I see. The thing is, Miss Leighton, they're not here.'

'What do you mean?'

'She and Miss Willow have gone. I have the flat next to Miss Willow's and I heard them moving around early this morning. They left before it was light.'

Ivy stared open-mouthed as the man walked away, leaving her standing in the doorway. She was about to leave when another man approached her.

'Excuse me, Miss. I am the building attendant. Did you say you are Miss Leighton's sister?'

'Yes, do you know where she is?'

'I'm afraid not, but she left a note asking me to give you this, if you came looking for her.' The man reached behind the reception desk and Ivy gasped. He held a battered, musty old bag. As he handed it over, she had no doubt. It was her mother's carpet bag.

'I don't understand. Why did she leave?'

'I'm sorry, Miss. I wish I could help you, but that was all she said.'

In the cab to Mrs Newbold's Ivy tapped her fingernails against the window. Had she been foolish to trust Mona? Had she driven her away by insisting she face her responsibilities? A musty smell rose from the bag, and she pushed it under the seat. Her foot connected with something inside. The smell grew as she unclasped the brass buckles. Her lip trembled as she stared at her mother's diary. Her footsteps were heavy and slow as she entered the house.

'Is Mrs Newbold in the parlour, Clara?'

'Yes, Miss. Should I bring tea?'

'No, thank you. I think Mrs Newbold will pour large brandies when I give her my news.'

She collapsed into a chair and took a mouthful of the expected brandy. The hot, sour taste helped to dislodge the lump in her throat. She related her tale, and the older woman shook her head.

'I cannot understand why any mother wouldn't be desperate to be reunited with her child.'

Ivy flushed; she knew of Mrs Newbold's despair at not having a child with her beloved husband. She shook her head, some people would give all their worldly possessions to be blessed with a child, yet Mona had discarded hers as if Evie was a dress she no longer wanted. Ivy couldn't defend her sister any longer. Mona had abandoned her daughter yet again.

'I know, and she does have a good heart. I think sometimes she forgets her responsibilities and grasps whatever new excitement is offered. I expected she would be there to meet me today. I believed she had grown up and was ready to be a proper mother.'

'What will you do now, my dear? Where could she have gone?'

Ivy stared then nodded, resolute. This wasn't her fault; she hadn't driven Mona away. Her sister had chosen to leave, the fault sat squarely on Mona's selfish shoulders.

'I don't know where she has gone but I know what I intend to do. And no part of my plan includes my sister.' Ivy wept and Mrs Newbold poured them both another large brandy.

Evie

The match rasped and she smelt sulphur as the glow illuminated her face. Her eyes flew open, and Jack smiled. She pushed him away. 'You idiot, you scared me half to death! What do you want?'

'I've been waiting for you because Uncle John had this to deliver.'

Evie's pulse quickened as she stared at the letter. Years earlier Jack's uncle had agreed that if any letters arrived addressed to Miss Eveline Brown, he would hand them straight to her. Lizzie had destroyed many of Evie's letters, this was only the second one she had ever received.

'Lizzie was drunk and raving in the street. Shouting she hadn't had any money for you again, saying things needed to change. Then she headed to the Globe.'

Evie's cheeks burned. Lizzie never tired of telling her she was only there because her aunt and mother sent money for her upkeep. After taking a letter years earlier and suffering a harsh beating from Lizzie, Evie had never dared to look again. She didn't know whether money arrived, and Lizzie wasted it in the Globe, or whether her aunt and mother had reneged on their promise.

Jack continued. 'Uncle John asked me to hand it to you in person. I've been waiting in the freezing cold, Miss Eveline Brown, a thank you wouldn't come amiss!'

His chin jutted out huffily and despite her despair, she laughed. 'Well, are you going to read it?'

She trembled as she took the letter. A sweet smell rose from the paper, her aunt's scent. She closed one eye and managed to make out her name, but her useless eyes couldn't read the sender's name and return address. She handed it back. 'Read it Jack, please.'

'It's a telegram from your aunt.' He smiled as he read the thin sheet.
'YOUR MOTHER AND I WILL ARRIVE IN GATESHEAD TOMORROW. WE WILL BRING YOU BACK TO LONDON WITH US.

YOUR LOVING AUNT, DINAH.'

Evie gasped. In the letter she had stolen from Lizzie years before, her aunt had promised that once she was married, Evie could live with her. Was Aunt Dinah getting married? Was her nightmare finally over? She closed her eyes, not daring to hope.

Her hand shook as she took the telegram. Suddenly, Jack dragged her into a doorway.

'Ow, that hurt, what are you doing?'

'Shush, look.'

She peeked out. She saw Harry pushing Lizzie towards the house. They staggered and swayed, and Evie's empty stomach heaved. She clutched the precious telegram and allowed herself to hope. For a better life, with enough to eat and clean clothes. A life where she wouldn't be mocked because her shoes didn't fit. Where she would be safe from brutes like Lizzie and Harry.

'Time to go.' Jack's voice brooked no argument.

'But…' She started then stopped.

Jack stared. 'But what? You're not considering staying here when you have a way out?'

'No, but there's something in the house.' Evie hesitated.

'What?'

'The picture of my mother.'

'And you're prepared to go into that midden of a house and tell those two disgusting creatures you're leaving? Haven't you had enough beatings at Lizzie's hands?'

Her cuts and bruises proved she had, but still she hesitated.

'I only have one picture of my mother and it's in there.' She had memorised her mother's beautiful dress, long necklace and fur wrap. And her wave. Whenever Evie looked at the picture, she imagined her mother was thinking about her, that she was imagining waving to her daughter.

'Where is it?' Jack barked the question.

'There's a loose floorboard under the table next to where I sleep.' She reddened, ashamed to admit she didn't have a bed, only a mangy old mattress. 'The picture and my mother's handkerchief, they're in there.'

Jack stared. 'Listen, I heard something the other day.'

'What?' Evie sighed; people had whispered about her for years. She was scruffy, stupid, her mother had run away because she didn't care about her. There was nothing she hadn't heard herself many times before. But what Jack told her was new, and it was worse than anything else.

'It's Lizzie…'

'What about her?'

Jack hesitated. 'Uncle John said everyone was talking about Lizzie and Harry Campbell. They were rolling drunk last night, arguing and fighting in the street at closing time. Then today Lizzie was stumbling around Pipewellgate with a massive cut on her head.'

Evie understood where the dry blood in Lizzie's room had come from.

Jack continued. 'And they carried on where they left off, drinking and fighting.'

'What's it all about?'

Jack looked away. 'I'm not sure I should say.'

'Why not?'

He shuffled his feet as he cleared his throat. 'It's something to do with you, that's why not. I overheard Uncle John talking to his friend about it. I'm sorry, Evie.'

'What? Tell me!'

Jack took a deep breath. 'Lizzie is planning to sell you to Harry Campbell.'

Evie frowned. She was a girl, not a bolt of fabric or a side of ham to be sold to the highest bidder at the quayside market in Newcastle. She frowned again, what had she read on the Crone's lips when she looked in through the window as she and Lizzie gossiped? It was about someone taking Evie and Lizzie could name her price. She swayed as she realised it was true. Lizzie had shown her true colours and was about to betray her in the most wicked way possible. Her thoughts were interrupted by a bellow of pain and the sound of breaking glass.

'I'm not going in there, it's too risky. We have to go Evie, right now.'

'But where? My aunt said they would arrive tomorrow. They won't know where to find me.'

'Come with me. I'll ask my uncle to leave a message for your aunt at Newcastle station. She'll get it when their train arrives, so they will know where you are.'

Still Evie hesitated.

'Listen Evie, your mother will be here tomorrow. Isn't that better than any picture?'

She considered the picture she had treasured for so long, but she knew Jack was right.

'Now hurry before those monsters come for you!' Jack grabbed her hand, and they ran.

True to his word, Jack asked his uncle to send a message to the station for Evie's aunt. Later, Evie clutched the precious telegram. She dared to believe that tomorrow, she would be reunited with her mother. Eveline Dinah Annie Brown smiled as she closed her eyes to sleep.

Ivy

As the train pulled out of Kings Cross, Ivy silently thanked Mrs Newbold. Her landlady had agreed Evie could stay at Chestnut Tree Avenue until she and Bertie were married in a few months' time. Until then, Ivy had decided to take a break from the theatre to look after her niece.

Ivy had hugged Mrs Newbold, grateful for her magnanimous gesture. She understood her landlady's anguish that a mother could abandon her child as Mona had, not once but twice. Bertie had offered to accompany her to Gateshead, but Ivy insisted on going alone. She removed her mother's diary from her bag. She stroked the soft leather, now cracked and peeling. She took a deep breath and turned to the first, yellowed page. By the time Ivy arrived in Newcastle she had relived her mother's life in Paris and London. She had also read her sister's immature notes about her journey from Newcastle to London. How like her to start with good intentions and quickly be distracted. She had learnt more about her mother's life in Newcastle and Gateshead and the circumstances of the debt to Aunt Agatha. But a piece of the puzzle was missing. Why had the Registrar helped them? As she presented her ticket at Newcastle station the guard's eyes narrowed.

'Are you Miss Dinah Jane Brown?'

She went cold and stammered her answer. 'Yes.'

'A note has been delivered to the station for you. You can collect it from the ticket office.'

She thanked him and directed her shaking legs to the office. The note from John Todd left her anxious. Why was Evie with him and not with Lizzie? She started walking towards Cross Street, she would avoid Lizzie if she could. She could bypass Pipewellgate, but not the workhouse. She squinted at the familiar skyline, but something had changed. The dark bulk of the workhouse had always hidden everything beyond, but now the terraced streets were visible, laid out in long, dismal rows. She shook her head. She could see the streets because the workhouse had gone. She stepped closer, the crows and gulls picked over the rubble. Rats still scurried around the ruins, but of the building, nothing remained. Ivy raised her eyes to the sky and cheered. Good riddance!

At Cross Street, John Todd met her at the door and ushered her in. A small, wasted figure stood inside. The dirty girl was painfully thin. A ragged, over-sized shapeless dress hung around her emaciated frame and her eyes darted around the room, like a rabbit caught by a lamper. Ivy moved slowly, concerned not to frighten her. As she got closer, she looked into the girl's eyes. There was no doubt, they were Louis's dark brown eyes, it was her niece.

'Evie?'

*

Evie saw a woman's outline. A green coat and skirt. The woman spoke. The long-awaited, familiar voice of Aunt Dinah. Evie connected with her aunt's unmistakable, piercing blue eyes.

*

Ivy took in Evie's dirty, bruised face. She was black and blue from a vicious beating.

'Oh, my dear Evie, whatever has happened to you?'

Evie moved towards her aunt's open arms. As they embraced, Evie whispered. 'Is my mamma here?' The child's desperate wish, from the young girl's mouth, shattered Ivy's heart into a thousand pieces. She shook her head. Ivy had questions for John, but not questions she wanted to ask in front of Evie. Instead, she ate some stew and tried to make conversation. Her eyes kept shifting to her niece, who ate as if her life depended on it but didn't speak. John offered Ivy and Evie a bed for the night, but Ivy explained she wanted to catch the train back to London that evening. She would gather Evie's belongings and they would be on their way. Evie flinched as if she had been struck. John explained.

'She doesn't have anything, Miss Brown. Jack wanted to get her away from Pipewellgate because your cousin and Harry Campbell were in such a state. Jack was scared for her.'

'I'm sorry if I did wrong, Miss.'

'No, Jack. I am grateful to you both, for the care you have shown my niece. Without you, I dread to think what might have happened to her.'

'I have something for you, Miss Brown. It makes no sense to me but perhaps you will understand when you read it.' John handed Ivy an old, yellowed envelope.

She blew the dust from it and read her name, written neatly on the front. *'Miss Dinah Jane Brown, daughter of Theodosia Brown.'* She frowned at John and shrugged her shoulders.

'Did you walk past the workhouse on your way here? Or where it used to be?'

'Yes, I didn't know it had been demolished but I can't say I'm sorry.'

'No. Well, before the demolition began the current Registrar cleared out the office. He had never used it, didn't want to set foot in the place. He preferred to sign the death certificates at the Registry Office. He waded through an avalanche of papers but thankfully did a thorough job and found this letter. He gave it to me, thinking as the postman I would know what to do with it.'

Ivy shook as she opened the old letter. How long ago had it been written? She raised a fist to her mouth as she absorbed the enormity of the words. Words from beyond the grave. She smiled at John. 'Would you look after Evie while I visit someone?'

'Of course, but what does the letter say? Who are you going to visit?'

'My despicable aunt, Mrs Agatha Brown.'

Chapter 37

Agatha Brown

Agatha stared from the window of her grand townhouse as the woman opened the gate. The loud knock at the front door echoed around the empty house. After Agatha's husband had died the previous year, her staff had all upped and left. She had always known this day would come, when one of the Frenchwoman's daughters grew a spine and tried to take matters into her own hands. She had always expected it would be this one. The other was too flighty, weighed down by too much baggage. This one, Dinah, was more like her mother. No, what was her name now? Ivy Leighton. Why did members of her family keep changing their names? Him she understood, but not this one or her slut of a sister. Agatha had kept tabs on them over the years. Her reach went far beyond Gateshead, and she could have hooked them back at any time. But she had reasoned, as long as one of them repaid their wretched mother's debt, she would leave them be. Ivy marched up the path and Agatha turned away from the window, smirking. She would have the last word. She held all the cards.

*

The women stood facing each other in Agatha's parlour. Ivy looked around. There was none of the splendour of Theodosia's parlour in Seymour Terrace. No light, no beautiful '*objet d'art*,' no joy. Only dusty, bitter old Aunt Agatha. Ivy smiled and the cavernous lines between her aunt's brows deepened. Agatha rubbed her hands together and jabbed a bony finger in Ivy's direction.

'What do you think you've got to smile about? You still owe me money, don't forget!'

Ivy drummed her fingers on her cheek before answering. 'What if I refuse to pay?'

Agatha blew her red, veined cheeks out then yelled. 'The police would be after you for an unpaid debt before you drew your next breath! Don't think I wouldn't do it!' She bent double; the effort of her outburst had caused a coughing fit. Ivy waited as Agatha struggled to breathe. Eventually Agatha eased herself into a chair. Ivy smiled. Agatha's brow furrowed.

'You must have lost your mind, like your whore of a sister and your stuck-up mother!'

Ivy shook her head, still smiling. 'Or, I have some information that will finally rid our family of you.' She spoke calmly and Agatha's eyes narrowed.

'What rubbish are you talking? What information?'

'This.' With a flourish Ivy produced the yellowed letter.

'What's that old thing?'

'You will find you recognise his hand-writing.' Ivy leant over and pushed the envelope into her aunt's face. Agatha tried to grab it, but Ivy snatched it away. 'I'll read it to you, shall I?'

As Ivy read, her aunt removed her glasses and pinched the bridge of her nose with her fingers. Agatha tried to stand but another coughing fit forced her back into the chair. She blanched as words came from beyond the grave. Words of truth she had worked so hard to bury. She wheezed as she tried to form words. 'I will deny it. I will say you faked the letter. Who will believe the word of a scullery maid over a respectable member of the community?'

Ivy squared her shoulders. 'I am a singer and an actress. And I have evidence of your money lending. I kept precise records over the years as the *"interest accrued"* on my mother's debt continued to rise. A good solicitor would soon uncover the extent of your criminal activities.'

The fight went out of the older woman, like a large, popped balloon sagging into an unrecognisable shape. Ivy closed the door to her aunt's house and didn't look back. As she passed the long-since filled in pond in the grounds of the house, she paused to fold the item her aunt had given her. She slid it inside the envelope with the letter then ran back to Cross Street to collect Evie.

Ivy

Bertie was waiting at Kings Cross. He hurried to shepherd Ivy and Evie into the waiting cab. Their journey to Mrs Newbold's was silent. Ivy berated herself. How could she have let this happen? She grew hot as she sensed Bertie's eyes on her. Could she have done more, tried harder to see Evie over the years? She had lost count of the number of times she considered reporting her suspicions about Lizzie to the authorities. She knew why she hadn't. She had dreaded her niece being returned to the workhouse and Aunt Agatha ordering her back into service. She thought about the letter John had given her; Aunt Agatha no longer had any power over them. Evie nestled her head into the crook of her aunt's arm and as the cab made its way to Chestnut Tree Avenue, she slept.

Clara and Mrs Newbold sprang into action as Bertie lifted Evie out of the cab. A bed was ready, and the adults tended to the wounded girl in silence. Clara prepared cocoa and after Ivy helped Evie into one of her nightgowns, she held the cup to the girl's mouth. The smell travelled up Evie's nostrils and she closed her eyes as she sipped at the hot liquid chocolate. Tears gathered behind her eyelids as the long-forgotten hot nectar soothed her dry throat. Evie drank greedily and when the cup was empty, Ivy laid her down and pulled the soft covers up to her chin. Evie closed her eyes as, between her sobs, her aunt sang her a lullaby. Evie slept as she had never slept before.

Ivy didn't want to leave Evie, but Bertie persuaded her to join him in Mrs Newbold's parlour. Before she left her niece, she whispered that she was safe and there was no longer anything to be afraid of. The girl didn't stir but Ivy prayed her reassuring words had filtered into Evie's mind. A sob caught in Ivy's throat. This wounded, scared girl bore no resemblance to the child she had left outside the workhouse. Before joining Bertie, she collected her mother's diary from her bedroom, the items that had changed their lives were folded neatly inside. Bertie handed her a brandy. She looked into his eyes and saw compassion, not judgement. She raised her glass and smiled. He frowned.

'I don't understand. I know you are upset about Evie and yet, you also seem happy.'

She embraced him. 'I am determined Lizzie will not escape unpunished, I intend to write to Andrew Glass and my aunt to inform them of her behaviour. But I also have reason to celebrate. For many years I have lived under the threat of my aunt's cruelty, but now I am free.'

Bertie refilled their glasses and Ivy opened her mother's diary. She removed the letter the Registrar had written years before. He had placed it in a drawer in his office desk at the workhouse, before he hanged himself. She started to read.

'Dear Miss Brown,

This letter will come as a shock, but I hope the contents will help you to confront the woman who blights your life, as she has blighted mine. My name is Arthur Armstrong. I am Agatha Brown's brother. I imagine your surprise at learning Agatha has a brother. She also has a twin sister. Harriet was an adorable, cheerful child, everything Agatha was not. We were not a happy family. Our mother died when we were all young and Agatha, never a pleasant child, became cruel. One day she pushed Harriet into the pond in the grounds of our family home. She watched Harriet struggling to breathe and as I ran to help, she tripped me, and I fell. By the time I righted myself our father was helping Harriet out of the water. My life changed that day. Agatha was her father's daughter; he believed every vicious word that left her mouth. Accused of trying to harm my sister, I was sent away to boarding school.

I shall draw a veil over my time away, suffice to say I understand some of what your niece endured in the workhouse. That is why I took steps to arrange her removal. I threatened to expose Agatha and in a rare moment of compassion she agreed. Or perhaps she made you pay for it in a different way? I would not be surprised to learn you were one of her many debtors and your loan payments increased over the years. Agatha inherited her skill as a pernicious money lender from our father. Harriet left home as soon as she could, sadly I have been unable to find her. Some years ago, I returned to Gateshead under an assumed name. I avoided my vile sister and hid in plain sight, working as the Registrar. I hope my actions helped to redeem some of my sister's wickedness. I hope your life, and that of your young niece, are happy, fulfilled ones from this day forward.

Yours sincerely,

Mr Arthur Armstrong.'

Bertie stared, open-mouthed. 'But why have you only received this old letter now?'

Ivy set out what she thought might have happened, although she would never know the full facts. Her understanding was based on something Agatha spat out as she read Arthur's letter.

'The coward. The weak, sinful coward. He came here, with this threat, but I told him in no uncertain terms how easy I would find it to have him incarcerated.'

'He was anything but a coward, Bertie. For Evie and for me, he was brave. But for himself, he must have been so terrified of Agatha's threat against him that he took his own life. And if the new Registrar had used the office at the workhouse, I might have received the letter years ago.'

Bertie rubbed his chin before he spoke. 'And you didn't hear anything about this man, this Arthur Armstrong, when you were at Hampson Hall? I'm surprised he wasn't the talk of the kitchen.'

'No, but I remember Mr and Mrs Jackson poring over the newspaper one morning, their heads close together. As I left to go for the dairy, I caught a snippet of conversation from the table.'

'Was it about him? The Registrar?'

'Now I know what he did, I think so. They said it was sinful, the act of a coward. But they didn't know what he had done, the risk he took to help Evie.'

Bertie asked how Agatha was when Ivy left. She smiled; she had lied when she told Aunt Agatha she kept precise records as the *'interest accrued'* on her mother's debt continued to rise. She had no idea how much she had paid, only that it was too much. Agatha had believed her and now Ivy delighted in repeating her aunt's final, bitter words. Agatha had lain slumped in her chair, issuing empty threats as she struggled to breathe. Spittle flew from her twisted mouth as she rasped.

'You don't have the guts to do anything about it! No one would believe you anyway!'

Ivy had smiled. 'Are you willing to take the risk? I will take a cheque for the "*interest accrued,*" thank you.' When she finished speaking Bertie embraced her, knocking the diary out of her hands. As the tattered old volume landed face down on the wooden floor, the spine broke. She knelt to retrieve it and her hand came up with pieces of the cover as loose pages floated around the room.

'My darling, I am sorry. How clumsy of me.'

'It's all right, I'm sure I can put the pages back in the right order.'

Later, Ivy leant against the door after seeing Bertie out. She hung her head, overwhelmed by the day's events. A gentle hand touched her arm and she turned to see Clara holding something.

'Miss Ivy, I hope you don't mind, but after you arrived with your niece I slipped out to the mission and collected some clothes and a pair of shoes. Enough until you shop for her.'

Tears spilled down Ivy's cheeks as she hugged Clara. 'That is very kind. Thank you, Clara.'

Upstairs Evie slept, free from the horrors of Pipewellgate and Lizzie Brown. Safe.

Lizzie

Lizzie struggled to open her eyes, the light stung, and her head pounded as if a marching band had taken up residence. The room was thick with silence, and she struggled to recall the events of the previous night. She found only a vague memory of being in the Globe and talking to Harry Campbell. But that could have been any day, any night.

She heaved herself out of the filthy chair and peered around the dirty room. Where was the girl? She frowned. She hadn't seen the brat for days. Or was it weeks? There had been no letters or money for a while. She had come to depend on the extra money her snooty cousins sent. She shuffled around the room, trying to focus and remember what had happened to change things. As she gazed at the girl's threadbare mattress, the loose floorboard caught her eye. Her bulk made it difficult to bend so she slowly lowered herself onto the mattress then reached over. A memory surfaced as she retrieved the picture. It was wrapped in a delicate handkerchief, once white but now grey and ripped in several places. The remains of a red 'M' stitched into one corner told her who this had belonged to. She frowned, the girl had hidden it, afraid of losing her precious possession.

She moved to push herself up, groaning as the pain in her head exploded like a firework. With difficulty she managed to sit on the edge of the mattress. She narrowed her eyes. Harry Campbell was standing in the doorway, hands on hips. What the hell was he doing at her door?

'Any news?'

'What are you talking about, man?'

Harry laughed, a deep, guttural sound that turned her stomach.

'Your cousin's precious daughter. She's mine, remember?'

A memory forced its way into her mind, and she heaved. She reached for the dirty chamber pot and vomited yellow bile and dark brown sherry.

'Where is she? It's been weeks now!'

Lizzie smiled, revealing rotten, yellow teeth. Despite her, the girl had escaped.

'She's gone. The deal's off.'

Harry roared and grabbed the chamber pot. He raised it and the stinking vomit flew out. As he charged towards her, he slipped. He descended in slow motion. His head hit the floor and connected with the rough edge of the loose floorboard and rusty nails that had hidden the precious picture. One pierced his right eye and the other the huge, bulging vein in his neck. Harry Campbell wouldn't be buying drinks in the Globe that night or ever again.

Ivy

After checking on Evie, Ivy walked wearily to her own bedroom. She sat on the bed with her mother's diary and the loose pages. Bertie had offered to have it re-bound, but she said she would bring it with her when she and Evie visited him. She didn't want to let it out of her sight. When she and Bertie gathered the loose pages, she had spotted something. She laid the scattered pieces of the diary on the bed. The front cover and each loose page, one after the other. Two pages were folded in half, and she put them to one side. She examined the back cover closely. On the inside of the back cover was a small pocket, now hanging loose. When she had read the diary years before and again more recently, she had noticed the pocket but didn't look inside. She picked up the two folded pages and turned them over in her hands. They slotted into the pocket perfectly. As she unfolded the first one, a line across the middle, yellowed with time, started to tear. She placed the page on her bed then unfolded the second one. Two pages, side-by side. On one, handwriting she recognised. A hand that warmed and cheered her. A final letter from her mother.

'Mes filles au chocolat,

I am so sorry to have left you. You and petite Evie are my world, and it would never have been my choice to go. I know you will look after each other and you will love Evie as I do. Please know I did my best; I hope you believe that. I tried so hard to rid us of a problem that blighted my life and the life of your dearly departed papa. Sadly, mes filles chéries, I failed you and I go to my grave with that on my conscience.

You may know by now that my shame is the debt I have left behind. I tried so hard to repay it, but it was an impossible task, as it had been for your dear papa. These rooms in Seymour Terrace are rented to us by your aunt. Your papa was a hard-working man, but the rent was never a reasonable one and we found ourselves in debt. Despite many appeals from your papa and myself, Aunt Agatha continued to increase the rent over the years. Worse, she added interest to what we owed. Oh, my darlings, I am so sorry to leave you with this problem. I would suggest you try appealing to Agatha's better nature, although in truth I doubt she has one. Tread carefully around her, I suspect she is a very dangerous woman. She was the only person to ever evoke anger in your dear papa. But in true 'Enri style, he never denounced her. Whispers of a scandal always followed her, but I never discovered the truth of this. If it exists, I hope you find it and have the courage to confront her, but beware, my darlings. She has the teeth of "une louve," a wolf.

Bonne courage my darling girls, I tried to prepare you for a rich life, full of colour, music, dancing and beauty. My heart goes into the world with you as you seek these precious things. Never settle for a life any less than your dreams and live every day as if it holds promise. Mes filles chéries, I love you truly and dearly, always remember that.

Your dear maman.'

The paper shook and her mother's words blurred in front of her eyes as Ivy's tears fell. She opened her mouth to scream, to tell her mother everything but most importantly, that she had confronted Aunt Agatha. To tell her of the long-hidden scandal and how defeated her aunt was, in the end. But all that left her mouth was a deep, desperate wail. Her shoulders shook as she sobbed, the paper still in her hand. As her sobs subsided, she picked up the second piece of paper. A hastily written, messy note. From her sister. Written after she fled from the Diamond.

'Dear Dinah,

I am sorry to have been trouble for you, but I know you will put everything right. You always fixed things after I made a mess of them. I am so sorry to have left Evie behind, but I will send money for her when I can. Louis said he loved me, I believed him. I was a fool. He did not love me, and he abandoned me in London. I had to work at the most terrible place doing vile dances and I nearly died but I am free now.

Before I left London, I did something I did not know I was capable of. For the first time in my life, I felt strong, and I fought back. I hope what I did will help to redeem my other actions. I am sure you already know about Maman's life in London before she came to Newcastle and met dear Papa, but you may not know about an evil man called Solomon Zettler. He scared our dear maman, he hurt her friend Jeannie and many other people. I attacked him, Dinah. I stabbed him and I think he is dead. I do not know what my life will be now or if we will ever meet again but I do love you, dear sister. And I love my own sweet Eveline. Please look after her for me.

Your sister, Margaret.'

Ivy held her breath as she read her sister's stark words. Words about abandoning her daughter and attacking a man. Messy words about life-changing events, written in haste as Mona continued to run. When they were reunited their conversation had covered Mona's time at the Diamond, but she had failed to mention the attack on Solomon Zettler. The truth was laid out in front of her, and Ivy smiled. Yes, she knew about her mother's experience at the hands of the odious man and while she couldn't condone Mona's actions, secretly she was proud. Two sisters from the grey streets of Gateshead had fought for lives no less than their dreams, as their mother had wanted.

*

Soon after Evie arrived in London, Ivy said she wanted to speak to her about her mother. As Evie sat, Ivy appraised her niece. The small child she had left behind in Gateshead all those years ago had grown into a beautiful, if unusual, young girl. Evie didn't say much, and Ivy often caught her talking to herself and making strange movements with her hands, as if she was having a conversation with someone Ivy couldn't see. A few times she thought she heard Evie say another girl's name. Nancy. Ivy had gone to school with a girl who had no brothers or sisters. The girl had conjured up an imaginary friend to combat her loneliness. Perhaps when Evie lived in Pipewellgate with Lizzie she had invented a similar friend. Ivy wanted to tread carefully; she didn't know what Evie had endured while they were apart.

'My dear niece, now you are feeling better, I would like to tell you about your mother.'

Evie stared. 'My mother? You mean the woman who gave birth to me?'

Evie's anger didn't surprise Ivy, but she persevered. 'She is still your mother, dear.'

'No, she lost that right a long time ago. All I want to know is why she abandoned me and where she has been all this time!'

Ivy swallowed. Evie had a right to know the truth about her mother and her childhood.

'Very well, my dear. But parts of the story are not pleasant.'

'Yes, but it is my story, isn't it?'

Ivy sighed. 'Yes, it is. You were born in Gateshead on the 22nd of May 1899. But everything changed for you on the 16th of June 1903, the day your grandmother died.'

Evie sat quietly as Ivy spoke. Ivy didn't tell Evie everything about her mother. When Evie was older Ivy would give her Theodosia's diary and Evie could read their words herself. When Ivy finished speaking Evie embraced her. She looked into her aunt's piercing blue eyes.

'Thank you for telling me my story, Aunt Ivy. I don't want to speak of it again.'

'Oh, but my dear, perhaps we should talk more about your mother?'

'No thank you. I would prefer to look forward.'

Chapter 38

Mona

Mona skipped along the path at the side of Southampton dock. The majestic ship towered above her, patiently waiting for its eager passengers to embark in the warm spring sunshine. Mona's stomach fluttered at the prospect of returning to New York. The busy city was packed full of the excitement and glamour her shallow soul craved. She had no doubt, New York was the place for her.

'Mona! Wait for me!' The high-pitched voice rang out behind her. Mona turned.

'Peggy! Isn't this fabulous? Look at this magnificent ship!'

'I know, we're going to have such fun.'

For the last few months, the friends had been performing in repertory theatre in different coastal towns, but Peggy had said it was time to return to New York. Mona pushed away thoughts of her daughter and sister, knowing she had missed her chance. When Peggy had explained her reaction to Mona's news about Evie coming to stay, Mona understood. The flat was no place for a young girl, given some of Peggy's less than honest activities. Mona was a lot more like Peggy than she cared to admit. Her demons had disappeared once she received her sister's forgiveness. Her confidence had returned, and she found herself enjoying performing on stage again. As long as she kept pushing away the images of her daughter and sister, she could be her old self.

Peggy touched Mona's arm. 'Are you sure? It's not too late to go back to London.'

Mona considered Peggy's question. Then she thought about Marv's offer for her and Peggy to return to work with his company in New York. As soon as Mona pictured the Paradise her mood lifted, she even thought she would be able to successfully dance the cancan in *'Marv's Fabulous Femme Fatales.'* She could do anything now! Some aspects of Peggy's life scared Mona but she didn't want to be separated from her again.

'No. Ivy will take care of Evie; she was always more of a mother to her than me. Besides, today is my 28th birthday, I deserve to do something spectacular!'

'Are you sure?'

'Yes! Let's leave this god-forsaken country behind and sail off to a better place!'

'Very well, Mona. We'll let the wind take us!'

Mona laughed. They would have a whale of a time in New York.

*

Peggy slid a glance at Mona. Delight that her friend's fear and paranoia had abated was tempered by the certain knowledge that Evie's shadow would follow Mona wherever she went. Peggy's own ghosts accompanied her on every voyage she took. She caught up with Mona and linked her arm as they walked up the gangplank.

Evie

Evie spun around, her arms outstretched and her head back, laughing.

'Get ready, Evie!'

She was having her picture taken with Bertie in Mrs Newbold's garden. She blinked as the flashbulb exploded. She closed her eyes, she still had flashes of her life before. She didn't want to remember Lizzie's threats and the filth of Pipewellgate. She had Aunt Ivy's wedding and a new life in Bournemouth to look forward to. She had removed her spectacles to have her photograph taken but now she carefully replaced them. It was the one thing Aunt Ivy had insisted on asking her about.

She noticed Evie didn't read well and often screwed her eyes up, or closed one to try and make out words or numbers. Before long, Evie was being examined by an eye-doctor. An array of mysterious contraptions was placed on her face, and she was instructed to read from a page of letters the eye-doctor held out in front of her. Suddenly, the letters on the paper were crystal clear! The eye-doctor nodded, saying he had found the right lenses. Evie didn't know what he meant but she smiled because Aunt Ivy was thanking him and shaking his hand. A few days later a package arrived.

'Your spectacles, my dear!' Aunt Ivy clapped her hands as Evie opened the box.

'Quick, put them on and read this!'

Aunt Ivy thrust the newspaper towards her and as she carefully positioned the spectacles on her face, the words on the page came clearly into view. A whole new, marvellous world opened up. Mrs Newbold and Clara gave her books and Aunt Ivy took her to a bookshop. At dinner one evening not long after her new spectacles arrived, Bertie reached into his jacket pocket and produced something which he proceeded to put on his nose. Aunt Ivy laughed.

'Bertie, you and Evie are two peas in a pod!'

Bertie's small *pince-nez* sat proudly on his nose. He winked at Evie, and she joined her aunt in falling in love with him. She refused to think about her mother's picture under the floorboards in Pipewellgate, the picture she would cherish was the one of her and Bertie.

Her aunt took her to a department store called Selfridges to choose her dress for the wedding. Evie walked behind her aunt, expecting to be thrown out. Her aunt's hand reached for hers. As they walked towards the lift Aunt Ivy smiled. Evie held tight to her aunt's hand. Ivy led Evie to the lift and asked for bridal wear. As they stepped out, Evie caught her breath. Plush red velvet curtains hid the secrets of bridal wear from prying eyes, but she was speechless as the assistant pulled the curtains aside with a flourish. Inside were racks of the most beautiful dresses Evie had ever seen. She pinched herself to prove it was real.

Her unease gone, she pointed excitedly at one thing then another. The delicate, tempting fabrics were protected by light covers but as she moved towards one, the assistant spoke.

'Is that one of interest, Miss?'

Evie snatched her hand back as if the cover had burned her. She studied the floor, convinced the assistant knew about her disgraceful beginnings in life. Convinced she knew Evie didn't belong in Selfridges, touching the beautiful bridal gowns.

'Would you like to take a closer look at it?'

Evie nodded as the assistant unwrapped the precious dress. It was luxurious; a layered, draped garment of soft white silk, accentuated with sprays of hand-made, embroidered silk flowers.

'Oh Evie, it is perfect! It will complement my dress wonderfully. And once we find you some pretty shoes your outfit will be complete. Would you like to try it on?'

Evie nodded at her aunt. She shook as the assistant helped her. The silk rustled as the assistant pulled the dress gently over her head. She sniffed; the dress smelt of happiness. As the assistant fastened the small pearl buttons travelling down the back of the dress, butterflies fluttered in her stomach. As she walked nervously from the dressing room, her aunt's beautiful blue eyes filled with tears.

'Yes, we'll take it, thank you!'

'Very good, Madam. We will have it packaged and sent to you.'

Shoes were next. Aunt Ivy found a pair to match the dress and Evie thought she would burst with happiness. The day didn't need anything else to make it perfect, until her aunt whispered.

'Now, let's be cocoa girls!'

As they sipped the luxurious drink Evie told her aunt about her idea.

'Aunt Ivy, I would like to change my name.'

'You would? What would you like to change it to, my dear?'

'Ena Leighton.'

'That is a nice name. Why have you chosen it?'

'Well, my name starts with an E and the *Na* is for my friend Nancy. The surname is the same one you chose, although I know yours will soon be Primavesi.' Evie crossed her fingers, hoping her aunt wouldn't object. After all, she and Evie's mother had both changed their names.

'Very well. From now on you shall be known as Ena Leighton.'

Ena sipped her cocoa and smiled, she had a new name for her new beginning, and she would always remember her dear friend Nancy. She was a cocoa girl. She was home.

The End

The Cocoa Girls is Annie Doyle's debut novel.
The story is based on her nana's life and was
inspired by long-hidden family secrets,
uncovered when Annie undertook some
family history research.
Annie lives in Gateshead and is currently
working on her second novel,
Village on the Hill.
You can find Annie on Facebook and Twitter.

Photo by ValeriejaiPhotos

Printed in Great Britain
by Amazon